DISGUISED PERCEPTION

HIDDEN BEHIND THE VEIL

MAGIC & PROPHECIES
BOOK FOUR

TIFFANY KAHAPEA

BLURB

Olivia appears to lead an ordinary life as a dedicated chemical engineer at Sutton Engineering. Yet, a mysterious and debilitating illness haunts her existence, defying medical explanations. She hides her secret visions, sharing them only with her best friend, Evelyn.

During a disorienting moment at work, Olivia experiences a vision that shatters her reality, leading to her abrupt abduction by a secretive society. Her world spirals into magic, chaos, and dark forces with unknown intentions.

As Olivia navigates this new world alongside unlikely allies, they engage in a battle that tests their very essence. The truth behind the secret society's motives unveils a chilling reality: their intentions reach far beyond what anyone could have imagined.

Can Olivia harness her newfound powers to thwart the organization's plans, or will darkness triumph, plunging their world into eternal chaos?

CHAPTER 1
SOMETHING'S DEFINITELY WRONG

I cannot believe I'm doing this. Being out with Mom is the last thing I want to do, especially when it involves shopping. My graduation is tomorrow, and they have assigned me the duty of giving the closing speech. I can't focus on what she's saying right now as I'm too worried I'll forget what I'm supposed to say.

Mom hovers around me as I attempt to perfect my graduation speech in my head. She's always been one for appearances, and graduation is no exception. She can be overbearing and demanding at the best of times and downright controlling at the worst.

"Olivia! You must make a lasting impression. All eyes will be on you, you know!" she snaps at me. She's irritated because instead of focusing on her lessons about making an impression, I'm running through the speech in my head, effectively ignoring her.

I nod as my anxiety builds by the second. The thought of facing hundreds of people, even from behind a podium, makes my heart race. The sun beats down on us, warming the air, and the distant hum of chatter from other people shopping does nothing to help my concentration.

"And darling," she continues, her tone dripping with disapproval, "I can't believe you don't know how to put on makeup. I've scheduled someone to come in the morning to fix you up properly. You can't represent our family looking like... well, like you usually do."

I glance at my watch, silently willing the hours to pass faster. We have already filled my day with shopping for an outfit that screams confidence and success despite my every instinct urging me to wear what's comfortable. As the day wears on, a growing sense of unease tightens its grip on me. It starts as a subtle discomfort, a nagging feeling in my mind.

But soon, my head hurts, I'm lightheaded and dizzy, and the world around me blurs as if I'm seeing it through a haze. The distant scent of the various restaurants and the delicate aroma of Mom's expensive perfume is not helping, either.

However, I trudge on in misery as Mom drags me from store to store. Through it all, the unease remains, making it hard to focus. Mom is likely annoyed with my lack of atten-tion, as she walks away in a huff before telling me we're leaving. I sigh in relief as we head to the car, eager to get home and into bed.

However, she doesn't stop talking the entire ride home. As soon as we arrive, Mom's voice becomes a distant hum as we walk inside, the weight of the shopping bags bearing down on my arms. All I want is to crawl into bed and let the strange sensations wash over me until they pass.

"Dinner will be ready in an hour, Olivia." Mom announces as we step inside the house. I feel a surge of nausea and realize that this strange feeling isn't going away. The headache intensifies and is pounding behind my eyes.

"I don't think I can eat, Mom," I mumble as my voice trembles.

She waves off my concerns, her attention fixated on the grandeur of tomorrow's graduation ceremony. "Oh, you're just nervous, dear. You'll see, once you've given that speech, you'll feel so accomplished."

I don't argue. Instead, I make my way to my room with heavy steps and an aching body. The sounds of her voice grow fainter as I close the door, leaving me alone with my discomfort. As I sink into the softness of my bed, I realize that tomorrow's big day might not be what's causing this strange illness. The unease, the headache, the queasiness - it all feels too intense to be simple nerves. I'm pretty sure Mom's presence there is what's gotten me so out of sorts.

I've never been the type of daughter she wants. There's always something wrong with my clothes or my hair. She always finds something to critique about me, and it's disheartening. Even with the stylist and makeup artist coming tomorrow, I still don't think I'll look good enough for her. But for now, I'm too exhausted to dwell on it. I close my eyes and hope that sleep will wash away these unsettling sensations, leaving me ready to face the daunting graduation ahead.

Today is the day I've been waiting for. It's my college graduation. With my chemical engineering degree, I should feel excited and proud. But the overwhelming sense of unease gnaws at me, making it hard to focus on the excitement that should bubble inside. The morning arrives with all the fanfare of my impending graduation. In her relentless pursuit of perfection, Mom bursts into my room, rousing me from a restless night's sleep.

"Olivia, darling, it's time to get ready," she chirps, and I groan inwardly.

The world feels like a distant, hazy dream as I sit up, trying to shake off the lingering discomfort that had plagued me last night. Mom insists I go through the motions of hair and makeup, something that seems utterly irrelevant given the strange sensations still coursing through my body.

A skilled stylist works magic on my hair, and a makeup artist does her best to transform my face. Despite my reservations, I can't help but admit that, when finished, I look stunning.

Mom beams with pride, but her boisterous enthusiasm is unable to penetrate my clouded state. She goes on about the designer dress, the elegant shoes, and the makeup that enhances my features. She's happy that she has accomplished her goal of having a beautiful daughter.

But I couldn't care less about designer labels, makeup, or fancy shoes. They're just not me. I long for simplicity and comfort, not this glamorous facade. However, Mom's happiness means everything to me right now, so I play my part to keep her content.

Fully dressed, I look in the mirror and admire the person staring back at me. The dress is an elaborate creation, shimmering with intricate beading and lace. It hugs my figure in all the right places, and I can't deny it's exquisite. The high-heeled and elegant shoes are more than I'd ever choose for myself.

My hair is an intricate work of art, styled into cascading waves that frame my face. The makeup accentuates my features, making me appear more confident than I feel. The reflection in the mirror is of a young woman who seems ready to conquer the world. But beneath the surface, I'm a bundle of unease and uncertainty.

As we make our way to the graduation ceremony, I can't shake the sense that something is wrong. The nausea returns tenfold, and my head pounds relentlessly. Mom's chattering about how proud she is of me and how everyone will watch me is a constant backdrop to my discomfort.

I try to convince myself that it's just anxiety, that once the ceremony is over, I can retreat into solitude and figure out what's really happening to me. For now, I paste a smile on my face and focus on the road ahead, determined to make it through the ceremony for Mom's sake. As we arrive at the graduation venue, I spot my dear friend Evelyn, who squeals with excitement as we approach each other.

"Olivia, can you believe it? We're finally graduating!" she screams, her eyes lighting up with enthusiasm. "And you look absolutely stunning!"

I manage a small smile in response to her effusive compliments. Not feeling well is affecting the enthusiasm I should have for such an occasion. Since we met freshman year, Evelyn has always been the more outgoing and energetic of us, the yin to my yang. We engage in a brief conversation, small talk about our plans for the future, and the excitement of finally closing this chapter of our lives.

Suddenly, Evelyn gets a strange look on her face. She scrunches her brows and stares at me intensely, her focus unwavering. After about a minute, her eyes widen before stepping back, as if she just had an epiphany.

"What's wrong?" I ask as I look around the crowd, thinking she saw something or someone.

She shakes her head before pasting a smile on her face. "Oh, it's nothing. I got lost in thought for a second before I realized I was staring at your face."

We both laugh just as the announcer requests everyone to find their seats. The time for the ceremony has arrived, and my classmates and I file in to take our seats. The long-anticipated moment has come, and I try to push aside the relentless discomfort and concentrate on the task at hand. Finally, the ceremony unfolds, and one by one, my classmates and I walk across the stage to receive our diplomas.

The crowd's applause fills the air, mingling with a sense of accomplishment and relief. And then it's my turn. Unsteady legs carry me to the microphone at the podium. I take a deep breath and begin my graduation speech. The words flow smoothly from my lips as I recount the challenges we've faced, the lessons we've learned, and the bright future that awaits us.

But suddenly, my voice falters, and I fall into silence. My body trembles uncontrollably, and my eyelids flutter rapidly as if I'm trying to dislodge something caught in them. The world around me blurs, and I'm transported to a place that is not the graduation stage.

At that moment, I see something shocking, something that shakes me to my core. It's as if I've been thrust into a different reality, one filled with images and visions that I can't comprehend. I watch as the scene plays out in front of me.

A woman exits a building and starts running down the street. Based on the look on her face, I assume she fears someone or something. Her shoes pound against the pavement as she frantically sprints away from whatever she's running from. Two figures in dark clothing exit the building soon after and give chase. The woman turns to see them following and speeds up, and her fear is palpable in the air.

She turns down an alley, only to stop at its dead end. There's no way out for her as she twirls around, searching for an alter-

nate escape. The two figures chasing her turn into the alley, effectively preventing her from running back toward the alley's entrance.

"Give up," one figure says as malice drips from his tone.

The woman scowls at them. "I won't let you take me. I know who you people are. There are whispers about you and what you've done."

"Then you know how that running won't help you. Come willingly, or we'll force you," the other figure says.

"I know what you're doing and can't help you. If I go with you, I'll never see my family again," she says vehemently.

The first figure shrugs. "Even if you manage to escape, we'll catch you, eventually. Then you will never see your family again."

Her features turn sad as her shoulders sag. "You're right. I won't see my family again either way. But I'll be damned if I let you do to me what you did to the others!"

She whips out a knife so fast that the dark figures barely have time to react. The knife plunges into her chest, striking her heart. There's a small gasp as her face scrunches in pain, then her knees buckle. She falls to the ground with a lifeless look in her eyes.

"NO!" I cry out so suddenly that I startle myself. Without thinking, I try to run forward to help the woman, but in the next instant, a searing pain shoots through my body, causing me to gasp in agony.

Suddenly, the graduation ceremony snaps back into focus. My head hurts, and I see the concerned faces of the school staff surrounding me, their voices a distant echo as they try to assess the situation. Embarrassment washes over me like a tidal wave, and I realize I've made a spectacle of myself in front of the entire graduating class and their families.

Without a word, I scramble to my feet, my cheeks burning with shame, and rush out of the ceremony, leaving behind a bewildered audience and a trail of unanswered questions. My escape from the graduation ceremony is short-lived as Mom soon catches up to me, her high heels clicking on the pavement like an ominous drumbeat. She is furious, her voice carrying an edge of anger and humiliation that slices through me like a razor blade.

"Olivia, you've embarrassed me beyond belief!" she hisses, her eyes ablaze with anger. "You stood there on that stage for nearly ten minutes, ignoring everyone. What were you thinking? You know how important this day is!"

I try to explain, to tell her about what happened, what I saw, about the overwhelming sensation that overcame me. My voice trembles as I recount the surreal experience, hoping she'll understand. But Mom's reaction was not what I expected. She doesn't express disbelief or concern for my well-being. Instead, her anger intensifies, and her face contorts with frustration.

"Are you having a mental breakdown?" she scoffs, her words laced with disdain. "Do you know how terrible this will look for my image? You should have told me you weren't feeling well sooner, Olivia!"

The accusation strikes me like a physical blow. I told her I wasn't feeling well, and like usual, she brushed me off. Now, she doesn't believe me when I tell her what happened on stage. Her concern isn't for my welfare but for the damage this incident might cause her carefully cultivated public image.

I feel a mix of anger and hurt, but the pain in my head becomes unbearable, drowning out everything else. I clutch my temples, gasping for breath as sharp, searing pain courses through my skull. Everything around me blurs, and all sounds seem to fade away, except for a single, piercing noise that shrills into my consciousness like a relentless drill.

The last thing I hear is Mom's voice, now tinged with genuine alarm, shouting my name in desperation before everything goes dark. The world slips away, and I plummet into an abyss of unconsciousness, leaving behind the chaos and confusion of graduation day.

My consciousness returns slowly like a distant, flickering light, gradually brightening the shadows of a dark room. I can hear muffled voices, and the sensation of a cool material against my cheek tells me I'm no longer outside in the unforgiving sun. As awareness seeps in, I try to move, but my body feels heavy and unresponsive.

"Olivia? Olivia, can you hear me?" a familiar voice calls out, its tone softer, filled with genuine concern.

It's not Mom's harsh, demanding voice. I open my eyes, squinting against the harsh artificial lights above. The room comes into focus, and I realize I'm lying on a bed in a small, white-walled room. With a look of concern, Evelyn leans over me, her eyes wide and searching for any sign of improvement.

"Evelyn?" I whisper, my voice barely audible.

"Thank goodness you're awake," she says with relief. "You had all of us so worried."

Memories of the graduation ceremony and the vision flood back, and I shudder at the surreal experience. "What happened? How did I end up here?"

Evelyn helps me sit up, and I notice Mom is also in the room, sitting stiffly in a chair, her anger from earlier replaced by genuine concern. She looks like she hasn't slept in days.

"Mom?" I say, my voice still weak. "What's going on?"

I'm met with silence, and all at once, the gravity of the situation dawns on me. Lying on the uncomfortable examination bed, I feel suffocated in the sterile hospital room. Mom sits in a stiff-backed chair by my side, her face etched with worry and impatience. Evelyn stands silently nearby, offering me a reassuring smile whenever our eyes meet.

"You passed out," Eve finally answers. "We brought you here to the school hospital. They ran some tests while you were out."

A moment later, the doctors walk into the room, and I don't like the looks on their faces. They furrow their brows in confusion, and the unease in the room is palpable. They explain how they've run countless tests, poked, prodded, and examined, yet they can't pinpoint the elusive cause of my recent fainting spell.

"I don't understand," one of the doctors murmurs, their eyes locked on the perplexing results on a clipboard. "All the tests have come back normal. There's no apparent reason for these episodes."

Mom, who has always demanded perfection, cannot fathom such uncertainty regarding my health. She rises from her chair, her heels clicking sharply against the cold, tiled floor.

"You mean to tell me that after all these tests, you still don't know what's wrong with my daughter?" Her voice is sharp as she questions their incompetence.

The doctors look at each other, unsure how to handle Mom's anger. Everyone knows about her formidable presence and unyielding expectations, and now she directs that force squarely at them.

"I assure you, Ms. Iverson, we're doing everything within our expertise to figure this out," another doctor offers, attempting to appease her, but Mom's frustration knows no bounds.

She paces the room like a caged predator, with her anger escalating with each step. "Everything within your expertise? This is unacceptable! You're supposed to be experts! If you can't find out what's wrong with my daughter, I'll have your licenses revoked, and I'll find someone else!"

I wince at the threat, knowing the weight of Mom's words. Her reputation and influence are substantial, and the doctors are acutely aware of the implications. Her words give me pause as I try to figure out how long I've been out and where I am.

Amid the turmoil, Evelyn approaches me quietly, her eyes filled with genuine concern. "Olivia, how are you feeling? Is there anything I can do for you?"

I offer her a weak smile, grateful for her presence in this chaotic moment. "Don't worry, Eve, I'm okay. I want to go home."

She nods, understanding the complexity of the situation. Eve knows that Mom's outburst is not about my well-being but an attempt to protect her image. It's a painful truth we've both come to accept. As Mom continues her tirade about finding the right doctor, I can't help but feel a weariness settling in the pit of my stomach. The prospect of being shuttled from one doctor to another in search of answers is daunting.

I fainted once, but that's one time too many if she thinks it'll make her look bad, which is why she's treating this instance like a life-or-death situation. All I can do for now is placate her, endure this grueling ordeal, and hold on to the hope that she will eventually give up or someone will give her an answer she'll accept.

With Mom's furious rant serving as a dissonant back-drop, I cast one last sad glance at the sterile hospital room, my temporary sanctuary from the storm that rages around me. Then, I'm unceremoniously ushered out, Mom's grip on my arm unyielding as she embarks on a relentless mission to find a doctor who can provide the answers she desperately seeks.

CHAPTER 2

IN SEARCH OF ANSWERS

The next day comes, and a new chapter in my search for answers begins. I tried to convince Mom that I felt fine upon wanking up, but as soon as I stepped out of bed, I fainted as a sharp pain shot through my head. Mom decides to seek the counsel of a prestigious doctor in another state.

We set out on a journey that transcends geographical boundaries, fueled by her unyielding determination to understand the mysterious fainting spells that have haunted me since graduation.

As we embark on this road trip, I sit in the passenger seat with the hum of the car's engine providing a soothing backdrop to my racing thoughts. I can sense the worry emanating from Mom as unspoken fear etched into the lines of her face. She doesn't say much, but her silence speaks volumes, revealing the depths of her concern.

Concern that I know is only about how she will spin this in her favor should word spread about my hospital visits. Everything about her has to be perfect, and that includes me. I wish I could ease her anxiety, but my own uncertainty casts a shadow over my reassurance.

The drive takes us through changing landscapes, the scenery morphing from the familiarity of our hometown into the unfamiliar territory of another state. It's as if we're leaving behind the comfort of the known world, venturing into the uncharted territory of my health. With every mile that passes, I feel the weight of Mom's frustrations baring down on me.

Finally, we arrive at the prestigious medical facility and walk inside to wait for the doctors. The anticipation in the waiting room is palpable as the minutes stretch into an eternity as we await our turn. My heart beats in rhythm with the ticking clock on the wall as my anxiety increases. I've never been afraid of hospitals or doctor's visits. It's Mom's presence that makes me uneasy.

I never know how she will act or what she will say, especially if she doesn't get her way. While I don't think all this fuss is necessary for fainting, I do believe something is wrong with me. So, if I have to endure Mom's relentless pursuit of bettering my health to find out what's going on, I will.

When the doctor finally calls my name, we follow him into an examination room bathed in sterile light. His demeanor exudes confidence, a reassuring presence in the face of Mom's resting bitch face. He greets us with a warm smile, but it quickly fades as he realizes his happy and warm demeanor won't work on Mom.

The doctor sticks out his hand for me to shake. "Hello, Olivia. I'm Dr. Johnson. Can you tell me when the fainting spells started?"

"Well, I started feeling ill the day before my graduation," I start. "The day of graduation, I saw something that shocked me, and I fainted."

Mom scoots closer to me. "Nothing happened, Dr. Johnson. She was on stage when she just froze mid-sentence. She says some woman stabbed herself in the chest, but nothing so atrocious happened that day. I believe the pressures of graduating and becoming an acceptable adult in society have broken her mind. What can you do to help my daughter?"

"Have you experienced any other symptoms besides fainting, dizziness, or nausea?" Dr. Johnson asks me as he ignores my mother.

"Only the day before and the day of my graduation. There's nausea, headaches, and dizziness, and then I'm unconscious."

He nods in understanding. "And have there been any significant changes in your diet or sleep patterns during this time?"

"No, I like to keep a routine," I reply.

"Dr. Johnson, my daughter is clearly having a mental breakdown," Mom interrupts. "Is there some sort of medication you can prescribe or a facility you can recommend that will help her?"

I start at her with wide eyes, amazed by her questions. Luckily, the doctor ignores her rude questions. He continues questioning me about my lifestyle, habits, and whatever else he deems necessary. I give him honest and accurate answers, hoping every detail may shed light on sudden fainting spells.

Unfortunately, the more he questions, it becomes increasingly clear that the puzzle remains unsolved. His expression mirrors my frustration. He stops his line of questions and starts a round of testing. I endure the standard rounds of examinations—EKGs, blood tests, and even an MRI.

The cold metallic surfaces of the machines and the rhythmic sounds of their operation became a disheartening background to my growing sense of anxiety. When all the tests are done, Dr. Johnson releases me and says he'll get in touch with the results. Days of waiting for results feel like an eternity. When the doctor finally calls, his tone is mixed with empathy and bewilderment. I put him on speaker-phone so Mom could hear.

"Olivia, I've reviewed the tests thoroughly and can't pinpoint a specific cause for your fainting spells. It's possible that these episodes are stress-related," he tells me.

"Stress? But I've never felt more relaxed in my life," I reply, knowing that was only the half-truth. Any time I'm around my mother, it's stressful.

I hear him sigh through the phone. "Sometimes, the body reacts to stress in mysterious ways, even if it doesn't manifest as conscious anxiety. I recommend staying hydrated and getting plenty of rest. It's possible that your body needs time to readjust."

"You incompetent, worthless—" Mom starts.

"Thank you, Dr. Johnson," I say quickly before hanging up the phone, effectively cutting off Mom's string of insults.

"Olivia, we won't stop here. If we have to, we'll travel the world to get you the help you need," she says before walking away.

I sigh in resignation, knowing there's no way to talk her out of this misguided mission. A moment later, my phone rings again, and I look to see it's Eve calling me.

"Hey Eve, what's up?" I say as I answer the phone.

"Hi, I'm calling to see how you're doing and if your

mother is still dragging you all over the world," she replies, her tone laced with sarcasm.

"You know she is," I say with a tired sigh. "She's got it in her mind that I'm mentally unstable and is determined to find a doctor to agree with her."

Eve hesitates for a moment before speaking again. "Are you sure you saw what you saw?"

Something in her voice gives me pause. "I know it sounds weird. Maybe through everything going on with graduation, my mind conjured up a scene from a movie or something."

"Yeah, that's probably it," she says, but she doesn't sound convinced.

I tell Eve I have to go because Mom is calling my name somewhere in the house. After saying goodbye, Mom and I drive to my school to pack my things in my dorm. With school finished, I'm moving back home until I can find a job.

Mom's house is the last place I want to be, but Eve doesn't have room at her house for me, and I don't have many friends. Hopefully, living back home won't be too stressful, and dealing with the many doctors Mom has lined up won't be too bad.

The days stretch into weeks, and the relentless pursuit of answers becomes an unending odyssey. Over the next two weeks, the process drones on—more doctors, tests, and sterile waiting rooms that blend in a never-ending loop of clinical surroundings. Each consultation and examination carries with it the weight of Mom's undying hope and my growing frustration.

The headaches worsen, the nausea intensifies, and I started fainting more. I don't mention the things I see when this happens, or Mom will probably lose her shit before locking me up in a mental institution. As Mom drags me across state lines and even overseas in search of the 'right' answers, my feelings become a storm of emotions.

At first, I cling to a glimmer of hope, believing that one of these renowned specialists would determine the cause of my mysterious ailment. But as the days transform into weeks, and the battery of tests yields nothing but exasperation, a sense of resignation settles within me.

"Olivia, please," Mom says, her voice tinged with frustration, as we sit in yet another sterile examination room. "Understand. I'm doing this for your own good. We need to find out what's causing these fainting spells."

I glance at her stern face etched with lines of irritation and sigh softly. "I know, Mom, but we've seen so many doctors already, and none of them have found anything wrong. Maybe it's time to consider that it might be nothing more than stress like they say."

"That's nonsense," she snaps. "There is something wrong with you, and I will sort this out, even if I have to tie you up and drag you around to do it."

Knowing I won't win this argument, I offer her a reassuring smile, though it's tinged with sadness. "I appreciate your determination, Mom. I really do. But I can't help feeling like a lab rat in this never-ending experiment. And I miss my life, hanging out with Eve, my routine."

She releases my hand, her shoulders slumping. "I miss your old life too, sweetie. But we have to prioritize your health above all else."

As the weeks roll on, my feelings of helplessness intensifies. I can't shake the impression that I'm merely a pawn in an elaborate game, moved from one specialist to another like a chess piece in Mom's relentless pursuit of a solution. Her determination is unwavering, but it's driven by something more than just a mother's love—it's fueled by a desire for control, an obsession with maintaining the image of a perfect family.

Mom has abandoned the quest for answers. She's given up trying to understand the mysterious ailment that plagues me. Instead, she's shifted her focus, aiming to either medicate me into submission or find a doctor willing to place me in a facility far away from prying eyes. It's a strategy designed to control the narrative surrounding my condition and preserve the illusion of a caring, doting mother doing everything in her power to help her troubled daughter.

For Mom, it has always been about image—about projecting the facade of perfection to the world. In this relentless pursuit of answers, she sees an opportunity to shape the story to her liking, to cast herself as the devoted, long-suffering parent seeking the best possible care for her afflicted child.

Here we are again with another doctor. In the cold, sterile examination room, where the air seems thick with uncertainty, I find myself adrift in a sea of medical jargon and well-intentioned yet futile efforts. Mom's voice advocating on my behalf in hushed tones echoes in my ears, making me feel like a science experiment.

"I want answers, Doctor," she snaps at the latest specialist, her voice laced with anger. "I can't bear to see my daughter like this. We've traveled across the country and beyond but still don't have a diagnosis. Her fainting has gotten worse, and she won't tell me, but I know she's still seeing things. Bad things, doctor."

The doctor, a middle-aged man with a kind but weary expression, sighs and runs a hand through his graying hair. "Ms. Iverson, we've conducted many tests and consulted with experts from various fields. I understand your frustration, but at this point, we can't pinpoint a specific medical cause for Olivia's fainting spells."

Mom's face turns to stone, and I know she's going to lash out. "What the hell am I supposed to do with a broken daughter? Do you know how bad it makes me look when I can't find a competent medical professional to help her? There must be something we can do."

The doctor nods sympathetically. "I recommend continuing to monitor Olivia's condition, as well as keeping a detailed journal of her episodes. It's possible that patterns or triggers may emerge. And, of course, maintain her general health with a balanced diet and exercise."

Clearly dissatisfied with the doctor's response, Mom looks at me with a mixture of resolve and concern. "We'll do that, Doctor. But we won't stop here. I won't rest until I find someone to help my daughter."

While tinged with a sense of resignation, I offer the doctor a smile of gratitude. I am beyond tired of traveling everywhere. I've been dealing with this long enough to be happy going through life this way. If seeing weird and sometimes shocking things a couple of times a week gets me away from my mother, I'd gladly deal with it. Mom may not like it because I don't fit her idea of the perfect daughter, but she's disrupting my life more than the fainting spells.

Finally, after an exhaustive day filled with probing questions and inconclusive tests, Mom and I find respite in a nearby restaurant. The establishment exudes a pleasant ambiance, with soft lighting and the soothing hum of conversation filling the air. However, as I glance at Mom, it's clear that her foul mood remains intact.

She lets out a heavy sigh as her gaze drifts toward the

menu, although her thoughts appear to be miles away. "Olivia, you really should straighten up. Let's take a picture to commemorate this moment."

I blink, surprised by her abrupt request. "A picture, Mom? Why?"

Her eyes flick to her phone, her fingers deftly tapping on the screen. "Just a little something to update my assistant with, you know? It's important to maintain appearances. After all, I've been away from work for too long."

As she sends the picture to her assistant, I can't shake the feeling that I'm being reduced to an afterthought in her grand plan to maintain appearances. It's clear that she views our quest as a mere inconvenience, a disruption to her carefully curated image.

Meanwhile, I struggled internally. On one hand, I yearned to discover if there was something profoundly wrong with me, something that required long-term medical attention. I couldn't dismiss the possibility of a hidden ailment lurking beneath the surface. Perhaps it wasn't as straightforward as making lifestyle changes—reducing salt intake or incorporating more cardio into my routine to ease stress.

But as Mom prattled on about the latest designer trends and the importance of maintaining a polished appearance, I reached my breaking point. I can no longer bear her overbearing, controlling indifference regarding my situation.

"Mom," I interject, my voice tinged with frustration. "This isn't just about appearances or updating your assistant. I'm the one going through all of this, and I'm scared, okay? I want to know what's happening to me and your support."

Mom's eyes narrow to slits, her expression shifting from

indifference to irritation. "Olivia, you're blowing this out of proportion. You're always so dramatic."

I clench my fists, my patience finally snapping like a brittle twig. "Dramatic? Seriously, Mom? This is my health we're talking about! And all you care about is how it might affect your precious image!"

The argument escalates rapidly, with our voices growing louder as the tension between us reaches its peak.

"You know what, Mom?" I spit out, my voice trembling with emotion. "You're incorrigible, and I don't care if it ruins your perfect image. I will not keep chasing doctors to make you look good. I'll get the help I need on my own."

Her eyes widen, and her face contorts in disbelief. "You can't do that, Olivia. You can't just abandon this."

Of course, Mom would make this all about her, and her words confirm my suspicions.

"I'm not abandoning anything," I shoot back with anger. "I'm taking control of my life and my health. You can continue playing your image game if you want, but I won't be a part of it."

With that, I push my chair back, leaving her sitting there with her mouth hanging open in the restaurant. Our relationship has always been strained, but at that moment, I feared I'd made it irreparably worse.

As I walk away from the restaurant, a mixture of emotions surge within me—anger, frustration, sadness—but above all, determination. I refused to be pulled in every direction based on Mom's whims. I graduated from one of the country's most prestigious universities and am determined to make something of myself, even if it means limiting my interactions with her.

The night air is cool against my skin as I step outside with a sense of liberation washing over me. I know the road ahead won't be easy, but I'm ready to face it on my own terms. I've taken the first step toward being on my own, and I'm determined to forge a path to my future without my mother's influence, one where I have control over my destiny.

CHAPTER 3

UNRAVELING SECRETS

"Olivia? Are you listening to me?" Mom asks on the other end of the line.

I roll my eyes even though she can't see me. Her voice rings loud and clear through the speakers in the car, and I can hear the irritation in her tone. She's been nagging me all morning, and I was almost late for work. I know she's hounding me because she cares, but it's getting tiresome.

Luckily, traffic is light, and I make it to work quickly. I pull into the parking garage, find my spot, and turn off the car. I'm still in shock that I landed my dream job, and every time I see Sutton Engineering on the building, I'm reminded of how far I've come.

"Yes, Mom," I reply as I grab my purse and exit the car. "I hear you. You don't have to keep calling to check up on me."

"Don't take that tone with me, young lady. I want to make sure you're okay. Especially given your condition," she replies in an angry tone.

I really hate it when she says that. It makes me feel like I'm invalid and incapable of doing things on my own. I'm a chemical engineer at one of Chicago's most prestigious engineering companies, but she doesn't care about that. It makes me sad that all she can think about is my condition, and it's the only reason she calls now. Despite my situation, I've come really far on my own.

"Mom, I just walked into the office. I really have to go," I tell her quickly. "I'll call you later."

I hang up the phone before she gets the chance to reply. Laying my purse on the desk, I remove my blazer and put on my lab coat. I smile every time I put it on because I worked hard to get where I am. I enjoy my job and like the people I work with, except for some guys that creep me out.

Since I'm still new, I'm worried that my job will be affected by my "condition," as my mom likes to call it, but so far, it hasn't been a problem. However, I go to great lengths to hide it because I don't want anyone to know.

Four years ago, something about me drastically changed. I finally found a doctor who gave a probable diagnosis, and I ran with it simply because I wanted my mother to stop her crusade of finding doctors. Gone is the carefree geeky girl who loved reading and having fun. I started having seizures, but not the full-body convulsing type of seizures.

The doctor called it "silent seizures" because, for those looking from the outside, I'm just standing there staring off into space with a blank look for various periods of time. Sometimes, it's a series of eye flutters while I'm frozen in place. I never know when or where it will happen; no medication has helped.

I was told this type of medical condition is uncommon

among adults, and they haven't figured out why it started. However, that's not why I'm hiding it, though. I don't believe I'm actually having seizures, and I can't really say what's happening, but I know it's not natural. During my seizures, I sometimes get glimpses of random things. Sometimes, I see people I've never met having conversations while out eating food.

At a different time, I saw a car crash with a little girl pinned inside a burning car. I called the police then, letting them know what I'd seen. Imagine my surprise when the news said the accident was somewhere in California, and I was at home in Chicago. It was then that I realized I was special in a unique sort of way. The only other person who knows about this is my best friend, Evelyn. She's been my rock through all of this.

"Good morning," Axel says as I enter the lab.

He's the CEO of Sutton Engineering and one of the few people who creep me out. It's how he looks at me as if trying to see into my soul. It's pretty disturbing, and I try to avoid him at all costs, though he will travel down to check on lab operations from time to time.

I give him a slight nod. "Good morning, Axel," I say as I scurry to the back of the room to grab a few beakers and flasks.

He doesn't seem to take the hint that I really don't want to talk to him because he follows me. "I wanted to see what you're working on today. Have we gotten any further with the fuels?"

I almost drop the flask I'd taken out of the cabinet when I feel his breath on my ear as he speaks. I spin around to see that he's actually two feet away from me, looking at me with that assessing gaze of his. Just then, Nash walks into the lab, and I sigh heavily because he's another one who rubs me the wrong way. I often wonder how he got this job.

He's close friends with Axel and Steele, another guy who works in the lab, so maybe that's how, but I can't deny that he knows how to do his job well. They all make me feel slightly uncomfortable but have done nothing to me besides stare, so I think I'm just making a fuss over nothing.

"I need to put sample SE4757 into the centrifuge machine for a couple of hours," I tell him.

"I thought you did that yesterday, Olive?" Nash says, using the unwanted nickname he gave me.

"No, I was working on another sample yesterday," I say with irritation.

He knows I didn't, but he can't pass up the opportunity to get on my nerves. Smirks pass between them before Axel questions me more about the current project. After I've answered to his satisfaction, he leaves to go back to his big, swanky office on the top floor. I bask in the silence for a few minutes, hoping that Nash will leave me alone today, but I can't be so lucky. He saunters his burly body next to mine while I start the centrifuge test on the sample.

"What do you want, Nash?" I ask him before closing the door to the machine and setting the timer. "I really don't have time for your shit today."

He smiles and puts up his hands in a friendly gesture. "Come on, Olive," he says. "I'm not doing anything but observing you."

That's the problem. I'm sick and tired of them observing me with their intense gazes and broody stances.

"You intrigue me," he continues when I say nothing. "There's something about you I can't quite figure out."

My heart quickens as I stare at him, unsure what to do or say. I want to keep my supposed seizures a secret so that no one treats me like a freak or turns me into a science experiment. I glance around the room before finally meeting his gaze.

"What do you mean?" I whisper, my throat suddenly feeling dry.

He steps closer to me, his deep brown eyes now almost smoldering. "I know you have a secret, and I want to know what it is."

My breath hitches in surprise, and I quickly turn away from him. "No, I don't." I walk to the other side of the lab quickly so he doesn't see the lie written all over my face.

"Oh, I think you do," he calls out before leaving the room.

I slump into a chair and drop my head into my hands with a groan. How could he know that I'm hiding something? I feel like I'm walking on a tightrope, and one wrong move could get me in serious trouble. Maybe I'm not as subtle at hiding it as I thought. The door opens, and a tall, middle-aged woman with auburn hair and icy-blue eyes walks in.

I immediately rise, not recognizing her, and prepare to tell her she's not permitted in the lab. She looks at me with an amused look before glancing at the timer on the centrifuge.

"Olivia," she says as if she knows me.

"Yes, that's me," I say with hesitation.

She walks forward with a friendly smile on her face. "My name is Barbara, but everyone calls me Barb. I'm from HR and wanted to see how you're settling in. I know you've been here a year, but I like to do my own observations."

Smiling, I bring a seat over for her to sit and answer all her questions. She's warm and inviting, giving me a sense of safety in her presence. I push the encounter with Nash out of my mind and enjoy our conversation. We talk for about an hour before she leaves me to finish my work.

There are a few analysis reports I need to get done, so I busy myself with that before taking lunch. I'm supposed to meet Evelyn downtown, and I'm running late. After grabbing my purse from my office, changing out of my lab coat, and rushing to the car, I hightail it down Michigan Ave to the little bistro.

"Liv!" she calls from her patio table. "Over here. I saved you a seat."

Laughing, I walk inside the restaurant before heading to the patio. "Still stating the obvious, I see," I tell her as I sit down. "I would have seen you as I got closer. No need to shout across the patio."

She rolls her eyes and hands me a menu. "Whatever. How's work coming along?"

I shrug with indifference. "It's been a great experience so far. The only difficult thing is learning all the calculations I'll need to know to succeed."

Eve takes a sip of her water as I look at the menu. "So, you're not having issues with the seizures happening more?"

With an exasperated sigh, I put down the menu. "No, but they're still there. I hide it, and so far, no one has any idea. Just Nash, Axel, and Steele stare at me often, and I suspect it's because they can tell I'm hiding something, which is not good. I do not want to be on the big boss' radar."

Her gaze jumps from the menu to mine. "Steele? Who is he?"

"Just someone that works in the lab with Nash and me. He's friends with Axel, too. He's tall, pale, and always wears black, so he stands out against everyone else."

"Ooh, mysterious," she says as she wiggles her eyebrows.

Just then, the waiter walks over and asks what we want. We quickly order our food and dive right back into our conversation. The food arrives quickly, and we sit quietly as we stuff our faces. Once finished, Eve tells me what has been going on with her.

The conversation turns to Evelyn's missing cousin, and the mood grows somber. She has been different ever since it happened. She never mentioned her cousin before, so it shocked me how hard she took her disappearance.

"I'm just not getting any closer to finding her," Evelyn says, frustration and sadness evident in her voice. "It's like she's vanished and left no traces behind."

I pat her hand softly. "You will find her, Eve. Don't worry."

Evelyn has been searching for her missing cousin for years. She doesn't know what happened to her, and it sent her on a never-ending mission to save her. All she knows is that her aunt and uncle murdered each other. She believes that whatever darkness surrounded their deaths had taken her cousin away from her.

Eve believes her cousin is still alive and is determined to bring her home, so she spends every waking moment scouring the internet and local newspapers for clues or leads to where she might be. She contacted anyone who seemed at least slightly connected to her disappearance to track down any information they might have.

Despite these efforts, Eve still feels helpless and hopeless in her search. She can't shake the feeling that something terrible had happened to her cousin and that she would never get justice for her. The only thing that keeps

Eve going is sheer determination; she refuses to stop until she finds her.

I listen and nod, adding comments here and there. After an hour of chatting, Eve looks at the time and gasps because we spent too much time here. I follow her out of the bistro with my mind returning to the conversation with Nash. It scares me to know he's watching me, so I have to be careful when I'm working. I don't know what he wants from me or what his intentions are if he finds out, but I'll keep my distance from him.

There's not much traffic on the way back to work, which is surprising given that it's lunchtime. I park in my usual parking spot and exit the car. The parking garage is across the street from the building, so I look both ways before crossing. Suddenly, a woman screams as a man with a mask over his face grabs her roughly.

No one is around to stop him as he drags her down the street toward a plain white van. She fights, kicks, and punches, but the man is too strong. The door to the side of the van opens, and he tosses her inside.

"Hey!" I yell before running toward the van.

I hear a horn blaring right before I hit the ground hard. I look up to see Steele lying on top of me, staring at me with a look of confusion. I realize I'm still in the middle of the street, between the parking garage and my office building.

I never made it across the street, and it's obvious I was having another episode. One that had Steele saving my life. Whatever was happening with that woman wasn't happening here. I lay on the pavement, eyes wide with shock as I stare at Steele.

"What just happened?" I ask breathlessly, my mind still trying to process what had just unfolded.

Steele takes a deep breath and helps me to my feet. "You

were just standing in the middle of the damn street, Olivia," he snaps. "I saw you cross the street, and you just froze there." He pauses for a moment and looks into my eyes before continuing. "You were completely out of it, and I had to tackle you out of the way, or the car would have hit you."

I nod slowly as my heart still races from the near accident. I open my mouth to speak, but no words come out. Instead, I can only look at Steele with embarrassment and a little gratitude.

Steele nods subtly, understanding what I mean without saying it out loud. "It's okay," he said reassuringly. "Are you feeling alright now? Do you need anything?"

I nod before finding my voice again. "Yes, thank you. I'm fine now. Thank you for saving me."

I look around at the crowd that gathered while we were talking, then back at Steele. "Thank you so much for your help."

Steele stares for a moment before nodding his head slightly in acknowledgment. He hesitates for a second before speaking again, unsure if he should say what he's thinking. In the end, however, he goes ahead with it anyway.

"You know," he begins cautiously, his gaze meeting me as he speaks slowly. "You don't have to keep secrets from me. I may understand what's going on with you better than most."

I look up at Steele as my eyes narrow before speaking. "I don't need your help, Steele. This is none of your business."

He takes a step back, surprised by my sudden outburst. He runs a hand through his hair and shakes his head in frustration.

"Look, I know there's something you're not telling me," he snaps, his eyes narrowing as he assesses me. "And I'm going to figure out what it is, with or without you telling me."

My mouth drops open in surprise. I'd been trying so hard to keep my episodes a secret, but Steele is determined to find out the truth no matter what. His sudden and unanticipated interest in uncovering my secret has perplexed and uneasy me. I cross my arms over my chest and sigh heavily before finally speaking again.

"You don't understand," I say, angry at his intimidation tactic. "It's not something I can control or explain. It just happens. I have seizures."

Steele's gaze narrows as he steps forward. "It's obvious that something is going on here," he says firmly. "I don't believe this bullshit seizure excuse of yours, Olivia."

My eyes widen, and I step back, shaking my head at his audacity.

"You know nothing about me, Steele," I snap, voice rising in anger. I gesture wildly with my hands and point my finger at his chest. "You have no right to judge me or my condition!"

"All I'm saying is that you're lying," Steele retorts, his voice sharp and demanding. He crosses his arms over his chest and looks at me with a barely contained fury. "I want the truth. There's something about you I can't quite put a finger on."

I glare at him momentarily before turning away with my fists clenched at my sides. I take a deep breath and slowly let it out before finally speaking again.

"Fine," I say, hoping he'll leave me alone after this. "It's true. I suffer from seizures that I can't control." I tighten her grip on my purse straps and meet Steele's gaze defiantly. "But don't think for one second you know everything about me or my situation. I will not let you ruin this job for me, so keep your mouth shut," I add sharply before stomping down the street without looking back.

I return to my office, switch out my blazer for my lab coat, and return to the lab. Luck is not on my side because Nash, Steele, and Axel are here talking in hushed tones when I walk in. Ignoring them, I sit at an empty desk covered with beakers, tubes, and various chemicals. Their eyes turn to me, and shivers roll down my spine.

I can't shake the feeling of unease that settles in my gut. I try to ignore it, but Nash, Axel, and Steele are still watching me, their eyes following my every move as I label the glassware. It makes me feel like I'm constantly under a microscope. I know Steele told them what happened, and now they're trying to figure me out, but I can't let them.

"Stop staring at me," I snap at them as their intense gazes become too much to handle. "I don't need your help or your scrutiny. I can handle this on my own. I am fine." Realizing I just snapped at the CEO, I take a deep breath before continuing more calmly. "Please, just leave me alone."

I stare at them a little longer before turning away and walking to the other side of the room without looking back.

Nash tilts his head as he assesses me. "You're not fine, Olive." He turns his head to Axel. "She could—" he starts but stops.

Axel sends them a scathing look, and something I don't understand passes between them. Steele and Nash walk to the other side of the lab and got to work without another word. Meanwhile, Axel cocks his head to the side and stares at me quizzically before walking over. He crosses his arms and glares at me.

"Lying will not get you out of this," he growls. "You

think I will not figure out the truth? I'll sort this out, no matter what it takes."

I cross my arms and glare at Axel. "You're standing in my space. Back the hell up." CEO or not, I will not let them gang up on me. "Why is this so important to you?" I question with an exasperated sigh. "I'm good at my job. Nothing in my life interferes with the quality of my work. You guys are fishing for something, and it's making me uncomfortable."

He narrows his eyes and steps closer to me. "I don't like liars," he says sternly. "You'd better talk if you know what's good for you."

I've never seen this side of Axel. While he's a straight-to-the-point kind of guy, he's never downright scary. Right now, Axel is the most intimidating of them all, and I don't know how long I can keep up this façade of not fearing them.

I scoff at him, shaking my head in disbelief. "Do you really think that intimidating me will do any good?" I ask indignantly. I step away from him and walk toward the lab door without looking back.

"I've had enough of your interrogation," I call over my shoulder. "It's time for you to leave me alone." I leave the lab and head home without a second thought.

It's late, and I'm at home, sitting on my couch and trying to relax. But my mind is racing with thoughts about my seizures and the secret I'm keeping from my coworkers. Suddenly, I feel a strange sensation wash over me, and my body freezes. It's happening again.

As I sit here, my mind transports to another place. I see flashes of images that make little sense. I see a dark alleyway with a hooded figure lurking in the shadows. Then, I see a glimpse of a face - a young woman with long blonde hair and piercing blue eyes. But before I can make sense of what I'm seeing, the seizure ends, and I'm back in my living room.

I sit here for a few minutes, catching my breath and trying to understand what happened. It's like my seizures are trying to show me something, but I can't quite decipher what it is.

DIVING INTO THE UNKNOWN

I wake up feeling refreshed and ready to start the day every morning. After a few stretches and breathing techniques, I make my way into the kitchen to prepare breakfast. First, I grind coffee beans for a freshly brewed cup that will give me an extra energy boost throughout the day. While waiting for it to finish brewing, I gather what ingredients I need for my favorite breakfast meal: oatmeal with banana slices and honey drizzled on top.

As soon as I finish everything, I sit at the table with my cup of coffee and enjoy every bite while savoring its deliciousness. Although it's just a simple meal, starting each morning this way has become one of life's minor pleasures that brings me joy every single time.

My phone rings, and I smile when Eve's name appears on the screen. I pick up, give her a morning greeting, and start recounting my terrifying experience from yesterday. I told her I'd been walking across the street to work when I suddenly felt a seizure coming on and lost awareness of my surroundings.

When awareness seeped in again, I realized Steele had pulled me out of the way just before I got hit by an oncoming car. I couldn't believe it—he'd risked his own life to save mine without hesitating. Then he, Nash, and Axel interrogated me relentlessly.

I sigh heavily into the phone. "It's so weird, Eve. I can't believe Steele actually put himself in harm's way to save me."

"Yeah, it really is something," she replies thoughtfully. "I mean, he was so angry and irritated with you but still jumped into action without a second thought."

"I know," I tell her as my voice softens. "I'm not sure why he did it, but I'm grateful that he did."

Eve pauses for a moment before continuing. "If it weren't for Steele, you could've been seriously hurt or worse. He must care about you on some level."

I sigh again and shake my head. "Yeah, maybe. I think it's because he's trying to figure me out, and he can't do that if I'm dead. I'm not sure how to make sense of it all."

"Well, whatever his reasons were for doing it, you should be thankful he was there when you needed him," Eve says.

"You're right," I agree reluctantly before changing the subject. "Anyway, what do you want to do for lunch today? I think we both deserve a break after all this craziness."

"Hmm, what shenanigans can I get up to with my best friend during lunch?" she replies, and I can hear the smirk on her face. "How about brunch with all-you-can-drink mimosas?"

"Mimosas during lunch, Eve?" I say with surprise. "And all you can drink? You know I can't do that in the middle of the workday."

My phone buzzes against my ear, and I pull it away to

look at the incoming message. "I just got a text from Nash. He's telling me that Axel says to stay home to recover from yesterday," I tell Eve.

"What? Is he serious?" She shrieks in excitement.

I nod, even though she can't see it over the phone. "Yeah, I guess so."

I sink onto the couch and grab the remote, flipping to my favorite news channel. As I watch, I absently shovel a spoonful of my breakfast into my mouth.

"So, you're coming over in a couple of hours, then?" I ask Eve over the phone.

"Yeah, that sounds good," she replies with excitement. "I'll bring lunch with me so we can have something to eat while we hang out."

"That sounds great," I tell her around a mouth full of food.

I take another bite of oatmeal as I stare at the television. I smile weakly as I watch the news report about the recent political turmoil in the city.

"Sometimes it feels like this world is spinning out of control," I sigh softly before hanging with Eve and turning off the television.

I almost didn't hear her when she said I don't know the half of it, but she'd already hung up before I could question her. I finish breakfast and prepare for Eve's arrival, feeling a little excited to spend my day off with my best friend.

Eve arrives with her arms full of books, and I wonder what she's up to and why she has such a strange selection.

"I don't think there's anything medically wrong with you, Liv," she says when she sees my confusion. "It's something magical."

I stare in disbelief as she spreads out the books before her.

I gesture toward the strange selection of books. "You can't be serious?" However, her tone tells me she's dead serious.

I let out a disbelieving laugh and shake my head. "Are you being serious right now? Magic isn't real, Eve."

"It might be," she insists, and her entire demeanor changes. She points to a particular book. "This one here talks about magical beings. I think we should look into it."

After some coaxing, I hesitantly agree to look at the books, still skeptical of her magical beliefs. I read through the titles and quickly realize they all relate to different magic and supernatural beings.

"Eve," I say, pushing the books away from me. "This is ridiculous. Magic isn't real."

"It might be," Eve says, her tone resolute. "Just entertain the idea for a moment. It wouldn't hurt to look into it more."

I nod and reluctantly agree again. I pick up one book and start looking through it, trying to make sense of what I'm reading. The book talks about ancient spells, magical artifacts, and powerful beings that can control time itself. As I read further, I realize that maybe there is some truth behind what Evelyn was saying - after all, if no one knows why I'm having seizures or seeing places in other times and locations, then maybe this could be an explanation.

With a newfound curiosity, Eve and I keep reading for a couple of hours with the news playing in the background, captivated by everything I'm reading about this mysterious magical world. Although it seems farfetched, I can't help but start believing in the possibility of magic being real - for if it truly existed, then perhaps it could be the answer to my own mysterious affliction.

We spend the rest of the day sitting side-by-side on the

couch, reading through books about different magical abilities. We discuss the various theories about how cool it would be to be one of these people. I mention how my life would be so much easier with magic and laugh, but Eve doesn't share the same sentiment. She gets a weird look on her face as if I'm crazy for saying that before it clears and passes it off as being lost in thought.

As we continue to read the books, I keep mental notes of any information I think relates to my mysterious affliction. While I'm not sure if any of it would make sense, I still feel compelled to search for answers.

Throughout our reading marathon, we take breaks to enjoy snacks or cook something together in the kitchen. After several hours of intense reading and debate, we finally call it a day - although we still have many more books to read through. I'm still amazed that Eve thought of this and how serious she is about magic. I never knew she believed in this stuff.

To give our minds a rest, we sit back on the couch and watch in horror as the news report details yet another kidnapping. This woman is the fourth reported case across the country, but they know there's probably many more that aren't being reported.

The reporter explains the women were taken within a matter of days and that their abductors hadn't left behind any traces of evidence or clues. The reporter also mentions that the victims are all young females between the ages of 19 and 25, which makes my stomach churn.

I feel a chill run up my spine as I listen to the news report. Every woman abducted was around my age, and they hadn't been able to locate them. I can't help but think that maybe I've seen one of them in a vision at some point.

I tune the news out and pick up another book. Reading

about magic seems like a better use of my time than hearing about women being kidnapped. I scan through a couple of pages before my eyes widen as I read a passage about a rare power known as world sight ability.

According to the text, this ability allows certain individuals to see into different places, times, and even other dimensions. I knew immediately that this had to be related to my affliction.

Eve leans over to ask what I'd found. I tell her there is a magical ability called world sight, and it could be what's wrong with me. The text explains that it's an ancient, very rare power. The book also describes how the wielders of this power could travel between dimensions, allowing them to gain insight into events happening in other places and times. They could also use this power to manipulate time itself.

I'm both intrigued and terrified by what I'm reading. I can't help but wonder if my seizures resulted from the world sight ability manifesting itself. As I look over at Eve with wide eyes, I see that maybe there is something special about me - something worth exploring further and potentially finding answers for.

My mind is racing with all the new information, and I'm amazed to think the seizures are connected to an ancient and rare power. On the one hand, I want to accept this explanation and learn more about what it means for me. On the other, I fear the implications - this power isn't something I asked for, and I had no control over it.

There is also a part of me that wishes I didn't have this power at all. It's made my life so complicated and, if left unchecked, could lead to dangerous consequences for me and others. We sit silently for a moment, both trying to comprehend what we read.

I turn toward Eve. "Do you think this could cause my seizures? Is it possible I have this 'world sight' ability?"

Eve nods, but she has this weird look in her eyes again. "It's certainly a possibility. But it's impossible to know for sure until we find out more information. I think you should try using your ability," she says so suddenly that her tone gives me chills. "The book says that wielders of world sight can use their power to see and walk through time. Maybe you can use it to help find my missing cousin."

Her request is so out of left field that I hesitate for a moment before finally nodding in agreement. There's no guarantee that anything would come of it, but at least we're taking action instead of sitting around waiting for something terrible to happen.

I sit there for a moment, unsure of what to do. I'd never willingly used this mysterious power before. A chuckle escapes my lips as I realize I've probably lost my shit. I'm trying to use magic when I didn't believe in it a day ago.

"What the hell are we doing?" I question Eve quietly. "I can't believe I let you talk me into this."

"I need to find my cousin, Liv," she pleads desperately. "This is important."

My brows scrunch at her desperation. "What's going on, Eve? You're worrying me."

She sits up straight. "Nothing. I'm grasping at straws here, Liv. If you have this ability, you're the only one that can help me."

"Why don't you let the police do their job? They'll find her." I tell her, trying to convince her how insane this all sounds.

"It's been too long already, and I must find her." Eve reaches into her pocket and pulls out a worn-looking photograph. She hands it to me. "This is my cousin. I know it's not a recent photo, but it may help you get an idea of what she looks like."

I take the photo and study it closely. Her cousin had a warm smile and deep brown eyes. Eyes that seemed to look right through me as she stared at them. I try to imagine what her cousin would look like now and how she would react if we ever found her.

"You seem hell-bent on finding her yourself," I say softly, handing the photograph back to her. "I'm still not sure I can help, though. I've never actively tried to bring on a seizure, Eve."

She smiles reassuringly and pats me on the shoulder. "You'll be fine. Just focus on your power and try to see where your vision takes you. If what's wrong with you is, in fact, the world sight power, I'm sure you'll find my cousin in no time."

My brows raise at her encouraging words. "I know you want to find your cousin, and I'm only slightly on board with all this magic stuff, but you can tone down the encouragement. I'm scared enough as it is."

She simply smiles and nods. She's been searching for her cousin for so long that I'm sure she's ready to believe anything. I don't want to disappoint her, but something about this seems off. However, she's been my rock through all this, so I'll try for her. But if there really is something magical going on with me, I am going to use it to help my best friend and maybe those missing women if this works.

I take a deep breath and let my mind take over. "Okay, let's see if I can do this."

I close my eyes and concentrate on bringing on a vision, visualizing what I think her cousin might look like now before trying to use my power to search for her in faraway places. As time passes slowly, I can feel myself growing tired as nothing seems to happen. Finally, with a start, I opened her eyes again, suddenly feeling exhausted.

"I don't think I can do this," I tell Eve.

"Yes, you can," she replies sternly. "Concentrate and try again."

My eyes widen at her tone, but I chalk it up once again to her desperation. I close my eyes and try again.

"Hmm. Hmm, Breeeaathee. Fooocccuuss," Eve hums and sings.

I open my eyes to see her gliding around the room with a candle. I sigh in exasperation as she lights several scented candles and continues to hum softly.

"What exactly are you doing, Eve?" I ask with a shake of my head.

She smiles mischievously and winks. "Just trying to create the perfect atmosphere to focus your powers," she replies.

"Focus my powers?" I reply, raising an eyebrow. "Are you serious?"

Eve chuckles. "You never know," she says with a shrug. "The book said the world sight ability is rare and mysterious. And let's face it, you've been having strange episodes for years." Suddenly, she looks so serious. "I know you have this ability."

Disregarding her tone, I tell her to sit down and stop playing around as I close my eyes again. I'm concentrating for so long; I think this won't work. Suddenly, a strange sensation flows over me, and I finally see Eve's cousin or, who I believe is Eve's cousin. She's sitting on a couch with two other girls as a group of adults speaks to them. I watch the scene play out in front of me.

"That's as calm as I'm going to get," a woman says as she paces back and forth with black wisps of smoke following her. "I

don't want to murder them anymore, but that doesn't mean I won't choke the shit out of them should they say something stupid."

Another woman speaks to them. "Explain. Tell me why you did something so stupid and reckless."

"I was trying to get some answers," the other girl says. This one has an angel-like aura about her. "I thought it would help."

The pacing woman points to two of the girls. "And tweedle dee and tweedle dumb thought it was a good idea?"

"For the record, I told her it was a bad idea," one of the girls replies. This one has pale gray skin and weird eyes.

"Well? Did you find out anything helpful?" the same woman replies.

This time, the angel-like girl answers. "We met a woman who is apparently my aunt, but she rubs me the wrong way. She told us they lived in peace. That each group lives on opposite ends of the world. One day, that peace was broken when they were attacked because they wanted control. They thought my parents took me to safety and didn't know I was kidnapped."

"That's it?" another woman says. "There's got to be more to the story. What does any of that have to do with Lucy?

"My aunt said my parents were trying to get me to safety when they were attacked. Maybe they intended to kill me but kidnapped me instead," the angel-like girl replies. "Maybe I became leverage against the Ylan. That's why they kept me alive and hidden."

Another adult speaks this time. "You'd have to be someone important to hold that kind of weight."

"I believe she was important," Eve's cousin finally speaks. "Everyone kept bowing at her and everything."

I take a deep breath as my surroundings come back into focus. I can't believe what I'd just seen. If that had indeed been Eve's cousin, then she looked perfectly fine. No fear.

No apparent abuse. She was alive and well. So why can't anyone seem to find her? I tell Eve what I just saw. Her cousin was alive and seemed to get scolded by a set of adults in a very parental manner.

I asked her if she knew someone named Lucy since I heard the name in the vision, but she tells me no. She's never heard of someone named Ylan, either. The mystery surrounding her cousin's disappearance is getting weirder by the second. It seemed like an ordinary family scolding their children when they'd done something wrong. Now, I'm not sure that was Eve's cousin because she didn't look like a kidnapping victim.

Evelyn shakes her head in disbelief. "Are you sure it was my cousin? It doesn't sound like she's in danger." Eve looks stunned, not sure if she's disappointed or relieved.

I am similarly perplexed by what I've seen, trying to make sense of it all.

"I don't know," I reply softly, "but I think so. Everything in the vision happened fast, and I can't be sure. It's possible it wasn't her, although it seemed so real..." My voice trails off into a thoughtful silence as my tired mind processes everything.

Evelyn seems torn between hope and suspicion. "Do you think you can see her again, to be sure?"

I nod my head slowly, and Eve looks relieved. "We'll have to be careful," I warn. "I'm not certain if the woman with white eyes was with your cousin or against her. Either way, we need to find out more before we do anything else."

Eve does a double take. "White eyes? Are you sure?"

"I know my colors, Eve," I snap. "Why is the woman with white eyes of interest? You looked shocked for a moment."

She shrugs as if it's no big deal. "It just sounded weird, that's all."

"Since you confirmed that she's alive, can you come over tomorrow to help me expand my search?" Eve asks.

"Eve, you read the text. I can see any place and any time. I don't know when that was happening. That vision doesn't prove she's alive now."

Anger clouds her features. "Don't speak that way. She has to be alive. She's important."

I feel for her because I would also be concerned for my family if something happened to them. Being the good friend that I am, I agree to take another day off work to help broaden her search. Maybe something good can come from this after all.

Eve smiles with relief and excitement, feeling hopeful for the first time since her cousin had gone missing. She thanks me for helping and suggests we take a break for the night before resuming our search tomorrow. We lay back on the sofa and cuddle up beneath the blankets. Abruptly, Eve gives me a tight hug.

"I know you think I'm crazy, but thanks for believing in me. Who knows, maybe this will all lead to something someday," she says cryptically.

I smile and hug her back. "You're my best friend. If you believed my crazy ramblings about women stabbing themselves and other weird shit, I can believe in your weird obsession with magic. Based on what just happened, there's got to be some truth to all the magic stuff."

After watching TV for a few hours, Eve gathers the books and stacks them neatly on the table. She grabs her shoes and tells me she'll be back bright and early in the morning to start our search. I'm a little apprehensive about the mysterious woman with the glowing eyes in the vision.

I want to help Eve find her cousin, but I don't want to find the scary woman while doing it.

I watch Eve silently as she moves around, feeling a mix of emotions twist around in my stomach. On the one hand, I'm excited about the chance to help her find her cousin. But on the other, I'm apprehensive about what might happen if we were to come across something bad doing this. I don't want to put either of us in danger, but I know this could be our best chance of discovering the truth about what happened to her cousin.

I walk over with her as she heads toward the door. "I'll be ready when you arrive bright and early tomorrow morning. We'll figure out everything then, okay?" I tell Eve just as she opens the front door.

Eve smiles and hugs me, reassuring me we'll be careful and that we'd find her cousin no matter what. She then heads out the door, leaving me alone with my thoughts and a strange feeling about magic.

CHAPTER 5

TROUBLING VISIONS

I've taken today off as promised and completed my morning routine. Nash, Steele, and Axel seemed to buy the story of me still not feeling well from the incident with Steele and agreed to give me the day off. Just as I finish getting dressed, Eve arrives with coffee and bagels. I smile at her gratefully as I accept the steaming cup.

"Ah, you know just what I need," I tell her with a chuckle. "You're a lifesaver, Eve."

She smiles back. "Well, I figured since you took the day off to help me, I might as well feed you and give you caffeine."

She laughs at my dramatic sip from the cup. Since I'm already ready, I reach over and grab my jacket before closing the door behind me. I hop into Eve's car and drive the short distance back to her apartment.

It's been a while since I've been over, and my jaw almost hits the floor when she opens the door. I know she's been searching for her cousin for years, but I never knew how much information she could collect about her disappearance.

She has every surface covered in newspapers, police reports, and other documents related to her long-lost cousin. Eve has been researching every detail of her mysterious disappearance, piecing together clues from different sources, connecting them in ways no one else has thought of before. Still, she couldn't catch a break until yesterday.

"You've been very busy, Eve," I tell her with raised eyebrows.

She shrugs like the state of her apartment is no big deal. "I was too tired to clean this up when I got home. Besides, it's a good thing I didn't. Maybe we can find something here that you can use your magic with."

I roll my eyes at her casual mention of me having magic. I survey the room again, trying to take it all in. This is more than just some casual investigation. It's an active search for clues related to her cousin's disappearance. She's left no stone unturned in her attempts to determine what happened to her. Her obsession became the sole focus of her life.

We get set up and start pouring through all the data she's collected. Eve points out various pieces of evidence and news reports she had gathered. We discuss plausible theories and ideas of what might have happened to her cousin for her to end up wherever she is now.

Everything from kidnapping to foul play seems like a possibility at this point. As we continue going through all the data, each piece of information seems to lead us further away from finding answers and deeper into an unsolved mystery.

Eve is silently sifting through a stack of newspaper articles about her cousin's disappearance as I read aloud from a witness statement.

"This guy said he saw your cousin get into a car around

the corner from her house," I said. "But he doesn't remember the make and model."

She nods at me. "Yeah, I've read that one. Keep reading further. His statement is just one of many peculiar ones."

I can see what she means. This supposed witness said he saw Eve's cousin leave her house and walk down the street before getting into a car. He describes the make and model of the vehicle in his statement, and my eyes grow wide as I read it.

"You cannot be serious," I say as I look at Eve.

She chuckles at my apparent disbelief. "As a heart attack."

"This guy just described a goddamn spaceship, Eve," I reply. "There's no way the police believed this load of shit."

"The funny thing is," she starts. "All the witnesses described the same thing."

I shake my head. No wonder she hasn't been able to make any progress in her search. The police reports are terrible. The news wants to report more on her aunt and uncle's domestic violence than her cousin's disappearance, and these witness statements seem like the police spoke to a bunch of five-year-olds. We continue going through everything, and I cannot believe the terrible police work that went into her cousin's disappearance.

"Nothing seems to point to how she ended up where she is. If it weren't for your magic, I wouldn't have known she was alive," Eve says tiredly.

We'd been sifting over the police reports for hours, and by the time I suggest we take a break and get lunch, Eve's eyes were glazing over.

"Let's take a break to eat and give our minds a rest," I tell her as my stomach grumbles.

"That sounds like an excellent idea," she says with a sigh of relief.

We gather our things, leave her apartment, and walk down the street. It's a lovely day out, and there are plenty of little shops in her neighborhood. As we're walking, Eve suddenly tells me something that catches me off guard.

"I believe my cousin has magic like you," she says.

I take a moment to process what she's saying.

"Are you sure?" I ask cautiously. "I'm still not sure if I fully believe in magic, Eve. This is all new to me."

"But was there anything that you saw that may suggest that?" she replies, looking at me as if I'm missing a piece of a puzzle she wants me to put together.

We walk in silence for a moment, as that is a complex question. "The girls I saw didn't exactly look normal, nor did the women scolding them." I put my hand up to stop her from replying. "However, it could have been how things looked in the vision. I'm still not sure how this all works, so I don't want to make more assumptions, Eve."

We walk in silence again, and thoughts run through my head. Eve seems like she's hiding something, but she would never hide something from me. Maybe she just wants me to believe in magic the way she does and is making me question my sanity to do it.

That doesn't seem like Eve's style, either. The most likely cause of my suspicions is probably her introduction of magic. I'm still trying to process it, and this is my mind's way of dealing with it.

We arrive at a little cafe. "Let's order some food," I tell her with a smile.

We sit by the window and peruse the menu for what feels like ages, as everything sounds delicious. We eventually decided to share a spinach salad with grilled chicken and roasted potatoes as our main course and two glasses of wine. Our food arrives quickly, and it smells heavenly.

They dressed the salad with just enough vinaigrette that every bite is fresh. The chicken is grilled to perfection, and the potatoes are crispy on the outside and fluffy on the inside. Our wine is just sweet enough for our tastes, with a hint of berry flavor.

We enjoy every bite of our meal as we discuss what we'd learned from the information she'd collected and continue to speculate about different theories for her cousin's disappearance. We end up forming some pretty crazy hypotheses by the time we're almost finished eating.

"That is the most ridiculous thing I have ever heard," Eve laughs. "Where did you come up with that?"

My shoulders shake with laughter as well. "Shut up. Considering that you brought your theory of magic to me, it's not that far-fetched. Your cousin could be a witch, hopped on a broomstick, and flew far away from here."

"Does this mean my cousin is around someone else with magic? You said you saw a woman with black wispy smoke flowing around her," Eve says cautiously.

"I'm still not sure, Eve," I tell her with a shrug. "Like I said before, it could be how the vision looks. I don't have definitive answers for you. I'm sorry."

We get back to talking and let the conversation flow easily. I keep Eve's mind off finding her cousin to keep the mood light. My brief vision of her has made Eve even more determined to find her, and it's a lot of pressure.

I don't want to disappoint her, but I also don't know if I can do what she asks. Maybe that vision was a coincidence, and it won't happen again. However, I feel that's not the case. There's more going on here, and I'm sure I'll find out eventually.

We finish our lunch and head back to Eve's apartment. We spend the rest of the day going through more files and calling anyone who might have information about her cousin's whereabouts. Anything that I can use to focus on and get a vision.

We're so overloaded with information that we don't know what to use and what not to use. This whole thing is a mess. As the day goes on, I feel a familiar tingling sensation in my head, and I know what's coming next—a seizure.

"Olivia, are you okay?" Evelyn asks, noticing the panic on my face.

"I'm fine," I lie. "Maybe I need to rest for a minute."

I close my eyes and let the seizure take over. A little girl is screaming and crying as water pours over her. This angel-like girl is glaring down at her with anger in her eyes.

"What are you doing to my little critter?" the intimidating woman with white eyes says.

She snaps her fingers in the blink of an eye; the water turns off, and the little girl is standing in front of her as dry as if water had never touched her. The little girl whines about the angel-like girl being mean to her and not getting any ice cream.

The woman with the white eyes glares at the angel-like girl, and they're in an intense stare as Eve's cousin walks into the room.

"Not this again. Will you two stop it?" she says to them.

My eyes snap open in shock. Eve had been watching from the sidelines and noticed the change in my demeanor.

She quickly sits down beside me. "Did you see something? Anything at all?"

I stare at Eve with a dazed expression. "Yes," I stammered. "I-I think I did... I saw your cousin standing in a bathroom doorway, talking to the angel-like girl again.

They were discussing something, and then I saw the scary woman with white eyes standing in the corner, yelling at the angel like a girl while a little girl was crying about ice cream. Your cousin was standing back, telling them to knock it off."

"What does this mean?" Eve asks.

"I don't know," I tell her.

I'm frustrated, though, because this is the second vision I've had of Eve's cousin, and I can't tell her anything about where she is. There were no identifying marks anywhere to help me out. All I know is that she's inside of a house. It's late now, and I want to go home. Eve drops me off at home, and I tell her I'll see her later before closing the car door. I've got work in the morning, and I want to get a good night's rest.

Every night, I make it a point to stick to my bedtime routine. As soon as I make it inside, I get ready for bed. First up, I brush my teeth and floss. Then, I take off my makeup using a gentle cleanser and some warm water. After that, I change into my pajamas and apply some moisturizer to my face.

Then, I set my alarm for the following day so I won't oversleep. I've always been a stickler about keeping to this routine. After I finish putting my hair up, I walk out of the bathroom and notice the bedroom window is open. I don't remember opening it when I came home, but I could have left it open this morning.

Walking over, I shut it before drawing the curtains shut and walking back toward the bed. My mind is racing from today's information overload, especially my last vision. To help calm my mind, I pick up the book on my nightstand and start reading.

I only read for about ten minutes before drifting off to

sleep. I turn over, snuggling deeper into the blanket as I feel a cool breeze blow through the room. My eyes snap open as I remember closing the window before bed.

As soon as my eyes open, I see a figure standing in front of my bed. I let out a shriek and frantically reach toward the nightstand to flick on the lamp. As the room illuminates, I look around in fear but see nothing unusual. I was sure I saw a figure standing before my bed. My heart pounding, I slowly look around the room, and everything seems to be normal.

The window is still open, and the curtains are blowing in the night air, but nothing else seems out of place. As I try to calm myself down, I hear a low whisper coming from the other side of the room. I gasp and quickly sit up, scanning the room for any signs of movement. All I can see is an empty room, but something doesn't feel right. My skin crawls with fear as if someone or something had just passed through me.

I hold my breath, not daring to make a sound until finally, after what feels like an eternity, my heart rate slows. I don't want to stay in my room any longer, so I get out of bed and run to the living room. I quickly turn on all the lights and sit on the couch, trying to process what happened. My mind is getting away from me. All this talk of magic, trying to find Eve's cousin, and the visions are all messing with my head.

Maybe I thought I closed the window before bed, and I hadn't really done it. There's no one else here with me, and there's no way the window opened by itself. My mind must have still been waking up because I imagined seeing someone in my room. Whatever it is, I know one thing for sure: there's no way I'm getting a good night's sleep tonight.

The incident leaves me feeling unnerved and scared but, strangely enough, also somewhat intrigued. I can't help but wonder if this is only the beginning of some strange magical occurrences that lay ahead of me. Whatever it may be, I vow never to drift off so easily into sleep without inspecting the house again. From here on, I will stay alert no matter how hard it might be while sleeping. I truly frightened myself and don't want to go back to sleep.

I try to stay awake, but my eyelids are heavy. My head keeps drooping, no matter how much I try to keep it up. The night is still and dark; nothing stirs in the silent room. It feels like a struggle to remain conscious as if I have to fight an invisible force that wants me to sleep. I feel like my body is being dragged down into the depths of slumber, and I have to fight tooth and nail against it.

I try counting to one thousand, reading a book, listening to music, anything that can keep me awake. But eventually, it all seemed futile. My eyes close of their own volition, and my head droops again. Unfortunately, my dreams are nightmares tonight.

"Help! Someone help me, please!" a woman yells.

She's running down the street frantically with tears streaming down her eyes. It looks like she'd just gotten off work because she's wearing a waitress uniform with a familiar diner logo. She works at the White Horse Diner down on Michigan Ave. The woman runs as fast as she can, her heart pounding in her chest and terror gripping every part of her body. She screams for help with all her breath, desperately looking for a way out of the terrifying situation.

She darts down streets and alleyways, zigzagging to lose her pursuer. However, with every turn she makes, she keeps looking back to see if the mysterious person is still chasing her. She sprints hastily through an unfamiliar neighborhood in a last-ditch effort to escape. I can't see who's chasing her but hear heavy footsteps thundering behind her.

She needs help, and there's no one around. Something flows through me, and I step forward, intending to help her. I look around to see that I'm a few feet behind her. My feet pound against the ground as I run after her, eager to help get her to safety. I put two fingers to my mouth and whistle, effectively getting her attention.

"Come with me!" I yell quietly. "Hurry!"

The woman turns around and runs toward me. "You have to help me! Some guys just tried to kidnap me."

"Follow me. I know a police station that's not too far from here." I tell her as I grab her hand and run.

We make it to the police station in under five minutes. I usher her in, and she grabs my hand, giving it a gentle squeeze before thanking me for my help. The police station is pretty empty tonight, and luckily, there's an officer there to help.

"Hello, I'm Officer McNeal. And you are?" he says as he sits at the desk he escorted us to. He gives me the feeling that he's one of those slimy officers you see in movies.

"My name is Alex," the woman whispers.

He leans back in his chair. "Okay, Alex. Can you tell me what happened?"

She recounts what happened. "I was walking home from work when I noticed a man lingering around the corner. He had an eerie presence and followed me as I walked. I panicked and began running, but he kept matching my pace and closing in on me." She looks over at me. "Luckily, she found me at that moment and helped me escape."

"What were you doing out so late, Ms.?" Officer McNeal says as he looks toward me.

"It's Olivia," I reply. "I wasn't out. I heard a woman screaming and helped."

"Hmm," is all he says before going back to speaking with Alex.

We're there for almost an hour before he has everything he needs, which wasn't much. She'd answered his questions to the best of her abilities but had no specifics. He offered to drive her home, but I declined when he asked me.

As I stand to leave, Alex grabs my hand and thanks me once again. Nodding, I turn to go to head back home. I stumble a few minutes into my walk when a realization sinks in. I was at home asleep in my bed. What I'd mistaken for a dream was reality, a vision. One that I'd inserted myself into without thinking.

CHAPTER 6

A FRIGHTENING ENCOUNTER

My alarm goes off at its usual time, and I am beyond tired. I could barely sleep, as I'd been on edge after last night's ordeal. Realizing that I'd stepped into my vision of a woman running for her life really shook me.

I complete my morning routine, but this time, I go through the entire house, securing the windows and double-checking that no one is here. As I check the lock on the last window, my phone rings. I sigh heavily as I see Mom's name pop up on the screen.

"Hi, mom," I say as I answer the phone.

"Olivia, you sound tired. It is your condition?" she says, not bothering to greet me good morning. "I swear, you need to take better care of yourself, or you will not get any better. It's bad enough that something is wrong with you. Don't make it worse."

I take a second before answering because I really don't want to rile her up. "Everything is fine, mom. I'm just tired, that's all. I didn't sleep well."

She huffs in agitation. "Well, why didn't you sleep well?

Are you not taking your medication? When is your next doctor's appointment? I'm going to come with you."

"I'm not a child, Mom," I snap, unable to help it. "The medication doesn't work, and the doctors don't know what they're doing."

"It's that kind of behavior that will keep you in the condition you're in. Is that what you want, Olivia?" Mom asks, her voice laced with anger.

I don't recognize the woman on the other end of the phone. She's never been so cruel to me. "Mom, why do you only call to ask about my condition? We haven't been out together in years. You never visit anymore, and whenever I plan to come by, you always have something else to do."

"Olivia," Mom gasps into the phone. "I can't be in public with you. What if you have an episode? People would stare and talk. I can't have that."

I am stunned silent by her response. I knew our dynamic had changed when all of this started happening, but I never thought she'd stoop to this level. It shouldn't surprise me that she's even more embarrassed by me.

Mom continues talking. "You would probably be better by now if you had gone to that treatment center like I told you to. Seriously, Olivia. You have to do better. Follow what the doctors are telling you to do. I can't have this making me look like I don't care about your health."

Now, it all makes sense. Mom is a state representative, and she doesn't want me to tarnish her reputation. Her image means everything to her, but it had never impeded our relationship too drastically until now.

That treatment center wasn't to help me get better. It was to hide me away or use it as promotional material. I'm seeing Mom in a new light, and I wonder if she's always been this way, and I just never saw it.

I snort into the phone. "If you're so embarrassed by me, don't bother calling again. I've got to get to work. Bye."

"Oliv—" she says, but I hang up the phone.

I leave the house in anger after the conversation with Mom. Luckily, traffic wasn't too bad, so that didn't sour my mood further. I park in my usual space and take a second to breathe. I will not go into work in a foul mood and a frown on my face.

After giving myself a few minutes to calm down, I grab my things and exit the vehicle. I head straight to my office, put on my lab coat, and walk straight to the lab. Nash and Steele are already inside when I arrive.

"Good morning, Olive," Nash says as I walk in. "Are you feeling better?"

The way he gazes at me makes my skin crawl. "Good morning, and yes, I am feeling better. Thank you for asking."

I know the next set of tests that need to be done, so I head over to the cabinets and grab the materials. These tests require all of us to work together, and I'm not looking forward to them assessing me all day.

I grab the book with the test procedures and sit it next to all the testing materials. Both Steele and Nash walk over. We each take a few test methods and get to work. We're working in blissful silence when Steele's whisper interrupts my serenity.

"Are you sure you're okay after the incident?" he asks. He sounds more curious than concerned when he asks.

I frown at him as he looks me in the eye. When I'm about to open my mouth to answer, I feel a sensation flow through my body, and I know what's about to happen. I close my eyes tight with my hands gripping the edge of the counter as I try to fight off the seizure, but I fail miserably. The vision comes on swift and strong.

"We have a situation that will require all of us," the woman I'd seen before tells them. "Some very dangerous men are after one of our people."

The angel-like girl frowns at her. "Why?"

What looks to be a ghost shimmers into the room. "Because their ability is one special ability, and the men know what it is. If they get their hands on that magic user, some terrible things will happen."

This time, the woman with the white eyes speaks. "Off we go on another adventure based on sketchy visions and half-assed information. When will we ever learn our lesson?"

The ghost laughs at her theatrics. "Yet somehow, with my help, you always win. A thank you would be nice."

"When you can tell us something that we don't have to decipher, then I'll say thank you," the woman with the white eyes replies. "Are we leaving or what?"

When I open my eyes again, I'm back in the lab, and it seems neither Steele nor Nash have noticed my lapse in focus. That's what I'm afraid of—having people catch me during an episode. I finally answer Steele and get to work on the tests.

Now and then, I'll feel their gazes on me, and goosebumps form on my skin every time. After running a few more tests, I excuse myself and hide in my office for the rest of the day. They can manage without me. I'll tell them I'm catching up on reports if they ask.

Unfortunately, I'm not lucky enough to be left alone. A couple of hours later, Axel buzzes my office and requests my presence. I have no choice but to see him since he is my boss. With a heavy sigh, I leave my office for the elevators. When I reach his floor, I walk to the receptionist's desk to let his assistant know Axel asked to see me.

She tells me to go straight in, and I find Axel sitting behind his large desk, talking to someone on the phone in a stern tone. When he sees me, he growls at the person on the phone to be more careful next time, or there will be consequences.

After he hangs up, he motions for me to sit in the chair in front of his desk. He looks and seems agitated, which only adds to his imposing demeanor. He stays silent for a few minutes, staring at me like he's trying to see into my soul.

"I know something strange is going on, Olivia," he says. "I've known since a month after you started. It hasn't interfered with your job, so I let it be. Steele and Nash have been observing you lately, and they're convinced it's something more than the seizure excuse you gave Steele. Especially after he saved you the other day."

Feeling like a deer caught in headlights, I stare at him with wide eyes. "I.. I don't know what you mean. It's a medical condition. Am I being fired? I did state that I had a medical condition on my application."

He leans back in his chair. "No, you're not being fired. It would be illegal to fire you for a medical condition. Here's the thing, Olivia. I don't like liars, so you better tell the truth before I fire you for being a liability."

He looks downright scary right now. The dark look on his face tells me he's probably done some bad things in his life.

"I have seizures, Axel. Sometimes, it causes me to space out. I know it happens at the most inopportune times, but I can manage it," I tell him, hoping like hell that he believes me.

He cocks his head to the side. "There's absolutely no reason to hide seizures, Olivia. Especially since you stated you already disclosed that information. If you really suffered from seizures, you would have asked for accommodations. In that regard, you're protected by law. So, I see no reason for you to hide seizures so fiercely unless you're lying."

He has a point. I look sketchy as hell, and I need to think of something fast before he fires me.

"Okay, I'm hiding some secondary complications associated with the seizures. I'm still being seen for a proper diagnosis. I didn't want it to be an issue since it's not something listed on my application," I tell hurriedly.

There's no way in hell I'll tell him that my best friend believes I have magic and that I believe it as well. They'll ship me off to crazy town faster than I can blink.

"If you say so. You can go back to work," he says in a dismissive tone. I can tell he doesn't believe me, but I'm not sticking around for him to question me further.

As soon as I return to my office, I lean back in the chair with my head toward the ceiling. Thinking back to the episode I had in front of Steele, I wonder what it was about. It was the same women I'd seen before, and this time, they were talking about magic and bad guys.

Not to mention, a ghost shimmered into their room, and they started talking as if it was normal to see a ghost. It's safe to say they are involved with magic, but I won't tell Eve this. She'll get too absorbed and want me to do all kinds of things that I'm not sure I want to be involved in.

My phone rings, and I see Eve is calling me. Her timing is always impeccable when I need to talk.

"My boss thinks I'm a liar and that I'm probably on drugs," I say as soon as I answer.

A brief silence ensues before she answers. "Um, what the hell, Olivia? Start from the beginning."

I tell her about the episode in the lab, trying to hide out in my office, and then my conversation with Axel. Ever since Eve brought her magic theory to me, everything's been going to shit.

"Well, he has a point, Liv," she says. "Everyone knows you're hiding something, and you're giving them a pretty shitty reason behind it."

"Thanks for your very astute observation, Evelyn," I reply. "My life has been getting weirder ever since you brought the theory of magic up. I would like to go back to my normal weird now."

She snorts into the phone. "Don't blame this shit on me, Liv. I figured out what was really happening to you. You should thank me."

"I'm not sure if I should say — thank you, you are an awesome friend, or a screw you, you messed up my life. I'll let you know once I decide," I tell her sarcastically.

Her laughter flows through the phone, bringing a smile to my face. I can always count on her to help me feel better.

"Hey, why were you calling?" I ask her. She must have called me for a reason.

"Your mother called me today. Five times!" she shouts into the phone. "She's raving about how you've lost your mind and won't take your medicine or listen to the doctors. She thinks you're intentionally trying to sabotage her image, if you can believe it or not."

"Oh, I can believe it," I tell her. "We had a very intense conversation this morning that ended with me telling her not to call me again. It is funny that she hasn't attempted to call me since, but she called you."

"Ugh, I cannot believe the balls on that woman," Eve

says. "Don't let it get to you, Liv. She's always been more concerned about herself. Everyone saw it but you."

"I guess you're right," I say sadly.

Eve and I talk on the phone for a few more minutes, making plans to meet for lunch tomorrow. Nash knocks on my office door to tell me they need me to run a few tests for them, and I have no choice but to help. This was originally a group effort, anyway.

There are no more stares, and I'm slightly put off by it. I wouldn't say I liked all the staring to begin with, but now they're avoiding looking at me altogether. It makes me wonder if Axel said anything to them about it. The rest of the day flows easily, and we complete all the tests.

The drive home is uneventful, but I have a feeling of dread the whole time. As if my conversation with Axel did not go well, and it could come back to bite me in the ass. I make it home in no time, eat, complete my night routine, and now I'm relaxing until bed. There isn't much on TV, so I settle for watching a B-rated action movie, and it isn't very interesting.

Something startles me awake. I hadn't realized I'd fallen asleep, but I'm more worried about what woke me up. Something grabs me and yanks me out of the bed, and I let out a loud scream. I'm utterly shocked as the intruder grabs me and pulls me down the hallway.

I feel the intruder dragging my limp body across the floor, and I try to scream for help, but only muffled cries come out. The cold, hard grip of their hands refuses to let go, and I feel myself losing consciousness from fear.

The intruder then stuffs a towel into my mouth, cutting off my already faint screams. They drag me further down the hall until we reach the bathroom. With one arm around my neck, the figure opens the door and throws me onto the cold tiles with a thud.

He runs the water in the tub, and the fear inside me grows to the size of a mountain. I yank the towel out of my mouth and scramble off the floor. Running through the hallway, I scream bloody murder as the intruder chases after me. There is no way I'm going to let him drown me.

He catches up to me, grabbing me by my hair before putting me in a chokehold. I gasp for air, desperately trying to break away from the intruder's iron grip. His hands are around my neck, and I feel myself slowly slipping away as I struggle to stay conscious. With all the strength I have left, I push him away and stumble into a chair nearby. He moves in front of the front door.

He lunges at me again, but I'm ready to block his attack, pushing him backwards with my force. My mind runs through escape routes, but there is no way out of this situation other than through him. He comes at me again and we tussle until he finally pins me down on the floor, pressing his weight against mine so hard that it feels like he wants to drown me in the ground itself.

My heart rate skyrockets as I realize that I'm in serious trouble. This could be the mysterious person who was chasing Alex home after work, and now he's here to kill me because I'd successfully thwarted his attempt to kidnap her. Frantically, I scan the room for something, anything, to use to my advantage, and then it hits me. Two feet away is the pair of heels I wore to work today.

I reach over and grab a shoe, hitting him in the head with the tip of the heel. He screams out in pain as it embeds a little when it contacts his skin, temporarily incapacitating him. Taking advantage of this opportunity, I scrambled back up and run towards the door, pulling it open just as he chases after me again.

This guy is fast because he grabs me before I make it out the door. I'm thrown back, and I fall to the floor. I watch as he stalks toward me slowly.

"What do you want?" I ask him frantically. "Why are you trying to kill me?"

He bends down, grabs one of my legs, and starts dragging me back toward the bathroom, where I hear the water still running. He never answers. Instead, he says nothing as he puts his hands on my body and throws me into the tub. The cold water that fills up the tub shocks my body, and I feel like I'm going to die.

Suddenly, he steps into the tub with me, and I'm confused. He trains his deadly eyes on me, staring intensely before hauling me to my feet. Water drips down as I shiver from the cold. He holds his hand down toward the water, and it swirls around, sloshing over the sides of the tub.

We spin around, faster and faster, until we fall through. Water surrounds me, and I hold my breath like it will save me from drowning. I'm pulled and tugged every which way, flowing through a vortex of water as I go.

I'm trying to fight the force moving me through the water with no success. Whoever this guy is, he obviously has magic, but I don't know what he wants with me. I don't have any enemies, and the only thing I'm guilty of is helping that woman. No good deed is my last thought before everything goes black.

CHAPTER 7
THE VEIL SOCIETY

I wake up in a dark room, and my head is foggy. Looking around, I see a small bed, a table with a lamp, and a small bathroom with no window. There isn't even a door to the room. I don't know how long I've been out or in this room, but suddenly, a door appears on one wall and swings open.

At first, I can't believe my eyes. Doors don't just magically appear out of nowhere, but I guess there is magic involved. A hooded figure appears in the doorway, distracting me from my thoughts. Refusing to cower, I lift my chin higher as the figure approaches, showing my defiance. The figure moves to grab me, and I pull away.

"Where am I?" I ask. "Where have you taken me?"

The figure grabs me again, this time faster than I can react. With a firm grip, I'm dragged out of the room as the figure tells me I'm going to meet the boss. I stumble when I try to keep pace as I'm dragged down a long, dark hallway until we stop at a closed door.

The figure knocks on the door, and a muffled voice yells

at us to enter. Upon entering the room, a gasp leaves my mouth because sitting behind a large oak desk is none other than Axel himself in an expensive-looking black suit.

He nods his head toward the figure escorting me, and he turns to leave the room, leaving me staring with shock on my face. Fear coursed through me once the shock wears off because if I thought he was scary before, he looks down-right dangerous now. He kidnapped me, and though I don't know why, I am worried.

He reclines in his chair. "Do you know why you're here, Olivia?" he asks.

"No," I snap at him without regard to the danger I'm in. "What the hell are you doing, Axel?"

He motions toward the empty chair in front of his desk and tells me to have a seat. I shake my head no and step back, intending to run through the door I just entered. Just as I turn to bolt toward the door, Axel's voice snaps in the air like a whip, telling me not to move another step.

I freeze with fear at his sharp command and turn around to look at him. Axel gets up from behind his desk and walks toward me, one menacing step at a time. I stumble back as he advances until I press my back against the wall.

Without warning, his hand whips out and grabs my jaw. His fingers dig in painfully as he presses me deeper into the wall as fear so strong courses through me. He looks menacing as his dark brown eyes peer into mine. I don't know what's going on or what he wants from me, but I mentally prepare myself for a fight should I need to.

He leans forward so his face is an inch from mine and bares his teeth. "I can smell your fear, Olivia. Are you afraid of me? Now, what does a woman like you have to be afraid of?"

Despite my fear, my brows scrunch in confusion. A woman like me? I'm just a chemical engineer with a medical condition. There's nothing exciting about me, despite my newfound belief in magic, but he doesn't know about that.

His grip tightens even more. "I expect my orders to be followed, Olivia. When I tell you to do something, you do it, or the consequences won't be nice. Now sit your ass down in that chair."

He lets go of my chin and stalks back behind his desk. He sends me another scathing look before sitting down again. I slowly slide into the seat, sitting as far back as the chair will allow. He sends a condescending smirk my way.

"Welcome to the Veil Society, Olivia," he says.

"What the hell is the Veil Society, and why am I here?" I ask him in confusion. "Have you lost your damn mind, Axel?"

"The Veil Society is an ancient society dating far back through history. Our sole purpose is to find the *byu na iko*, pair of powers," he starts. "They are the individuals who, together, will reshape the world to what it's supposed to be."

I sit here quietly, listening to his story and how he believes I am part of this mysterious pair they're searching for. Why he thinks that, I don't know.

"How is the world meant to be?" I ask, interrupting his story.

His eyes shoot daggers at me for interrupting. "The world is meant only for people like us."

"Like us? What about people.... not like us?" I ask, trying to understand what he means.

He shrugs carelessly. "They'll be gone. Extinct. There is no place for them amongst us. We will use the *byu na iko* to find Thodara and make her pay for not protecting her world."

I hop from the chair in anger. "You're crazy! Delusional. Kidnapping is illegal, Axel. I'm not like you, whatever the hell that means!"

His phone rings before he can reply, and he answers on the second ring. He sits straighter in his chair when someone speaks on the other end. He snaps his fingers, and someone enters the room. I turn around, and again, a gasp leaves my mouth.

He covers the phone with his hand. "I see you've met Barb. She's like us, but her ability is unique. With just one touch, she can get a sense of what another one of us can do. Imagine my surprise when she told me your ability enables you to know and see all. Now, that's a priceless ability that will work to our advantage."

"This is insane. Let me go," I plead with him without taking my eyes off Barb's smiling face.

"I tried to give you a chance to come clean, Olivia. To tell what was going on, but you refused and lied," Axel replies.

I stare at him in disbelief. "Come on, Axel. All of this would seem insane to normal people. Excuse me for trying to stay out of mental institutions!"

"I could have helped you see the big picture you're a part of, but you forced my hand," he says. "You are a vital piece to our plans."

I recover from the shock, and anger blazes in my eyes. I tell Axel that I want no part in whatever illegal activity he's got going on, but he ignores me and returns to his call. Barb grabs my arm and leads me out the door, and I run for it.

The hallway is dark, and I can't see very well. I stumble

on something before falling to the ground. Suddenly, Barb is there, pulling me up by my hair. She's stronger than she looks, and she drags me away.

I struggle to keep up with her pace, and she shoves me face-first into a wall. Suddenly, an open door appears in front of me, and I fall through to the ground. Before I can get up to go back through, it disappears again, leaving me in the room alone. I'm left alone to think about what Axel said to me.

I've never heard of Thodara before and don't know what she's done to earn the anger of this Veil Society. However, everything about this situation seems crazy. I tell myself that I'll wake up any moment, and this will all have been a dream.

Unfortunately, that is not the case. A few hours later, a small opening appears in the wall, similar to the size of a doggy door, and they push a tray of food through before the opening disappears again. Slipping off the small bed, I walk over to the tray to see a burger and fries but no drink.

At first, I suspect the food is poisoned, but then I eat it to maintain my strength. If I'm going to escape, it's better not to be tired or starving.

The next couple of days pass in the same manner. I'm in the room for hours, and three times a day, a small door appears, and I push food through. Today is different, though. A door appears, and the hooded figure returns, grabbing me by the arm and dragging me out of the room.

"I have ears, you know," I say as I tug back. "All you have to do is ask me to follow you."

The figure ignores me and continues to drag me. We walk down a series of hallways until I'm led back to the same door as Axel's office. He's sitting behind the same desk, apparently waiting for my arrival. This time, the hooded figure led me to the chair and pushes me into one before leaving.

"I trust you've had some time to think about what I've told you," Axel says when the hooded figure closes the door.

"What exactly was there to think about?" I ask. "I don't know what your little crazy story has to do with me or what you want from me."

He sighs in frustration. "You're smart. I thought you'd figure it out, Olivia. You are part of the pair of powers, and you will help us find the second half. I don't care how many we have to kill to do it," he snaps.

I gape at his command. I can't even control what's happening to me, and he wants me to use it to help him? To find other people like me?

"How am I supposed to do that, Axel?" I snap at him despite the dangerous aura he emits. "It's not like tracking a beacon, and people don't walk around with signs that say 'I have magic' with them."

He's around the desk and is standing in front of me before I can react. "Show some respect when speaking to me. I don't care how you do it, but you will do it, Olivia."

I stare up at him in defiance. "I will not help you torture and kill innocent people."

He grabs me by the throat. "So, you'd rather I'd torture you than do what we ask willingly? I can arrange that."

I'm ushered out of the room before I can protest, and fear shoots down my spine at what's coming. The following days were torture indeed. After I left Axel, they took me to a room where someone strapped me to a chair. The first person came in and tried to freeze me to death. Still, I refused to help them. The next day, someone continuously electrocuted me. It was a pain I'd never felt before, but I held firm.

The following person broke certain bones and mended them before breaking them again. I don't know how much more I can hold out, but withstanding torture is much more brutal than they make it seem on TV. After a few more days of this, Axel comes into the room.

"Are you ready to comply now, Olivia?" he snaps.

I only stare at him with fire in my eyes, conveying all the hatred I feel for him at this moment. He continues when I refuse to speak.

"The torture will continue. Is that what you want? To die?" he says frantically.

I smirk at him. "You won't let me die, Axel. You need me, remember? I'll withstand all the torture in the world to keep from helping you kill innocent people."

He punches me in the face, and my head snaps back. Black dots cloud my vision as I lean back in a daze.

"You think you're so smart? Trust me. You will aid in our endeavor," he says before storming out of the room, leaving me exhausted from this ordeal.

I'm glad to say that my bravery put an end to the torture. I'm escorted back to my room. My body hurts, I'm hungry, and I'm exhausted. Luckily, food arrived shortly after I'm led into the room, and I inhale the food like my life depends on it. All too soon, I fall asleep on the bed.

Screams of pain wake me up instantly. It's weird because I rarely hear anything inside this room. I guess someone else refused Axel's request and is now being tortured. I notice an open door on the other side of the room and look around in fear. There's not usually a door to this room, so I'm highly suspicious. This could be a mistake or a trap, but I'm willing to chance an escape.

I walk into the hallway, holding my breath, waiting for someone to appear, but no one does. More screams reach my ears, and I know someone is being tortured for sure. I can feel the pain in the screams down to my bones. I continue to maneuver slowly through the hallways, trying to find a way out of the place.

Another scream pierces the air, this time clearer. "Please! I...don't know...What...You're...Talking...About!"

I freeze as terror seizes my entire body. It feels like ice is flowing through my veins as I shiver and fear flows through me. It. Can't. Be.

The scream sounds again, and I take off running in the direction it came from. "No, no, no," I mumble as I run.

I turn a corner and run into a dead end. Just as I turn around to return the way I came, a wall appears, closing me inside four walls with no exit. The wall in front of me turns to glass, and I can see my worst fear clearly.

The tears stream down my face. "No! God no!"

A door appears behind me, and Axel steps through. He pins me to the glass by my throat when I turn around.

"You were right, Olivia," he says. "You are too important to the cause to die." He inclines his head toward the glass. "But she's nobody. I don't have to kill you. I can kill those you love. You'll still have blood on your hands. Who's it going to be? People you don't know or your loved ones?"

Tears stream down my face in defeat. The choice is simple. "Fine. Let Eve go. She has nothing to do with this."

He stares at me for a moment longer before letting go. "Wise choice, Olivia. But I think she can take a little more. Just in case you don't understand the position you're in."

I slide down the wall as tears stream down my face, and Eve screams in the background. This is an impossible position to be in, but I will not let my decisions affect my loved ones. I'll have to do what he asks until I figure out how to escape. I hope Eve will be okay because I will never forgive myself if something worse happens to her.

CHAPTER 8
CONFRONTING A PAINFUL DILEMMA

I had no choice but to watch as he hit Eve repeatedly, screaming in anger and pain at the same time. His men pulled me away before I could do anything else and took me back to my room. My heart shattered into a million pieces seeing Eve suffer like that, with tears streaming down my face all night long.

I know that the only way to keep her safe is for me to do whatever they ask of me. I can only hope and pray that it will be enough so she won't have to endure any more torture like this. But in the back of my mind, I fear what might happen if I fail. I can only try my best and hope to get out of this.

All I can do is wait in fear, with nothing to keep me occupied but my own thoughts. The days could have passed like hours or the other way around. A door appears on the other side of the room again, and in walks Axel with the hooded figure trailing behind him.

"Time for you to uphold your end of the bargain, Olivia," Axel says as he stops in the middle of the room.

The hooded figure darts forward so fast I don't have

time to react. He grabs me and drags me down the hall into a pool room. I realize what's going to happen a second before we jump in. Water swirls around us, and I struggle in his arms to get loose and make my way to the surface. The vortex of water gets stronger, and my tired limbs can't fight much longer. I give up and let it take me to my destination.

"Olivia, wake up," I hear Axel's voice off in the distance.

I struggle to open my eyes, and when I finally do, I'm staring up at the night sky. I sit up quickly, with my heart pounding in my ears. Axel is now standing a few feet away, surveying the area with his hands shoved into his pockets.

"Where are we?" I whisper as I try to get my bearings.

"We are in Aurora. A friend told me that there may be more people like us in this city," he says with a tired sigh. "You have the power of sight. You know things no one else knows, and you can see things others can't. I want you to use your ability to find out where the other power is and then bring it back to me."

"I can't control it, Axel. I don't know the times or places these visions take place," I try explaining.

He scowls my way. "You better hope you narrow it to this area, Olivia, or you will not like the consequences."

My stomach drops at his implication. I understand his words and my purpose here. I know I'll do what he asks, but I don't want to. This is wrong, and I know it. Unfortunately, if I want Eve and my family to remain safe, I have to put other families in danger.

It's a lose-lose situation for me. I close my eyes and take deep breaths, trying to bring on the sight. The funny thing about this ability is I have no way of knowing when or where the vision is taking place.

The same sensation as before flows over me, and I finally see someone, a woman. I describe what I see to him.

The house has deep red walls and lots of plants on the windowsill. Her furniture is chic, with a bright yellow couch and several other pieces of brightly colored furniture. I tell him the woman's husband seems happy as they laugh together, and he points out some wildflowers growing outside their window.

"I don't give a rat's ass if they're happy and in love or their sense of style, Olivia," Axel snaps. "Give me something useful to use. Landmarks, familiar surroundings, something."

I switch to describing the outside, hoping that it's something useful to him. I don't want to fail my first time helping him.

"I think I know where she is now," Axel says confidently. "That's a statue found in one specific place in the middle of the city. Follow me."

He walks off without a backwards glance. I run to keep up with him and almost fall over from lack of nourishment. We arrive at the house I'd seen in my vision, and I can see the woman and her husband in the window. Axel walks up to the door, knocks without hesitating, and the woman answers.

Confusion crosses her face. "Yes? Can I help you?"

"I believe you possess a power that I want," he says coldly, and I can feel a chill in the air.

She looks between us, and something clicks in her mind because her eyes harden. I'm sure she realizes what he means.

"What do you want?" she whispers harshly, turning slightly to see her husband standing behind her.

Axel coldly looks at her and steps forward, towering a few feet away from her. "We need your power."

She narrows her eyes. "Charles," she calls to her

husband. "I'm going to need you to go upstairs for a moment. I need to have a friendly chat with our visitors outside."

"Yes, dear," he says. "Remember, try not to destroy the entire neighborhood like the last time. I don't want another visit from those crazy women. That one with the white eyes scares the shit out of me."

Suddenly, she pushes Axel hard, and he stumbles back a few feet. She approaches us with determination, her energy crackling around her. She charges the energy inside her and focuses it into a burst of lightning that illuminates the night sky. Surprised, The hooded figure staggers back in fear as he feels the power emanating from her.

Axel lets out a loud laugh. "You've got some power, I'll give you that. I can tell right now that you're not who we're looking for. However, I'm going to kick your ass for daring to touch me."

"Axel," I say, but my voice falls on deaf ears. He attacks the woman swiftly, but she's holding her own against him.

Her movements are graceful yet precise as she aims exactly where each strike would cause maximum harm. Waves of force ripple outwards with every strike she causes, sending shockwaves through the air. Sparks fly here and there as she fights with determination and skill.

With one final jolt of energy, she pushes Axel back, and they fill the night with the sound of their heavy breathing. The woman stands victorious in the aftermath, her power still crackling around her as she lets out a triumphant yell that echoes through the night.

Once again, Axel lets out a manic laugh. Despite his bruised and battered state, he seems not to care for his wellbeing. Suddenly, his body vibrates before he lets out a painful yell, and a tearing sound fills the air. I stumble back with a gasp. He just shed his skin.

"I can shed my body or skin and emerge with a new body, even after dismemberment," he says. He spreads his arms out wide. "See, I'm good as new."

He whips his hand in a blur and a knife embeds in her throat. Surprise flickers across her face before she falls to the ground, the sound of her choking on her blood filling the silence.

"Unfortunately for you, there will be no round two," he says before walking away. "Let's go, Olivia. It's time to find another one."

Too shocked to move, the hooded figure shoves me forward. We walk for a little while, and fatigue is setting in. Luckily, we stop at a park, and I sit heavily on one bench. Axel yells for me to start, so I close my eyes and summon another vision.

This time, it's of an older man in a supermarket. He's a middle-aged man wearing a sharp suit sitting behind the counter, counting money. I assume he's the manager or owner of the establishment. Shelves with food items surround him, and customers are shopping in the background. I tell Axel the name of the market, and we head in that direction.

Fortunately, the man didn't put up much of a fight. He cowered in a corner like a baby, but not before turning into a little rat first. Unfortunately for him, Axel squashed like a bug before he could scurry out of the office. Now, Axel is pacing in the parking lot in frustration. I guess he's not happy with the magic users I found for him.

"Dammit! This is not going as planned," he shouts.

"Axel," I say, my voice barely a whisper. I'm too

exhausted to speak any louder. "I swear, I did what you asked me to do."

He stalks over to where I am standing, his rage barely contained. "This is unacceptable! I want better results, or there will be consequences."

I stiffen at his words, but I say nothing. Axel stares at me briefly before he turns and stalks off. I sink down onto the ground with my entire body trembling. Disbelief filters through my head as I realize I just killed an innocent person and destroyed another's life. I took part in crimes I never should have. I have to do it for my family, but I will never forgive myself.

I close my eyes once again and summon another vision. However, this one feels slightly different. In this vision, I see a familiar woman cowering on her couch. I stand up and step forward, touching her shoulder. I'm so eager to see the face of this familiar woman I hadn't realized I had stepped through the vision to wherever she was. The woman turns around.

"Ms. Lock?" I question in surprise. There's no way she's who my vision brought me to.

"Olivia? What are you doing here? Where did you come from?" she asks as she sits straighter on the couch.

I wave her off. "Never mind that. What's wrong?" It looks like there'd been a fire recently.

She cocks her head to the side, studying me with an intensity that makes me uncomfortable.

"You're one of them, aren't you?" she asks.

I must look like a deer caught in headlights because she continues talking without waiting for me to reply.

"I knew something was special about that girl, and I tried to help her, but she's too headstrong," Ms. Lock says.

A commotion sounds outside before I can ask her what

she means, and I run out the door to see what's going on. I see people running in fear right before a little girl, and female voices catch my attention.

"How old are you, five?" Eve's cousin asks.

The little girl's face gets angrier. "I'm nine years old, idiot. Are you blind?"

I realize it's the same child and girls from a previous vision.

Eve's cousin's smile falls away instantly. "Listen here, you little snot-nosed brat. You may have everyone else here scared of you, but we are not. Do not test us. What are you doing, anyway?"

"Ms. Lock wouldn't let me have the ice cream I wanted, so I got mad, and the table caught fire," she states in a matter-of-fact tone.

"Seriously? Where's the lighter? You can't go around setting shit on fire because you get mad," the ethereal girl says. "You need to come with us, Dakota. We can help you."

"What did you call me?" the little girl asks as she rages. "MY NAME IS FLARE!"

She's a little girl one moment, and the next, her whole body catches fire. She's literally a little torch, and she runs our way.

The girl with the pale skin puts up a shield to block her advancement. "Seriously, kid? You need to calm down before I douse you with water," she yells.

Dakota bangs her fiery hand against the shield. "I will douche you! I'm in charge, not you old ladies."

The ethereal girl flicks a wrist and lifts her twenty feet into the air. All the little girl's anger morphs into fear instantly. "You need to calm down. We're here to help you, but if you call me old again, I will drop you," she says. The little girl calms down instantly. "Much better."

She places Dakota back on the ground, and she stands there, unsure of what to do.

"It's douse, not douche," Eve's cousin tells her. Dakota gives her a puzzled look. "Just to clarify. Douse is when you pour a liquid over something. Douche is when you—,"

"Vik!" the ethereal girl shouts, cutting off her inappropriate explanation. "Do not go there. Seriously, now is not the time for that."

The pale-skinned girl walks forward and places a hand on Dakota's shoulder. "Don't worry. You're coming with us, and we'll help you."

A woman comes running out of her house. "You can't take her. That's kidnapping!"

"Shut it, lady," the pale-skinned girl snaps. "You were hiding in your home when we arrived. You can't let her run around wreaking havoc when she has a damn tantrum."

"Technically, she's right," Eve's cousin comments.

The pale girl sends her a look that says shut your mouth. "All we're doing is helping her. I'm sure we can arrange for her to visit. Once she's finished learning our ways, she's free to go if she wants."

The woman cries as she sends them a confused look. "Our ways? I don't understand."

"There are things you can't know. The world is full of things you can't even imagine," the ethereal girl tells her.

"Don't worry," the pale girl says as she opens a portal in the middle of the street. "You won't remember a thing after today."

I run inside and shut Ms. Lock's door. "Oh my God! What the hell have I gotten myself into?"

"Sit down before you pass out," Ms. Lock says as she pats the seat beside her.

I shake my head vehemently. "Oh my God, I have to go.

I've seen those girls before. They seem scarier in real life. I've seen those other women, too. I need to go back now."

"Go back where?" she asks in confusion.

"Shit, shit, shit," I say as I pace in her living room. I run out of the door with no idea of how to get back to Axel. All I can do is go home and pray that he's not pissed when he finds me. I don't care how mad he is or what he does to me. I will not lead him to a little girl just for them to torture and kill.

CHAPTER 9

THERE IS NO ESCAPE

Axel found me at my apartment in the early hours of the morning. He hauled out of bed and slammed against the nearest wall. I can feel the anger radiating off him, and my eyes zero in on the blood staining his shirt. The ruthless air radiating from him in waves has me swallowing hard, wishing I could find a spot to hide.

"Your disappearing act will not get you out of this, Olivia. Unless you want your family's deaths' on your hands, you'll never do that again." his voice carries a dangerous growl that vibrates through my entire body.

I refuse to show him fear and narrow my eyes in disgust. "It will never happen again, so will you back the hell away from me?"

"How the hell did you disappear, and where did you go?" he says as he steps away, straightening his shirt.

There's no way I'm telling him what happened. Especially not the little girl I saw in my vision.

"At that moment, I was trying to bring on another vision. I told you I can't control it!" I scream at him despite the dangerous aura surrounding him. "All I kept thinking about was being home in my safe, warm bed. The next thing I know, I'm at home. That's it."

He looks at me through narrowed eyes. "Are you telling me you can disappear and reappear in locations you think about?"

"I am saying it was a one-off occurrence that I don't know how it happened," I tell him, trying to downplay what actually happened. "It could have been this other person you want me to find trying to get me out of danger."

I hold up my hand to stop him from speaking. "All I'm saying is that I don't know what happened, and before you get your head wrapped around me having abilities I do not have, consider outside forces."

"Okay, I believe you, Olivia," he says as he walks toward the bedroom door. "But that means we need to find this other person sooner rather than later. I'll see you at work tomorrow and don't be late.

My eyes widen in shock. Holy shit. This is happening. I have to be social with a man who just threatened me and the safety of my family—a man who seriously acts like the devil. And I still have to work with him like everything is fine.

"Fine, let's just agree to ignore each other while working," I tell him.

He adjusts his shirt once again. "Let's get one thing straight so there are no misunderstandings, Olivia. Things will be normal while at work, and you will continue to aid our efforts afterward."

He walks out of the house without a backward glance and slams the door. That was two months ago, and I am tired of finding people for him to torture and kill. Axel is sure his threat keeps me in check because he allows me to go home instead of holding me hostage like he did before.

I've called Eve every day, hoping she'll answer and I'd know that she's okay, but she never answers. This increases my anxiety, but I have to continue doing what Axel says and hope he sticks to his word. I walk into the office like it's a typical day, and Nash and Steele are already in the lab running tests.

"Good morning, Olive," Nash says as I walk in.

"Eat a dick, Nash," I lash out at him. The stress of what I'm doing is eating me up inside, and I'm tired of pretending.

"Whoa, what has your panties in a twist," Steele laughs.

"I've told him repeatedly that I don't like him calling me Olive, like some term of endearment," I tell him in agitation. "Now, let's focus on the lab test. How are the new fuels coming along?"

I work diligently with Nash and Steele to run the lab tests on the new fuel, ensuring it is fit for use, before taking a break for lunch. As I walk down the street to the usual restaurant, my heart is heavy in my chest as I hoped Eve would show up. I've been coming here daily, hoping to see her to ensure she's okay. Luck seemed to be on my side today as I see her approach from across the street.

"Oh my God, I'm so sorry, Eve. I can't believe what happened to you." I say as she sits down at the small table.

Eve smiles, the kind of smile I haven't seen before. "It's alright, Olivia. I'm okay now. Don't worry about me."

"But the fear and pain that you must have felt..." I start but choke up.

"It was terrifying. At first, I thought he was going to kill me or worse. All I could think about was never finding my cousin. But then he put me in this tiny room and locked the door behind him. The only light came from a crack under the door, but even that couldn't keep away the sense of dread that filled every inch of that place," she replies.

I nod sadly and can't help but feel as if I'm the one to blame. "That must have been horrible for you."

"It was, but somehow I got through it," her calm tone over the situation surprises me, but I suppose this is her way of dealing with what happened.

I grab her hand on the table. "I'm so glad you're alright. Maybe I could have done something more to help."

She squeezes my hand gently. "You did more than enough when you got him to stop the torture. You saved my life, Olivia — and for that, I will be forever grateful. Things are exactly as they are supposed to be."

"Yeah, but you wouldn't have been there if it weren't for me in the first place," I tell her, sadness etched deep in my voice. "And why are you speaking so weird? No one is meant to be tortured, Eve."

She waves a hand in the air. "Enough talk about what happened to me. What's been happening to you? Since you're here, I assume you're done helping Axel?"

As we eat lunch, I tell her all the things Axel is having me do and how I still have to go to work like normal. This situation is enough to make me go crazy, but I don't know what else to do. I've been hiding my visions from Axel whenever I have them at work.

I don't want to interact with him more than I need to. Aside from forcing a vision when he asks me to, I don't volunteer any information. Hell, sometimes I fake not being able to force a vision to get him to back off. I can tell his frustration is growing by the day, so I need to come up with a plan.

Eve and I finish our food, and she tells me she's staying

somewhere safe to ease my worries. I head back to work, but unfortunately, Axel asks to see me as soon as I return. Now I'm in the elevator, heading straight to his office, hoping like hell that he hasn't caught on to what I've been doing. I walk into his office without knocking and notice he's on the phone.

"It's taking a little more time than we expected, but we're getting closer every day," he says in a serious tone.

The person on the phone says something that makes Axel's eyes flash with anger before he trains them on me. "That will not be necessary, sir. I have everything under control. I will have better results for you by the end of the week."

"We won't be finished testing the fuels by the end of the week," I tell Axel when he hangs up the phone. "You shouldn't have promised results without discussing our progress first."

He stares at me momentarily before slowly getting up from his chair. He stalks toward me like a predator that's found its prey. His eyes are on me with barely controlled anger.

"Do you have a death wish, Olivia?" he asks. "I saw you with Evelyn. Were you two hatching a plan against me?"

"Are you insane!" I yell at him. "No one's hatching anything against you. I wanted to make sure she was okay. It's not like you volunteered that information, Axel."

He pushes closer to me, causing me to stumble back against the wall. "This stops now, Olivia. You will do what I say, when I say it, and where I say it. I will not tolerate your behavior. You will follow every order I give you, or it will be the last time you see her."

I take a deep breath and look him in his eyes, not

faltering as I reply. "You're right. I will do what you say. I'm sorry."

He steps away from me and takes a seat. "I will not be lenient if you do this again. If I tell you to do something, you will do it without question, or I will kill everyone you love."

"I understand." I nod.

He looks at me for a long moment before waving his hand toward the door. "That's all. Return to work and get the fuel working properly by the end of the week."

I turn and walk out of his office, feeling the heavy weight of his warning in my every step. By the time I arrive back in the lab, Nash and Steele have already left. I take a deep breath and start getting to work. I might be tired, I might be scared, I might feel like I'm out of options. But I can't give up. It is time to take my life back, and I am determined to make it happen.

Later that night, Axel shows up on my doorstep, demanding that I come with him. He seems even more desperate to find this other half of the pair of powers than before.

"Time for you to do your job and find your other half, Olivia," he says. "Time is of the essence."

I pull on my shoes and run to catch up with him. This time, we get in a car to go wherever the hell he's taking me. I'm surprised when we pull up to Sutton Engineering. When we get to his office, there are people I've never met before, and I'm a little nervous. There are two guys and a woman that look menacing.

Axel sits behind his desk. "This is Ajax, Archer, and Angel. Go ahead, Olivia. Get started."

My eyes dart to the other people in the room, wondering what they're here for. I take a deep breath and close my eyes, calling on the powers inside of me. I can sense the surprise from the others in the room, but I pay them no mind as I concentrate on my task. Suddenly, I'm looking around someone's living room. As I look around, I notice a woman standing before me, and she's glowing orange.

She opens her eyes, and they flash brightly. "Ah, there you are. I've been sensing you, Olivia. You have been very hard to find."

I can feel my mouth drop open in surprise as I take in what all this might mean. I step back, my heart racing.

"I found her. Grab her and get back here quickly," the woman says, looking off to the side, talking to someone I can't see. "And for the love of God, do it quietly and don't leave a mess."

"I don't understand," I say to her.

She smiles as her eyes flash once again. "Don't worry, Olivia. You'll find out soon enough."

She raises her hand, and with a simple flick of the wrist, I'm pushed out of the vision and land on my ass back in Axel's office.

"Olivia!" Axel yells. "What the hell just happened? I told you to summon a vision, and you fell on your ass like a child!"

He stalks toward me, and by the look in his eyes, I know he will hurt me.

"I wouldn't do that if I were you," comes a female voice. "If you lay one hand on her, I'd be forced to beat your ass, and I promised my aunt that I'd get in and get out without leaving a mess."

Two of the females I saw at Ms. Lock's house are standing at the office door. They were standing outside with that little girl.

"Who the hell are you, and what are you doing here? This is a private building," Axel shouts.

"I'm Danielle, and this is Lucille. We're here to take Olivia, and if you know what's good for you, you'll stay the hell out of our way."

Axel laughs at their threat. "Two little girls are no match for me or my guys. I don't know who put you up to this, but run along before I hurt you."

"Hey, Olivia?" Lucille says. "Why don't you move to the side of the room while we handle these guys? If you get hurt, we'll never hear the end of it."

I stand up and back away in confusion. It's like I've been thrown into the twilight zone, and things are getting more mysterious by the second. Suddenly, Danielle and Lucille change appearance. Danielle's skin changes to a pale gray with black veins cascading all over, while Lucille takes on an ethereal glow.

"What the hell are you?" Ajax says in disgust.

Danielle cocks a brow. "I'm a half-demon, and she's basically a goddess. You guys are severely outmatched in power."

The air crackles with anticipation as sparks dance along Danielle's skin. Moonlight peeks through the towering buildings, casting an eerie glow upon the room. Her eyes glow with an otherworldly radiance, and a swirling aura of magic envelopes her form, dripping with untamed power.

Suddenly, steel pipes and debris shoot from the walls, twisting to form an impenetrable shield around Ajax. Energy surges from Danielle's fingertips, hurtling toward Ajax's metallic shield.

"Is that what you call your little magic show? I've seen scrawny low-lives display more power than that. You really need to step up your game, sweetheart," Ajax taunts.

"Sweetheart? How original. Maybe I'll start calling you Tin Man since you look like a can of soup right now. But hey, I'll give you credit for creating that shiny suit of yours. Fashionable if you're into that industrial chic look." Danielle replies with a bored expression.

With a wave of his hand, the metal shield expands outward, flying toward Danielle with sharp tips. Undeterred, Danielle unleashes a torrent of fire, engulfing the room in a blaze of flames. The searing heat threatens to melt Ajax's shield. He concentrates his power, causing the metal around him to contort and reshape into a towering golem of steel.

"Dude! Keep the flames contained. Remember, we can't destroy the office or the building," Lucille scolds as she faces off against Angel.

In an instant, Angel's body shimmers, and a transformation unfolds. Limbs dissolve, flesh melts away, and bones become nothing but vapor. In the blink of an eye, she disintegrates into a cloud of swirling insects, her essence scattering throughout the office. The swarm moves with a synchronized purpose, weaving through the air in a mesmerizing dance.

"Ew, your ability is to become tiny insects?" Lucille says. "Damn, did you get the shit end of the stick?"

She raises her hand to summon an energy blast. But before she can unleash her divine energy, the horde of insects swarm around her, enveloping her in a twisting vortex of wings and stinging bites. Lucille tries to resist, but the woman's fragmented form proves elusive, slipping through her fingers like mist.

The insects attack from all directions, each delivering a tiny but potent blow. They bite and scratch, their little bodies giving a thousand pricks. Lucille thrashes, struggling to defend herself against the relentless assault. Suddenly, power blasts from her body, disintegrating the insects instantly.

"You killed Angel!" Archer yells from the sideline.

"Oh, was that your girlfriend?" Lucille retorts. "You should thank me then because that ability should make your skin crawl."

Archer attacks Lucille, and he jumps and punches her in the face. Her head snaps back, and blood trickles out of her nose. Her eyes flash in anger.

"Uh oh," Danielle says from off to the side. "You should not have done that. Seriously, she has an attitude problem, and therapy hasn't worked."

Lucille flicks her wrist, and he soars toward her. She raises her fist, and he flies right into it. She does this repeatedly before kicking him to the other side of the room.

"You can't hurt me," he says with a laugh. "I don't feel pain."

Lucille doesn't answer. She conjures knives and throws them rapidly, each embedding in his body before he can react. "It doesn't mean I didn't enjoy that," she says with a smile.

She looks toward Danielle. "Come on. We've played around enough. We need to grab Olivia and get back."

Just then, Axel grabs me from behind and backs us behind his desk, his back against the window as we face the others.

"No one is going anywhere with Olivia." he snarls.

"Ow, motherfucker!" Danielle shouts.

Axel grabbing me distracted her, and Ajax used that opportunity to stab her in the back. A little blood trickles from the corner of her mouth as her eyes flash with untamed anger.

"You piece of shit!" she snarls as she yanks the metal out and turns toward Ajax, who now looks scared shitless.

The entire building shakes as Danielle's fury builds. Her aura glows brighter as she levitates.

Lucille huffs on the side. "Now you've really done it. You just had to take a cheap shot, didn't you?"

She flicks a hand toward me. "Come here, Olivia. We need to take cover."

I sail through the air, and as soon as I land in front of her, she covers us with a bright pink shield. The building shakes even more now.

"Calm down, Danielle!" Lucille yells through the shield. She looks back at me. "Listen, when we get back, tell them that what's about to happen was not me, especially if the building falls down. I've had enough of getting in trouble because she can't control her anger."

Danielle looks over at us. "You're one to talk, Lucy. But you're right. Mom will have a cow if I knock this building down."

She looks back toward Axel, Archer, and Ajax. "I hope you can fly because you'll be squashed like a bug in the next few minutes."

She claps her hands, and a blast of energy explodes in the room, sending the men flying out of the windows and destroying the office.

She floats back to the ground, looks around, and turns her gaze towards me. "If my mom asks, those guys made this mess."

Lucille nods her head. "Yeah, we have to stick together if we don't want to be put on extra duty because we drew attention to ourselves."

Before I can reply, we disappear and reappear in the living room I saw the woman with the glowing orange eyes.

I step away and put up my hands. "Stay away from me! I don't know what you want, but I will not let you bully me like Axel. I will fight you every step of the way."

"Will you now?" a female voice says. "I love a good fight. Want to take this outside, Olivia? There's nothing but space and opportunity. Let me stretch first, and then I'll be ready."

I turn around to see a woman with glowing white eyes. The same woman from my visions, and she looks even scarier in person. The other women from the vision walk into the room behind her, and their power fills the air. I realize I do not know who these women are or what they want from me. Sheer terror takes over, and I pass out.

CHAPTER 10

UNEXPECTED ALLIES

I wake up on the couch after passing out, looking at my strange surroundings and wondering how I got where I am until everything comes rushing back. Danielle and Lucille showing up to rescue me from Axel and his goons, the fighting, Axel holding me hostage, and Danielle blowing up his office. All of it.

"Finally, you're awake," says a female voice. "There's no time to sleep all damn day. We've got shit to do, and time is wasting."

"Shut up, Ashley," another female says with a sigh.

I look at the women standing in front of me in confusion. Sure, they look very intimidating, but I don't think they mean me any harm.

One woman steps forward, pointing to herself and the other women in the room. "I'm Miranda. This is Mary, Stephanie, Sydney, Annie, and Ashley. We are the Over Lords, leaders of the Mutane Sihiri. You can address us as Over Lords."

I sit up on the couch. "I don't understand what any of that means. Really, I just want to go home. I don't want any part of whatever this is. I've had enough people trying to control me, and it's pissing me off."

"Good!" Over Lord Ashley says happily. "Being pissed off means you won't take any shit. It means you'll learn to stand up for yourself and learn to fight. You can't join our band if you don't pull your weight around here."

"Okay, Ashley. Settle down before you scare the poor girl," Over Lord Annie says.

Over Lord Sydney takes a seat next to me on the couch. "We don't want to scare you, Olivia. We're all a part of a magical race called the Mutane Sihiri. That includes you. Our roles as leaders of this race are to protect our people and keep our existence a secret."

"Sydney tells us you are one extraordinary person and that your ability can endanger everyone," Over Lord Miranda states in a serious tone.

She asks me about everything that's happened and how I came to be with Axel. I tell them about my visions of them, Axel kidnapping me, the Veil Society and their mission, and how he forced me to help them find and kill their people.

"Wait, wait, wait," Over Lord Stephanie says. "There's a whole secret organization out there intending to find an ancient powerful being to do what now?"

"According to Axel, he wants this goddess or whatever to pay for what happened to some other world," I tell them.

"But that makes little sense," Over Lord Miranda replies. "Why would they have a vendetta against her? That was like eons ago."

She steps off to the side to talk to Over Lord Mary. Over Lord Sydney tells me I'm on Orchard Landing, a magical community that houses our people. Then she tells me I will live here, and they will teach me to control my ability, learn their ways, and how to fight.

Danielle and Lucille walk into the room. "You called," Danielle says. "I was about to head home to take a shower and go to bed. It's been a long day."

I didn't hear them call anyone, let alone pick up a phone. Things are very weird around here.

"Speaking of a long day," Over Lord Mary says as she turns to glare at the girls. "Want to tell me what happened to the office building? News reports about an explosion at Sutton Engineering are floating around."

Danielle takes a step back. "Mom, I can explain. It wasn't our fault."

"I told you to go in, get Olivia out, and do it quietly," Over Lord Sydney says in an irritated tone.

"They put up a fight. There was even a lady who turned into a bunch of little insects," Lucille adds. "It was pretty disturbing if you ask me."

"Well, I didn't ask you," Over Lord Mary scolds. "I know how you two work. Always covering for each other." She turns toward me. "Olivia? What really happened?"

My eyes widen in shock that she would ask me. "Um, they really put up a fight, and I'm just glad I got out of there alive."

The Over Lords stare at me, and the room is silent for so long that I'm starting to feel uncomfortable.

"Psst!" Danielle says, and I look over at her. "You can call me Dani and her Lucy. I know this seems weird, but they're talking to each other. They do this when they don't want anyone to know what they're talking about."

"I hope they're not talking about us and what happened to the office. I really don't want extra duty," Lucy whines.

I spend about thirty minutes looking around and playing with pieces of lint on my clothes. This silence gets to me while Dani and Lucy sleep on the other couch.

They're startled awake, and I nearly jump out of my skin when the Over Lords talk again.

"We have decided that because of the special nature of your existence, you will live with the girls," Over Lord Miranda tells me in a tone that gives no room for argument.

I assume she means Dani and Lucy, and I'll take that overstaying with the Over Lords, even though I want to go home.

"What about my job? My home? My family and friends? I can't just disappear. People will worry," I say as I panic in fear of being imprisoned once again. "I can't just give up my life for you."

Over Lord Ashley steps forward. "News flash, Olivia. Your life was over the moment you realized your power. You are not a prisoner here. Once we train you in our ways, help you control your ability, and eliminate the threat to you, you are free to go wherever the hell you please."

Her eyes flash brightly as she displays her power. "But make no mistake. We are the most powerful there are. As long as you don't cause any problems, we'll leave you alone."

Lucy gets up. "I hate to interrupt this intimidation tactic, but there's no room for her at our place."

"Alright, Lucy," Over Lord Ashley says. "You and me. Outside. Right now. I'll show you intimidation." She walks out the front door with Over Lord Stephanie trailing behind her, telling her to stop acting crazy.

"I knew that would rile her up," Lucy laughs. "She was scaring poor Olivia."

Over Lord Miranda glares at Lucy. "I know this is a little game you two play, but I wish you'd stop antagonizing her." She looks at Dani. "It's already taken care of, Dani. We sent Kyle to make adjustments to your house."

"Now, if there is nothing else, I have to go calm Ashley down before she does something rash," Over Lord Miranda says before waving her hand.

Suddenly, we're standing in the living room of another home. It's beautiful and homey, but I'd rather be back at my place. Seeing as I have no other option but to stay here, I flop down on the couch with a heavy sigh.

"I'm so glad to be home," Dani says as she walks through the house. She comes back a second later. "I'm guessing the new bedroom and bathroom are for you. I'll get you some pajamas, and we can all head to bed."

Dani and Lucy leave the room, and I sit here wondering how my life has changed so drastically in a short amount of time. Just then, the front door opens, and in walks another female.

"Whoa, what happened to our house?" she says. "Did you guys tell Kyle we needed a bigger house?" she yells out.

I sit up straighter, unable to believe my eyes. "Viktoria?"

Her eyes snap to mine. "Who the hell are you? Stranger danger! Stranger danger!" she yells before pulling out a knife and throwing it at me.

I scream in fear, but the knife stops an inch from my face. It hovers in midair before sailing into Lucy's hand.

"How many times do I have to tell you to stop yelling stranger danger whenever you see someone new on the property?" Lucy says with a shake of her head.

Viktoria shrugs and takes off her shoes. "It's good to know when someone new comes. However, the new person never comes to our house, and it surprised me. How does someone I've never met say my name like we're long-lost friends?

"I know Evelyn," I tell her. "She's been looking for you after you disappeared." I hesitate before continuing. "And I saw you. I saw you here and told her you were okay. She feared the worst."

Viktoria narrows her eyes. "What do you mean you saw me?"

"Vik, this is Olivia," Dani tells her. "She has the special ability that the Over Lords have been trying to find."

Viktoria nods in understanding. "Ah, okay. Wait, you know my cousin? Evelyn?" She pulls out another knife. "What do you know about Eve? She better not be caught up in your shit."

I tell them how I know Eve and what she thought happened to Viktoria. I also tell them what Axel did to her, and they were not happy that he involved an innocent human in his twisted game.

"Listen, I don't mean to sound rude, but you all are weird," I tell them. "Will I get in trouble for not saying what really happened back in the office?"

"Let's get one thing straight," Dani says. "My mom and aunts know everything. If we get away with something, it's because they let us. They let us because it either didn't cause any problems for them, or they're going to make us do something we don't want to do."

They must see how tired I am because Lucy suggests everyone go to bed, and we'll pick up this conversation in the morning.

Dani hands me a pair of pajamas and spare clothes and leads me to my new room. Once I'm alone, my thoughts run wild, and I can't sleep. I'm too worried about what may happen to me, my family, and my friends. As soon as the thought pops into my head, I hop out of bed. Unfortunately, I don't make it far.

Over Lord Annie pops into my room. "Going somewhere?"

"Ah!" I scream before falling on my ass. "Holy shit! You guys really know everything."

"Well, your racing mind is keeping me awake. I'm here to put you to sleep so that we can all rest," she says, her tone laced with annoyance.

I don't even get the chance to respond. She snaps her fingers, and everything goes dark.

I wake with a start, disoriented by my unfamiliar surroundings. I take a few moments to orient myself before getting out of bed and heading into the ensuite bathroom. The hot shower feels invigorating against my skin, washing away any lingering traces of fatigue or confusion. After showering, I dry myself off and go over to the bed to put on the clothes Dani gave me.

I pull on the jeans and T-shirt she chose for me—they fit well. Feeling more put-together than before, I head out of the bedroom to the kitchen in search of breakfast. As soon as I open the door, a horrible smell greets me. They must have left something cooking on the stove. I walk into the kitchen to find Dani and Vik yelling at Lucy.

"What the hell were you thinking, Lucy?" Dani asks, sounding shocked.

"I was trying to do something nice to make Olivia feel welcome," Lucy snaps.

"By putting eggs in the toaster?" Vik yells at her. "How on earth did you think that was going to work?"

"I don't know. I figured it would toast it or grill it or something. How was I supposed to know it would just slide to the bottom?" Lucy says, sounding embarrassed at her lack of culinary skills.

"Because it's a fucking liquid!" Vik yells again. "I don't understand how your mom and dad didn't teach you how to cook."

Dani grabs Lucy by the shoulders and stares into her eyes. "What is the most important rule of this house, Lucy? Come on, say it with me."

"Never, ever, under any circumstances, not even in life-or-death situations, let Lucille Carsewell attempt to cook any food, to include boiling water, as it can cause a catastrophic failure so severe that we may never recover from it," they all say in unison.

I take a seat at the table. "Don't you guys think that's a little harsh?" I ask them.

"Tell me something, Olivia," Dani says. "Have you ever had your ass set on fire by someone attempting to bake cookies in a frying pan on top of a stove?"

I'm speechless by the absurdity of the question. I can't think of a single person who would bake cookies in a frying pan on the stove. Baking implies the use of an oven, and everyone should know that.

"I can tell by your expression that you haven't. I have. By Lucy. She's a walking culinary disaster, and if you know what's good for you, you'll never let her near a kitchen unsupervised," Dani says as she laughs.

Dani and Vik take over making breakfast while Lucy and I watch some TV. Despite being in an unusual situation, they seem like ordinary people. They call us into the kitchen when the food is ready, and we sit around the table to eat.

Dani, Lucy, and Vik tell me about life on Orchard Landing. They are so proud to be soldiers in their army—it seems like a big part of who they are. They tell me about all the places they've been and the people they met on missions to find more people just like them. I can tell that this matters to them, and it makes me even more curious about their stories.

"Do you think Axel is dead?" I ask suddenly, ruining the easygoing atmosphere. "Will my family be safe now?"

"I threw him out of the window of a high-rise office building," Dani says. "I'd be surprised if he's able to be scraped off the ground."

"My mom and aunts won't let anything happen to your family and friends," Dani tells me. "Let's go tour the property. Since you'll be living here for a while, you might as well know your way around."

The three of them walk me around Orchard Landing, pointing out everything that makes it special. They mention how everyone here uses magic to help with the daily tasks and chores. Dani even shows me one of her abilities she uses to clean up the garden after harvesting vegetables. It's incredible to see this new world.

I can tell they're really proud of their community and how everyone pulls their weight to keep things running smoothly. It was great getting the tour from Dani, Lucy, and Vik. I can tell they want me to feel welcome.

Dani stops walking and turns toward me. "I know you're worried, but the best thing you can do right now is to worry about yourself. You need to learn our ways, train hard, and learn to control your ability."

"And how am I supposed to do that?" I ask.

"The same way we all did," Vik answers. She grabs my hand and pulls me until we reach a clearing with a large building standing before us. "Welcome to the Institute of Magical Arts. It's a school for people like us."

I look at the building and then back at them. "School? You're telling me I have to go to school? You cannot be serious."

"We're as serious as a heart attack," Dani says. "Come on. We'll take you to meet Jade."

I follow them into the school and into an office of a very stern-looking woman. She looks up from her desk and frowns when she sees us.

"Danielle, Lucille, and Viktoria, it is nice to see you," the woman says. "Is there something you need?"

"Hey, Jade," Dani says. "Not sure if Mom told you about Olivia, but we brought her over so she can get started."

Jade looks at me with a raised eyebrow. "Over Lord Miranda has informed me of Olivia's arrival. I have prepared a list of readings for her to get started on. Please, leave her with me. I'm sure you have better things to do."

She turns and walks back to her desk without another word. Dani, Lucy, and Vik turn to leave, and I take a seat in front of Jade.

"You are new to our culture and, therefore, behind in our ways. My job is to teach you. I run a tight schedule, and I expect obedience," she says.

She hands me a book, and our fingers brush. That familiar sensation happens again right before a vision of Jade takes over.

Jade ran as fast as she could, her heart pounding in fear. She had been walking through the small town where she lived when a group of angry people appeared out of nowhere and suddenly started chasing her.

Her throat constricted with fear, and tears blurred her vision. She tried to focus on running faster, but it felt like no matter how hard she tried, the people were still gaining on her.

Finally, after what seemed like an eternity, Jade found a hiding spot in an abandoned alleyway. Her breathing was ragged from exertion and terror. She slowly peered around the corner to make sure the angry mob was gone before finally emerging from her hiding place.

"You won't get away, Jade," a man with hatred in his eyes says from behind her.

Something hits her from behind, and she's knocked out cold. She wakes up with her arms tied to a wooden post. There's an angry mob shouting and throwing things at her.

"We have found you guilty, and your punishment is ten lashes," he says, spittle flying from his rotten mouth.

"Please! I did nothing!" Jade cried in fear.

Her cries go unheard as the whip flies through the air. The sound of it hitting her skin echoes all around. The man made it to six lashes before Jade started shaking uncontrollably, and it didn't seem like it was from the pain. Suddenly, electricity flies from her hands, striking a few people in the angry crowd.

The electricity singed the rope holding her hands, and they drop like heavy weights. She stands on shaky legs with fire in her eyes. She raises her hands, and electricity shoots all around, striking everyone in sight. When she's finished, nothing but ash lays where people used to be.

The room comes back into focus, and Jade is still standing before me, both hands still on the book.

"What happened to you? Why did you do that to those people?" I ask before I can stop myself.

Her brows shoot up in surprise before morphing into anger. "This will be the last time you touch me, Olivia," she says before stomping back to her desk. "Why don't you take the book home, and we will resume later. I will send the time, and do not be late."

Her tone holds a sense of finality, so I got up and returned to the house. I hope I didn't get on Jade's bad side because I don't know these people, and the last thing I want to do is make them hate me. I guess only time will tell.

CHAPTER 11

EXPERIENCING THE MAGIC

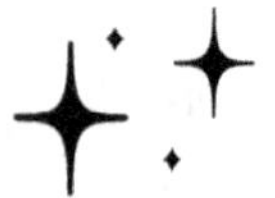

Yesterday was eye-opening. I'm grateful for being rescued, but I've gone from one scary place to another. Everyone seems nice enough, especially Dani, Lucy, and Vik, but I won't let my guard down.

I have to stay here to learn the culture of the Mutane Sihiri, whether I want to or not. Luckily, I got introduced to this world during the week of trials at the Institute of Magical Arts, so everything they wanted me to learn was paused until the trials are over.

From my understanding, the school does the trials to test the student's proficiency with magic and combat. They go through an entire week of different trials, and I get the unfortunate luxury of tagging along with Dani, Lucy, and Vik to watch it all.

"Tell me again why I have to go to the trials?" I ask them as we go to the field for day 1 of trials.

"You have to go so that you experience what our world of magic consists of," Dani replies.

Vik nods in agreement. "You'd think that having magic

would make life easier, but nope. Magic brings chaos and destruction."

"Isn't it wonderful?" Lucy adds with a smile.

As we approach the field, I can't help but feel a mix of anticipation and trepidation. The Institute of Magical Arts is a massive, sprawling complex, and it seems like they gathered the entire student body here for the trials. The atmosphere is charged with energy, a palpable buzz of excitement and nervousness.

Dani leads the way, her confidence shining through as she navigates the crowd. She's a half-magic user, half-demon hybrid, a fact that still boggles my mind. Lucy walks beside me, radiating an air of otherworldly grace. She's essentially a goddess, and I'm not sure I'll ever fully grasp her true nature. Vik is a master of compulsion, and she's been warm and welcoming, just like the others since I arrived.

As we find a spot to watch the trials, I can't help but ask, "So, what kind of trials are these, anyway?"

Dani grins, her white teeth glinting in the sunlight. "You're in for a treat, Olivia. The trials cover everything from elemental magic to combat simulations. It's a week-long extravaganza of magic, mayhem, and a lot of drama."

Lucy adds, "And don't forget the intense rivalries between the groups of students. It's great."

Vik chimes in, "You'll see magic used in ways you never thought possible. And, of course, some truly spectacular failures."

I raise an eyebrow, intrigued despite my reservations. "Failures?"

Dani laughs. "Oh, yes. Magic doesn't always go according to plan. That's why it's important to learn how to use it. But that's what makes it exciting."

We arrive at the field, and Olivia stands off to the side with Dani and Lucy as groups of students stand on the field, receiving directions from their teachers. Day 1 is Strategic Maneuvers. No magic is allowed in this trial because the students must learn to use their skills without magic aiding them. The students must work together against hazardous terrain and surprising hurdles to get a flag and make it to the building at the back of the property. Seems simple enough.

The trial unfolds with a captivating blend of strategy and athleticism. The teams quickly learn to cooperate, with some students acting as scouts, carefully navigating the tricky terrain ahead, while others stay back to provide cover and support. Their communication is impeccable, with hand signals and brief verbal exchanges guiding their movements.

The hazardous terrain includes treacherous patches of quicksand that threaten to engulf anyone who steps on them. With my breath held, I watch as a student teeters on the edge of one such patch, only to be saved by a teammate who throws out a rope just in time.

The rocky outcrops become a natural vantage point for some teams, allowing them to gain a tactical advantage. However, these positions are not easily defended, and the students soon find themselves in a fierce struggle to hold their ground. I can feel the tension in the air as the trial unfolds.

The surprising hurdles thrown at them include concealed traps that trigger with a click, sending nets or streams of water spraying out to disrupt their progress. Students react with lightning-fast reflexes, either leaping out of harm's way or using their friends as shields.

"I can't believe she just did that!" Dani laughs at the

student who used their teammate to block a net coming toward them.

"I would never have done that," Lucy says. "That team won't win this if they continue to throw each other under the bus to save their own ass."

Some teams attempt to outwit their opponents by setting clever traps of their own. It's a game of cat and mouse, where one wrong step can mean the difference between victory and defeat.

Despite the physical and mental strain, there's a noticeable sense of camaraderie among the students. They encourage each other, shout instructions, and provide a helping hand when needed. It's clear that these trials forge bonds among them, friendships that will be essential to the trials that lie ahead.

As the teams draw closer to getting the flag and reaching the designated building, the intensity of the competition escalates. Students use their last reserves of energy, employing every bit of cunning and determination to achieve their goal. It's a thrilling race to the finish, and the spectators, including myself, are caught up in the suspense.

Finally, one team emerges victorious, hoisting the flag triumphantly as they reach the building. The sound of applause and cheers fills the air as the trial ends.

Dani, Lucy, Vik, and I exchange impressed glances. "That was incredible," I remark, realizing that these trials are not just about individual strength but also the ability to adapt and work as a team. It reminds me of the school where I grew up.

Lucy smiles and lets out a little laugh. "And that was just the beginning. Each day brings a new challenge, testing different aspects of their abilities."

The excitement from the first day of trials carries over into Day 2, and I can hardly contain my anticipation as we head back to the school. The students talk with each other, and the excited chatter flows through the air as they prepare for the challenges that await. This day brings a unique set of trials. Combat 101 and the Obstacle Course. These trials are bound to be as thrilling as the first day, if not more so.

Dani, Lucy, Vik, and I arrive at the designated area for the trials, and I can't help but notice the palpable tension in the air. Combat 101 is first on the agenda. As we approach the combat area, I see students pairing up some wielding knives, swords, and other weapons. The teacher blows the whistle and the Combat 101 trial starts.

The clashing of steel against steel fills the air as the students engage in intense hand-to-hand combat. I watch as two students face off against each other. One has a set of knives, and the other a sword.

The student twirls the knives in her hands before lunging toward the other student. His sword comes down, blocking her strike with the blades, and he trips her. She falls on her back but rolls out of the way before his sword pierces her chest.

I watch in awe as their movements blur, their skills a testament to years of training. It's clear that magic isn't the only aspect of their abilities they've been taught to perfect. The precision and control they exhibit are nothing short of impressive.

Lucy leans in to explain the dynamics. "Combat 101 is where they put their combat skills to the test. It's not just about magical prowess but also physical combat. They must learn to defend themselves and attack with precision using all kinds of weapons."

Vik adds with a huge grin, "And let's not forget, a little flair can go a long way. Style points aren't officially counted, but everyone secretly hopes to impress with their moves."

I see what they mean when the girl knocks the sword out of his hand, and he quickly pulls nun-chucks from his cargo pocket. He spins it around with expertise before attacking once again.

The intensity of the trial draws me in. The students' determination and tenacity are inspiring, reminding me of the strength I'll need to develop if I want to survive in this world. As the trial advances, the sun climbs higher in the sky, casting a warm, golden hue over the vast property.

As Combat 101 concludes, we move on to the Obstacle Course, and I'm utterly captivated by the spectacle before me. The course is a labyrinth of physical and heart-racing challenges, an actual test of the student's abilities. Ropes dangle precariously over pools of shimmering water, nets sway in the breeze, and targets spin unpredictably, challenging their agility and control.

Dani, Lucy, Vik, and I find a prime viewing spot near a challenging section of the course. I can't help but be impressed by the students' adaptability as they navigate the obstacles with grace and determination. Lucy, her eyes sparkling with excitement, leans in to explain the intricacies of the Obstacle Course.

"This is where they prove their vigor, Liv," she says, and I smile at her use of a nickname. "It's not just about physical prowess; it's about creativity and ingenuity. Often, magic comes into play in our everyday lives, but it's not always the most straightforward solution."

Vik chimes in with a grin. "And you'll see some spectacular fails along the way, too. It's all part of the learning process."

At that moment, a student gets caught in a fiery onslaught of arrows soaring towards her. She loses her footing and falls in the mud, getting it everywhere. I can tell by the look on her face that she's embarrassed, but she gets up and continues.

I watch in awe as students use physical prowess I don't possess to conquer the course. Throughout the day, I alternate between cheering on the participants and absorbing the lessons these trials offer. The Mutane Sihiri's dedication to their craft is nothing short of inspiring, and I can't help but feel a growing sense of admiration for their skill.

As the trials draw to a close, the students celebrate their achievements, their faces lit up with pride and exhilaration. Dani, Lucy, Vik, and I make our way back to the house, and I'm brimming with excitement.

"You guys, that was amazing!" I shout. "I've never seen anything like it. The way they tackled the obstacle course is incredible."

Dani grins, her eyes reflecting my enthusiasm. "And this is just the beginning, Liv. In the rest of the trials, the students get to use magic. Now you'll really see what our kind can do."

"You're part of this world now, Liv," Lucy adds, using my new nickname. "The trials are just one facet of what it means to be Mutane Sihiri. There's magic, history, culture —all waiting for you to discover."

Vik nods in agreement. "We're here to guide you every step of the way, Liv. You're not alone in this."

The atmosphere crackles with anticipation as Day 3 dawns, heralding the offensive magic trials. Today, the students are allowed to unleash the full extent of their magical abilities, and the grounds of the Institute are transformed into a battleground of swirling energies and mystical clashes.

Dani, Lucy, Vik, and I look on, our eyes fixed on the first group of students preparing for their challenge. I can feel the tension in the air as the students coordinate their attack against the teachers who have taken on the roles of enemy insurgents.

"Here we go, Liv," Dani says with a grin, her eyes sparkling. "You're about to witness some truly spectacular magic."

The students launch their assault with a dazzling array of magic. Fireballs streak across the sky, leaving trails of crimson and gold, while bolts of lightning crackle and dance with lethal precision. Shields of shimmering energy spring up to deflect incoming attacks, and the very ground beneath their feet seems to respond to their commands.

Lucy leans over to explain the intricacies of the battle. "This isn't just about raw power, Liv. It's about strategy, creativity, and teamwork. They have to work together to overcome their opponents."

Vik nods in agreement, her eyes never leaving the unfolding spectacle. "And watch for the unexpected twists. Magic can be unpredictable, and that's what makes these trials so thrilling."

One teacher, I believe his name is Kyle, raises his arms, and the ground lifts into the air. He's constructed a small maze around the students attacking him. With the students preoccupied with finding their way through the maze, the teachers successfully infiltrate their building and take the other students hostage, effectively ending that group's trial. Now, it's time for the next group of students, and I'm dying to see how it plays out.

As the day progresses, we witness breathtaking displays of elemental manipulation, body morphing, and even the summoning of animals to aid in the student's quest to capture the enemy leader. Each group brings unique strengths and tactics to the battlefield, and the fights are nothing short of mesmerizing.

The air is filled with magic, and the ground trembles beneath us as the students give their all. The sky itself seems to react to the magic being unleashed, with brilliant flashes of light and bursts of color that paint a vivid tapestry against the azure backdrop.

This time, I lean toward Dani. "How can you all do this without drawing attention to the property?"

"The Over Lords hide it," she replies. "Don't ask me how. I'll tell you like I tell all new comers. No one knows just how much power they have. There's nothing they haven't been able to do, and I've seen them do everything."

I sit back and marvel at everything this community can do without the outside world knowing. I'm still marveling when the day is over, and we head home for the day. Day 4 arrives, and with it, the trials of defensive magic. The challenge is to protect their territory from the insurgents, which are the teachers.

The students gather in formation and prepare to ward off the impending threat. I'm breaking out in a sweat just thinking about the start of the trial. When it starts, the students waste no time attacking the teachers.

"This is incredible! They're so skilled," I say out loud.

"Defensive magic is about protecting what's important to you. It's not just about brute force; it's about resilience and adaptability." Dani says, as her eyes gleam with pride.

Lucy nods in agreement. "These trials teach them to

defend not just their territory but also their people. It's a test of unity and strength."

Despite the students' valiant efforts, victory does not come easy against the teachers. The teachers have what I assume are decades of experience over the students, so it's not surprising that they're struggling.

I get the sense that these trials are not about winning but about unity and doing for the greater good. Wave after wave of magical attacks batters against the students' defenses, and the tension mounts with each passing moment.

Vik offers words of encouragement with a steady voice. "Even in defeat, they're learning valuable lessons. It's all part of their journey to becoming skilled Mutane Sihiri."

As the trials of Day 4 come to a close, I can't help but admire the sheer dedication and talent of the students. The trials have revealed the depth of their magical prowess and the strength of their skills. Each challenge, whether won or lost, has left a lasting mark on their journey toward reaching their potential.

I turn to Dani, Lucy, and Vik. "Thank you for bringing me here, for showing me what an incredible world you live in."

Dani smiles warmly. "You're one of us now, Liv. This is your world now, too."

As we leave the trials, I feel happy that I've found people I have something in common with. It makes me want to call Eve to tell her everything she believed about magic is true. However, I don't think they'll like me telling her about Orchard Landing. The people here seem easy-going but are very protective of each other. Especially from outsiders.

Today is the last day of trials, and it's supposed to be

the most important trial. The students, who are usually split into groups, are now one united team, pitted against the entire school staff. It's a challenge meant to simulate a full-scale magical battle or war, as Dani had explained to me earlier. The teachers, Elliot, Kyle, and even Torri, are fighting with the students.

As we watch from the sidelines, I can't help but feel a sense of awe and trepidation. The sheer power and experience of the school staff are apparent, and facing them as a united front is no small feat. The trial begins with a silent understanding among the students. It's a battle of pure magic and raw skill. The ground beneath us trembles as the magical staff launches their offensive.

I watch Elliot as he steps forward with a wicked grin on his face. His body morphs, sprouting additional arms and legs until he resembles a multi-limbed behemoth. My mouth hangs open as I take in his new form as he engages the students. His body spins around, and his many arms grab students in firm holds before tossing them a few feet away.

Kyle stands calmly as he observes the trial. With a simple wave of his hand, he conjures towering structures of stone, a stronghold for the teachers against the students. Torri walks around as if she's not afraid of the magic the students are hurling her way because she turns them to stone with a simple gaze.

"Holy shit!" I yell in shock.

"Don't worry, we can undo it," Lucy says as she laughs at my flabbergasted expression."

However, despite the fight the teachers put up, the students continue to fight back. A student raises her arms and summons a cyclone of air, creating a swirling vortex of wind that lifts the teacher off their feet before dropping them to the ground. Kyle had enough forethought to summon the ground up to meet them before slowly settling them down.

Flames dance and crackle in the air as a student sends fireballs soaring toward the stronghold that Kyle constructed. A few of the walls crumble from the force of the hits. Then he summons a fiery inferno that heats the entire field before it suddenly burns out quickly. The student looks around in confusion, and I realize someone has put out his fire.

"Do not incinerate the school staff!" Over Lord Miranda yells. "Linda will be pissed if she has to stay up all night healing people."

The trial continues, and the struggle is intense and relentless. Water surges forward, forming a protective barrier around the students before swirling around and launching toward the teachers. The water turns into sharp pieces of ice before embedding into a wall of stone Kyle erected.

Dani, Lucy, Vik, and I watch in rapt attention, our faces reflecting the ebb and flow of the battle. There's no need for words; the spectacle before us speaks volumes about the students' determination and the staff's expertise.

However, as the minutes turn into hours, it becomes increasingly clear that victory is a distant dream for the students. The school staff's experience proves overwhelming. Slowly but surely, they whittle away at the students' defenses, gaining ground with each passing moment.

I can't help but feel a pang of empathy for the students. Despite their valiant efforts, the overwhelming power of the staff is too much to bear. It's a testament to the staff's mastery of magic and their role as educators. As the trial concludes, the weary and battered students yield to the staff's unrelenting force. The battle-worn students gather in defeat but with their heads held high with pride.

I turn to Dani, Lucy, and Vik, my heart heavy with the weight of the student's efforts. "The teachers could have let them win."

Dani shakes her head in disagreement. "It's not about winning every battle, Liv. It's about learning from each one and growing stronger."

"These trials prepare them for the challenges that lie ahead. They'll emerge from this experience wiser and more resilient." Lucy adds.

"Real life isn't fair, and people are going to let you win just because you're weaker than them," Vik says. "Defeat is just another step on the path to mastery. They'll come back stronger next time."

One by one, the Over Lords emerge, commanding attention and respect. They exude an air of wisdom and power that makes even the most battle-hardened students stand at attention. Over Lord Mary steps forward with pride and understanding in her expression.

Her voice carries effortlessly across the field. "You have all shown remarkable resilience and determination throughout these trials. Today's challenge was not about victory or defeat but growth and learning."

They meet her words with a collective nod of agreement.

Over Lord Miranda offers a reassuring smile. "It's important to remember that failure is not the end, but a stepping stone on your path to mastery. Those who faced setbacks today will learn and improve. Your journey has only just begun."

Over Lord Annie adds her own perspective. "Each trial has revealed your strengths and areas for growth. Embrace these lessons, and you will emerge from this experience stronger than ever."

Finally, Over Lord Sydney imparts her wisdom. "These trials are not just about honing your magical abilities but also forging bonds and trust with your peers. Unity is your greatest strength."

With their words of encouragement delivered, the Over Lords' return to the main house, leaving behind a field of inspired students. As the sun begins its descent, casting a warm, golden hue over the field, the students exchange stories of their trials, laughter mingling with tales of challenges overcome.

As we walk back toward the house, Dani, Lucy, and Vik can't resist a little teasing at my expense.

"So, what did you think of trials?" Dani asks with a wiggle of her eyebrows.

"Well, consider me amazed," I tell them with a wide smile.

"You should have seen Dani and me at our trials," Lucy replies. "We totally kicked ass."

"I wish I was there," Vik chimes in. "I would have totally kicked ass too!"

"You barely kick ass now, Vik," Lucy laughs.

"So, Liv," Dani begins with a mischievous grin on her face, "Are you ready to dive headfirst into our world of magic?"

I glance at her, my apprehension bubbling up again. "Honestly, I'd rather not dive at all. As fun and exciting as it seems, I like my nice and boring life."

"Oh, Liv, you can't escape it now," Lucy says with a click of her tongue. "You're already a part of this world, whether you like it or not."

"And trust me, once you get a taste of the chaos that

comes with the territory, you might find it hard to resist," Vik adds.

I sigh, realizing that they're right. There's no turning back now. I've been thrust into a world of magic, and there's no escape. It's a daunting realization, and I can't help but feel a sense of trepidation as I prepare to face the unknown.

As we reach the house, I retreat to my room, grateful for the solitude. I lie down on the bed and stare up at the ceiling. The events of the day replay in my mind, and the weight of my new reality settles in.

Leading a magical life won't be easy. There will be trials, challenges, and dangers I can't even fathom. But as I close my eyes, I also acknowledge that there will be moments of wonder, discovery, and perhaps even a sense of purpose I've never known before.

With these conflicting thoughts swirling in my mind, I drift into an uneasy sleep, knowing that tomorrow will bring fresh adventures, challenges, and a world waiting to be explored.

CHAPTER 12

A WHOLE NEW WORLD

I wake to the insistent buzzing of an alarm clock, still groggy from sleep. It's way too early for anything productive, and my body protests as I reluctantly push the covers aside. The pre-dawn light seeping through the curtains dimly lit the room, casting a soft blue hue across the walls.

"Dani?" I mumble as I squint at her. She's standing by my bed, a barely discernible silhouette in the dim light.

"Liv, get up. We have something special planned for you," Dani whispers as she barely contains her excitement.

I rub my eyes, trying to shake off the remnants of sleep. "Why are you waking me up at the ass crack of dawn, and what's with the outfit?"

Dani is holding out a sports bra and leggings in my direction. Confusion mingles with curiosity as I reluctantly accept the clothing. With a sigh, I slip out of bed, then hastily change into the clothes. The sports bra and leggings cling to my skin, and I feel exposed in a way I hadn't expected. The cool fabric sends a shiver down my spine as I try to shake off the drowsiness.

As I stumble out of my room and into the living room, the early morning chill hits me like a bucket of cold water. The living room is dimly lit, and I can make out the outlines of Dani, Lucy, and Vik standing there, each wearing similar athletic outfits.

"Liv, you're here," Lucy says with excitement. She's hopping from one foot to the other with a wide smile.

"Yeah, but what's going on?" I reply, still trying to wake up fully.

Dani steps forward with a grin on her face. "We're going to do something different today. Follow us."

They lead me outside, and the cold air rushes over me, sending goosebumps racing across my skin. As the pre-dawn sky glows with shades of pink and orange, I feel a sense of anticipation building within me.

We walk across the dew-kissed grass towards a small field tucked away behind the house. It's a serene spot, surrounded by trees that whisper in the early morning breeze. A thin layer of dew covers the field, giving it an almost ethereal quality.

As we reach the center of the field, Vik finally speaks. "Liv, today you're going to have your first fight training session with us."

I blink in surprise because I know this cannot possibly be what their excitement is about. Fight training? I don't know what the hell are they talking about. Clearly, all three of them are badasses. I, on the other hand, had never thrown a punch in my life.

"Wait, we're doing what now?" I stammer, trying to make sure I heard them correctly.

"Your first fighting lesson," Dani answers.

I frown at all three of them. "Why?"

"Because, Liv, you're part of our team now, and it's time

you learn to defend yourself. Plus, it's going to be so much fun!" Lucy replies.

Despite my apprehension, I can't help but smile. The idea of learning how to fight alongside these amazing women makes me feel good.

"But first, Dani, Vik, and I will demonstrate the badass you're going to be by the time we finish with you," Lucy adds.

I watch as they square off against each other. Dani lunges forward with her right fist, slicing through the air with a hiss. Lucy, quick on her feet, pivots to the side, narrowly avoiding the blow. The air crackles with the whoosh of missed punches as they circle each other, searching for openings.

A sudden flurry of blows erupts between the three of them as fists collide with flesh. Vik's jab lands on the jaw of Lucy, causing her head to snap back with her hair flying in disarray. Pain flares through her face, but she retaliates with a swift knee aimed at Vik's midsection. It connects with a thud, forcing the air out of her lungs.

Lucy does a brutal roundhouse kick that connects with the side of Dani's thigh, sending a jolt of agony down her leg. She stumbles momentarily as she grunts with pain, but stays on her feet. They grapple and wrestle, trying to gain the upper hand over each other.

The next thing I know, each of their fists sails through the air, each one aiming for one. Dani toward Lucy, Lucy toward Vik, and Vik toward Dani. Their fists connect with their intended target, sending them flying back on their asses.

They look at each other in shock at what happened before bursting out into laughter. I'm appalled at how hard they went at each other as I see their bruised and battered state. They can't possibly think that I'd willingly do something like this. They kicked each other's asses like it's a regular Tuesday.

"You guys are crazy!" I yell. "If you think I'm going to do that, you're dead wrong."

"Relax, Liv," Dani says as she stands.

She waves a hand over herself, and I watch as she heals and cuts and bruises. Lucy waves a hand and does the same thing to her and Vik.

I throw my hands up in the air. "No wonder you have no problem beating the shit out of each other like it's normal. You heal yourselves when it's over."

"Doesn't mean the fighting doesn't hurt like hell, Liv," Vik replies while rolling her eyes.

"Come on, Liv. It's your turn." Dani says.

I'm about to shake my head no when Dani hands me something, and I realize it's padding. As Dani explains the basics of self-defense, I take a deep, steadying breath to prepare for my first lesson. I put on the protective gear and gloves and take another deep breath to steady my nerves. Dani cracks her knuckles and flashes a mischievous grin.

"Ready to fight, Liv?" Dani asks, her eyes glinting with excitement.

I square my shoulders as determination replaces any lingering anxiety. "As ready as I'll ever be."

"I won't take it easy on you because that's not how the real world works, but I won't pummel you to death either," she tells me as we start.

With a nod, we circle each other, feet shuffling through the dew-kissed grass. Dani moves with a grace and precision that leaves me terrified. She's a force to be reckoned with, and I know this lesson won't be a walk in the park.

Dani wastes no time attacking first. She launches a

flurry of kicks and punches, a whirlwind of motion that keeps me on the defensive. I block as best as I can, but her strikes come with lightning speed and impeccable accuracy.

I try to throw a punch, but she grabs my arm and twists it behind my back before throwing me to the ground and following up with a flurry of punches and kicks. Thank god I have on the padding because her hits still hurt. I'd hate to know what it'll feel like without it.

"Come on, Olivia! Show me what you've got!" Dani taunts as she backs away, her voice teasing.

I grit my teeth and gather my resolve before standing up. This time, I try to mimic what I'd seen her do, throwing a jab followed by a roundhouse kick. It's sloppy, and I nearly fall over, but Dani easily sidesteps and counters with a quick jab of her own, catching me off balance.

"Not bad, but you've got to be faster," she quips with a grin.

I leap onto her like a monkey before grabbing her in a chokehold. She's laughing at my tactic to overpower her before flipping me over. Round after round, Dani continues to outmaneuver me. Her kicks are precise, her punches are powerful, and her timing is impeccable. I have a long way to go before I can match her skills.

I try to punch her, but she grabs my arm and uses my momentum to throw me off balance before delivering a kick to my chest.

"You make it look so easy," I say as I lay on the ground, panting.

Dani chuckles as she stares down at me. "Well, that's why they call it practice, Liv. You're doing great, and you're getting better with every minute."

I nod as I stand, determined not to let this beat down

get the best of me. My arms feel heavy, and my legs are tired, but I focus on my breathing and try to anticipate Dani's next move. She lifts her leg like she's going to kick me, so I twist to the side, but at the last moment, she puts her leg down and backhands me. However, she pulls the power of her hit because it was a little tap on the cheek.

"Don't anticipate what your opponent is going to do," Dani reprimands me. "Your focus will only be on one thing instead of remaining alert for multiple attacks."

I throw a jab, followed by a quick low kick, aiming for her legs. She dodges my punch but barely evades my kick.

"Nice one!" she grins at my sudden attack. "There you go! Now you're getting the hang of it."

The lesson continues, and I find my rhythm. I block hits more effectively, and my strikes become crisper. Dani doesn't hold back, but provides just enough resistance for me to grow. Our banter becomes more playful, even as we exchanged blows.

"Liv, you're so uncoordinated," Dani teases as she evades my still sloppy high kick with a graceful backwards leap.

I roll my eyes, trying to hide my amusement. "Well, shouldn't we have started with lessons in proper form or something?"

"I have learned that experience is the best teacher," Dani replies. "Nothing helps you learn faster than continuously getting your ass whooped."

My sparring lesson with Dani ends and I am breathing heavily from exertion. I'm battered and bruised, but couldn't have felt prouder of my progress. Thankfully, Lucy healed me after.

Dani grins at me. "You did fantastic, Liv. You're already getting better."

"Yeah, right," I snort. "You kicked my ass all over the field."

She laughs before walking away. Now it's my turn to spar with Lucy. I think they're having fun with this. Lucy has her own unique set of skills, as I've witnessed when they were fighting each other. Despite being tired, I can't help but feel excitement as I get ready for our fight.

"Ready to dance, Liv?" Lucy asks.

I nod as my nerves and anticipation form a tangle of knots in my stomach. "Let's do this."

We circle each other. I'm cautious, keenly aware of the potential power behind each of her hits. I watch Lucy's movements carefully, searching for any opening to exploit. She's agile and quick, and I know if I can keep up with her.

Lucy starts the exchange with a sharp jab. I block it in time, feeling the force of her hit against my forearm.

"Nice block, but can you handle this?" Lucy taunts, her leg snapping out in a blur.

I try to dodge, but I'm just a fraction too slow. Her kick connects with my side, sending a jolt of pain through my ribs. I wince, but refuse to show any signs of weakness.

I go low, attempting to do the leg sweep Dani did to me, but she jumps over it before delivering a series of punches. My determination grows stronger as I shake off the discomfort. I have to counter Lucy's relentless onslaught. I launch a series of quick punches, aiming for her chest, but she effortlessly deflects them and counters with a powerful left hook. The force of the blow sends my head snapping to the side.

"Come on, Olivia, you can do better than that!" Lucy teases, her eyes sparkling with mischief.

I grit my teeth, refusing to let her get into my head. I

take a step back, reassessing my approach. Maybe I can't out-muscle her, but I can try to out-think her.

I back away, circling Lucy cautiously, looking for an opening. Her laughter fills the air as she taunts me, "You're like a punching bag with legs, Liv."

I can't help but smirk, even during our heated exchange. "Well, at least I'm a well-dressed punching bag."

Lucy chuckles as I move to attack. Despite my best efforts, Lucy's experience and speed are overwhelming. She moves with the grace of a dancer, her punches and kicks flowing seamlessly together. As the minutes pass, exhaustion takes its toll. Lucy, on the other hand, seems tireless. She launches a final devastating roundhouse kick that I can't evade, and I tumble to the ground.

She offers me a hand with a wide smile. "Good effort, Olivia. You'll get there."

I accept her hand, pulling myself up with a mixture of frustration and admiration. "Thanks, Lucy. You're incredible."

She winks, her playful spirit shining through. "Well, don't tell Dani, but I'm the best fighter in the house."

"Bullshit!" Vik says. "I am, and now it's my turn to kick Liv's ass."

I snort at her comment. "Glad to know it's kick Olivia's ass day today. I'm glad you're having fun."

I prepare for my sparring session with Vik. After taking on Dani and Lucy, my body is aching, and my muscles are protesting. I'd held my own against Dani and Lucy, even though I struggled. Now, I'm ready to face Vik.

"Let's see if you've still got some fight left in you, Liv," Vik says.

I nod in anticipation. "I'm ready, Vik."

As we square off, I can't help but notice the differences

in Vik's fighting style compared to Dani and Lucy. She has a boxer's stance with her fists held close to her face, and her footwork was steady and precise.

Viktoria starts with a punch to my face, but I move and come back with my punch. She's testing my defenses. Dani and Lucy may joke about Vik's fighting skills, but I don't think they give her enough credit, or maybe it's just me and my lack of skill. She follows up with a powerful right hook that I narrowly dodge and stumble back.

"Getting quick on your feet, aren't you?" Vik remarks with a playful smirk on her lips.

I grin, glad that I'm making progress. "Gotta stay light on my toes if I want to keep up with you guys."

We continue to trade punches, and I'm pleasantly surprised that I can anticipate some of Vik's movements. Her punches are strong, and she has an uncanny ability to dodge every single strike I make, but I'm gradually getting better at reading her rhythm.

Vik throws a series of jabs and hooks, and I evade most of them. I counter with a left hook to her side, causing her to wince. I shout in excitement that I land the hit.

"Not bad, Liv," Vik admits, rubbing her side. "You've got some power behind that punch."

I chuckle. "I'm glad I hit one of you."

As the rounds continue, I can feel the rhythm of the fight changing. I'm becoming more comfortable finding my groove amidst the punches and footwork. Vik's coaching and guidance are paying off.

I land a few solid punches of my own, my jabs and hooks finding their mark. Vik's playful banter continues, and we exchange snarky remarks between punches.

"Is that all you've got?" I taunt as my confidence grows.

Vik grins, her eyes dancing with amusement. "Not even close, Liv."

Despite my newfound confidence, Vik's experience and technique ultimately win. She lands a powerful hook that sends me stumbling back, and I know the match is over.

"Alright, alright, you win, Viktoria," I concede, removing my gloves and shaking out my sore hands. "You didn't have to let me get confident just for you to knock my ass back down."

"But it was so much fun, Liv. You need confidence, but don't turn that confidence into cockiness, especially at your skill level. But you did well. Keep it up, and you'll be a force to be reckoned with." Vik tells me.

I roll my eyes in frustration when they tell me we're not done yet. Now they want to teach me the fundamentals, and I'm positive that kicking my ass was all fun and games for them. With a simply flick of her fingers, a padded dummy appears on the field.

We spend a few more hours on the field. Dani teaches me the fundamentals of karate. Her movements are precise and graceful. Lucy's kickboxing expertise came next, her powerful kicks making me wince with each impact on the padded target. Vik shows me how to throw punches with precision and speed.

The surroundings seemed to come alive as we train. Birds chirp overhead, and it gets warmer by the minute, revealing the vibrant colors of the awakening world. The hot air warms with our exertion, and I feel sweat trickling down my back as I throw punches and kicks for practice.

Throughout the rest of the day, my body protests, muscles I never knew existed ache from the strain. Yet, with each punch and kick, I grow more confident. Though, I know it will take a lot of time to become proficient in fighting and even more time to reach the levels of Dani, Vik, and Lucy.

"Thank you," I tell them suddenly. "I never thought I'd be doing this, but I'm so glad I am."

Dani grins and claps me on the back. "You're doing great, Liv. This is just the beginning. We're going to turn you into a force to be reckoned with."

Lucy nods in agreement. "And we're going to have a lot of fun along the way."

After our intense training session that left me battered but invigorated, I tell them I'm still not sure I can live this life. I have family and friends back home that I can't forget about. I had a life before all of this happened and I'd like to get back to it.

Dani surprises me by insisting that we had to meet the Overlords. The thought of facing the powerful and mysterious figures who governed Orchard Landing fills me with a mixture of curiosity and apprehension.

As we make our way to the main house, Dani senses my unease. "Don't worry, Liv. They're not as intimidating as they seem."

I can't help but raise an eyebrow. "That's easy for you to say. You're practically family to them."

Dani chuckles. "True, I am family, but they'll like you. Just be yourself."

We enter the main house, and I find myself face to face with Over Lords' Miranda, Mary, Annie, Sydney, Stephanie, and the always scary Ashley. They sit on the couch with unreadable expressions.

"Olivia, meet the Overlords," Dani said with a grin.

Over Lord Miranda gives me a warm smile. "It's nice to see you again, Olivia. How are you settling in?"

I try to keep my composure despite the awe that washes over me. "Everything is fine, thank you."

Dani nudges me forward. "Go on, Olivia. Tell them your concerns."

I hesitate for a moment, wondering if I should even share my worries. Then I take a deep breath and begin. "Well, it's just that... I'm not used to all of this. Orchard Landing, the training, everything. Then there's my life back home, my friend Eve, and even my mother."

Over Lord Mary speaks kindly. "We understand, Olivia. It's a lot to take in, but we'll take care of everything while you're here. Your friend Eve, your mother, your life back home—consider it all taken care of."

Over Lord Stephanie nods in agreement. "You don't have to worry about a thing. We have resources and connections that can handle any situation."

I can't help but feel a sense of relief wash over me. "Thank you. That means a lot and I want to get back to my life."

"Newsflash, newbie. This is your life. Whatever you were doing before, whoever you were before, no longer matters." Over Lord Ashley chimes in.

Over Lord Sydney elbows her, her expression scolding. "Show some compassion, Ashley."

"Enough, you two," Over Lord Miranda snaps. "Olivia, we're here to support you. Orchard Landing is a haven for those who need it, and we've got your back."

Over Lord Annie adds with a warm smile. "You're part of our family now, Olivia. And families take care of each other."

As I absorb their reassurance and warmth, I feel a sense of gratitude. These influential figures aren't the distant and imposing figures I had imagined. They are people who genuinely care about me and my well-being.

Dani squeezes my shoulder as she smiles. "See, Liv? I told you they'd be on your side."

I nod, feeling a newfound sense of belonging and purpose. Orchard Landing might have been a world away from my old life, but it's becoming a place where I can learn, grow, and find support in the most unexpected ways.

Dani and I leave the main house with the weight of my concerns lifted by their reassurances. A sense of contentment envelopes me as we return to the house for the night.

Inside the cozy living room, the warm glow of the table lamp welcomes us. It's become my refuge since being here, a place where I could unwind and relax. Once everyone's showered, we set out to make dinner. Plates of food balance on our laps, and the movie we started earlier fills the room with suspense.

As we watch, Lucy whispers something to Dani. Their brows furrow as they turn their attention back to the movie.

"Dani, Lucy, is everything okay?" I ask, sensing that something isn't right.

Dani shrugs and looks confused. "Yeah, Liv. Lucy was telling me something she forgot to mention earlier."

Just as I resume watching the movie, the lights in the room suddenly dim to an eerie, blood-red hue.

My heart skips a beat, and I looked around in bewilderment. "What the hell is going on?"

A tense silence hangs in the air, and I look over to see that everyone has disappeared. Then, with a sudden and spine-tingling jolt, the room plunges into complete darkness.

I shriek in fear. I don't know what's happening, but I

don't like it one bit. My breath hitches, and I feel a shiver run down my spine. I'm about to call out to them when a hand grabs my shoulder.

I scream and jump off the couch. I run to the front door as fast as I can, wrenching it open and running out.

"Liv! Liv! Stop running," Dani yells from behind me.

I gasp as I stop, and my heart is pounding. "What's happening?"

Before I can react, I'm transported back into the house and am surrounded by their laughter. Dani has tears streaming down her face from laughing so hard.

"I'm sorry," Lucy says through her laughter. "We didn't mean to scare you so bad."

"This was a prank?" I yell, anger lacing my tone. "You guys need to grow up!"

I flop down on the couch, letting out an angry sigh. Unfortunately, their laughter is infectious because I can't help but laugh at the freight they gave me.

"You guys are ridiculous," I say, joining the laughter.

Vik emerges from the shadows with a playful grin. "We couldn't resist having a little fun. You were so stiff with anxiety and concern. You need to loosen up a bit."

As the tension eases, we settle back into the couch, still chuckling at the prank. The movie resumes, and I watch for any other pranks they may pull.

CHAPTER 13

LET THE TRAINING BEGIN

True to their word, the Over Lords worked their magic, and my family won't worry about me. To be honest, I was more worried about my mom and Eve. I don't know what they told her, and I don't have my phone to call her, but I trust they did what's best.

As for Eve, she wasn't home, and they can't seem to find her. This has me worried that something terrible has happened to her. I freaked out on the Over Lords because they're supposed to know everything, and they can't seem to find my only friend.

"Olivia, you need to calm the hell down," Over Lord Mary snaps.

"How can I calm down when the powerful, all-knowing Over Lords can't see to find my friend?" I snap back, so lost in the haze of worry that I have no fear of them at that moment.

Over Lord Ashley steps forward. "Alright, I'm going to kick her ass. Right now."

Suddenly, she flies back into the far wall as I'm lifted into the air. "Everyone calm the fuck down," Over Lord

Miranda says as her power fills the room. "We will find Eve, Olivia. There's no need to lash out. I understand that you're worried, so I'll give you this one time. Step out of line again when talking to us, and I'll beat your ass myself."

She puts me down slowly, and some of my worry for Eve dissipates. They are more attuned to the Mutane Sihiri, not the humans, so it may be difficult to find her. However, before letting me go, they assured me they would ensure she was safe.

I've been on Orchard Landing for so long that I take a leave of absence from Sutton Engineering. No one knows what happened but Axel and Barb. To anyone looking in, it's an ordinary request that was approved.

I spend a few more weeks at the Institute, learning about my magical heritage and abilities. The Over Lords are patient with me and teach me everything they can about the Mutane Sihiri when they aren't busy.

There are so many abilities that I'm amazed the Over Lords can keep up with them all. Jade never mentioned what happened the first day we met and has been cordial with me ever since. Lucy and Dani tell me she has a stoic demeanor all the time and not to let her stand-offish personality get to me.

I'm not like the other people here. Most of them seem to have been born with some magical ability, though there are some here, like me, that came into their power at some random time. The good thing is that I learned where our magic came from. I also learned some challenges the Over Lords have been through, and I'm amazed they're still standing strong.

Despite my many protests, I have to learn how to fight, and it's a non-negotiable requirement for all of us. Every-one's ability is physical, whereas mine is invisible, and I feel intimidated. Even though I try my best to keep up, some-times I feel wholly inadequate and incompetent compared to everyone else. It's a constant reminder that I'm different from most other students.

Sometimes, I want to disappear into the shadows and observe rather than take part. Even then, I feel out of place, as these kids seem more at ease with their abilities than I am with mine. It's hard for me to be around them without feeling inferior or unworthy.

Yet, I'm determined to keep trying and not give up, no matter how hard it is. I know I can learn and grow if I work hard enough. It will take some time for me to become accustomed to this new world of magic, and that's okay.

I've grown closer to Dani, Lucy, and Vik and am grateful for them. It's like we've been friends for years. I feel foolish for keeping them at a distance initially, but they've done nothing but try to make their home my home, too.

To take the pressures away from training with the other students, Dani convinced the Over Lords to let her, Lucy, and Vik train me. We've been training for weeks, and it's my least favorite thing to do. This morning is another training day, and I'll train with each of them every day this week.

"Come on, Liv," Dani says as she yanks the blanket away from me. "Get your ass out of bed. We've got training to do today."

I roll over, turning my back to her. "Go away, Dani. I don't feel like getting my as kicked today."

The next moment, I'm falling onto grass covered in dew. The sudden wet sensation causes me to hop up with a shout. "Seriously! Next time, give me a warning."

"I told you to get up," Dani laughs. "We either train, or mom will make you return to the school to train with the other students."

"Fine, let's get this over with," I reply with a sigh.

Dani snaps her fingers, and I'm instantly in training gear. "I know we've been working on your hand-to-hand. I'm going to spar with you a little, and then we can mix things up with some weapons."

One positive thing about living with Dani, Vik, and Lucy is the confidence boost. When the visions started happening, I folded in on myself and became this shell of a woman. They remind me of the young and confident person I used to be, even if I was a quiet nerd. I'm slowly getting back to that. I'm not on the level of awesomeness they're on, but I'm getting there.

"Alright, Dani, let's see what you've got," I say as we square off in the open field.

I've been training for weeks, and I'm ready to show her what I can do. The sun is shining brightly overhead, but neither of us pays much attention. We're both too focused on the fight. We circle each other warily, sizing up our opponent before making a move. It doesn't take long for me to make mine. With a yell, I charge forward and throw a punch to her head.

Dani blocks my strike easily and counters with one of her own that sends me flying backwards into the grass. I land hard on the ground, moaning in pain as I struggle to my feet. If I thought she would take it easy on me, that hit proved me wrong. She had some serious power behind it, but I'm ready to give up yet. I get back on my feet and ready myself for another attack, determined to show her how good I've gotten.

I take a few steps back as Dani charges forward, throwing punches like a wildcat. I quickly block Dani's fists with open palms and retaliate with swift jabs that send her staggering back. At least I've gotten stronger during my time here, and it shows. Dani recovers quickly and goes for another round, but this time, she feints right to distract me before launching a full-force attack. I handle my own, but she won this match.

"Good job, Liv," Dani says as we take a break. "Now we can try fighting with weapons. We'll start with knives first."

I shake my head. "Are you sure? I don't know about this, Dani. What if one of us gets hurt?"

"Then either Lucy or I will heal you up, good as new," Dani tells me, as if getting hurt should be the last thing on my mind.

"But what if I don't want to get hurt?" I whine, imagining the pain of being cut or stabbed with a knife.

Dani throws her head back and laughs. "I'm going to break this down for you, Liv. Getting hurt is a part of fighting. Weapons are a part of fighting. My job is to teach you to fight and to use weapons while doing it. Your job is to protect yourself from getting hurt."

"You guys know we're not in a war, right?" I ask Dani. "There's no need for all of this."

Dani shakes her head sadly. "You didn't grow up in our world. You do not know the monsters that lurk in the dark and what we had to endure. But I'll give you an example when we leave here."

She conjures two knives, one for her and one for me, and we start. We both charge forward, slashing and dodging our way around the field. Somehow, Dani seems to know exactly what move I would make before I made it, almost as if we were competing in a high-stakes game of chess rather than an intense knife fight. I try my hardest, but she always stays one step ahead of me.

The fight goes on like this for what feels like hours. In the heat of battle, Dani and I switch between offense and defense in a wild dance of martial arts. Sweat beads on our faces as we kick and punch with newfound vigor, neither giving an inch to the other. Finally, after sparring for so long, I make a mistake and slip as I swipe at Dani. I can't dodge Dani's punch, and the impact sends me flying back, landing with a loud thud.

"Sorry, Liv," Dani says as she helps me back up. "That was quite impressive. I think we can call it a day."

I give her a small smile, and we head home to shower, change clothes, and relax for the rest of the day. I step into the shower, allowing the hot water to cascade over my aching body. Taking a few moments, I allow myself to relax before quickly washing up and changing into clean clothes. Though I am exhausted, my stomach grumbles hungrily as I head toward the kitchen. With any luck, there'll be something edible left in the pantry.

"Can you come here for a second, Liv?" Dani calls out before I make it to the kitchen.

I walk into the living room to see Dani standing there, her expression unusually serious.

"Hey," she says, her voice tinged with anticipation. "Come, take a seat."

Nervously, I sink into the nearest armchair, my mind racing with a mix of curiosity and trepidation. There's an air of secrecy, of something momentous about to unfold. As I settle into the chair, Dani steps forward, her eyes alight with a mischievous glimmer.

"I have something to show you," she says, a hint of laughter in her voice.

My curiosity piqued further, but I've seen the jokes they play on each other and know I should be wary of whatever she's about to do. Without another word, Dani raises her hand, and a pulsating light emerges from her palm.

My eyes widen as the shimmering light merges into a magical portal, swirling with otherworldly hues. I watch, spellbound, as the portal widens, revealing an ominous darkness beyond. I feel a chill run down my spine and my breath catches in my throat.

Then, four colossal figures step out of the portal, their forms looming over us like towering shadows. I gasp as my heart pounds in my chest. These are demons. I learned about them at the Institute, but seeing them in the flesh is an entirely different experience.

Their eyes glow like fiery coals, and their massive bodies cast ominous silhouettes across the room. Fear gnaws at me, and I involuntarily scoot back in my chair, my body tense like a coiled spring.

"What the hell, Dani!" I scream at her. "You brought demons into the house!" I squeeze my eyes shut. "Holy shit, demons are real. I must be sleeping because there's no way demons are standing in our living room."

Dani lets out a boisterous laugh. "Don't worry, Liv. They're my uncles. They might look scary, but they won't hurt us. These are the -she throws up air quotes- good demons."

I try to calm down, reminding myself that Dani wouldn't put me in harm's way. Still, the sight of these fearsome creatures standing before me is unlike anything I'd ever encountered. It is as if the boundaries between fantasy and reality have blurred, and my mind struggles to comprehend the surreal scene unfolding before me.

"Little niece, it is nice to see you," one of them says. "It is always nice when one of your portals appears. To what do we owe the pleasure?

As the demons greet Dani with a mix of respect and playfulness, I can't help but marvel at the magical world I'd unwittingly stumbled into. The fear gradually subsides, replaced by a sense of awe and wonder.

She gives the demon that spoke a hug. "Hi, guys. We've got a new member in our group. Our little trio of misfits is now a quartette. I'm just showing Liv there are scary things in our world that she hasn't encountered yet. That's why her training is so important."

The demons turn their black eyes my way. "It is a pleasure to meet you. I am Buranath. These are my brothers, Astroloch, Salgremas, and Urathel."

"Um, hello," I squeak out.

Dani's demon uncles stay for a little while and tell me stories about their world. I also learn just how powerful Dani and Lucy really are based on what Buranath told me. There are worlds out there that prove we are not alone. At that moment, I knew my life would never be the same. After their visit, we settle in for the night. Dani tells me we'll have to step up my training if I hope to be as badass as them.

A few weeks flow by, and I've gotten better at fighting. Today, I'm sparring with Lucy, and I can't wait. I stand in the open field, the tall grass swaying gently in the breeze. They sunbathe the landscape in a warm glow, setting the perfect stage for my training session with Lucy. As I adjust my grip on the wooden staff she provided, I can't help but feel a mix of nerves and excitement. Lucy stands opposite me with her own staff poised and ready.

"Alright, Olivia," she says with a reassuring smile. "Let's begin."

With that, she lunges forward, her staff whirling through the air with a fluid grace. I react instinctively, blocking her attack with my staff. The impact sends a jolt through my arms, but I hold my ground. Lucy is skilled, and I know she's challenging me to become better.

We engage in a dance of parries and strikes, our staffs clashing and echoing across the field. Lucy's movements are swift and calculated, and I struggle to keep up with her speed. But she's patient, offering encouragement and guidance as we spar.

"Remember to breathe," she reminds me, her voice steady. "Find your center and maintain your balance."

I take a deep breath, trying to calm the fluttering nerves in my stomach. With each exhale, I feel myself becoming more grounded. As our training continues, I get the upper hand. I expect Lucy's moves countering her attacks with greater precision. The wooden staff feels like an extension of me, an instrument through which I can express my newfound abilities. With a swift twirl, I disarm Lucy, sending her staff flying in the air.

She grins, genuinely impressed by my progress. "Well done, Liv," she praises. "You're getting the hang of it. You'll be kicking ass and taking names in no time."

"Thanks, Lucy," I tell her as I smile at my improvement. "Do you know when we'll work on my ability?"

The smile wipes off her face instantly. "The Over Lords will help you with that."

The sudden change in her demeanor has me narrowing my eyes. "Spit it out, Lucy. What are you not telling me?"

She huffs with agitation. "For the record, you did not hear this from me. Have you had any visions since the last one with Jade?"

"How did you know about that?" I ask her in surprise. I had told no one, but I wasn't aware Jade did. "Wait, come to think of it, no, I haven't. Why is that?"

"Jade told the Over Lords you had another vision, and

that she worried you'd start scaring the students," Lucy explains. "So, Over Lord Sydney came by that night while you were sleeping and suppressed your ability. To help you focus on training. She was going to release it when the time came."

"She did what!" I shout. "She had no right!"

Anger crosses over Lucy's face. "She had every right! It was only to help you, Liv."

My shoulders sag in defeat. "Well, it has given me peace. I guess I should be thankful, but I feel so violated."

Lucy laughs at that. "Trust me, we've all felt that way a time or two. Come on. Let's call it a day and chill the rest of the night."

"Okay," I tell Lucy. "Seriously, just how powerful are the Over Lords?"

"That is a question that everyone asks but will never get an answer to because the Over Lords don't even know how powerful they are," Lucy says as we walk back to the house. "And trust me, they have a lot of power."

Things are still going well for me on Orchard Landing, and while cleaning my room this morning, I find my phone. I've been so wrapped up in training that I hadn't realized I hadn't talked to my mom or Eve in months. It takes a while to charge, but when it does, I decide to call them. I take a deep breath to steady my nerves as I dial Mom's number.

"Hey, Mom," I say as she answers the call, trying to sound cheerful despite the turmoil inside me.

"Olivia, sweetheart! How are you doing? How do you like your new position overseas? Are you enjoying it?"

I swallow hard, my mind racing for the right words. "Oh, you know, Mom, it's going well," I reply, trying to sound convincing. "The position is interesting, and I'm learning a lot."

Mom seems pleased with my response, but my heart sinks. I hate lying to her, but I can't bear to tell her the truth about my magical ability and the world I've stumbled into. Not yet, at least. I don't know what the Over Lords did, but Mom seems to believe I'm away for the opportunity of a lifetime with my job.

"That's good to hear, dear," she says. "I knew you'd excel in your career. This overseas opportunity will open so many doors for you. Especially given your condition, I'm glad it's working out for you. You wouldn't believe how many questions they have asked me about your sudden departure, Olivia."

Her words sting, and anger flares within me. I'm angry at her assumption that my condition has been a hindrance to my potential. I'm angry that she thinks I had to go halfway across the world to find success. But most of all, I'm angry at myself for not being honest with her.

"Mom, my seizures have nothing to do with my potential," I reply, my voice trembling with emotion. "The seizures don't define me, and they certainly don't hold me back."

There was a moment of stunned silence on the other end of the line. "Don't take that tone with me, Olivia. I want the best for you. Do you know how this makes me look?" she snaps.

Tears well in my eyes as I struggle to find the right words. "I know, Mom, but you need to understand that I'm more than my job or my condition," I tell her, my voice steady now. "I'm not here to help or uphold your image. God, Mom, do you hear how you sound?"

There was another pause, and then Mom speaks with sincerity. "You're right, sweetheart. I'm sorry if I made you feel that way. I'm proud of you."

I take a deep breath, feeling the weight of the touching moment. "Thank you, Mom," I whisper. "I love you, and I promise to keep in touch."

"Great, now that that's out of the way. Do you think you can send some pictures? I want to show everyone how well you're doing," she says with impatience.

I'm silent for a moment, wondering if everything I say goes through one ear and out the other. I thought I just had a moment of understanding with her, but I need to come to terms with this is how she'll always be.

My anger boils over. "I will not be sending any pictures for you to show around and pretend that you have a picture-perfect life! I'll call again when I have some free time."

I hang up the phone and immediately dial Eve, but her number is disconnected. My worry for her well-being has intensified, and I don't know what to do. Unfortunately, I can only do what the Over Lords say, and I hope things work out for the best.

CHAPTER 14
A SECRET MISSION

The weight of worry clings to me like a second skin as I lay awake in my quiet, dark room. Last night, I had been restless, with my mind plagued by the inability to reach Eve. My concern for her has grown into a gnawing fear that something is terribly wrong, and I know I can't ignore it any longer.

I've been on Orchard Landing for months, learning about magic users and being trained as one of their fighters. At first, I had paid close attention to their soldiers' patrol routines. Not because I intended to spy on them, but because my initial plan was to escape this place as soon as possible.

However, over time, I'd grown comfortable here, forming connections with Dani, Lucy, and Vik and finding peace in this magical community. Still, I monitored the patrol routes, and now that knowledge is about to come in handy.

My mind races with thoughts of Eve. We had been through so much together, and she's always been my anchor to keeping my sanity. That I hadn't been able to reach her for weeks is twisting my insides. I can't shake the feeling that something has happened to her. As I slide out of bed and pull on my dark, weathered jacket, I grab the I.D. I hadn't used it since I got here. I don't go anywhere without it, but I haven't needed it since I haven't left the property.

The night air is cool as I tiptoe out of my room and into the dimly lit hallway. I move with practiced stealth, my bare feet making no sound on the nice floor. I've learned to become quieter since being here because Dani, Vik, Lucy, and the Over Lords seem attuned to everything.

The front door creaks slightly as I open it, and I freeze for a moment, listening to see if either of the girls woke from the slight sound. Luckily, they didn't, and I quickly step through the door before closing it quietly. The moon is a silver sliver in the inky sky, and as it casts ghostly shadows, I tiptoe through the courtyard and into the woods beyond.

I move through the trees as silently as possible, not wanting to rustle any wildlife as they would give away my position to anyone walking about. Orchard Landing is like a small city that never sleeps. People are always around doing one thing or another.

I've been awake and out with Dani, Lucy, and Vik at all hours since being here and memorized the patrol routes of the soldiers. Tonight, that knowledge is my lifeline. I know they usually take a break near the eastern edge of the property around this hour, their chatter and laughter serving as a beacon for my escape.

My heart races as I navigate the winding paths I know so well. Each rustle of leaves and crackle of twigs underfoot feels like a betrayal of my presence, but I press on, my determination to find Eve pushing me forward. I heighten my senses as I tread softly through the underbrush. Every noise I hear as I make my way seems amplified, magnifying my fear of getting caught.

My heart pounds wildly in my chest and it feels like it's echoing in the quiet night. Every shadow, every whisper of wind through the trees, feels like a potential threat. The forest seems to close around me. The trees reach out like gnarled fingers, ready to ensnare me in their grasp.

As I approach the edge of the property, I slow my pace. I know the soldiers' patrol will soon resume, and I have to be careful not to cross their path. I crouch behind a dense thicket, careful to control my breathing t as I watch a few soldiers pass by, oblivious to my presence.

One misstep, one careless noise, and they'd know I'm here. I can't afford to be caught, and my doubts gnaw at my resolve as I question my decision. If the Over Lords discover my absence, they will want to punish me for my disobedience. They aren't evil people, but I know they don't take kindly to disrespect either.

With the soldiers safely on their way, I continue my journey, each step taking me further from the safety of Orchard Landing. I cautiously slip past the entrance gates, and my breath catches in my chest once again in fear of getting caught. I run for it, straight ahead, until I pause when I make it through the thick forest of trees. Orchard Landing isn't in a small town like I thought. It's a tiny island. However, we must not be far from civilization because I see a city skyline off in the distance.

The island turns out to be smaller than I thought. My footsteps are slow and deliberate as I move through the underbrush, doing my best to stay hidden from any potential eyes that might be watching. After what feels like hours of creeping through the woods, I finally stumble upon the key to my escape—a small ferry boat moored along the shoreline. My heart leaps with a mixture of excitement and trepidation. The boat means I can reach the city and, hopefully, find Eve.

I approach the boat with caution. My eyes scan the area for any signs of guards or unexpected obstacles. The boat is a beautiful, modest size, even if weathered by the elements, but it seems good enough for my purposes. The controls, however, are a puzzle of knobs, levers, and buttons that baffle me.

My face scrunches in frustration as I fumble with all the controls. My fingers slid over slick surfaces, trying to decipher their purpose, but every attempt to start the engine yields only the same hollow silence.

"This is bullshit," I say as I get angrier by the minute. "It cannot possibly be this hard to start a damn boat."

Time seems to stretch on, each minute an eternity as I fumble with the controls. I'm getting more anxious as seconds tick by, fear of someone catching me, so I can't afford to waste any more time. Finally, after what feels like an eternity, I find the control that turns on the engine. The engine roars to life, and I look behind me to see if anyone heard it.

"Yes!" I say with a triumphant smile, but my relief is short-lived as I realize I don't know how to steer this thing.

The boat lurches forward, sending me stumbling in the dash. Panic settles in as I desperately try to regain control, but my efforts only seem to make matters worse. The boat sways in a haphazard direction, tossing me about like a rag doll. It takes a few minutes as I battle my frustration and fear before getting the hang of the steering. Soon, Orchard Landing fades away as the city grows closer.

As the boat takes me closer, I see homes along the

shoreline with their decks extending to the calm waters. I guide the boat toward the nearest dock, hoping no one notices me. Making it to this side was simple, as I now face the daunting task of finding Eve in this unfamiliar area.

I hop out of the boat quietly and make my way up the dock. My plan to go unnoticed is ruined when I realize someone is sitting in their backyard, just a few yards from where I stand. My heart sinks as I watch them hidden behind the bushes, hoping they won't notice my presence.

Unfortunately, luck is not on my side as I step on a few sticks. The homeowner, a middle-aged woman, turns her head and locks eyes with mine. Panic surges through me as I debate whether to flee or come up with a plausible explanation for my presence here.

"Who's there?" the woman yells out. "Come out, or I'll get my shotgun. You're trespassing, so I can shoot you and get away with it."

I quickly put my hands up before standing. "Don't shoot! Please, I mean you no harm. I'm just trying to get home."

"Do you need help, dear?" the woman calls out, her voice filled with concern.

Surprised by her sudden concern, I scramble for an excuse. "I'm so sorry to bother you," I stammer. "My mother and I were out boating, and we got turned around. I think we're lost. Can you tell me where I am?"

The woman frowns as sympathy appears in her eyes. "Oh dear, that must be quite frightening. You're in Washington State."

I can't help but gasp at the realization. Washington State is a considerable distance from where I'm headed. Getting back home to look for Eve will be even more challenging.

The woman continues as I stare in silence. "Are you sure you're okay? Do you need any help?"

I force a smile, desperate to get my hands on a phone to find a way back home. "No, thank you. I think I'll be fine. Do you have a phone I can use just to let my mother know I'm safe?"

The woman nods sympathetically and grabs her phone before handing it to me. I pretend to speak to someone on the phone to keep up with the lie before stepping away to search an airline's website and find a last-minute flight back to Chicago.

My fingers fly across the screen, and I pay for the ticket using my bank information, thankful that I had the forethought to memorize the information for emergencies. I never thought I'd need it, as I always had my purse and cards, but I'm glad for my paranoia.

"Can you print this out for me?" I ask, my voice filled with gratitude.

Without hesitation, the woman takes me into her home, where she kindly prints out my ticket. As I hold the printed document in my hand, relief washes over me. Before I leave, she offers me a ride to the airport. I gladly accept as this is not something I expected to do.

I knew I wasn't in Chicago anymore after they rescued me, but I never thought I was in an entirely different state. In the car, she wishes me luck with finding my mother, and her niceness makes me feel bad because she's unaware of the real reason I'm in such a hurry.

Getting through the airport is easy, and my worry for Eve continues to grow throughout the entire flight. The flight is long and tiresome, and my heart pounds hard as I step off the plane. This clandestine experience has been a whirlwind of anxiety and uncertainty, and now I'm finally back where I'd last seen Eve.

I hitch a ride from the airport to Eve's house, and my anxiety grows with each passing mile in anticipation of seeing her for the first time in months. The thought of seeing her again fills me with both hope and dread.

As I pull up to Eve's house, I notice the lights aren't on. I hope she's sleeping because I don't know where to search for her if she's not home. I rush through the lobby, up to her apartment, and knock furiously.

"Eve! It's me, Olivia! Open the door," I shout, my voice getting louder with each knock.

But there's no response, only the eerie silence of an empty apartment. I knock again and again, my desperation growing with each unanswered call. My heart sinks as I finally realize Eve is not home, and the dread that has been growing returns with a vengeance. Helplessness washes over me, and I continue to pound on the door until one neighbor comes out of her apartment, irritation etched across her face.

"Hey bitch, knock it off, or I'll call the police!" she yells, her annoyance palpable.

My shoulders slump in defeat as I step away from the door. I need to find Eve, but my current approach is not working. With a heavy heart, I walk the streets of her neighborhood, hoping to come across her on her way home. I can't give up. Not when she might be in trouble because of me. But as I walk the familiar streets, my hope dwindles with each passing minute. The city is enormous, and Eve could be anywhere.

The adrenaline that had sustained me through this journey ebbs, leaving me more exhausted and vulnerable. Suddenly, I realize how much colder it is here in Chicago than in Orchard Landing. The wind cutting through my clothes chills me to the bone. I wrap my arms around myself, shivering as I walk the streets, desperately searching for any sign of Eve.

I won't make it much longer in this cold, and I need to warm myself up before I freeze to death. With a heavy sigh, I decide to return to my place and grab some warm clothes and a coat. I'll be no good to Eve if I'm freezing and exhausted. The trek home is a sizable distance from Eve's, and I can't feel my fingers and toes when I make it home.

As I walk through the door, memories wash over me. It's just as I'd left it on the day Axel demanded that I go with him. The same day, Dani, Vik, and Lucy rescued me, and an eerie stillness still hangs in the air. The memories of that dark time seem to seep from the very walls.

I move cautiously through the rooms, my footsteps silent on the well-worn floor. The impulse to turn on the lights is strong, but I quickly realize that doing so will give away my presence. If anyone is watching, I don't want them to know I'm home.

I go to the bedroom, carefully pulling open the drawers and the closet door, digging out some clothes and a coat. I need to get warm, but I also need to stay hidden. As I change, the tension in my body slowly eases. The familiar feeling of my clothes offers a small measure of comfort in this strange and dangerous situation.

Just as I'm about to finish dressing, a noise sends a shock of adrenaline through me. The front door had opened, and I can hear the soft click of it closing. Panic wells up inside me, and I freeze as fear travels through my body.

I creep behind the bedroom door, pressing myself against the wall, hoping whoever entered the house won't realize I'm here. My ears strain to catch the voices that follow through the house.

"I know I saw someone walk in," one voice says as I hear doors opening and closing. "She's here, and we need to find her and bring her back."

My blood runs cold at those words. These intruders are looking for me, and I should have known coming here was a mistake, but I had nowhere else to go. Fear grips me, but I know I must stay quiet and hidden. Their footsteps echo around the house as they search room by room. I hold my breath, willing myself to keep quiet and still. Meanwhile, my mind races, trying to devise an escape plan.

As they enter the bedroom, I know it's now or never. With every ounce of strength I can muster, I lunge out from behind the door and sprint toward the front door. The element of surprise helps me, and I reach the door just as they turn around. In a flurry of motion, I swing it open and dart outside as my heart pounds with terror and anxiety.

I'd barely taken a few steps when a hand grabs me and yanks me with a force that sends me stumbling backwards into the house, and the door slams shut behind me. Panic surges through me as I whirl around, only to find myself surrounded by the three intruders who had infiltrated my home. I'm scared, but not as terrified as I'd been the first time someone broke into my house.

Months of training with Dani, Lucy, and Vik gave me courage, so I'm not a helpless victim anymore. I know who they are and what they want. I will fight because I won't let them take me without a struggle.

I dart around the coffee table in the living room to put some distance between us. "Look, guys, I don't want any trouble. Let me leave. You can pretend you never saw me and go back to staking out my house like nothing happened."

They only stare at me, but I knew asking was a long shot, anyway. I look around, searching for something to use as a weapon. I'm sure these are magic users, and I have no physical magic to fight against them with. It will be challenging, especially since I don't know what kind of magic they have.

I see one of them produce tape and rope and know it's now or never. As they move closer, attempting to subdue me, I kick the coffee table with every ounce of strength I have. One trips over it and falls onto the table, but the other two keep their balance and come at me again.

I grab the remote to the TV and smack one in the face with it as one lunges forward, arms outstretched, to grab me. The remote smashes to pieces, and he screams in pain. As the other moves closer, I twist to the side, grab one arm, and use his momentum to slam him face-first into the wall behind me. The other grabs me from behind, and I elbow them on the side of the face, forcing them to let me go.

I stumble forward just as the one who tripped over the coffee table throws a punch. My head snaps back from the force of it. Blood pours out of my nose as I groan in pain. I'm in a daze and can't stop the next hit. One kicks me in the stomach, and I fall to my knees. I've pissed these guys off and they're trying to beat me into submission.

I will try my damndest to get the hell away from them. We continue to fight. My fists fly, and my kicks land with precision as I fight to fend them off. Furniture topples, glass shatters, and the walls bear the marks of our struggle.

I'm losing momentum as these guys out-power me and outnumber me. I'm bruised, battered, and bleeding. With one last hit to the side, I fall to the ground, gasping and groaning in pain. In my weakened state, they tie me up and place tape over my mouth. One intruder hoists me over his shoulder before they turn to leave.

Bound and gagged, I watch in astonishment as three familiar faces burst into my chaotic house. Dani, Lucy, and Vik suddenly appear, and their arrival takes the intruders by surprise. They hesitate for a moment, clearly taken aback by their sudden arrival.

"Put her down before I break every bone in fucking your body," Dani says to the figure holding me.

The grip on me loosens slightly. I glance at Dani, Lucy, and Vik with disbelief and confusion, but the tape over my mouth muffles my words. At seeing my predicament, Dani, Lucy, and Vik seize the opportunity to scold me, expressing their displeasure and ignoring the intruders.

"Really, Olivia?" Lucy says to me. "I cannot believe you had the audacity to sneak away!"

"Or the stupidity of coming back to your house when you know a group of asshats want to kidnap you," Vik says with a hit of disappointment. "Have you learned nothing from what we taught you?"

However, the intruders grow frustrated with being ignored. The figure tightens his hold on me and changes his stance. "Move out of our way. Pretend you saw nothing, and we'll let you live."

Lucy cracks her knuckles with a smirk. "How about you put her down, and I won't break your goddamn face?"

Dani's and Lucy's appearance change as they display their power. Dani only lets half the change take over because she doesn't care for how she looks when her demon half entirely emerges. Anger flares in his eyes, and he drops me unceremoniously to the floor. Pain shoots through my body as I hit the ground with a thud, and I groan again in agony.

I watch silently as they attack each other. Dani punches one so hard in the face that he flies back and slams into the wall. However, it didn't faze him one bit. I watch in surprise as he changes his appearance. Now, there are two versions of Dani fighting each other.

"So you can clone someone else's appearance, I see," Dani says. "Unfortunately, I can't see how that will help you in a fight. I'm still going to kick your ass."

I see Lucy fighting against another intruder, and they trade punches and kicks as their bodies are a blur of motion. A left hook crashes into his cheek, sending a spray of sweat and blood into the air. Grunts and gasps fill the room as they battle it out.

One of his bruised knuckles hits Lucy in the ribcage with a sickening thud, eliciting a sharp cry of agony. She flings an arm out, and he sails through the air into the wall. She holds him there as intense anger covers her features. Suddenly, all the knives in my kitchen fly through the air and plunge into his body.

I look toward Vik to see her fighting the air. She looks crazy, moving about in every direction as if there's some-thing there.

"You slimy shit stain," Vik growls. "Can't take getting your ass whipped by a girl so you turn invisible to get the upper hand?"

I hear laughter, but I can't see him. A grunt from Dani snags my attention, and I see them pummeling each other, though one Dani looks worse than the other. I know it's the imposter Dani that's beaten like that.

A knife embeds into Dani's back, and she gasps in pain. She stumbles back, reaching behind her, trying to pull it out. Vik's actually been fighting the air because the invisible magic user has stabbed Dani in the back.

"Enough!" Vik yells. "Show yourself," she demands.

Slowly, the magic user returns to normal, but I can see the strain on his face as he tries to fight the compulsion. The other magic user changes back to his original appearance.

"Stand right there and don't move," she tells them.

I snatch the tape off my mouth. "Why didn't you just do that in the first damn place? Then all of this could have been avoided."

"This could have been avoided if you'd stayed your ass on Orchard Landing," she snaps back.

That silences me because she's right, but before I can reply, the house shakes. I look over to see a very pissed Dani, and the complete change has taken over. Horns have sprouted from her head, her hands changed to sharp black claws, and black veins travel along her pale skin. She looks downright scary.

"Dani, calm down," Lucy says cautiously.

Dani isn't listening because she has the remaining two magic user's throats in her hand faster than I can blink. I gag a little because seeing the inside of their throats is disgusting. The dead magic users fall to the ground with surprised looks in their now lifeless eyes.

Dani and Lucy exchange glances as their power still crackles in the air. They return their attention to me, and I can feel the irritation coming off them in waves.

"What the hell, guys?" I snap. "There are dead bodies in my fucking living room! Who's going to clean this up?"

Dani snaps her fingers, and the bodies are gone. "A thank you would be nice." She says before snapping her fingers again, and all the destroyed furniture is gone, leaving the room empty. "We didn't have to rescue your ass."

"How did you know I was gone, and where to find me?" I ask, wondering if they can track me somehow.

"I went to get you for breakfast, but you were gone," Lucy replies instead. "We hoped you were somewhere on the property. When that search turned up nothing, we hoped you didn't come to Chicago to look for Eve, given the meltdown you had when the Over Lords couldn't find her. When she wasn't home, we hoped you didn't return to your house."

Dani looks at me deadpanned. "As you can see, your stupidity knows no fucking bounds."

Vik chuckles at that. "You always seem to find trouble, don't you?"

That pisses me off. "I don't find trouble. Trouble finds me. I was perfectly fine living oblivious to all of this. How did you guys leave the property with no one knowing?"

Lucy's expression turns stern as she fixes her gaze on me. "That's the least of your concerns right now, Olivia," she says firmly, her voice filled with urgency. "You need to understand that if the Over Lords find out that you snuck off Orchard Landing and almost got yourself kidnapped again and possibly killed, they're going to be pissed."

"And don't think that just because you die, that's the end. They will still get you, even in death." Dani says in a cryptic tone.

Her words send a shiver down my spine, and I stammer, "What are they going to do to me?"

"Nothing, because right now they don't know we're gone. We should get back before they notice." Vik answers.

I can't help but voice my confusion. "But I thought you said they know everything? Wouldn't they know—"

Before I finish my sentence, Vik swiftly covers my mouth with her hand. "Do not speak it into existence," she whispered urgently. "The Over Lords are like an omen. As soon as you speak it into existence, they know, and then we'll all be in for it."

Lucy laughs softly, shaking her head at Vik's words. "Vik, that's not how it works, and you know it. Stop trying to scare Olivia. We don't even know how they know things. We just know they do. Let's head back."

With a last glance at my ransacked apartment and the lingering sense of danger, I nod in agreement. There are still many unanswered questions, and the mysteries surrounding Eve's disappearance still have me worried more.

CHAPTER 15

FRIENDSHIP AND A PACT

As we materialize in the middle of our living room, a collective sigh of relief escapes our lips. The absence of the Over Lords waiting to confront us is a minor victory. Perhaps, for the moment, we have evaded their watchful gaze.

Dani wastes no time and approaches me. Her fiery eyes soften with concern as she examines the bruises and cuts I'd gained during our altercation with the magic users. With a silent gesture, she channels her healing magic, and I feel a soothing warmth spread through my body, mending my injuries and giving me an extra burst of energy.

"Thanks, Dani," I whisper gratefully. "I truly appreciate this."

She gives me a reassuring smile before turning to Vik and Lucy, who are both already heading towards their respective rooms to change clothes. The tension that had been building during our search for Eve seems to lift slightly to a more relaxed state now that we're home.

I slip out of my damaged clothes and began changing. Just as I'm about to pull on a fresh pair of jeans, the door to my room burst open, and Dani, Vik, and Lucy enter without warning.

I let out a high-pitched shriek, clutching my shirt to my chest in a futile attempt to preserve some modesty. "Do you mind?" I yell, as my cheeks burn with embarrassment. "I'm getting dressed."

Dani rolls her eyes, clearly unbothered by my half-dressed state. "I don't care about seeing your lady bits, Liv," she says with a small laugh as her eyes dance with amusement.

Lucy laughs at my shocked expression. "We've each had our share of nakedness. I've come home a few times with my ass hanging out from fighting."

"Yeah, modesty is not a thing here, Liv," Vik adds while wiggling her eyebrows playfully.

I hastily finish putting on my clothes as I feel a bit flustered. "Well, what do you guys want?" I ask.

Dani exchanges a glance with Vik and Lucy before stepping forward. "We need to talk," she says in a serious tone.

With my clothes hastily arranged, I turn to face them, my earlier shock giving way to a sense of curiosity mixed with a touch of concern. Whatever they want to discuss has an air of seriousness about it, and I can't help but wonder what prompted this sudden interruption.

"We realize you must feel trapped here," Lucy starts. "Evil shit stains kidnaped you, then we rescued you and basically confined you to the property."

"Yeah, you haven't seen your mother in months. Your friend was missing when we rescued you, and no one has any idea where she is," Vik says. "No wonder you snuck away. You're filled with worry, and things haven't been normal for you in a long time."

Dani smiles at me. "So, we want to help you look for

Eve." She puts up her hand to stop me from saying something. "This will be our secret, and we can do it in between your training."

"Believe it or not, Liv, the Over Lords have been out looking for the Veil Society and Eve," Vik says in a soft tone. "It may seem like they're not doing anything, but trust me, they are. They're frustrated because they are the most powerful magic users, and somehow, whoever took Eve has kept her hidden, with no trace of where she could be. This is personal."

I lean over and give each of them a hug. "Thank you. Really. I don't know what I would do without you guys."

"Clearly, you'd die without us," Vik laughs.

Dani takes a deep breath before speaking. "Liv, we need to have a candid conversation about what we're getting ourselves into."

Her words hang in the air, but I nod, urging her to continue.

"We know little about the Veil Society. They could be more dangerous than we think," she says slowly. "You have to be sure that you want to do this because we could be in a lot of danger."

Lucy nods in agreement. "The Over Lords are not to be underestimated. Their power and influence extend far and wide. If you want to stay away from the danger, trust them to find her."

"I already feel like I'm just here, doing whatever I'm told to do. I want to be productive. To help. I can't just sit here where everything's great while who knows what is happening to Eve," I reply. I look toward Vik. "How come you're not more worried about your cousin?"

Vik shrugs at the question. "Honestly, I don't know her that well. It's not that I'm not worried. I trust the Over

Lords to find her. You're obviously a lot closer to Eve, so you feel differently."

"Okay, so when do we start?" I ask.

Dani shakes her head at my eagerness. "We have to be careful. The Over Lords may not have caught us this time, but they're bound to notice, eventually. We need to be prepared."

I furrow my brow as my mind races with questions. "Prepared for what?"

Vik leans in closer, her eyes intense. "Prepared for the consequences of our actions. For the risks we're taking to help you. For the possibility that the Over Lords may catch us."

"Not only that. These people are dangerous, Liv. We're not invincible. We have our strengths, but we also have our vulnerabilities," Lucy adds.

I understand where they're coming from since I'm still new to all the dangers their world offers. They're not willing to help me for long because the longer we do this, the higher the chances of getting caught. So, we compromise on one week. For one week, in between training sessions, we will sneak away from the property to search for Eve. With that agreement, we head out for my training.

The afternoon sun bathes Orchard Landing in a warm, golden light as we prepare for my fight training session. Once again, we're in the clearing behind the house. I'm still amazed at how beautiful the property is. The sprawling grounds, with its gnarled trees and lush greenery, are beautiful even on the most dreary days.

As her long hair sparkles in the sunlight, Dani stands at the forefront of our small group, her expression serious as she looks at me. "Remember, this training is not just about improving your fighting skills. It's about survival. Should we encounter the Veil Society, they won't hesitate to kill us. We need to be prepared for anything."

Vik gives me a playful grin before speaking. "That means pushing ourselves to the limit. No holding back."

Vik charges me with a kick to my stomach, but I block it with my arm and follow up with an elbow strike to Vik's face. She twists out of the way, taking me with her as she moves. She weeps my legs out from underneath me and follows up with a punch to the face. My head snaps back, and blood seeps from my lower lip.

"I said no holding back, Liv," Vik says with a smirk.

I wipe the blood off my mouth with the back of my hand before smiling right back. "You're on."

I punch her in the face before delivering a kick to her stomach. Our training lesson passes in a blur of motion. We engage in combat drills, practice defensive and honing our offensive maneuvers. The energy that crackled in the air was palpable, a reminder of the power that lay within us.

When the session concludes, we're sweaty, breathless, and beat the hell up. This training lesson allowed me to let go of my reservations. I realize just how dangerous magic users can be, and I can't let my fear of getting hurt or hurting someone else get in the way.

Dani looks at me like she's proud of how far I've come and tells us we should head home to change clothes before leaving. We exchange weary but resolute glances, silently acknowledging the secret mission we're about to embark on.

As night falls, we prepare for our covert mission. We wear warm clothing because it's bone-chilling cold in Chicago. Sneaking away from Orchard Landing is no simple thing to accomplish.

However, we move with a fluidity that makes me think

that even the most proficient soldier wouldn't be able to keep up with us. Once we're far enough away from the entrance, Dani opens a portal directly into my living room. We sneak out of the house and start our search for Eve.

The city looms before us, with its towering skyscrapers seeming to reach up to touch the sky. Dani, Lucy, and Vik stand there, their eyes wide with wonder, as they marvel at the sheer size and energy of the urban landscape. They seem captivated by the city's vibrancy, as if they are seeing it for the first time.

I can't help but give them a slightly weird look. "Are you impressed by the city?"

With her eyes still fixed on the tall buildings, Dani chuckles before speaking. "More like overwhelmed. We've never really experienced anything like this."

Lucy's eyes dart from one skyscraper to another. "Yeah, Dani and I grew up on Orchard Landing. We rarely leave it, and when we do, it's usually to hunt down magic users. We don't really go exploring, as we're too busy with the mission."

I can't suppress my laugh. "Well, welcome to the Windy City, where the streets are dirty, everything is loud, and the people are rude."

Vik grins and points at me. "Exactly! You're not missing out on anything. Trust me."

Dani sighs, with a hint of longing in her eyes. "I've had a few trips outside of Orchard Landing, but I've never really gotten to experience a city like this."

"We've gone shopping in a few places, but we never stay for long," Lucy adds. "Why are all these stores and restaurants still open?"

"Well, you know what they say. The Windy City never sleeps. One day, we'll all have to have a day where we can have fun, go shopping, eat at fancy restaurants, and do whatever we want." I tell them with a smile.

Dani snorts with laughter, her eyes twinkling with amusement. "Good luck getting that approved by the Over Lords." She motions up ahead. "Come on. Enough staring at the large metal structures. We need to continue our search."

Our first stops are the locations where Dani, Vik, and Lucy had encountered magic users before while they were out apprehending them. The city's dark alleyways and abandoned buildings are eerie under the moonlight, casting long shadows that seem to dance with secrets.

Lucy's voice breaks the silence as she examines the surroundings. "Look for any traces of magic," she instructs Dani and Vik, who nod their heads in understanding.

We comb the area meticulously, our eyes scanning for any signs that might lead us to Eve. The clock is ticking, and our one-week window is limited. We search the dimly lit alleyways and abandoned buildings where Dani, Vik, and Lucy had previously confronted the magic users. Our steps are cautious, each corner we turn with anticipation, and our senses alert for any threat out to get us.

As we move deeper into the city's maze of streets, I can't shake the feeling of unease that hangs in the air. The night is eerily quiet, even though people are still walking about. The usual bustle is dimmed by the late hour, and the shadows cast by the moon seem to stretch endlessly.

Then, in a secluded corner, we found her—a lone magic user with a defiant glare leaning casually against a graffiti-covered wall. Her presence is unmistakable, like she doesn't quite fit. We approach her cautiously with a stern expression, but mine is filled with curiosity. The magic user, a young woman with a sassy demeanor and a cocked eyebrow, eyes us with a hint of amusement.

Vik speaks first as she holds up the picture I gave her of Eve. "We're looking for someone," she tells the girl. "Have you seen this girl?"

The magic-user takes a leisurely glance at the photo before rolling her eyes. "It's the city. People go missing here all the fucking time."

Lucy narrows her eyes before pointing a finger at her. "You'll go missing if you keep up with the attitude. It was a simple yes or no question. Have you fucking seen her?"

The young magic user let out a theatrical sigh, as if she were humoring them. "Look, I see many people in this city. It's a veritable sea of faces. What makes your girl so special?"

Dani leans in closer, getting in her face. "She's special to us. We need to find her."

The magic user's grin widens. "Special to you, huh? Well, I hate to break it to you, but she's not special to me. I see many people, and your precious girl doesn't exactly stand out."

"I'm going to punch this bitch in the face," Vik growls before taking a step forward.

The magic user's smile widens more. "Try it and see what happens."

Suddenly, her nails turn long and sharp like thick, large needles. She moves to take a swipe at Dani.

"Stop!" Vik yells and the girl freezes mid-slash. "Point those nails toward your torso."

The girl's eyes widen as she moves to do what Vik says. I see her struggling against the compulsion, but it's useless.

"Now, I'll ask one last time. Have you seen the girl?" Vik snarls at her.

"No, I haven't. Honestly, even if I did, there's no way I'd remember if I did. I live in an alley lady. I see tons of people every day," the girl replies.

Vik nods, content with her honest answer. "Fine, you can put your hand down. Clearly, you don't know who we are, and luckily for you, you're not a priority." She nods her head toward the magic-user and gives a small wave. "You can leave, but we'll see you again soon. Oh, and there's nowhere you can hide that we won't find you. Til next time."

The magic-user runs out of the alley as fast as she can. Dani, Lucy, and Vik exchange frustrated glances. The sassy magic user gave us no helpful information, and her attitude leaves us with more questions than answers. We continue well into the night, and we're still no closer to finding Eve. My hope for finding her is slowly dwindling down to nothing.

We have been searching for Eve for a week, tirelessly combing the streets of Chicago and revisiting the places where Dani, Vik, and Lucy had encountered the magic users. Our one-week search for Eve has been a rollercoaster of emotions, marked by long nights, fruitless leads, and frustrating dead ends.

We've walked the gritty streets of Chicago, delved into its hidden corners, and questioned countless magic users with little to show for our efforts. The city's sprawling expanse has felt both overwhelming and eerily empty.

One particularly eventful evening, we found ourselves in a lively downtown neighborhood. The neon signs blinked above us, casting a kaleidoscope of colors onto the bustling streets.

Dani couldn't resist a bit of humor. "Who knew searching for a missing person could make us experts in late-night city exploration? This city is like a hub for magic users."

"Maybe we should start a side business as bounty hunters for the Mutane Sihiri. We'll be called 'The Magic Stalkers.'"

I laugh at her enthusiasm. "Aren't you kind of already that?"

"Yeah, but we don't get paid for it," Dani laughs.

Lucy rolls her eyes but can't hide a small smile. "That sounds ridiculous. Let's not quit our day jobs just yet, shall we?"

As our agreed-upon time draws to a close, a sense of unease settles over us again. We've come up empty-handed, and our mission to find Eve is left hanging in the balance. Our covert efforts have gone unnoticed by the Over Lords so far, but their watchful eyes are always lurking in the shadows.

We trudge back to Orchard Landing, our footsteps heavy with disappointment. The sun dipped below the horizon, casting long shadows that seemed to mirror the weight of our hearts. Despite our best efforts, we could not find any trace of my missing friend.

My shoulders slump with the weight of failure, and I have a feeling of guilt that is twisting in my stomach. I had been the one to bring Eve into this world behind the Veil, and now she's missing because of me. When we arrive back at our shared house, Dani, Lucy, and Vik gather around me, their expressions filled with empathy and understanding.

Dani speaks first. "Olivia, this doesn't make you a fail-ure. We did everything we could."

"Sometimes, these things take time. We can't control every aspect of this world, no matter how hard we try," Lucy says.

Their words of comfort ease the burden of disappointment, and I nod, my gratitude clear in my eyes. "I just wish we could have found some clue, some lead to follow."

Dani places a reassuring hand on my shoulder. "We will find Eve, Olivia. I promise you that."

"Remember what I told you. Trust in the Over Lords. They won't let you down," Vik reminds me of her previous words.

"Damn, skippy!" Over Lord Ashley says as the Over Lords pop into the room. "I trust your little -let's find Eve without the Over Lord knowing- secret mission didn't yield any results, huh?"

My mouth hangs open in shock before speaking. "You guys knew? And you let us do it anyway?"

"Of course," Over Lord Ashley snorts. "It takes some of the workload off us. If you succeeded, then great. If not, then we'd still have the duty of finding her."

"Yup," Over Lord Mary adds as she stares at me. "As long as you don't get yourself kidnapped or killed in the process."

My shoulders slump as I sigh. "You know what happened."

"Of course, we know," Over Lord Miranda answers. "Like usual, we trust Dani, Lucy, and Vik to handle business. You're lucky they rescued you from your own stupidity, Olivia."

"But understand this," Over Lord Mary says in a commanding tone to all four of us. "No more stupid shit. We let you get it out of your systems because we understand how it is to worry about someone. No more sneaking off of Orchard Landing. No more searching for Eve. We don't know how dangerous the Veil is, and we're trying to find out."

"Alright, Olivia," Over Lord Ashley says as she suddenly claps to get my attention. "Time to get down to business. We've been getting some seriously bad vibes about this Veil Society, and we don't like bad vibes."

I raise an eyebrow at her casual approach, considering the gravity of the situation. "Bad vibes? You mean like a gut feeling?"

Over Lord Ashley offers a creepy smile. "Precisely. Whenever we get a bad feeling or start getting anxious, bad shit usually happens. Really bad shit. So we'd rather be prepared than sorry."

With a reluctant sigh, I acknowledged the importance of their words. "Alright, but what exactly do you want me to do?"

"We're going to start with some basic exercises to help you focus your ability. Think of it like training a muscle that needs to be strengthened." Over Lord Stephanie answers instead.

"We'll start immediately," Over Lord Miranda adds.

Just before they leave, Dani calls out. "Mom?"

"What's up, Dani?" Over Lord Mary replies.

"There's something we encountered during our search for Eve that we should probably tell you," she replies.

Over Lord Mary lifts an eyebrow as if to say 'really.' Her eyes narrow ever so slightly. "Go on. Say what you have to say and get it over with."

Dani hesitates for a moment before continuing. "We came across some magic users while searching. We didn't bring them back to Orchard Landing, though."

The room seems to grow colder as silence settles over us. Over Lord Mary's expression shifts from curiosity to stern disapproval. "You encountered magic users, our people, and you didn't bring them back here?"

Dani winces at the scolding tone in her mother's voice. "Well, we thought it was a secret mission, and if we had known you knew what we were doing, we would have brought them back," she explains, her voice tinged with irritation.

Over Lord Miranda leans forward with a stern gaze. "Whether or not you were worried about being caught, you should have brought them back. You underestimate the importance of every one of our people, Dani. Especially with the Veil Society kidnapping them."

Dani's shoulders slump in resignation. "I understand, Aunt Miranda."

Over Lord Miranda nods. "Very well. Go retrieve the magic users you encountered. I don't care if you take all night."

The Over Lords then abruptly teleport out of the room, leaving us to deal with the consequences of our actions. Dani, Lucy, and Vik groan in unison, their frustration clear.

As they magically change into their uniforms, Vik shoots me a wry smile. "Consider yourself lucky, Liv. You get to enjoy a peaceful night's sleep while we deal with our punishment."

Lucy smiles with a little laugh. "Just remember that the next time you're tempted to venture off on your own."

With a collective sigh, they turn to me as Dani speaks. "We'll see you in the morning, Liv. Get some rest."

After Dani, Vik, and Lucy teleport away to retrieve the magic users, I find myself alone in the dimly lit room. The weight of the day's events presses down on me, leaving my mind racing with thoughts of the Veil Society and their terrible plans.

Fear and anxiety well up within me as I contemplate the upcoming training sessions with the Over Lords. The consequences of any misstep during my attempts to control my ability weigh heavily on my mind. What would they do if something went wrong?

The mysterious nature of the Over Lords leaves me with more questions than answers, and the uncertainty gnaws at my conscience. As I settle into bed, tossing and turning in the dimly lit room, my thoughts churn in a whirlwind of doubts and worries.

Suddenly, Over Lord Annie appears in my room. Her presence is unexpected, and I blink in surprise as she addresses me. "Your thoughts are so loud right now, it's getting on my nerves."

Before I can reply or process her words, Over Lord Annie reaches out, touching two fingers to my forehead. A strange sensation washes over me, and the world blurs and twists. The last thing I hear before falling into a deep and dreamless sleep is her calming voice saying.

"Go to sleep, Olivia. Everything will be alright."

Everything fades as I fall into a deep sleep.

CHAPTER 16
A LOOK TOWARD THE FUTURE

Breakfast this morning was another eventful affair. Lucy tried to convince Vik to teach her to cook, and their argument about it was hilarious. In the end, Lucy pouted at the table like a baby. After we finish breakfast, Vik dismisses herself to go on a mission, and the house is a little quieter with her gone.

"So, Liv, you've been kicking some serious ass during our training sessions," Dani says with a grin as her eyes twinkle mischievously.

My smile is bright as I think of the skills I've developed. "Damn right I have," I reply, winking. "Who knew I had it in me?"

"Well, we did," Lucy says as she leans back in her chair. "You're a natural, Liv, and you're getting stronger every day."

I bask in the praise, but then Dani's playful tone shifts to something more serious. "You know, Liv, we could use someone like you in our army. We'll kick some ass together," she says.

I raise an eyebrow at her. "Oh, really? And what exactly do the soldiers do?"

Dani smirks before leaning forward as if she's about to say something secret. "Oh, you know, just defending the world against dark forces, saving our people, and being badass all the way around."

I roll my eyes but play along with her theatrics. "Well, I suppose you can try to convince me to join such an elite group."

Lucy shakes her head and laughs. "You'd fit right in, that's for sure. But remember, with great power comes great responsibility."

I hold up a hand dramatically, like I'm taking an oath. "Fear not, oh wise ones, for I shall use my newfound badassery for good."

Dani laughs and claps her hands in excitement. "Looks like we've created a monster, Lucy. I like this sassy version of Liv. Maybe we should unleash her on the demons."

Still playing along, I grin and put my fists up. "Oh, believe me, I'm ready to kick some demon ass. They won't know what hit them."

As we laugh and joke around, I reflect on everything that's happened in the past few months. Dani, Lucy, and Vik had become my best friends, mentors, and partners in this magical world. Our fun is cut short when we're summoned to the meeting room at the main house, a place I've never been to.

Upon arrival, a bunch of people I've never met are there, and they make introductions. Will, Courtney, Taylor, and Deborah sit at the table with the Over Lords, discussing a way to stop the Veil Society from kidnapping more Mutane Sihiri. They are all tense, worried about the safety of their people and the consequences of the Veil's actions.

"This cannot continue. They've managed to escape us every damn time we got close. I say we find them, torture them for information, kill them, and let me torture their souls for eternity," Over Lord Ashley says.

"You want to do that with everyone, Ashley," Over Lord Miranda tells her. "Sit down and be quiet unless you have an actual solution to our problem."

"The Veil Society has been growing bolder," she continues, her eyes flashing with intensity. "Their obsession with finding the second half of the 'pair of powers' threatens not only our world but countless others."

"We've tracked their movements and discovered their next target—a small city in Georgia. They plan to kidnap more of our people from there," Deborah tells them.

I sit up straighter in my chair. "How do you know this?"

"We have people all over the world. Some are in some very influential positions. If we want to find out something, they give us the information," Over Lord Annie replies.

"That's why we're here," Courtney chimes in. "We provide this information." She looks toward Over Lord Miranda. "We need a coordinated attack. Divide and conquer. Hit them where they least expect it."

The conversation fades off as something catches my attention. Something is shimmering off to the side of the room. I look to the side, squinting to see what it is, when a ghost finally comes into view.

"Ah!" I scream and slide back into my chair. "What the hell is that?"

"What's up, guys! Did you miss me?" the ghost says.

Over Lord Miranda sighs heavily. "What the hell do you want, Rebecca?"

"I come bearing a message from the beyond," Rebecca says in a silly voice.

"We don't have time for your cryptic shit today," Over Lord Mary tells her.

Anger crosses Rebecca's face. "Well, you better make time. You need to hear this." Rebecca closes her eyes and takes a deep breath before speaking. "The Veil is dark and thick. Their latest intentions are a trick. Shadows move quickly and quietly. The Byu Na Iko shall act defiantly. The coming night will go as you believe. Though you should beware of the coming eve. Ancient power is at play. Watching and waiting for their prey."

Over Lord Ashley groans. "Can you just be straight with us for once in your miserable fucking afterlife?"

"You know how this works," Rebecca deadpans. "Why must we go through this every single time?"

Over Lord Mary's brows raise. "Maybe because you keep showing up, providing unwanted help. If you're going to give us help, at least provide specifics."

"Ungrateful bitches say what?" Rebecca mumbles.

"What?" Over Lord Stephanie replies in confusion.

Rebecca bursts out in laughter, causing me, Dani, and Lucy to laugh as well.

"Don't make me go back to blocking you," Over Lord Ashley says as she points to Rebecca. "Everything is so much more peaceful without your rhymes and riddles."

"Promises, promises," Rebecca sings. She looks at me. "Olivia, you are causing quite the mix-up around here."

I don't know how she knows my name, but I won't let her intimidate me. She can't possibly do any harm as a ghost.

"Nope, I'm not doing anything," I tell her, holding my head up high. "I was fine being left alone. I didn't ask for this shit."

She smiles and laughs a little. "I like you. You've got spunk. You'll fit in just fine here."

Rebecca shimmers and fades from the room. That is the weirdest thing that's happened to me since I've been here. The Over Lords dismiss Will, Deborah, Courtney, and Taylor, leaving me, Dani, and Lucy in the room.

"I know you've all been having fun getting trained, but there's something we need to discuss." Over Lord Mary says to us.

"As you all know, Olivia here has the ability of World Sight. Unfortunately, her power is very unstable and, if left unchecked, could be a very dangerous weapon." Over Lord Annie adds.

"That is why we said we'll train her. Things are getting tricky. From now on, we will train Olivia to control her ability better and to use it at will. Your fight training will be on hold until further notice. Her ability is what they want, so we need to focus on that," Over Lord Miranda states.

They dismiss Dani and Lucy, and they teleport me to another location on the property.

"I know you know I've suppressed your ability, Olivia," Over Lord Sydney says. "There is a possibility that once it becomes unsuppressed, visions will come swiftly and strong, and we'll be here to help."

Unfortunately, I don't get a warning before it's done, and that familiar sensation I get before a vision happens before it takes over.

I find myself on a vast, ethereal battlefield. Dani, Lucy, Vik, and the Over Lords stand bravely side by side, surrounded by a swirling sea of shadows. The darkness seems to writhe and pulse with an ominous energy, and the air crackles with the power of magic.

Every member of our group fights with unmatched prowess,

their movements fluid and precise. Dani's fire lights up the shadows, Lucy's ice encases them in icy restraints, Vik's punching and kicking with precision, while the Over Lords' combined elemental forces unleash a symphony of magic.

Magic intertwines, creating dazzling bursts of light that illuminate the battlefield. Their power is immense, but despite their united strength, the shadows are relentless, constantly shifting and reforming.

As the battle rages on, my heart pounds with awe and fear. The shadows seem almost overwhelming, their sheer numbers and ethereal nature making them difficult to combat. The ground trembles with the force of the battle, and the air echoes with the clash of magic.

The dark shadows encircle Dani, but she shows no fear. Her magic pulses within her, an energy that resonates with her demonic heritage. With a swift, fluid movement, Dani's hands glow with an otherworldly light. She summons her power, unleashing a surge of raw magic that ripples through the air. The shadows recoil as if sensing the potency of her magic.

As the shadows lunge at her again, she twists and dodges, her magic forming a protective shield around her. The shadows strike her barrier with a menacing force, but it holds steady against their assault. Dani's eyes narrow, and a mischievous grin tugs at her lips. She doesn't fear the shadows; she embraces them as a challenge. With a flick of her wrist, she sends a surge of magical energy forward, tearing through the shadows like a blazing comet.

They hiss and writhe, but Dani is relentless. She moves with a dancer's grace, evading their attacks while simultaneously launching her own. Her magic surges and swirls around her, a mesmerizing dance of light and power.

In another area, the shadows lunge toward Lucy, but she dances gracefully out of their reach, her movements almost hypnotic. With a mere thought, tendrils of light extend from her fingers, weaving through the air like luminous ribbons. The tendrils coil around the shadows, restraining their movements and containing their malevolent energies.

Lucy's magic is a force of nature, a manifestation of her divine essence. As she focuses her power, the light intensifies, illuminating the darkness in an awe-inspiring display. The shadows squirm and struggle against the magical restraints, but they're no match for her celestial power.

With a flick of her wrist, Lucy sends a surge of energy through the tendrils, causing the shadows to disintegrate into wisps of smoke. Her power expands with each vanquished shadow, becoming radiant and bright.

The ground rumbles with the raw power she channels magic, and the air hums with energy. It's as if the very fabric of reality acknowledges her as a formidable force that stands against the darkness with unwavering determination.

Unfortunately, the shadows keep coming back. Over Lord Stephanie is fighting ruthlessly off to the side. Closing her eyes, she envisions a celestial storm swirling above her. Thunder booms and clouds gather, crackling with lightning. With a sweeping motion, she directs the storm toward the shadows.

The onslaught of wind and rain, their forms wavering under the elemental assault, pummels the dark figures. But they persisted, attempting to overpower Over Lord Stephanie's magic with their evil force.

Over Lord Mary is facing an attack but is holding her own. As the shadows lung at her, she stretches out her hand, and tendrils of fire move in the air, scorching the darkness. With a swift motion, she encases her hands with earth and stone, forming powerful gauntlets that allow her to deliver crushing blows.

Just when it seems like the darkness might overcome them, a figure descends from the heavens. Encased in a blinding light so brilliant that it's almost blinding, this unfamiliar presence radiates an aura of pure power. The figure moves with grace and determination, their movements swift and purposeful.

As they join the fray, their light seems to dispel the shadows, leaving trails of sparkles in their wake. With a wave of their hand, they summon an explosion of magic, creating a powerful shockwave that sends the shadows scattering.

The vision unfolds like an action movie, with each member of our group contributing their unique abilities to the battle. The powerful light figure and our group fight together in perfect harmony, with our strength bolstered by our unity. I still strained to see our opponents and the unknown figure's faces as they remain obscured by the brilliance of the light and the chaos of the battle.

As the vision slowly fades, I find myself back in the room with the Over Lords, my heart still racing from the intensity of what I had witnessed. It's clear that a great battle looms ahead of us, and I don't know if I'm ready for it.

"What did you see, Olivia?" Over Lord Annie asks me.

I shake my head to clear it, unsure of what I just saw. "I saw you guys and Dani, Vik, and Lucy fighting. However, I couldn't tell who or what you were fighting."

"What the hell does that mean?" Over Lord Ashley asks in confusion.

"It means exactly what I said," I snap, forgetting that I'm talking to the leaders of our kind. "There were shadows everywhere, and you were fighting the shadows."

They're silent for a few minutes, no doubt talking to each other telepathically again.

"Tell us what you know about your ability, Olivia," Over Lord Mary says. "That would be a good place to start."

"I don't know anything," I reply with a sigh. "Like I said in the beginning. I was told by doctors that I was having seizures, and then my world descended into chaos. From being kidnapped by Axel and his evil organization to aiding this organization in kidnapping. Then you rescued me, and that's it."

"The World Sight ability is tricky, Olivia," Over Lord Miranda tells me. "You can see anything, anytime and anyplace. The tricky part is differentiating when the vision occurs: in the past, present, or future."

Over Lord Stephanie walks closer and puts her hand on my shoulder. "This ability enables you to walk through life through your ability to see. We're going to help you control it."

We start with breathing techniques to help calm my racing mind. We do this for so long that I'm almost asleep when they direct me to move on to the next thing. This time, I'm stretching. I don't know why this is relevant, but Over Lord Annie says it helps relax the body and could be helpful. Now, I'm standing in the middle of the room, waiting for what to do next.

"Now, open your mind," Over Lord Annie's voice penetrates my thoughts. "Steady your breathing and let your thoughts flow. Think of something you want to see and will it to your mind."

I want to see how Mom is doing, so I think of her, willing my mind to take me to her. As I concentrate, I feel the familiar sensation before the vision comes. I see my mom sitting in a restaurant, talking to her friends.

She's telling them about my new position overseas and how well I'm doing. She's doing what she usually does. Painting a picture-perfect life to help maintain and maybe even boost her image. I shake my head in disgust and let the vision fade away.

The room comes back into focus, and I see the Over Lords staring at me. "Good, Olivia," Over Lord Miranda says. "Now try again."

"How do you even know I had a vision?" I ask, puzzled that they knew.

"I know when any of our people are using their ability," Over Lord Sydney says. "Now try again."

I repeat the process, but this time, I focus on Evelyn. I still have been able to contact her, and I'm still worried about her well-being. No matter how hard I concentrate, no vision comes to mind. I try to think of the last time we spoke at the bistro and try to get a vision off that, but it doesn't work.

I concentrate a little longer, hoping to get something when it happens. A vision swirls through my mind, and I see a field of green before me. There's a figure encased in light straight ahead. I inadvertently walk through with wonder, guiding my steps. I only make it a couple of steps before the figure turns.

"You should not be here," a distorted voice whispers in my mind. I can't tell if it belongs to a man or a woman. "Go back. Now!"

The light gets brighter, and I'm knocked back from a hard push. I fall on my ass and look up to see the Over Lords looking at me with concern.

"I'm fine," I tell them as I stand back up. "I just had a vision of a mysterious place, but a creepy voice told me I shouldn't be there. That I should go back, and then I was pushed."

"It seems like someone is trying to stop you from seeing what they don't want you to see," Over Lord Miranda says.

"We're finished for today. My sisters and I need to discuss some things."

I'm teleported back home without another word. Neither Dani, Lucy, nor Vik are home. I'm assuming they're out on a mission. With nothing else to do, I shower, eat, and relax a little, waiting for them to come home so I can tell them what happened.

CHAPTER 17

A LOOK AT THE PAST

Despite yesterday's blunder with the weird vision, the Over Lords request my presence at the main house today. Alone. Dani, Lucy, and Vik are all out on missions, leaving me to face this daunting task alone. It's strange how quickly things have escalated. Just a few months ago, I was a college graduate with a chemical engineering degree, and now I find myself in a world of magic, demons, and secret evil organizations.

I stand at the entrance of the imposing main house with my heart pounding like a drum in my chest. I've never really enjoyed being around the Over Lords on my own because they are scary. Not that it's happened much, but their presence is imposing. They're like legends in this magical world, and their presence has always filled me with apprehension.

I take a deep breath and remind myself that I must do this. There's no turning back. Dani, Lucy, and Vik have their own missions to attend to, and I can't let them down by acting like a wimp. I knock gently on the ornate wooden door, and before I can even register the sound of my knuckles against the aged wood, it swings open by itself. It's a peculiar sensation I've grown accustomed to in this world of magic and mystery.

Peering cautiously into the dimly lit living room, I take a hesitant step over the threshold. As if responding to my presence, the door slams shut behind me with a resounding thud, causing me to yelp in startled surprise. The echoing sound reverberates through the house, and I can't help but feel a little intimidated by being here. It never felt this eerie the few times I've been here.

The house is quiet as I take a few more steps forward, the only sound being the soft rustle of my footsteps on the lush carpeting that lines the floor. The air is heavy with an old, almost oppressive, presence that seems to seep from the walls themselves.

I glance around the room, searching for any sign of the Over Lords. The living room presents an intriguing paradox of charm and eeriness, a space that appears entirely normal yet leaves an unsettling undercurrent in its wake. At first glance, it exudes an inviting warmth that lures you in, but as you take in the details, an eerie sense of melancholy creeps in.

Soft, diffused sunlight filters through the curtains, casting a gentle glow over the room. Tasteful artwork and family photographs cover the walls, framed in rich, dark wood that adds a touch of elegance to the space. A plush sofa with inviting cushions sits at the center, its uphol-stery a soft, earthy tone that beckons you to sit down and relax.

The room's color palette is warm and inviting, with hues of caramel, beige, and soft blues that create a cozy atmosphere. But it's the subtle details that give rise to the eerie feeling. The family photographs, while charming, feature faces that seem to stare a little too intently, as if they're trying to stare into my soul.

The room's silence, broken only by the occasional tick of a clock and the distant sounds of the hustle and bustle of Orchard Landing, adds to the eerie ambiance. It seems like the room carefully preserves secrets, stories, and memories, waiting for the right moment to unveil them.

"Over Lord Miranda?" I call out tentatively, my voice echoing in the stillness.

The absence of their immediate response only adds to my growing anxiety. As I walk deeper into the house, my mind races with wild thoughts. The Over Lords requested my presence, yet they didn't seem to be home. I'm not sure if I should have waited outside or not. I'm not sure I should wander through their house either.

Despite the unsettling surroundings, I can't deny the curiosity that gnaws at me. The Over Lords must have brought me here for a reason, and whatever that reason may be, it's undoubtedly tied to what's happening with the Veil.

As I cautiously make my way further into the house, a sudden, unexpected presence materializes behind me. Strong arms encircle my neck, and instinct takes over. Without thinking, I grab the arm, pivot forward, and swiftly flip my assailant onto the ground with a practiced maneuver.

The figure lands with an undignified thud before bursting into laughter. My heart races and it takes a moment for me to realize that the unexpected assailant is none other than Over Lord Ashley.

"Damn, I was not expecting that," she says with a hearty laugh. "You're definitely getting better."

Before I can respond, the house loses its eerie aura and

is back to normal as the other Over Lords walk into the room, their presence adding an air of authority.

"Knock it off, Ashley," Over Lord Miranda chastises her. "We've got shit to do today."

I give Over Lord Ashley a scowl, still a bit ruffled from the surprise attack, and then walk over to sit on a plush old couch that seems strangely out of place compared to their other furniture.

"What? You're not going to help me up?" Over Lord Ashley asks with a mischievous grin as she picks herself up from the floor.

With a faux pout, she disappears and reappears next to me just as I'm about to sit down. My eyes widen in surprise at her sudden appearance, and I can't help but roll my eyes as she's the crazy one of all the Over Lords.

Over Lord Miranda clears her throat, drawing my attention away from her sister's antics.

"Alright, Olivia," she says in her composed, authoritative manner. "Today, we're going to work on helping you get a better handle on your ability."

Over Lord Stephanie chimes in, her soft voice resonating with seriousness. "We can't afford any more incidents like yesterday, especially with the Veil's shitty plans hanging over our heads."

I nod in understanding, my earlier apprehension giving way to nervousness about mastering the ability that's made my life hell. The Over Lords may be enigmatic and, at times, intimidating, but I can't deny that their guidance is essential for my survival in this world.

With a resolute nod, Over Lord Miranda explains the day's agenda. "First, we'll focus on honing your control over your visions. The ability to see the future is a potent gift, but it can also be dangerous if not properly harnessed."

Over Lord Mary approaches me with a reassuring smile. Her calm presence is a welcome contrast to the intensity of the day's training.

"Olivia," she says gently, "It's time to work on your spatial awareness. This is a critical skill for someone with your gift of sight. You need to be able to move swiftly and accurately when the situation demands it."

Over Lord Mary directs me to concentrate, closing my eyes as I attempt to attune myself to the magic inside. It's a strange sensation, like tuning into a frequency beyond my normal senses. I focus on the subtle shifts in energy, the ebb and flow of power within the room.

"Feel it, Olivia," Over Lord Annie encourages. "The magic is all around you. It's an extension of yourself. Let it guide you."

I take a deep breath and try to let go of my doubts. Slowly, I sense the currents of my magic, like invisible threads weaving through the air. They beckon to me, tugging at my consciousness.

As I focus my thoughts and let the magic flow within me, the familiar sensation of impending vision washes over me. It's a curious mixture of excitement and trepidation, like stepping into an unpredictable dream.

My mind drifts, subconsciously drawn to thoughts of Dani, Lucy, and Vik. I can't help but wonder how their mission is going, and a pang of longing tugs at my heart. The three of them have become my closest friends, and right now, I want to be with them, laughing and joking as we watch TV in the comfort of our home.

Unbeknownst to me, this longing and connection to them influences the vision that unfolds before me. It's like a window opening to reveal a scene from a distinct reality.

The vision unfurls before me like an otherworldly tableau, vivid and filled with the electric charge of magic.

It's a snapshot of a gritty urban landscape. A dimly lit alleyway nestled between towering, forgotten buildings that loom overhead like ancient sentinels.

Dani stands at the forefront, her long silver hair cascading around her shoulders like a shadowy veil. Her gold-slitted eyes blaze with a fierce resolve that's only enhanced by the intense gaze on her face. A pair of horns unfurls from her head, their tips sharp as a razor blade.

Lucy stands with an ethereal presence, her long, white hair cascading down her back like liquid moonlight. She radiates an otherworldly grace, her aura shimmering with an iridescent glow.

Her narrow eyes gleam with intelligence that belies her apparent youth, and she wields her power with a gentle authority. A luminous shield hovers around her, deflecting any threat that dares to approach.

Vik remains slightly concealed in the shadows, her presence almost unnoticeable. Dressed in sleek, dark attire, she exudes an air of confidence. Her emerald-green eyes gleam with a mischievous glint, and her hands ball into fists as she prepares to fight. I've never seen them in all their powerful glory before, but whoever they're against is obviously putting up one hell of a fight.

The atmosphere crackles with tension, and the alleyway seems to narrow as the magic users confront them. They're a motley crew, their expressions ranging from defiance to fear as they face the formidable trio.

Dani steps forward, her voice a low growl that echoes in the confined space. "You guys are seriously going to get your asses kicked. We don't want any more trouble. Surrender peacefully, and we can resolve this without anyone getting hurt."

"Take her advice," Lucy adds. "You caught us by surprise the first time. I guarantee you, this won't end well for any of you."

One of the magic users, a young woman with fiery red hair and trembling hands, scoffs. "You think you can just waltz in here and tell us what to do? We won't be your pawns."

Lucy raises an eyebrow and sends an evil smirk her way. "We're not here to control you. We're here to ensure the safety of everyone, magic users included. But if you leave us no choice..."

Vik's compulsion ability comes into play. Her voice is like a velvet whisper, and her emerald eyes gleam with a subtle command. "You don't want to fight. You want to resolve this peacefully and find a better way to use your magic."

The magic users' resistance wavers, their expressions clouding with confusion as Vik's magic takes hold. Yet, one of them, a defiant young man with sparks of electricity dancing in his eyes, resists.

"We won't bend to your will!" he shouts, raising his hands to conjure a crackling lightning storm.

I'm left with mixed emotions as the vision fades and reality reasserts itself. On the one hand, I know they can take care of themselves. On the other, I can't shake the feeling that I should be out there with them, helping them like they helped me.

Over Lord Mary's voice brings me back to the present. "Olivia, you've had a vision. Tell us what you saw."

I take a moment to compose myself, to push aside my longing, and focus on the task at hand.

"I saw Dani, Lucy, and Vik on a mission," I begin, my voice steady. "They were apprehending new magic users, but it seemed like one of them was immune to Vik's compulsion. He resisted her command."

"Well, that's interesting," Over Lord Annie says. "Maybe we should check on them?"

Over Lord Ashley snorts at the question. "Don't worry about them. We taught them well. They can handle themselves." She turns to me. "Try again, Olivia."

I concentrate again, and the sensation and vision became much easier this time. The vision swirls into view.

"The previous events were unfortunately caused by a few rogue groups of our people and are no longer a threat. I can assure you that we will continue to deal with them. The truth is, we've been partnering with your government with an organization called the USSNA for some time now. The facilities that were attacked were, in fact, USSNA facilities, and there are more. All we want is peace, and your government lured us into a partnership under the guise that they wanted peace as well, but they lied. They kidnapped, tortured, and experimented on our people. The rogues found out and attacked. We tried speaking to the previous president about the atrocities committed against us, but he was no help."

"Lies!" a man snarls. "You have some nerve showing up here and telling lies. Your people attacked us because you think you're better. You and your people committed an act of terrorism, and that is punishable by death. Do it now!"

Shots ring out, and I watch in horror as they kill the Over Lords. Each one falls to the ground with a dot in the middle of their foreheads and a lifeless stare in their eyes.

The vision abruptly ends as I hop from the couch, panicking at what I just saw.

"Oh my god, you guys just died!" I yell as I pace the living room.

"Which time?" Over Lord Ashley asks calmly. "Or is this a new death you foresaw? Let me know if it is. I want to be prepared."

"What!" I scream. "You were standing at a podium talking about USSNA and a rogue group or something like that. Then a man called you liars and told these soldiers to kill you."

"Oh! You saw the start of the war," Over Lord Ashley replies in understanding. "That's ancient history. We killed the president and his army of idiots before setting the world right again."

I'm borderline hyperventilating, as I'll never get used to seeing a person die. I just saw their deaths, and they act like it's a common occurrence. They are genuinely crazy. I'm shaking uncontrollably now, and I've lost what little control I had. I can't stop the visions from coming.

The visions hit me like a tidal wave, a relentless torrent of anguish and despair crashing into the fragile walls of my mind. I can't escape it, can't control it. My gasps for air are drowned out by the din of death and destruction echoing in my head.

I pace the dimly lit living room with my heart pounding like a drum in my chest. My palms are clammy, and my breaths are shallow and erratic. Over Lord Mary's voice, calm and composed, drifts through the haze of my panic.

"Olivia, you need to calm down," she urges, her words a soothing melody that I can't quite grasp. But how can I calm down when the visions threaten to consume me?

I can't. I'd lost control, and my ability is spiraling out of my grasp. With each chaotic whirlwind of thoughts, I'm transported into another vision. People, animals, and even beings I can't identify materialize in the living room, startling me and the Over Lords.

"Stop!" Over Lord Mary yells, voice growing sharper with a hint of urgency slipping through her facade of calm authority.

Unfortunately, I can't stop. It's as if the fabric of time is unraveling, and I'm caught in a never-ending loop of visions, unable to distinguish past from present. Each vision pulls me in deeper, as if I were reliving the Over Lords' past deaths, their agonizing moments of defeat.

"Olivia, focus! We need you to regain control. You're altering time, and it's becoming dangerous." Over Lord Miranda snaps, her voice firm and harsh.

Tears blur my vision as I try to obey and wrestle my abilities back under control, but it's like trying to tame a beast with an insurmountable force that rages within me.

Over Lord Annie and Over Lord Sydney move closer, their magic intertwining as they attempt to quell the storm of my emotions. The surrounding air shimmers with their combined power, and slowly, the chaos in my mind dies down.

Drained of strength, I stumble forward and collapse onto the couch. Over Lord Annie's soothing magic covers me, a gentle cocoon of calmness that seeps into my very core. My breathing steadies and the visions recede like a tide reluctantly retreating from the shore.

As I sit here, my trembling hands slowly coming to rest, I watch the Over Lords move with precision and efficiency to dispel the remnants of the beings I had unwittingly summoned. They are a well-oiled machine, working in perfect harmony to clean up the commotion I'd caused.

As I sit on the couch, feeling the calming effects of Over Lord Annie's magic wash over me, I hear their hushed voices, a soothing backdrop to my racing thoughts.

Over Lord Annie leans closer, her expression soft with concern. "Olivia, are you feeling better now?"

I nod, my voice still shaky. "Yes, thank you, Over Lord Annie. I'm sorry for the mess I caused."

"It's alright, Olivia. These things happen when you're

learning to control your abilities. We're here to help you." Over Lord Sydney says in a gentle tone.

Over Lord Annie's eyes bore into mine, her voice filled with sincerity. "You're not alone in this, Olivia. We'll work together to strengthen your control over your visions."

The weight of their support washes over me like a comforting embrace. "I appreciate it, all of you. I want to learn, to understand my abilities better."

Over Lord Annie's fingers brush my shoulder lightly, her touch comforting. "We believe in you, Olivia. You have a unique gift, and it's our duty to help you harness it."

As the calming effects of Over Lord Annie's magic enveloped me, I notice Over Lord Ashley lounging on a nearby chair, her signature smirk playing on her lips. She has been observing the chaotic events with keen interest, and now that the situation is under control, her snarky comments can't be far behind.

Over Lord Ashley leans back, propping her feet up on a nearby table and her eyes glinting with mischief. "Well, well, Olivia, you certainly know how to put on a show. I must say, I haven't been this entertained in ages."

Over Lord Sydney shoots a reproachful look in Over Lord Ashley's direction. "Ashley, show some respect. Olivia is going through a difficult time."

Over Lord Ashley waves her hand dismissively, completely unfazed. "Oh, come on, Syd. It's not every day we get to witness a time-bending, reality-altering meltdown. It's practically a live-action drama."

I can't help but roll my eyes, even in my vulnerable state. "Glad I could provide you with some entertainment, Over Lord Ashley."

"Oh, you have no idea, Olivia. I was on the edge of my

seat. Bravo!" She replies with her words dripping with sarcasm.

Over Lord Miranda gives a wry look at Over Lord Ashley. "You realize that Olivia's abilities are nothing to be trifled with, right? This isn't a game."

"Of course, Miranda. I was merely testing her. You know, making sure she can handle the pressure," she replies.

Over Lord Annie chuckles softly. "Testing, huh? More like tormenting."

"Alright, enough for today," Over Lord Mary says. "Why don't you head home to relax your mind, Olivia?"

I nod, eager to get home and leave this day behind me. As I step out of the main house, I can still feel the lingering effects of the intense magical training session. Over Lord Miranda had finally called it a day, claiming that further attempts to help me control my unpredictable abilities would be counterproductive. Over Lord Mary has advised me to head home and give my mind a break, suggesting that relaxation might be the key to finally mastering my magic.

The long walk home is a mix of relief and apprehension. I welcome the chance to unwind, but the constant struggle with my newfound abilities weighs on me like an invisible anchor. I wonder if I will ever gain the control I so desperately need.

As I approach the house, a wave of warmth and familiarity washes over me. It is my new home—the one place where I feel safe and truly myself. Upon entering, I'm met with an unexpected sight. Dani, Lucy, and Vik sit in the living room, their expressions a curious blend of relief and concern. The relief is evident in the smiles that greet me while the concern lingers in the depths of their eyes.

"Olivia, you're back," Dani shouts, rising to her feet and approaching me. "We were starting to worry."

I give a weak smile, suddenly grateful for their presence. "It's been a long day, but I'm here now."

"Tell us, how did it go with the Over Lords? Any progress?" Lucy asks with excitement.

I hesitate for a moment, the memory of the chaotic, vision-filled meltdown still fresh in my mind. Dani, Vik, and Lucy would understand. They'd offer me the reassurance I need to master this.

"It was a disaster," I admit, my shoulders slumping as I relay the events of the day. "I lost control completely and had visions of their past deaths. It was... overwhelming."

Vik raises an eyebrow, concern all over her face. "That doesn't sound good. Are you okay?"

Once again, I nod, though my turmoil was far from settled. "I'll be fine. Over Lord Mary suggested some rest, and she's probably right. It's just I'm overwhelmed with being here. Everything here is weird. They acted like dying is normal. You guys train like you're in a war. Like, how is this a normal life for you?"

Dani exchanges a knowing glance with Lucy before motioning for me to sit down. "Well, Olivia, if you think that's something, then wait until we break everything that's happened down for you."

I sink into the nearest chair with my curiosity piqued. "What are you talking about, Dani?"

"You know my mom and aunts haven't always been this way," Dani starts. "It was foretold many eons ago that they would inherit their magic. I'm going to give you a brief version of everything that's happened since then, including Lucy's and my stories. Then you'll realize why they are the way they are."

With that, Dani launches into a tale that seems too unbelievable to be real. Dani tells me about the magical war that raged between the Over Lord and the humans. She tells me of her disturbing time when she attempted to rule over magic users, demons, and humans. She explained how Lucy had discovered her divine lineage and the extent of her powers, the celestial heritage that set her apart from the Mutane Sihiri.

When Dani's wild stories conclude, my mind is a whirlwind of disbelief and astonishment. I can only stare at them, wide-eyed, as the weight of her story settles upon me.

"Well, shit," I say, at a loss for words. "So, crazy seems to run rampant around here?"

Lucy leans back and laughs. "That's one way to put it."

"I can't believe they fought a war for that long," I say in amazement. I point to Dani and Lucy. "Or that you tried to rule the world and that you went world hopping to find your family."

Vik throws her arm around my shoulders. "Yup, Liv. It's always a wild ride around here. Things never get boring."

I leave them to shower, relax, and head to bed. I need to get today out of my mind. Before falling asleep, my last thought is that I don't think I'm cut out for this kind of excitement in my life. Maybe when the Over Lords determine this is all over, I can return to my normal life.

CHAPTER 18

THE OMINOUS DEMON'S ARRIVAL

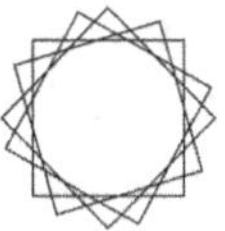

I stand frozen in the middle of the sprawling field on Orchard Landing. My heart is pounding like a relentless drum. Chaos surrounds me as students rush past, screaming and hollering, a cacophony of panic that sends shivers down my spine. I've seen nothing like this before. The sheer terror on their faces startles me into taking an unconscious step back, flustered by the scene in front of me.

Out of nowhere, a student I don't recognize charges toward me with such force that I have to sidestep at the last moment to avoid a collision. It's as if everyone around me has gone mad, and I'm thrust into a nightmarish scene.

I frantically scan the chaos, trying to make sense of the hysteria. That's when I spot Dani and Lucy. Relief washes over me at the sight of familiar faces, but something is undeniably off about them. Their eyes, usually warm and inviting, now gleam with an unsettling intensity. However, I can't dwell on it further because something abruptly draws my gaze to something far more ominous.

Standing before Dani and Lucy is a figure that defies all reason and sends a shiver of dread coursing through my veins. I *have only been at Orchard Landing for a few months, but even I know this is no ordinary man. He is a demon, an embodiment of terror and malevolence.*

His skin is an eerie, pallid gray, like the lifeless surface of the moon. Slitted, golden eyes pierce the chaos with an otherworldly intensity, making me feel as though he can see straight through to my very soul. Long, dark hair cascades down his back, a stark contrast to his inhuman features.

But it isn't just him that sends waves of fear crashing over me. Flanking him are creatures that defy description. They are the stuff of nightmares, with gnarled, grotesque features and eyes that seem to glow with a sinister hunger. I can't tear my gaze away from the horror scene before me.

As the surrounding frenzy continues to escalate, I realize that this is something beyond the ordinary activities of our daily lives. Though Orchard Landing has always been a place of mystery, it has become a place of unimaginable darkness and danger. I do not know what had brought these menacing creatures to the property, but one thing is clear—I'm in the midst of something far more terrifying than anything I have ever imagined.

My mind races with questions, but there is no time for answers. The demon's chilling gaze shifts, locking onto me with a predatory intensity. Panic surges through me, and I know I have to get out of there, away from this nightmarish scene.

Without another thought, I turn and start running, following the stream of panicking students as we all make a mad dash for the safety of the dorms. The distant wails and screams echo in my ears, a constant reminder of the terror that has descended upon Orchard Landing.

As I neared the dormitory, I risk a glance over my shoulder. The demon and his grotesque companions are still there, looming ominously in the distance. I can't comprehend what had brought them here or what they want.

As I approach Dani and Lucy, I feel the weight of the unknown pressing down on me. Every step I take, I have to be cautious, careful not to draw the attention of those grotesque creatures that flank the demon.

My time at Orchard Landing has been brief, and I had only scratched the surface of the enigmatic world hidden within the property. Taking on one of those monstrous beings is beyond my capabilities and a grave threat to my mortality.

I approach Dani and Lucy with a sense of trepidation, my eyes darting between their bizarre, calm expressions and the menacing figure standing before them. I can't comprehend the connection they seem to share with this demon or how they can maintain their composure in the face of such hostility.

Then the demon moves. It happens so fast that I barely register the blur of motion. He comes to a halt in front of Dani, and a twisted smile curls across his unnaturally gray face. My heart races and I instinctively press myself further into the shadows, hoping to remain unnoticed.

He inclines his head toward Dani, and my heart constricts with dread. "It is nice to see you, Danielle," he says, his voice dripping with an eerie familiarity that made Dani's brow furrow in confusion.

Lucy pushes Dani behind her and glares at the man—or whatever he is—approaching them. Her eyes bore into his as if daring him to come any closer. His gold-slitted eyes remain fixated on Dani, and he reaches out toward her.

Before he can make contact, Lucy's arm snaps forward, a forceful motion that sends the demon flying across the field. The creatures flanking him hiss and growl in frustration as they scramble to their feet. However, Dani and Lucy don't wait around.

With remarkable agility and speed, they take off running, disappearing from my view in the blink of an eye. Panic surges through me as I lose sight of them, and I desperately hope they can escape whatever nightmarish fate this demon has in store for them.

The world around me shutters, and the next moment, I see something that defies explanation. It's like skipping scenes in a movie, and I missed an important moment leading up to this. Dani glows like a bright, fiery star in the middle of the field. Her radiant light cuts through the darkness of the situation.

The ground beneath me trembles, and a powerful surge of energy radiates from her body. The force is so immense that I'm pushed back, stumbling and falling to the ground. It's as if a tidal wave of raw power had erupted from her, washing over me and sweeping me away.

When I open my eyes, I find myself in a place unlike any I have ever seen. It's dark and cold, with an eerie stillness that settles over me like a suffocating shroud. The air feels heavy with foreboding, and an unsettling silence envelopes everything.

I stand amid this desolate expanse, my breath forming misty clouds in the frigid air. The ground is uneven and rocky beneath my feet, and the sky above is a vast, starless void. The atmosphere is heavy with a sense of isolation and abandonment, as if I'd been cast into a forgotten world, far removed from the world I know.

Confusion and fear plague me as I try to make sense of my surroundings. I do not know where I am or how I ended up here. My first instinct is to find Dani and Lucy, but I hear movement behind me before I can even take a step.

My heart pounds in my chest as I turn around quickly, my hands raised instinctively to defend myself. I'm acutely aware of my vulnerability, knowing I am ill-equipped to confront whatever threat lurks in this strange place.

Movement came from my right, and I whirl around to face it. Then it happens again, and I find myself turning every which way to confront the unseen danger, but nothing materializes. It's as if the shadows themselves are playing tricks on my senses, toying with my fear.

Suddenly, with a force that knocks the breath from my lungs, something tackles me to the ground. We fall hard, and I thrash and wiggle, desperate to dislodge the being on top of me. Panic courses through me as I realize how utterly defenseless I am in this unfamiliar and eerie place.

With every ounce of strength I can muster, I managed to squirm out from beneath the figure and scramble to my feet. My racing heart seems to echo in the silence as I take in my surroundings once more. That's when I realize where I am.

I'm standing inside my bedroom in the house I share with Dani, Lucy, and Vik. This had become my sanctuary from all the magical weirdness I've experienced. But everything here is wrong. The room is shrouded in darkness, and an ominous chill hangs in the air. Fear gets trapped in my throat, and I can't shake the feeling that I am not alone.

A figure, barely discernible in the gloom, stands before me. I take in the deepest breath I can, and I let out a piercing scream as the figure slowly rises. The darkness seems to coil around it, obscuring its features, and I have a sinking feeling that whatever I am facing is not of this world.

Dani, Lucy, and Vik run into the room, ready to take on any threat they find. Dani and Lucy move to form a protective barrier in front of me while Vik stays behind the dark figure. However, both Dani and Lucy freeze upon looking at the imposing demon.

"Uh, Dani?" Lucy whispers in shock. "Isn't that—"

"Yup," Dani answers, cutting Lucy off. "It sure is."

"Can someone tell me what the hell is going on?" I ask no one in particular.

Just then, the Over Lords pop into the room.

"What's wrong?" Over Lord Sydney asks. "I felt your fear and anxiety."

Dani points to the demon standing quietly in the room.

"Volkath?" Over Lord Mary asks as shock coats her tone. "It's really you."

As the seconds tick by, Volkath's eyes remain fixed on Dani, his expression an unsettling blend of adoration and malevolence. The Over Lords now wore expressions of shock and disbelief. They exchange glances, their thoughts racing to comprehend the impossible.

Volkath's voice cuts through the palpable silence. "I have returned, my daughter."

The room seems to hold its breath, and Dani's face contorts with a mix of emotions I can't decipher. Her voice, when it finally comes, trembles with a complex blend of anger, sorrow, and confusion. "How can you be here? I thought I killed you."

The room crackles with tension, a myriad of emotions swirling within its confines. Volkath stands before us, an enigma wrapped in darkness. His presence is both eerie and captivating, a stark reminder that we are entangled in a web of mysteries that defy explanation.

The tension in the room grows thicker, and I feel like an intruder in a family drama far beyond my understanding. As I grapple with the surreal circumstances, I wonder how my vision, or dream—or whatever it was—had led to this inexplicable reunion.

Over Lord Sydney breaks the silence with a furrowed

brow. "Are you here to stir up shit again? We don't have time for your vendetta right now, Volkath."

Over Lord Mary takes a step forward, and her voice holds an odd mixture of relief and trepidation. "Volkath, how is this possible?"

He regards her with a soft look before sending me a look that sends a chill down my spine. "She did it. The girl brought me back from a dark and cold place."

Over Lord Ashley huffs in annoyance. "Just great! I thought this asshole was gone for good. Alright, stand back. I'm going to incinerate this fucker into nothingness."

Volkath's eyes turn deadly as he directs a venomous glare at Over Lord Ashley. The tension in the room escalates, and I have a feeling that this situation is far from resolved.

My impatience grows, and I clear my throat, drawing all eyes to me. "What the hell is happening here, and who is this demon?"

Dani's eyes softened as she regards me, her gaze filled with a mixture of gratitude and regret. "Liv, Volkath is my father. I thought I killed him while struggling to control my demon half. I told you about that."

"You never said you killed your father. You conveniently left out that part, Dani," I snap.

Her eyes narrow at my outburst. "Would it have mattered if I did? Would it have changed what happened? How was telling you of any relevance, Liv? Would you pity me? Really, Liv. I'm trying to understand your anger for not knowing."

The room falls into another heavy silence, the enormity of the revelation weighing on all of us. I know she's right. Telling me wouldn't have mattered. I'm sure she still felt remorse and left that out of the story. Now, I feel bad about my outburst. This whole surprising situation got to me, and I'm taking it out on her.

"I'm sorry, Dani," I whisper.

She gives me a small smile. "It's okay, Liv. I'm just glad he's alive and that he's back."

Over Lord Miranda directs her attention towards me. "That brings the question of what is he doing here and how did he get here? In your room, no less."

"I went to bed like normal, and I thought I was dreaming, but I guess it was a vision. It's never happened in my sleep before," I reply.

Over Lord Stephanie pats my shoulder. "That's okay, Olivia. You didn't know. What exactly happened in this vision?"

I tell her about the vision, and they know exactly what I'm talking about. Apparently, it was during the time Dani lost her shit, and I can't believe I didn't put it together sooner.

Over Lord Miranda shifts her gaze to mine as she sighs heavily. "We have much to explain, Olivia. But for now, we need to deal with the immediate threat Volkath poses and figure out how to send him back to where he came from."

"Where did you bring him back from?" Over Lord Sydney asks.

"Well, after Dani went nuclear in the vision, I found myself in a dark and cold place, just like the one he described earlier. I thought I was alone until Volkath grabbed me, and then everything went dark. Somehow, I threw us out of the vision, and we landed in my room."

I look at Volkath. Though weak, he seems more composed than when he had first appeared. I take in his appearance and notice his sunken eyes and even paler skin.

He meets my gaze, his eyes carrying the weight of years

of separation and suffering. "Dani grievously wounded me during our encounter. She struck a blow that sent me into a dark and cold place, a realm unlike any I had experienced. I was trapped there, unable to teleport, and it took me time to heal. I had resigned myself to my fate until Olivia arrived in that very place."

Silence settles once more, but this time, it's different—a contemplative hush filled with the collective realization that we intertwine our fates in ways we could not yet comprehend.

Over Lord Ashley speaks up with her voice laced with distrust. "So, what now? Are we just supposed to welcome Volkath back with open arms?"

Volkath's features harden, and his voice takes on a tone of earnestness. "I understand your apprehension, but I am not here to sow chaos. I am here to seek answers, understand what transpired in my absence, and perhaps find a path toward redemption."

Over Lord Sydney moves to ease the tension. "We have much to discuss and plan, but for now, let us focus on understanding the circumstances that brought us to this point. Olivia's ability is our priority, and we can handle Volkath's return later. There's too much shit to deal with already."

"We need to determine if Volkath's return poses a threat," Over Lord Annie adds. "You heard Rebecca and her puzzling prophecy. We've yet to figure out what it means, and Volkath's appearance is not a coincidence. "

I can feel the weight of the situation pressing down on me. I'd unwittingly played a role in this unfolding drama and want to find answers and control this ability. My gaze meets Dani's, and she offers a reassuring nod, silently conveying her gratitude for my willingness to become involved in their world, no matter the risks.

As the room buzzes with conversation and contemplation, an unexpected disturbance shatters the uneasy calm. A portal materializes, its shimmering surface giving way to the arrival of Dani's demon uncles. They step through with an air of familiarity and casualness that belies the gravity of the situation.

"Little sisters, it's always a pleasure to see you," Buranath greets with a wry smile.

"Well, I don't know how pleasant this visit will be. Look at who Olivia found," Over Lord Ashley remarks, her gaze pointedly directed at Volkath.

Astroloch, the more stoic of Dani's demon uncles, can't hide his astonishment. "It cannot be. You are alive."

"We'll leave you to catch up with Volkath. Take him back with you, and we'll get in touch at a later date." Over Lord Miranda states in a tone that gives way for no argument.

I watch the demons leave through the portal, their departure as sudden as their arrival. The room falls into silence once more as everyone processes the whirlwind of events that had just transpired.

Over Lord Ashley breaks the quiet with her abruptness by clapping her hands. "Well, this has been entertaining, but I need my beauty rest." She walks toward the door before turning back to me. "Olivia, try not to bring anything else back from your visions."

With that weird piece of advice, Over Lord Ashley disappears without another word, leaving me with more questions than answers.

Genuine concern softens Over Lord Miranda's face as she approaches me. "Don't worry, Olivia. Things will get better. Tomorrow, we'll work with you again on controlling your ability, and you'll learn to navigate this world more effectively."

The Over Lords depart, leaving the room with a sense of emptiness and unresolved tension. Dani, Lucy, and Vik, their faces etched with weariness, retreat to their respective rooms, leaving me to confront the restless night that awaits me.

As I lay in bed, the events of the evening swirl in my mind like a windy storm. My involvement in this magical world has grown far beyond my initial curiosity, and I can't help but feel a sense of responsibility for the consequences of my actions. The visions, Volkath's return, and the baffling presence of the demon uncles are all threads in a tapestry of intrigue that I had unwittingly become a part of.

My thoughts drift to the visions that had brought me here, visions I had initially dismissed as mere dreams. The realization that they were a manifestation of my latent abilities had opened a door to an entirely new world of possibilities. I know I need to gain control over this newfound power, not only for my sake, but for the safety of those around me.

The night is long, and sleep remains elusive. My mind is a whirlwind of questions, doubts, and determination. I'm determined to find answers, to uncover the secrets that lay hidden within the Veil Society, and to protect the friends who had welcomed me into their world. Then maybe my life can return to normal, and I can put all of this behind me.

With the first light of dawn breaking through my window, I rise from my restless slumber and make my way to the kitchen. The scent of brewing coffee fills the air as I prepare a steaming cup, the comforting routine a small anchor in the tumultuous sea of uncertainty.

As I sip my coffee, I reflect on the previous night's events. The Over Lords had assured me they would work with me to hone my abilities, a prospect that both excites and terrifies me. The visions had already shown me glimpses of various things, and I know that there is so much more to discover.

With determination in my heart, I know the challenges ahead will not be easy, but I'm willing to face them. Orchard Landing had become my second home, and the bonds I had forged with Dani, Lucy, Vik, and the Over Lords have become an intrinsic part of who I am.

As I finish my coffee and gaze out the window at the dawning day, I know that my path in this magical world is just beginning. There are mysteries and wonders that await me. I'm ready to embrace them, to learn, to grow, and to protect those I care about so that I can return to my normal life.

With newfound resolve, I set down my cup and make my way to the main house, where Over Lords will do everything they can to get my ability under control.

CHAPTER 19
THE SURPRISE VISITOR

My training with the Over Lords is proving to be an absolute disaster. I always train in the main house, surrounded by their powerful presence, yet I still feel utterly lost. Try as I might, I can't seem to gain control over my ability. They are becoming more unpredictable as the days go on.

Every time I attempt to harness my power, it slips through my grasp like a wisp of smoke. I can feel the Over Lords' mounting frustration, their impatience with my lack of progress. The Over Lords now look at me with a mixture of disappointment and annoyance. Deep down, I know it's not me specifically, but the mounting threat of the Veil Society. They want me for my power, and not controlling it makes me more dangerous.

The visions themselves are a whirlwind of chaos. They come to me unbidden, striking like lightning, taking me to places I can't control. Sometimes, I find myself transported to the distant past, witnessing events long gone, as if I am a ghostly observer of history.

Other times, I'm thrust into the present, seeing snippets

of the world through different eyes, experiencing moments that are not my own. Then there are the glimpses of the future, hazy and uncertain, like fragmented dreams that offer no clarity or guidance.

I can see faces, places, and events, but they are like puzzle pieces scattered in the wind, impossible to assemble into a coherent picture. The harder I try to focus, the more elusive they become, slipping away like water through my fingers.

The Over Lords watch in silence as I struggle, their expressions growing increasingly inscrutable. It's as though they expect me to unlock the secrets of my power easily, and my inability to do so is a disappointment they can't hide. Each attempt leaves me mentally and emotionally drained, my confidence crumbling with every failure. However, we keep going because I'm determined to get this under control.

I've been training with the Over Lords for a few weeks now, learning to control my visions. Soon, I'm able to conjure the visions more easily. It's a minor feat compared to learning to pinpoint when and where the visions take place. They let me know that while I may bring them on at will, there will be times they'll happen without my control.

That's just how it works with visions. So far, I've been able to help them find more of our people. As a small reward, they have allowed me to go on a mission with Dani, Lucy, and Vik. I'm filled with excitement and nervous anticipation as I prepare for my first mission with them.

"The magic user is in the abandoned warehouse on the outskirts of town," Over Lord Sydney tells us. "Grab her and bring her back. And for the love of all things holy, do not draw attention to yourselves. No explosions. Do not do big displays of magic. No doing anything that will be in the newspapers or on television. Understood?"

"Yes, we understand," we say in unison, with me feeling like a newcomer eager to prove herself to the task at hand.

In a whirlwind of motion, Dani extends her arm, her fingers crackling with magical energy, and she instantly transports us to the location of the magic user. It's a dimly lit and lonely place, the stale air thick with an unsettling smell.

Dani turns to me with a firm look. "Liv, you're here to observe. Do not engage unless you are defending yourself. I really don't want to deal with explaining your injuries."

I shake my head in agreement, my apprehension palpable as I take in my surroundings. The warehouse is large, its windows shattered and its walls worn and weathered. As we cautiously walk through the warehouse, the magic user comes into view. She's standing in the center of the vast, open space, looking at us with contempt. Her power is unlike anything I have ever seen—she seems to manipulate the very darkness itself.

"Hi, I'm Dani," she starts. "I'm here to take you with us back to Orchard Landing. It's a haven for people like us."

"You know as well as I do that I'm not going anywhere with you," the magic user responds.

Dani's gaze remains steady. "We're not here to harm you. We simply need your cooperation. Nothing will happen to you. We're all in this together."

The magic user scoffs as she narrows her eyes. "I've heard of Orchard Landing. The feared Over Lords. You take people, and they're never seen again. I don't know your grand plan, but I am not interested in being a pawn in your games."

"We understand your hesitation, but we promise

Orchard Landing is not what you're assuming it is. There's nothing nefarious about it. We just want to help." Dani tries to convince her again.

"And if you come willingly, it'll save us all a lot of trouble," Vik grumbles from off to the side.

The magic user crosses her arms with a stubborn expression. "I don't care about your promises or your convenience. I won't let you take me against my will."

Dani, Lucy, and Vik exchange glances before bursting out into laughter.

"I tried to take the calm and easy approach for your sake," Dani says when she looks at me. "We wanted to make your first mission simple and easy, but like usual, the magic users are stubborn."

Lucy directs her gaze to the magic user with a sinister smirk. "We can do this the easy way or the hard way. It's your choice."

The magic user's response is swift and defiant. "I chose the hard way."

Without warning, the magic user unleashes her power, twisting dark tendrils and lashing out at us. Panic surges through me, but I push it deep down. Amid the chaos, I draw upon my training and instinctively dodge the encroaching shadows. Without magic at my disposal, I rely on my physical abilities, using agility and quick reflexes to evade the sinister tendrils.

It is a heart-pounding dance of survival, and it feels invigorating. In the end, they prevail against the magic user. She's exhausted and outnumbered, and they apprehend her with ease.

We'd just returned from our latest mission and delivered our newest member to the main house to speak with the Over Lords.

"Great work, girls," Over Lord Mary says with a smile. "You all will take the newcomer to get settled. We need a moment with Olivia."

Suddenly, we're standing inside the ancient library on the property. I've only heard about this place from Lucy because a while ago, she had to get some books to help her figure out what type of demons were hunting her. However, I've never been here for anything because the books are in a language I can't read.

"I don't know why we didn't think of this until now," Over Lord Stephanie starts. "Jade brought up an excellent point the other day. We've only been teaching who the goddess was that gave us our power and what we've done with it as a race so far, but we've never delved into who this goddess is."

"Well, she did seem kind of lonely," Over Lord Ashley adds.

I take a seat at a nearby table. "Wait a minute. You guys actually met this goddess?"

Over Lord Ashley scrunches her face in thought. "I wouldn't say met. When we died saving the world, Thodara decided to spare our souls and give us a chance to live again. That crazy bitch thought we'd rather live a life without each other over dying."

"She didn't really give us a choice to accept or reject her gift," Over Lord Stephanie adds sadly. "She just gave it to us, and we were reborn as different people."

"Whoa, that is really crazy," I say in disbelief. "But you're here now. Together."

Over Lord Ashley smiles brightly. "That's right! Because our bond is unbreakable. That's because we're stuck together like glue. We're inseparable, like glitter at a craft party sticks to everything and is impossible to get rid of.

We're tighter than a pair of skinny jeans on taco night. Our sisterhood is like a GPS; we always find each other, no matter how lost we might be. We're—"

"That's enough, Ashley," Over Lord Sydney laughs. "I think she gets it. Now, let's move on to why we're here."

Just then, Jade walks through the doors to the library. "Good afternoon, Lords," she says as she bows. She looks at me with an unreadable expression. "Olivia."

That's all the greeting I get before she walks past toward a bookshelf and pulls down an old scroll. "Ancient scribes did an excellent job of recording the events that took place. While aiding Lucy, I found this book with multiple gods and goddesses inside. Perhaps this may be useful in obtaining more knowledge about the goddess of magic and what she has to do with this Veil Society."

"How is this supposed to help me control my ability?" I ask them.

"To harness and control your ability, you must first understand its origins." Jade begins. "But that is not the main point. We need this information to help combat the Veil Society since they have a vendetta against the goddess."

All at once, the Over Lords' eyes snap up and flash brightly as their power fills the room. "Someone is on the property," Over Lord Miranda says, her voice fills with anger.

Suddenly, we're transported from the library to the field in front of the institute. Dani, Lucy, and Vik appear on the field as well. Just as fast as the Over Lords appeared, they disappeared. They're only gone for a second before reappearing with someone in their grasp.

"Who the fuck are you, lady?" Over Ashley asks as she

drops the woman on the ground. "How the hell did you get onto Orchard Landing?"

The woman crawls back away from them in fear. "I took a boat."

My brows raise in shock. It can't be. I walk a little closer, unable to help myself and the surprise presence.

"Bullshit!" Over Lord Ashley snaps. "No one comes to Orchard Landing without our knowledge, let alone makes it onto the property."

She takes an intimidating step forward. "Are you a bad guy? Wait, you're a woman. Are you a bad woman? A bad woman working for the bad guys? Wait, women can be in charge, too. Are the bad guys working for you, bad woman?"

"Stop spouting nonsense, Ashley," Over Lord Miranda says, pulling her away from the frightened woman. "Give her a chance to answer your stupid questions."

"Evelyn?" I ask, afraid my eyes are deceiving me.

"Liv!" she shouts before getting up and running toward me.

We clash, hugging each other so tight that there's no air between us. I've missed my friend, and I was worried sick about her. I can't believe after all the searching we've done, she'd make her way to me.

Suddenly, she's ripped from my arms. "No touching the merchandise until we know you're not a threat," Dani snaps.

"Is that you, Evelyn?" Vik asks from behind me.

Her eyes widen in surprise. "Viktoria!"

Now Evelyn hugs Vik, as Vik stands there unsure what to do. However, she's once again ripped away.

"Are you deaf? Cousin or not, I will hurt you if you

touch them again without telling us how you got onto the property." Dani tells her with suspicion coating her tone.

"I'm good at researching," Eve starts. "When I couldn't find Liv, I started researching and searching for her. It led me all the way here."

I step toward Eve. "I tried calling you. You never answered your phone, and then it was disconnected. I couldn't even get a vision of you. We tried searching for you and found nothing. What the hell happened?"

"I was scared, Liv. They kidnapped you! Once I found out you took a leave of absence from Sutton Engineering shortly after the news reported about an explosion, I knew something wasn't right. So, I ran. While I was hiding, I started looking for you," she tells me.

"And I shit glitter. Stop bullshitting a bullshitter, Evelyn," Over Lord Ashley snaps. "To the outside world, we are upstanding citizens. We're wealthy women who run a school for the young and gifted. No one thinks otherwise and there's no way in hell that you followed an imaginary trail all the way here to find Olivia. No matter how small the breadcrumbs were, we have people that eat that shit up before it leads anywhere near here."

Eve shrugs as if she's not worried about her accusations. "I don't know what to tell you. There are reports and groups out there that say Orchard Landing houses a cult that sacrifices people in exchange for eternal life. Given recent events surrounding Liv, that was a pretty damn good breadcrumb to follow. Especially since I found her."

"Cult? Sacrifices?" Over Lord Ashley questions with glee in her eyes. "Tell me, how do they say we sacrifice these people? Is it gruesome? Am I the queen of sacrifices?"

"Not the time, Ashley," Over Lord Miranda chastises her.

The Over Lords stand silent, no doubt communicating with each other again. Various expressions cross over their faces, and I can't tell what they think. Meanwhile, we stand in silence, staring at each other, unsure what to do now. Suddenly, Eve's hands are shackled in front of her with a magical binding. The sudden action doesn't startle her, but I gasp in surprise.

"Alright, because we're such nice people, you can spend a little time with Viktoria and Olivia," Over Lord Sydney says. "But you will not be free to roam. The girls will watch you. When your time is up, you're going back to wherever the hell you came from."

I open my mouth to say something, but Eve shakes her head, telling me to leave it be. With that final declaration, we take off toward the house, with Eve following behind like a prisoner. I can't say I like it, but she doesn't seem to mind. Either way, I'm glad that she's here and that she's safe.

"You can stay in the living room," Dani says to Eve as we enter the house. "No roaming around."

Dani and Lucy leave, and now it's just me, Vik, and Eve.

"I can't believe you're here," Eve says in awe as she stares at Vik. "When I heard about your parents, I thought the worst. I thought that maybe somebody had kidnapped you."

"I'm fine, Eve," Vik replies. "You read what the police reports said. My parents killed each other. Why would you think I got kidnapped?"

Eve shrugs as she looks around the room, avoiding looking her in the face. "What else was I supposed to think? You were missing."

"You didn't think that she simply ran away?" I ask.

The thought had never crossed my mind before now.

But now that I've spent time with them, I wonder how Eve concluded Vik was kidnapped. Now that I remember, many of the reports say Vik walked away. Not that someone took her. But the reports were loaded with weird stories that I know now were the Over Lords' doing.

She ignores the question and takes Vik's hand. "What happened, Viktoria? How did you get here? I'm guessing you're not a prisoner here?"

"I resent that!" Lucy shouts from the back of the house. "She's never been a prisoner and is one of my best friends. If you insinuate one more negative thing about us, I will cut you!"

Me and Vik laugh at Lucy's outburst while Eve sits there with a pensive look on her face. She's staring at Vik, analyzing her like she's trying to figure out something.

"I've never been a prisoner here," Vik answers when she stops laughing. "At first, I was scared, but then they took the memories away, and when I adjusted, they gave them back, and I remembered everything that happened.

Eve assesses Vik again. "So, what is your power? Do you know what it is? How much about your ability do you know?"

"Look, Eve," Vik starts. "Not to be rude, but why were you looking for me? It's not like we were close. Honestly, I barely remember you. I saw you once before I disappeared, and sorry to say this, but I thought you were weird."

"We're family, Vik," Eve says nervously. "So, tell me what really happened. Was it one of these people that killed your parents?"

Dani's voice floats into the living room. "Okay, now I'm going to punch her in the damn face." She appears in front of Eve, glowing from releasing her power. "We don't kill needlessly. Imply that one more time, and I will seriously hurt you."

I'm amazed that Eve doesn't seem scared. Maybe it's because she's already experienced the worst with Axel.

"I do not intend to imply anything," Eve says calmly. "I'm simply asking some questions."

"Well, your questions are offending me and my friends," Vik snaps at Eve.

I jump in to relieve the tension in the room. "Why don't you tell her what happened, Vik? Maybe that will ease her worries."

She huffs in agitation. "Fine, but it's not a pretty story. My home life was not always pretty. My parents went from loving to straight-up mean. That night, they were arguing like usual. They're always going at it, verbally and physically. All the yelling got to me, and it pissed me off. So, I yelled at them. I yelled and told them that if they hated each other so much, just to kill each other."

"I didn't know that. I'm sorry you had to witness something so gruesome. However, it's not your fault if their argument turned so violent, Vik." I tell Vik.

Vik gives a humorless laugh. "It is my fault, Liv. You don't know my ability because I don't use it unless I have to. That's why they rarely see me using it."

"I'm so sorry that happened to you," I reply.

Eve sits forward on the couch. "You made them do it."

"Yup," Vik says, popping the p. "Now that we've gone over the sordid details of my previous life, let's never discuss it again. I hope I have eased your worries, Eve, but as you can see, I am fine."

Eve stares at Vik again, assessing her in a way that has me confused. I feel terrible that her ordeal with Axel has shaken her so much that she's different.

Over Lord Annie pops into the room. "Times up! You need to come with me, Evelyn. You're going back to wherever the hell you came from."

Eve stands, and I walk over to hug her. "I'm glad you're okay. Please stop reading those crazy books about magic. I know you discovered a new world, but this isn't for you. I'd hate to see something else bad happen to you. Now that we know you're okay, please return to your normal life. I will keep in touch. Okay?"

"I'm glad you're okay, Liv," she says. "We'll keep in touch, okay?"

I nod as she turns to Viktoria. "I'm also glad you are safe. It seems like you've found a new family here. I'm happy for you. I'll see you soon."

"No, you won't," Over Lord Annie confidently says.

"Be safe, Eve," is all Vik says to her.

Over Lord Annie teleports them out of the room in the next moment. I think about how Eve seemed different and the changes in demeanor. I'm not used to this new version of her, and I hope she gets help because I'd hate to see my friend suffering long term because of me.

"Since that awkward encounter is over, Mom says we need to head to the main house," Dani informs us.

I'll never get over how they seem to communicate telepathically. As usual, we pop over to the main house to find all the Over Lords, except Over Lord Annie, sitting in the living room.

"We need you to see if you can get a vision on the Veil," Over Lord Stephanie tells me. "We still can't find them, which is unusual for us and worrisome."

I concentrate for a long time, trying to get a vision of the Veil, but nothing happens. They're hidden very well. I try a couple more times, and still nothing happens. Then, that familiar sensation takes over, and a vision forms in my mind. The world around me blurs and shifts, and suddenly, I find myself standing in the dimly lit room.

I watch Axel pace back and forth, his face illuminated by the soft glow of his phone's screen. His voice is low and filled with urgency as he speaks into the device.

"We've been searching for years, and finally, we have a solid lead on the other half of the pair," Axel says, his tone a mixture of excitement and trepidation. "I can't believe it's taken this long, but we might finally finish what we've started. But first, we have something to do."

I strain to hear every word, my heart pounding in my chest. As Axel continues speaking, I notice a hint of vulnerability in his eyes, a glimpse of the man beneath the tough exterior. "I know it's risky, but we can't let this opportunity slip through our fingers. The longer we wait, the greater the danger of being discovered. We must strike now or never."

Axel's conversation continues, and I can feel the weight of responsibility in his words. He looks around the room, and I'm so focused on Axel that I don't notice the others in the room.

"Gather the team and meet me at the location in an hour. We'll discuss the next steps there. And be cautious. We don't know if Olivia knows what we're doing," he says with a hint of finality.

As the vision fades, my mind races from the gravity of what I just saw. Taking a deep breath, my eyes flutter open, back in the real world. Everyone stares at me, waiting for me to explain what happened because they knew I had a vision. I stand there thinking about everything I saw in the vision.

"Well? We don't have all damn day," Over Lord Ashley says, breaking the silence in the room. "What did you see?"

"Axel is planning something," I tell them. "They have a

lead on the other half of the pair of powers. He said something about striking now because I may know what they're doing."

"Okay, what was his location?" Over Lord Stephanie asks.

"I don't know," I reply. "I couldn't tell, and the vision didn't last long enough for me to find out."

"You guys go back to the library to learn more about this pair of powers nonsense," Over Lord Miranda tells us. "We have enough shit to deal with as it is."

Over Lord Sydney nods in agreement. "Every time things calm down, something else pops up. Why can't we catch a damn break?"

"Right?" Over Lord Ashley says. "First, we have to take on some big, bad demons. Then, we had to deal with Dani going fucking psycho. Next were more demons, but this time, they were trying to kill Lucy. Now, we have to deal with Olivia and another Mutane Sihiri because of something Thodara did before we were sperm in our daddy's nut sack. Hell, their daddy's daddy's nut sack. And their daddy's, and their daddy's."

Over Lord Ashley starts pacing back and forth. "Let's not forget the Veil. Haven't we had our fair share of secret organizations? There was the USSNA, and let's just say people are right when they say to never trust the government. During all that, there was the unruly and the rising. That shit was irritating as hell. Now, there's the Veil Society. What the hell is going on around here?"

Over Lord Sydney waves a barrier behind Over Lord Ashley as she paces away. When she turns around, she slams right into it.

"Calm your ass down, Ashley," she tells her. "We'll figure this out just like we did all the other times. If you need to blow off some steam, go spar with your husband. No need to wear a damn hole in the floor."

My eyes widen in shock. "You guys are married?"

The Over Lords laugh so hard they have tears coming out of their eyes.

"Yes, Olivia, we are." Over Lord Stephanie replies. "All of us except Mary. She had to be all weird and fall in love with a demon, spawn Dani over there, and almost destroy the world in the process."

Dani huffs in agitation. "That's not what happened, and you know it. Can we please get back to the topic at hand?"

"Do you think the pair of powers are more powerful than you are?" I ask, worried that there may be more to this problem than they can handle.

Over Lord Mary's eyes flash. "You may have been here a few months, but you have not seen us in action, Olivia. We're pretty badass when we need to be, but let's get one thing straight." All the Over Lords' power flares in the room. "Nothing and no one is more powerful than us."

"We're pretty badass too, you know," Lucy adds with a fake pout.

"Alright, enough talk about our badassery." Over Lord Miranda says. "Go find out more about Thodara and this pair of powers nonsense while we head out."

With that last command, the Over Lords teleport out of the room.

CHAPTER 20
THE LOSING BATTLE

The ancient library is a vast labyrinth of dusty scrolls and crumbling books. We huddle around a worn-out table with expressions of frustration. We'd been searching for hours, trying to uncover any trace of the elusive Goddess Thodara and the mysterious "pair of powers" Axel had been talking about.

I run a hand through my hair in frustration. "This is insane. Thodara should have an entire section dedicated to her, but it's like she vanished from history."

"It's not like we have much to read through," Dani says, irritation coating her voice. "These ancient texts are written in the old language. It's like trying to decipher hieroglyphics. Mom knows we can't read it, and she sent us here, anyway."

Vik groans and lays her head on the table. "Can we take a break? I'm starving and can't concentrate on magical mumbo-jumbo when all I can think about is food."

"You're always hungry, Vik," Dani laughs. "I guess we can take a break and pop over to the house to eat."

Just as we pack up our things, the library door swings open with a bang, and Torri storms in, her nose held high with an air of superiority. Dani and Lucy groan, and I look at them in confusion because I've never met this woman. I've seen her because of trials, but can't remember her name.

I elbow Dani to get her attention. "Who is that?"

"That is Torri," she replies while scrunching up her nose. "She teaches at the school, and she's insufferable."

Just then, Torri reaches our table. "The Over Lords sent me to help you, since you failed to learn the language of our people."

Vik pops up and glares at Torri. "Oh, look, it's our knight in shining arrogance. How nice of you to grace us with your presence, even though we didn't ask for it."

I stick my hand out toward Torri. "Nice to meet you. I'm Olivia."

She glares down her nose at me. "It is, isn't it?"

"What is?" I ask, as confusion coats my tone.

"Nice to meet me," she says before walking toward a bookshelf with a roll of her eyes.

Dani giggles beside me. "She's just so thrilled to be here."

"What crawled up her ass?" I ask them, whispering so that Torri can't hear me.

Vik shrugs. "That's just Torri. She has permanent PMS and resting bitch face. Don't pay her any mind. She's like that with everybody."

Torri returns, reluctantly taking a seat, and starts reading the text. As she's reading, she translates it into English so we can understand. We pour through book after book and scroll after scroll for a couple of hours.

"Can we find anything about Thodara already?" Vik

whines. "I'm getting hungrier, and I can eat a horse right about now. Or at least a dozen cupcakes."

Dani scowls at her. "Keep it together, Vik. You're acting like a starving maniac."

"I am a starving maniac, Dani," she replies as her stomach rumbles. "Do you know how many calories I've burned today?"

"Can we focus!" Torri snaps, startling us. "I believe I've found something about this Goddess Thodara."

"Really? What does it say?" I ask in excitement.

Torri huffs and rolls her eyes before she reads aloud. "Thodara, Goddess of Magic, vanished from the mortal realm after gifting the mortals their magic. It is believed that she is in hiding after completing this task. Some believe it's because she used up all of her magic, and others believe she is running from something or someone. Her whereabouts are unknown, and those who ventured to find her never returned."

Torri finishes reading and sits back in her chair.

"Well, that's helpful," Dani says sarcastically.

"I was hoping for something like 'Go to the mystical taco stand and chant guacamole three times to unlock the secrets', something like that," Vik says.

I laugh at her rambling. "Wouldn't that be nice? But I guess we have to figure out where she is on our own. Especially since these texts have nothing about a pair of powers."

"As if that'll be a piece of cake," Torri snorts.

Vik smiles widely. "Did you say cake? Can we go get some now?"

Dani chuckles at that. "Let's call it a day. We'll come back tomorrow with fresh eyes and maybe a less grumpy Torri."

Torri doesn't bother to reply or say goodbye. She stands up, places the books and scrolls back, and walks out the door.

We pack up our things, with Vik leading the way as her stomach audibly growls. We make our way out of the library and pass through the field when a large explosion happens right before us. It sends us flying back, and we land on the ground hard. I groan in pain from the impact.

"Liv!" Dani shouts. "Are you alright?"

I stand up slowly. "I'm fine."

The Over Lords appear in front of us just as I look across the field to see Axel walking forward with a large group following behind him. There have to be at least a hundred of them.

"How the fuck did they get onto the property?" Over Lord Ashley asks no one in particular. She looks at her sisters. "Remind me to maim our patrol when we finish kicking ass here. Seriously, how hard is it to keep intruders from accessing the property?"

"Let me guess," Over Lord Miranda says as the intruders stop their advancement. "You must be the mysterious Axel." She points to the people standing behind him. "And you're his merry band of idiots."

Axel lets out an obnoxious laugh. "And you must be the fearless Over Lords." He takes a bow. "It is an honor to be in your presence."

"I assume you want Olivia?" Over Lord Mary asks.

"You assume right," he replies. "But that's not all. You have an entire community here filled with potential candidates for the pair of powers, and as soon as I'm finished with you, I will sift through every single one of them to find the person I'm looking for."

Just as I tell Dani and Vik that there are too many for

them to fight, the ground rumbles. Marching toward us is a medium-sized group of Mutane Sihiri soldiers, ready for battle.

Axel smiles, and it's so evil it makes my skin crawl. "I was hoping you'd put up a fight. It will make my victory that much sweeter."

Over Lord Ashley turns toward me. "Who the hell is this delusional asshole?" She doesn't allow me to reply as she addresses Axel again. "You think you can come into my home, threaten me and mine, and get away with it? Oh, you are so going in the box, mister!"

Axel looks just as confused as I am. I don't know what the box is, but it doesn't sound all that threatening.

Lucy must see my confusion. "Trust me, nobody wants to go in the box."

"Aunt Ashley has a mean streak, and she can hold a grudge," Dani adds.

"As amusing as this conversation has been, I'm growing impatient," Axel says after a moment. "Stand aside now, and no one will get hurt...yet. If you pursue this, we will kill you."

"Get ready for battle," Dani says. "Now, you're about to see us in action, and our badassery is like no other."

With a simple wave of her hand, I'm dressed in battle gear with Dani, Lucy, Vik, and the others.

"Time to put your skills to the test, Liv," Lucy says. "Don't worry, though. We won't let you get hurt."

Dani conjures her Sai, Lucy summons her knives, and weapons appear in my and Vik's hands. She has a sword, and I have a staff. My heart races in anticipation because I've never actually been in an actual fight. Training with my friends doesn't count since they weren't trying to kill me.

I'm scared shitless, but I will fight until my dying breath not to return with Axel.

Axel signals his goons to attack, and all hell breaks loose. Both sides clash, bodies mixing together in a battle of wills. I'm pushed off to the side by some unknown force.

"Stay there and stay safe," Lucy says. "Do not fight unless you have to."

She disappears into the crowd of bodies, and I stand there like a deer caught in headlights, unsure what to do. I watch in amazement as the Over Lords, Dani, Lucy, Vik, and the soldiers, fend off Axel and his goons.

I stand in awe as Over Lord Miranda unleashes her power in a display of dazzling magic and martial prowess. The air crackles with energy as she readies her attack. She's surrounded by about twenty people, and their eyes hold contempt.

With a swift movement, Over Lord Miranda conjures a shimmering portal, and from it emerges a flurry of throwing knives. They hover around her like deadly satellites, waiting for her command. With a smirk, she flicks her fingers, and the knives shoot toward the people surrounding her in a deadly dance of steel.

Her opponents attempt to avoid the knives, but some get hit, the knives sticking out like pin dolls. The rest move forward, attacking swiftly and brutally, but Over Lord Miranda's power is as fluid as her fighting, seamlessly weaving together like she'd been doing this her whole life.

In an instant, Over Lord Miranda disappears from one spot and reappears behind one of them, her fists charged with energy. A series of precise punches and kicks sends her attackers hurtling backwards, crashing into the ground. With a simple snap of her fingers, the attackers break down into tiny particles and float away with the strong wind. It's then that I notice how strong they are.

I turn to see Over Lord Stephanie controlling the elements. She's the master of nature magic and steps into the center of the clearing. Her eyes glint with mischievousness, and her hands are poised in a stance that combines the grace of Muay Thai with the raw power of nature.

A magic user sends a torrent of flames hurtling toward her. With a swift wave of her hand, she summons a swirling water vortex, extinguishing the fire before it can even reach her. The water then transforms into sharp ice shards, which she directs at the other magic users, attacking them with precision. They struggle to dodge the icy onslaught and soon find themselves trapped in vines she summoned from the earth, holding them firmly in place.

Before she can dispatch them permanently, dark clouds, crackling with lightning, gather overhead. The wind howls, and rain pours down in torrents. This magic user can manipulate the elements, too, but Over Lord Stephanie doesn't seem worried about their ability.

She raises her arms, and a dome of swirling air forms around her, deflecting the lightning strikes and repelling the heavy rain. With a forceful push of her hands, she sends a gust of wind barreling toward the magic user. They're thrown off balance and fall to the ground, giving her the upper hand.

Suddenly, she's stabbed from behind and stumbles to the ground. A knife appears in her hand, and she flings it at the person who stabbed her. The knife hits dead center in their forehead, and they fall in a lifeless heap on the ground.

She pulls the knife out. "Motherfucker! That hurt like a bitch."

I am amazed as she heals herself and leaps back into the fight. I turn to see Dani, Lucy, and Vik tag-teaming their attackers. The air crackles with energy, and the ground trembles as they take on their attackers.

Dani's eyes blaze with fire and anger as she unleashes a wave of powerful energy to push back their attackers. Lucy flicks her wrist, and tendrils of magic wrap around two magic users, immobilizing them before she stabs them. Using her voice, Vik commands a few of them to turn against each other.

I marvel at their prowess, each wielding their unique abilities with precision and skill. They're a formidable trio, and I'm proud to call them friends. One approaches Lucy from behind, intent on delivering a fatal blow.

She reacts instantly, spinning around to create a bright pink shield to deflect the attack. I'm paying so much attention to the battle that I'm unaware of my surroundings. Something strikes me on the back of the head, and I fall forward.

"Ugh," I groan as I land on my hands and knees. "Fuck, that hurt."

I see movement in my peripheral and roll over just as a foot lands where I used to be. Still dazed from the blow to the head, I stand slowly to fend off my attacker. I see Nash and Steele standing in front of me, and my mouth hangs open.

"What the hell are you guys doing?" I ask in shock. "I should have known you were involved with Axel's bullshit. So, I take it you're magic users, too. What kind of magic do you have?"

"If you put up a fight, I'll show you," Nash says with a smirk.

"Olive, I've missed you at work," Steele says. "It's been

so lonely without you there. We really don't want to hurt you. Why don't you come with us?"

"Why don't you kiss my ass," I snap back. They don't think I'm a worthy opponent, but I'm about to show him just how badass I've become.

My comment pisses them off, and they attack quickly and swiftly. My heart pounds in my chest as I face off against Nash and Steele. They outmatch me in terms of magical ability, but I've been training, and I'm not going without a fight.

I dodge to the side as Nash sends a sharp piece of metal toward me. I think it's safe to say he manipulates metal. As I duck out of the way, I lunge at Steele, aiming for a swift strike to his midsection. He spins out of the way, and I stumble before falling to the ground.

Steele laughs loudly. "Come on, Olive. You're no match for us."

"Stop calling me Olive," I snap. "You're not as tough as you think, Steele."

As I'm focused on Steele, Nash takes advantage of the distraction and moves to strike with another sharp piece of metal. I pivot on my heel, barely avoiding being stabbed.

Letting out a fierce yell, I attack. My fist flies, striking Nash and Steele with precision and speed. They meet my blows with steel-hard defenses, but I refuse to back down. For every strike I land, they retaliate with equal force.

I kick Steele in the stomach, and he stumbles back with a laugh. "Not bad, Olive. You've been learning a few tricks. You're good, I'll give you that."

I wipe the blood dripping from my nose and smile. "You're not bad for a big brute."

I lunge forward, spinning the staff as I move. It slices through the air with a hiss before striking Steele on the side of the face. I spin around and use the staff to sweep Nash off his feet, and he falls to the ground hard. They recover quicker than I expect, and Steel throws a punch in my direction. I twist to the side, narrowly avoiding the blow.

I feel the air move across my face as his fist brushes past. We clash again, and I land a few good hits, but my advantage is short-lived. Steele's eyes glint with dark intensity as he focuses, and in an instant, he grows in size, towering over me.

Steele smiles down at me. "How's this for a big brute?"

"Your size just makes you a bigger target," I tell him as I back up a few steps.

He attacks, and thankfully, I'm agile with my moves as I dance around him, looking for an opening. Before I can exploit his new size, Nash intervenes, hurling shards of metal at me from all directions. I deflect some with my swift movements, but a few grazes my skin, drawing blood.

"Having trouble keeping up, Olivia?" Nash jokes.

I wince at the stinging pain, but I refuse to show weakness. "I've had worse."

We go at it again, but despite my best efforts, I find myself backed into a corner, Nash's metal barrage narrowing my escape route while Steele closes in with menacing steps. I have to think fast, but my options are dwindling.

Then, a commanding and powerful voice cuts through the chaos. "Stop. Now."

Nash and Steele freeze in their tracks, and their eyes glaze over as Vik's commanding voice takes hold. It's a sight to behold as they drop to their knees, unable to resist the compulsion.

Vik steps forward, a sly smile playing on her lips. "You two think you're so tough, don't you? Olivia has some badass friends now. I'd make you kill yourselves, but I'm feeling generous today. Perhaps Over Lord Ashley will torture you before you die. I'd pay to see that."

I can't help but chuckle at her bravado. "Vik, way to make an entrance. Thanks for helping me."

"Of course," she says with a smile. "We've always got your back, Liv."

The fight dies down, and there's only Axel, Steele, Nash, and about twenty of their goons left.

"Enough!" Over Lord Miranda shouts.

The ground shakes, causing everyone to stumble. The Over Lords release more of their power, and the air feels thick. They float to about thirty feet in the air as they glow brighter. Axel and his goons shout in pain before being lifted into the air.

"You had the nerve to attack our home," Over Lord Stephanie says.

"I don't know if it's bravery or stupidity," Over Lord Ashley states. "My vote is for stupidity because brave people fight for a noble cause that they have a chance of winning. I don't know if anyone told you, but you never had a chance of winning the fight you picked with us. Your stupidity has led to your demise."

Then, Over Lord Ashley looks at her sisters with puppy dog eyes. "Can I please, Miranda? I promise I will only play with him in my off time. I promise."

Over Lord Miranda sighs. "I don't know why we put up with your shenanigans. If I catch you sticking his soul in a dead body to put on a Broadway show with the others, I will seriously hurt you."

"I did that once, and I never hear the end of it," Over Lord Ashley huffs and folds her arms.

"Take it or leave it. I'm ready to kill them and be done

with this bullshit," Over Lord Sydney says, her voice laced with boredom.

"I'll take it!" Over Lord Ashley says quickly. She smiles and points to Axel. "Your soul is mine, and you're going into the box. We're going to have so much fun!"

Suddenly, Axel and his men scream in agony. I don't know what the Over Lords are doing to them, but it sounds painful. Shadows start to swirl around them, covering them so thickly we can barely see them.

Axel and his men's screams stop abruptly as a blast happens, sending a shockwave throughout Orchard Landing. The shadows disperse quickly, as if they had never been there. When the area clears, I see the Over Lords falling toward the ground. They look limp, as if they're lifeless.

"Mom!" Dani shouts.

Lucy waves a hand and stops their fall before they slam to the ground. Both of them teleport over, leaving me to run across the field. By the time I reach them, Dani is holding her mom's head in her lap, and Lucy is squatting over the other Over Lords with worry.

"What happened to them?" I ask as I approach, breathless from running all the way there. "Where are Axel and his men?"

"I don't know, but they're barely breathing," Dani cries. "We need to get them to the infirmary. Someone alert Linda."

"What the fuck happened?" Lucy shouts. I can hear both anger and fear in her tone. "How did they manage to do this?"

Orchard Landing rumbles. The buildings shake, and the wind blows hard. Dani glows, and her eyes flash as she lets her power loose. I've never seen her fully change in person before. When her demon side fully takes over, she looks downright scary.

"I don't know, but I'm sure as fuck going to find out," she says in a voice straight out of a horror movie.

Lucy and Dani transport me and the Over Lords to the infirmary. I stand back and watch them talk to a woman named Linda, who looks more worried than they are. My thoughts race, and my anxiety over what just happened goes through the roof.

As far as I know, the Over Lords are the most powerful beings alive. So how did Axel and his men manage to almost kill them? I'm starting to think that stopping the Veil will be more complicated than we initially thought.

CHAPTER 21

THE SEARCH FOR ANSWERS

The night hangs heavy with tension as Dani storms through the dimly lit alleyways, her eyes ablaze with anger and determination. Her fists clench, and her magic simmers beneath the surface, ready to burst forth at any moment. Axel and his goons had gone too far this time, and Dani's on a mission to seek vengeance for the near-fatal attack they had orchestrated on the Over Lords.

We've been following her everywhere she goes to ensure she doesn't do something stupid in her quest to find them. She has been tirelessly searching for Axel and his men, her anger leading her to different areas.

The Over Lords have been in the infirmary for the last two weeks, and their slow recovery has ignited a burning rage within Dani. Despite her relentless pursuit, Axel and his goons seem to have vanished, leaving no trace of their whereabouts.

As she rounds a corner, she spots a group of four magic users huddled together, their eyes widening with a mix of surprise and fear as they notice her angry approach.

"Who are you?" one of them stutters, their voice trembling.

Dani's gaze is steely as she steps closer, her eyes narrowing. "I know you're a magic user. I'm here to find out about the Veil Society. You're going to give me answers."

"I don't know what you're talking about," he replies, trying to sound confident but failing miserably.

Dani snarls. "Don't play games with me, asshole!" She lets the change partially take over, showing her demon side to the magic user. "I'm more powerful than you, and I have ways to make you talk."

The magic users exchange nervous glances. Dani is a sight to behold when she's like that. Her mere presence seems enough to unnerve them, but she needs information and is not about to leave empty-handed.

"Look, we don't know much," another one stammers. "We've heard whispers and rumors, but we're not part of any group. We just want to be left alone."

Dani's patience is wearing thin, and without warning, she lunges forward, her fist connecting with the nearest magic user's jaw. The impact is swift and powerful, and the magic user stumbles back with their face contorted in pain.

"I'm not playing games here," Dani growls in a low and dangerous tone. "You're going to tell me everything you know about the Veil Society, or things will get much worse for you."

Fear flashes in the magic users' eyes, and they stumble over each other's words as they try to explain themselves. "We've... we've heard whispers of a secret organization. They operate in the shadows, but we don't know where or who they are."

Frustration wells up within Dani, but she fights to keep

it in check. She needs concrete information, not vague rumors.

She takes a step closer, her presence looming over the group. "You're going to give me more than that. You're going to tell me who you heard these rumors from, where they meet, anything that might lead me to them."

The magic users exchange anxious glances once again, their desperation clear. "We... we really don't know. It's all hearsay. We're just trying to survive. Please, just leave us alone."

Dani's fists clench at her sides as her frustration boils over. She had hoped for a breakthrough that would bring her closer to the Veil Society's elusive trail. However, there is no point in continuing to intimidate these genuinely scared and uninformed magic users.

"Fine, I believe you. However, I can't leave you here. You are Mutane Sihiri, and you will go to Orchard Landing to meet with the Over Lords," Dani says before she opens a portal to Orchard Landing and blows them through with a powerful gust of wind.

Unable to contain her rage any longer, Dani unleashes a burst of raw energy, sending sparks crackling around her. The alleyway lights up briefly, revealing her fierce determination.

"I won't rest until I find them all," she vows, as her voice trembles with emotion. "They will pay for what they did!"

Lucy speaks up gently. "Dani, we'll find them, but we need to be patient and smart about this. Charging in without a plan will only put us all in danger."

Dani looks up with her jaw clenched in anger. "I know. It's just... they hurt my mom and aunts. They almost killed them!"

Vik nods, her expression serious. "I understand your

anger, but we need to think strategically. We'll gather information, follow leads discreetly, and strike when the time is right."

Dani nods, and we teleport back to the infirmary to check on the Over Lords. Their vitals slowly have stabilized, but they remain unconscious. The sight of them lying still and vulnerable is unusual to see, especially since they're such strong and imposing figures.

Linda places a gentle hand on Dani's shoulder. "I know, and trust me, I share your anger. We need to be patient and focus on what we can control. The Over Lords need time to heal. Their bodies have endured a great deal of trauma."

Tears well up in Dani's eyes as she looks at her mom and aunts lying still on the beds.

"They're strong," Linda reassures her. "But even the strongest warriors need time to recover. We've done everything we can for them. Now it's up to them to wake up."

I place a hand on Dani's back, offering silent support. "Linda's right. We can't lose hope. The Over Lords are strong, and they've survived worse."

Dani takes a deep breath to steady her emotions. "You're right. I just... I want to make them pay for what they did."

"And we will," Lucy chimes in. "We won't rest until Axel and his goons are dead."

Suddenly, an idea pops in my head. "We haven't looked at Sutton Engineering," I tell them. "I'm almost sure that's where we'll find him."

They send a skeptical look my way. "No offense, Liv, but that's the stupidest thing I've ever heard," Vik says.

I shake my head, dismissing her statement. "Think about it. Axel has an image to uphold to the public. I'm sure he'll be working to keep up normal pretenses."

"There's only one way to find out," Dani says as she walks out of the room.

We follow her out and teleport to Sutton Engineering. I use my credentials to gain access to the building, thankful it's still valid, and take the elevator up to his office. Sure enough, he's at work, and Lucy, Dani, Vik, and I strut into his office like we own the place, surprising Axel with our sudden appearance.

He masks his surprise just as quickly as it crosses his face. "I'm surprised to see you here," he says as he leans back in his chair. "I heard that you guys like to keep a low profile, and I never would have guessed you'd show up here to cause trouble. Especially with what happened to your beloved Over Lords."

Dani shoots an energy blast toward Axel and splits his desk in two. "I will kill you," she snarls at him. "Tell me what you did to them."

He tips his head to the side. "I don't know what you're talking about. I didn't do anything. Shouldn't you be here apologizing to me for almost being killed?"

I snort at his absurd comment. "You attacked us. You're the one going around kidnapping people, Axel."

He flicks some small pieces of wood off his pants before standing. "No, Olivia. They attacked me first the night they came to kidnap you. We never did anything to them."

"Oh, come off your damn high horse, asshole," Vik shouts, anger clear in her voice. "You're going around kidnapping and killing our people, and you have the nerve to act offended when we rescue them? It's our fucking job to protect our people."

"I'm not sure how you're still alive after I blasted you out the window last time," Dani snarls. "You're lucky to still be alive after encountering us, asshole."

He shakes his head in disappointment. "Be that as it may, you interfered with my business, destroyed my office, and took something precious to the cause. Olivia is mine. I had no choice but to retaliate to bring her back. It just so happened that you have an entire property filled with potentials that I couldn't pass up."

At that moment, a vision comes, and I gasp as it takes over.

"Axel, we've captured ten more potential candidates," Nash says as he and Steele stand in front of his desk. "We secured them in the building's basement. The guys are waiting for further instruction."

"Take Barb with you to the basement so she can feel them out," Axel replies. "I have an important meeting that I can't miss. I'll check them out in the morning."

Nervous looks pass over Steele's and Nash's faces when Axel mentions his meeting.

"Go back to work now," Axel tells them just as he sits down to make a phone call.

The vision fades, and Dani's phone rings just as I'm about to say something. It's Linda telling her that the Over Lords have awakened and that she needs to return to Orchard Landing.

"You're lucky we have to go, or else I'd break your face," Dani says.

"Pity," Axel replies with faux sadness. "Do give the Over Lords my best. I hope they recover soon. They should be in top shape for what we have planned. I'd be disappointed if we killed them too easily."

Faster than I can blink, Lucy whips out her knife and hurls it towards Axel. It spins around midair, and the butt of the knife hits him in the nose before returning to her hand. She sheathed the knife just as quickly as it came out.

"Until that time comes," Lucy starts. "There's a little parting gift."

Blood pours out of Axel's nose as he glares with fire in his eyes. With a smirk, he sheds his nose, and in its place is a new, perfectly unharmed nose.

"No wonder you were in good shape after the fight," Lucy says. "That's a nifty ability to have, I'll give you that. But it won't save you when it comes down to killing you."

She whips out her knife and does it again, and we teleport away as he groans in pain. We appear in the infirmary to see the Over Lords talking to Linda.

"We're fine, Linda," Over Lord Miranda whines. "I promise nothing is wrong."

Linda shakes her head. "I don't care how much you promise. You will sit down while I look over at you one more time. When I'm satisfied you're okay, you can go."

Her tone leaves no room for arguments, and my eyes widen as they each walk to their beds to wait for Linda to do her assessment.

Dani laughs at my expression. "Linda is the only one who can boss them around like that. She's like a mother to them, and they're like daughters to her. They will listen to her."

I pull the girls to the side. "I had a vision in Axel's office."

"What was it about?" Lucy asks.

"They have more of our people held in the basement of Sutton Engineering. Axel will go there tomorrow morning. I'm afraid of what he'll do to them." I tell them.

"Then we have to get to them before he does and bring them back here," Dani says. "Maybe we can kill them in the process."

"Look, I'm all for killing these guys, but I don't think we

should do this on our own," Lucy tells Dani. "Maybe we should let the Over Lords know and see how they want to handle this."

Dani shakes her head. "No, they're still recovering. It'll be quick and quiet."

Vik shakes her head with a smile. "Nothing is ever quick and quiet with you, Dani. This is a bad idea. A terrible idea. What if Axel isn't alone? He and his goons almost killed the Over Lords. I know you and Lucy are almost as powerful as the Over Lords, but what do you think they'll do to us? Your aunt will raise us from the dead just so your mom can kill again if we die doing this."

"That's why we're going there tonight," Dani huffs. "Hopefully, Axel won't be there, and we'll just have to knock a few goons out to get our people out of there."

We finish our conversation just as Linda releases the Over Lords, telling them they must come back to see her at least once a day until she's satisfied that they're okay. We follow the Over Lords back to the main house, and they immediately sit on the couch once we arrive.

"What happened to you guys, Mom?" Dani asks.

Over Lord Mary shrugs. "I don't know. We were about to deliver the final blow to those asshats when they suddenly broke free of our hold. Then we were stuck and couldn't move. No matter how hard we tried."

"The shadows made it hard to see what was happening," Lucy adds. She looks toward Over Lord Ashley. "What was with all the shadows? Was it for flare?"

Over Lord Ashley shakes her head. "I know I'm known for my creepy, scary vibes, but that wasn't me. We don't know where those shadows came from."

"While it held us, a blast came out of nowhere, hitting

us and then lights out," Over Lord Annie says. "It hurt like hell, too."

"How long were we in the infirmary?" Over Lord Miranda asks.

"Two weeks," I tell them, watching their expressions change from tired to surprised.

"That explains why I've been feeling so antsy. I sensed quite a few magic users while I was unconscious," Over Lord Sydney tells us. "There are a few of them out there causing havoc. We need to apprehend them before they unleash more chaos."

"Consider it done," Dani replies quickly. "Tell us where they are, and we'll take care of it."

"Cincinnati, Ohio, and Oklahoma," her voice whispers in my head.

"Whoa! I heard you speak, and your mouth didn't move!" I shout in surprise. "Dani always told me your moments of creepy silence were you communicating tele-pathically. It's definitely a weird feeling."

Dani laughs. "Imagine your mom or aunts constantly popping into your head to dish out orders all day."

"We're getting off-topic," Over Lord Annie interjects. "Divide and conquer. Two teams will take each location. Dani, you and Lucy can go together, and Vik, you'll pair up with Olivia. Move quickly and efficiently, but most impor-tantly, do it quietly. Do not draw attention to yourselves."

With our roles assigned, we teleport to our respective destinations, ready to face whatever dangers await us. Thanks to Over Lord Sydney teleporting us, Vik and I appear inside a secluded old warehouse. We're instructed to call when we need them to bring us back, since neither of us can teleport. There's a group of people huddled around, lost in conversation.

"Remember," Vik whispers. "Let me do the talking. I want to grab them and get home without a fight, but be ready to defend yourself should you need to because, unfortunately, they always put up a fight."

I nodded, feeling a mixture of adrenaline and anxiety.

"Hey, guys," I call out, my voice steady despite the fluttering nerves in my stomach. "We're not here to fight. We just want to talk."

Vik slaps a hand over her face. "What the hell happened to let me do the talking? And what's up with saying we don't want a fight? Now, they're going to fight."

A guy turns around, his face twisting into a scowl at being interrupted. "Who the fuck are you, and how did you find us? You better get out of here before we kick your asses."

"We're not your enemies," Vik says calmly. "We're here to take you someplace safe. Please come peacefully, and we might be able to help you."

Without further warning, the guy attacks, sending rocks soaring our way. I deftly roll out of harm's way before getting hit.

"So much for peaceful," Vik mutters as she prepares to fight them.

Rushing forward, I engage the first magic user. We square off, throwing punches and kicks as we dance around each other. I'm surprised she's not using magic against me.

Meanwhile, Vik uses her agility and combat skills to fend off another magic user, her movements fluid and graceful. But she's careful not to use her compulsion ability just yet. I know she wanted to give them a chance to listen to her. But every time she tries to talk, he keeps attacking.

As I continue to fight fiercely with the magic user, I see an opening. With a well-timed kick, I send the magic user sprawling to the ground. Her head snaps toward mine with anger flaring in her eyes.

Before I can make another move, she raises her hands, and my surroundings blur. The warehouse fades away, and I find myself in the dimly lit room Axel kept me in when he kidnapped me.

The memory before her unfolds like a nightmare. Axel stands there with a sinister grin on his face. He taunts me with cruel words, his voice echoing in my mind as he unleashes a barrage of punches and kicks upon me. The pain is excruciating. My hands tremble as I try to break free, but I can't move. The pain feels too real, too vivid, and I scream in agony. But as the memory seems endless, Vik's voice penetrates the darkness.

"Enough," Vik speaks, her voice carrying an irresistible aura. "Surrender and submit."

The memory slowly fades, and I find myself back in the warehouse, on the cold, hard floor, breathing heavily and disoriented. I look up to see Vik standing beside me, her eyes blazing with anger.

"Liv, are you alright?" Vik asks with concern.

"I'm fine," I say as she helps me up.

I look around the warehouse. The magic user's eyes glaze over as they await Vik's next command. Vik takes out her phone and calls one of the Over Lords to teleport us back to Orchard Landing. We arrive back just as Dani and Lucy return, and we deliver the newcomers to the Over Lords.

The missions took us all night, and we were tired. Unfortunately, this also impeded our plan to rescue our people from Sutton Engineering, and we'll have to get there in the morning before Axel arrives.

THE SECRET MISSION

Morning arrives quicker than I'd like, and we're standing in the living room checking our gear before we head out to rescue our people from Axel. The living room is a controlled chaos of weapons, gear, and tension.

We're gathered around, each of us meticulously inspecting our arsenal for the upcoming mission. Vik has her eyes on a dainty dagger, Dani is checking her Sai with a critical eye, and I'm double-checking the clasps on my leather armor.

"Remember, ladies," I said with a wry grin. They told me I could take the lead on this mission since I found where Axel was hiding our people. "We're not here to throw a magical carnival. Subtlety is the name of the game."

Dani looks up from her daggers, a mischievous glint in her eyes. "Well, that's disappointing. I was really hoping for some fireworks and confetti. You know, if this whole magic thing doesn't work out, I can make a killing at a circus."

I shoot her a sideways glance. "Focus, Dani. We're going

in to rescue, not to audition for 'Knife Jugglers Anonymous.'"

"Hey, if it comes to it, I can dazzle them with a light show they won't forget," Lucy says, cracking a joke to lighten up the atmosphere with a floating orb of light.

I smile, playing along with the lightheartedness. "Right, because blinding them with a disco ball is definitely going for the 'quiet and stealthy' approach."

Vik chimes in with a smirk. "Yeah, and maybe a parade while we're at it." She smiles at me. "Don't worry, I've got their minds on lockdown. If anyone gets curious, I'll whisper 'nap time'."

I grin as the tension momentarily eases. "That's the spirit, Vik. Nothing says 'rescue mission' like a bunch of grown men suddenly needing a group nap."

A small chuckle escapes Lucy's mouth as she rolls her eyes. Leave it to my new partners in crime to inject humor into the most serious situations.

"Okay, okay," I say, trying to steer us back on track. "Let's make sure we have everything we need for a quiet, efficient rescue mission."

Dani flicks her wrist before sending a dagger spinning through the air and catching it effortlessly. "Don't worry, Liv. I've got enough pointy things to handle anything that comes our way."

Vik swings and twists her dagger with expert precision. "And I've got the moves they won't see coming."

I rub a hand down my face. "You guys are so lame. I guess that makes me your conscious, the one who will keep you focused and not cause a scene."

As we make our final gear checks, I think of all the challenges we may encounter. However, I hope we can do this without causing more trouble because the Over Lords will be pissed if they find out.

"Alright, ladies," I say. "Let's remember our goal. We're here to rescue our people from Axel's clutches. We go in, do what needs to be done, and get out. No unnecessary theatrics."

Dani salutes dramatically with a smirk on her face. "Loud and clear, old lady who never likes to have fun."

"Quiet and efficient it is," Vik adds with faux seriousness.

"Right," Lucy agrees as she puts her knives away. "Stealth mode engaged."

Vik can't resist a parting shot as we head for the door. "Remember, quiet as a mouse. Got it, Dani?"

Dani grins back at her. "Absolutely. Just as quiet as the time you tried to sneak into the kitchen for a midnight snack and knocked over the entire box of cereal."

Vik mock-glared at Dani. "Hey, that was one time!"

"Okay then, if you don't want me bringing it up, stop repeating about being quiet, as if I'm always the one causing drama," Dani replies.

We share a laugh and the tension easing once more. As we step out into the morning, determined to rescue our people and face whatever Axel had in store for us, I know that no matter what, we'd face it with a healthy dose of attitude and a whole lot of magic.

It's early morning, and the streets are relatively quiet, which works for us. We need to get in and get out with no one seeing us. We approach Sutton Engineering, and with a last shared glance, we slip through the entrance and into the building.

The air is musty and heavy, and our footsteps are muffled on the carpeted floor as we move deeper inside. We descend a flight of stairs into the dimly lit basement with our senses on high alert.

As we reach the bottom of the stairs, the sight before us sends a surge of anger through me. Our people, some in cages, others tied up or bound to chairs, are scattered across the room. Fear and exhaustion cover their faces, but their eyes light up when they see us. Clearly, they know we're not a threat.

Dani's fingers tighten around her knife as her eyes lock on the guards in the room. I hold up a hand, signaling for her to wait. We need to approach this carefully, and taking out the guards one by one will be our best chance. Unfortunately, Dani's temper gets the best of her.

I see the intent in her eyes before she even moves, but faster than I can stop her, she launches a knife into the chest of one guard. I watch in shock as he jolts back and falls to the ground.

The room erupts in chaos as Dani, Vik, and Lucy square off against the remaining guards, their movements calculated and precise. Dani lunges first, her agility and combat skills on full display as she weaves through the guards' attacks. Her knives flash in the dim light as she disarms one guard with a swift, fluid motion, the blade clattering to the ground.

Vik's eyes narrow as she focuses on the guard nearest to her. Her compulsion ability comes into play as she subtly whispers and manipulates his movements, causing him to stumble and lose his balance. It's a momentary distraction, but it's all Lucy needs.

Lucy waves a hand and summons an energy barrier to shield herself from the sharp shards of glass soaring her way. With a swift motion, she sends the fragments back at the guard, the force of his own attack knocking him off his feet.

Meanwhile, I focus on our captured people, working to free them from their bonds. My fingers deftly manipulate the knots as I try to untie them. As one of our people's hands finally comes free, she jumps up and tries to run out of the basement.

"Stop!" I yell, trying to catch her before she gets too far.

Luckily, Lucy appears in front of her and knocks her out. "I've got you, Liv. She'll wait right here for you."

She disappears back into the fight again. The room is a whirlwind of movement and energy. Dani's knives find their marks with deadly precision, Vik's compulsion powers keep the guards off balance, and Lucy's barriers shield us from incoming attacks.

Dani incapacitates another guard with one strike, leaving just one remaining. Vik's voice flows through the air, and the guard's movements slow, his eyes growing distant. She forces the guard to his knees, rendering him defenseless. Lucy's knives hover menacingly overhead, ready to strike if he dared to resist.

"Give it up," Dani's voice is low and commanding, her knives glinting in the dim light. "It's over."

The guard's shoulders slump as defeat comes across his face. Sighing, he raises his hands in surrender before lying flat on the ground.

With the guards subdued, the tension in the room eases. We share a collective breath and the weight of the fight lifts as our people gather around us, their faces a mix of relief and gratitude.

"Nice work," Dani says with a grin. "You're a natural leader, Liv."

I roll my eyes at that. "Sure, like you guys listened to me."

Vik's lips curve into a satisfied smile. "Not bad for a quiet and stealthy rescue, huh?"

"Maybe next time we can bring a disco ball for some ambiance," Lucy says as she tosses an orb of light for flare.

"You guys clearly don't know the meaning of quiet or stealthy," I deadpan, happy that things didn't escalate farther than they did.

"Alright," I say to the group. "We need to get out of here quietly and quickly."

"What about Axel?" Dani asks.

I meet her gaze with a slight shrug. "We'll deal with Axel later. Right now, our priority is getting everyone to safety."

"Not so fast, Olive," Nash says from behind us.

I turn around to see Axel, Steele, Nash, and a large group of his goons standing right behind us, blocking the exit.

Vik turns toward Dani with a serious look. "Now is not the time. We have people to protect. We need to get them out of here. Open a portal now."

We're standing there for a minute, waiting for Dani to open a portal or teleport us back to Orchard Landing.

When nothing happens, I send an impatient look her way. "Dani, let's go!"

Her worried eyes turn toward us. "What do you think I've been doing? For some reason, I can't!"

"I can't either," Lucy says suddenly, and I get an awful feeling.

"I've been told everything about you and your people," Axel says with a smirk. "I never know what Olivia will see, so I have taken extra precautions since you stole Olivia from me. You won't be getting out of here. Not alive, at least. Well, except for Olivia, we need her."

"How are you doing this?" Dani asks with irritation clear in her voice. "How did you manage to beat the Over Lords?"

Axel tsks at her. "That's my secret. I have more power behind me than you know. The real question is, what am I going to do with you?"

Lucy laughs, long and loud. "Dude, you need to work on your bad boy vibe. We're not scared of you. The real question is, when we get out, will you be alive or not?"

Suddenly, Dani's knives slice through the air, finding their marks with deadly accuracy as she fends off the random guards that just attacked.

Lucy's magical energy swirls around her, creating a protective barrier that deflects incoming magical attacks. She moves gracefully, her every motion a dance of light and magic as she shields our people from harm.

Vik moves around using her compulsion once again as she subtly manipulates the guards' movements, sowing confusion and discord among their ranks. I'm glad to see her using it willingly, so maybe this unexpected altercation can be over quickly.

I hold my ground at the center of the chaos, and my focus is regrouping our people and defending them against the assholes attacking us. My fists are a blur as I deliver powerful punches, each strike calculated to disarm and incapacitate.

Amidst the flurry of action, we pushed our way to the basement's entrance. Lucy sends a powerful energy ball and blasts an enormous hole where the door used to be. We run outside, intending to teleport or portal back to Orchard Landing, but we're met with an onslaught of Axel's goons.

Now, we're fighting in the middle of the city, where people can see this fierce magical battle for dominance, and that isn't good.

With a fierce snarl, Dani conjures fire, flames dancing along her fingertips before erupting into a searing blaze. She hurls a fireball towards the first magic user, the intense heat causing the air to shimmer and distort. The impact sends the magic user stumbling back, with their magical defenses faltering.

Unfortunately, his was no one-on-one duel. Two more magic users close in from either side, their attacks converging on Dani. She vanishes away and reappears behind them. Her Sai glints in the sunlight as she strikes with blinding speed, disarming one opponent while a surge of energy courses through her fist, delivering a devastating punch to the other. She stabs him through the heart, giving the final blow.

As she turns to face her next adversary, the ground beneath her rumbles as the elements conjured by the magic users surge forward. Streams of water and jagged rocks arc toward her, and with a fluid motion, Dani summons her own elemental powers, a vortex of fire swirling around her, colliding with the water and evaporating it instantly.

In her determination, Dani miscalculates the sheer force of her elemental counterattack. A wave of intense heat collides with the nearby storefronts, their structures groaning under the strain before finally giving way. Bricks and debris cascade to the ground in a thunderous crash, leaving behind a scene of chaotic ruin.

I can see the debris stretching down the road. I don't know how many buildings she just leveled, but thankfully, the fighting moves us closer to the smaller buildings in the city, not the skyscrapers. People will surely notice if she knocks down skyscrapers.

Dani's eyes widened as she realizes the unintended consequences of her actions. The surrounding battle momentarily freezes, magic users and our team momentarily pause to assess the damage.

"Seriously, Dani!" I yell in frustration because this is getting way out of hand. "I don't even know how many city blocks you just leveled, but please contain your damn chaos!"

Dani's voice is apologetic and coated with regret. "My bad, guys. Note to self: control the fire vortex near fragile structures. Got it!."

Without missing a beat, she redirects her focus to the ongoing battle, her energy blasts slamming into the remaining magic users. The sheer force of her attacks has them sprawling, their magical defenses crumbling under the relentless assault.

Lucy's eyes glint with determination, and with a focused gesture, she sends parked cars hurtling toward her enemies, creating a barrier that temporarily halts their advance.

As the magic users counter her attack, sending gusts of wind and waves of energy in her direction, Lucy's teleportation abilities come into play. She disappears in a flash of light and reappears several meters away, her movements fluid and graceful. She evades their attacks, her instincts guiding her as she weaves through the chaotic onslaught.

Drawing a set of throwing knives from her belt, Lucy's fingers move expertly over the blades. With a swift, precise motion, she launches the knives toward her opponents, each strike finding its mark with deadly accuracy. The magic users stumble back, their magical defenses faltering under her relentless assault.

As the remaining magic users close in, she abandons her knives and engages in close-quarters combat. Her movements are a blur of strength and agility, each punch and kick a calculated strike against her opponents.

The cityscape bore witness to their battle, the impact of Lucy's telekinesis, and the crackling energy of her enemy's magic sending shockwaves through the environment. Small cracks appear on the pavement, and debris flies through the air as their powers clash in a symphony of chaos.

With a last surge of power, Lucy summons a vortex of energy, sweeping the magic users off their feet and disarming them in one sweeping motion. The magic users stumble and fall, and their magical abilities halt as Lucy's combined strength and skill prove too much to overcome.

Suddenly, tendrils of shadows that lash out like whips flow down the street toward us. Goosebumps break out across my skin as it sneaks toward us. The same shadows that covered the Over Lords, and I wonder how Axel is doing all of this.

"Give up now, Olivia, and we'll let your friends live," Axel calls out.

"Hey, Lucy?" I call out. "You remember that move we practiced during our sparring lesson?"

Her eyes light up in delight, and she nods her head. She waves her arm and sends me soaring toward Axel with blinding speed. Faster than he can react, I raise my fist and slam it into his face. My momentum knocks him several feet back. In the distance, I hear Lucy, Dani, and Vik yelling for our people to run. They make it to me and Axel just as he's picking himself up off the ground. Dani quickly slaps energy cuffs on Axel.

As Axel struggles against his restraints, I step forward, my gaze unwavering. "It's over, Axel."

His laughter is a bitter echo as he glares at us. "You may have won this round, but you have no idea what's coming."

Lucy's energy encases Axel in a shimmering barrier, ensuring he can't escape. "Save your threats. We've faced worse than you."

She lifts him into the air, and he follows behind us as we run away from the mysterious shadows slinking toward us.

Lucy groans as we continue to run. "Well, Dani, you've really done it this time. There's no way the Over Lords won't know what happened here."

Vik sighs heavily and scrubs a hand down her face. "I knew this was a bad idea. I told you this was a bad idea!"

Dani rolls her eyes and a sheepish grin tugging at her lips. "Alright, alright. Next time, I'll aim the fireballs away from anything breakable."

"If there's a next time," Lucy says. "They're going to kill us for sure this time."

My eyes widen in shock. "This time? Do you make it a habit of starting magical fights in the middle of busy city streets?"

"No, but we've had our share of bad ideas that's gotten us in trouble a time or two," Vik shrugs.

Once we're far enough away, Dani is able to open a portal back to Orchard Landing.

With Axel securely contained, we walk through, where Jade meets us with a look in her eyes. It's a look that has fear trailing down my spine. Then she regards Axel with a steely gaze, her presence commanding and unwavering.

"Jade," Dani said, her voice firm. "He's all yours."

Jade nods, her grip on Axel unyielding. "Thank you,

girls. We'll make sure he faces justice for his crimes. However, I am truly sorry for you."

I don't like the tone in her voice, and as she leaves, my eyes follow her just to come face to face with the Over Lords themselves, and they look beyond pissed. They grab each of us, turning us this way and that to ensure we're alright.

I can see how much they care for them, and now I'm included, too. It's touching and brings a tear to my eyes. I've never had this kind of love or care from my own mother. Unfortunately, that feeling vanishes as soon as the yelling starts.

CHAPTER 23

PUNISHED BY ASSOCIATION

"What the fuck were you thinking?" Over Lord Mary shouts.

Vik runs a hand down her face before looking at Dani. "I knew this would happen. Didn't I tell you we should wait? We're about to get our asses reamed because of Dani's anger issues. If we get put on extra duty again, you owe me a lifetime supply of cookies. Oh, and ice cream."

"Mom, I can explain," Dani starts, then pauses.

"Well? Go on, tell me what you were thinking." Over Lord Mary says.

"Olivia—" Dani begins, but her mother interrupts her.

"Don't go blaming this on Olivia," Over Lord Mary snaps. "You weren't thinking. You leveled ten city blocks! Do you know how much power we'll have to use to undo everything you just did?"

"I'm—" Dani starts again but doesn't finish.

"You don't know! Especially after waking up from such a blow, we're not back to normal yet, Danielle," Over Lord

Mary continues as power laces her voice. "Danielle Eshar, Lucille Carsewell, Viktoria Graham, and Olivia Iverson."

"Oh no, she used our full names," Lucy sighs heavily. "Nothing good comes when she does that."

"Whoa, wait a minute, why am I included in this punishment? I didn't do anything." I exclaim loudly, feeling Over Lord Mary's power over me when she says my name.

"You're guilty by association," Over Lord Stephanie informs me with a raised eyebrow.

Vik hooks an arm over my shoulders. "Yup, we're the all-for-one and one-for-all type of girl group. It's equal opportunity punishment for us. Unfortunately, you and I are the only ones in this girl group who can't resist Over Lord Mary's calling."

My brows scrunch in confusion. "Calling? What the hell is that?"

"Fun fact, Liv." Vik starts. "Over Lord Mary can command the entire Mutane Sihiri race. We call that ability the calling. At least those with active abilities. Once they discover their abilities, they're puppets, just like the rest of us."

Dani shoves Vik's shoulder. "We're not puppets. She rarely even uses it."

"And it doesn't work on Dani and Lucy?" I reply, wondering just how powerful the Over Lords really are.

Over Lord Mary narrows her eyes. "Correct, but if Danielle and Lucille know what's good for them, they better heed the calling." Then she says three words. "Tier 1 duty."

I look around in confusion as Dani, Lucy, and Vik groan in unison. I don't know what Tier 1 duty is, but it must be bad if they're reacting like that.

"Specifically, lower Tier 1's," Over Lord Mary clarifies with a smile.

"Mom, please don't make us do that. It's cruel!" Dani whines.

"Can someone please tell me what she's talking about?" I ask, fearing the worst.

"You and I grew up with the humans, Liv," Vik answers. "At the institute, Tier 1's are basically elementary school kids. The lower Tier 1's are kindergarteners and first graders."

I tilt my head, still confused. "Okay, what's so bad about that?"

"These are magic users, Liv," Dani says. "Specifically little shits who can't control their abilities and get into all kinds of shit because these are five-and-six-year-olds."

Lucy sees my confused look change to dread. "Exactly. Imagine overseeing screaming, crying, little germ buckets with magic. It's going to be hell."

"How long must we endure this punishment?" Dani asks with a defeated sigh.

"Since you leveled ten city blocks, your duty is ten days," Over Lord Miranda replies.

"Do we get some time off our sentence if we've captured Axel?" Dani asks with all the sweetest smile she can muster.

"No, but thanks for letting us know," Over Lord Miranda answers. "I assume Jade took him?"

We nod our heads. "Good, we'll deal with him as soon as we get back from cleaning up your mess," she says before they disappear from the room.

Everyone is in a solemn mood as we head home. As we were getting ready for bed, Over Lord Mary telepathically informs Dani that we're starting our Tier 1 duty tomorrow.

I've been around kids growing up, and there's no way it's as bad as they're making it seem. The silver lining through all this is at least we rescued our people.

Today can not get any worse. Dani was right when she told me about these little terrors. I've had to deal with two five-year-olds today, one with the ability to influence water and the other influences fire. Neither can control their ability, and it was not fun.

I sigh as I look around the room, my gaze settling on the Tier 1 student assigned to me for help. A five-year-old with a phasing ability that seems to have a mind of its own. Just my luck.

"Alright, kiddo, let's try this again," I say with forced enthusiasm while bending down to Emily's eye level. "We're just going to make a simple paper flower. Remember, focus on keeping yourself solid."

She nods eagerly, her eyes wide with determination. I hand her a piece of construction paper and safety scissors, hoping today's arts and crafts session won't end in a disaster.

She grasps the paper and scissors with a determined frown, and her brow furrows in concentration. As she tries to cut out a petal shape, her hand passes through the paper, leaving a jagged, hole-ridden mess in its wake.

"Uh, that's okay," I mumble, trying to hide my frustration. "Let's, uh, try gluing the pieces together instead."

She nods again with her face, a picture of pure innocence. I hand her a bottle of glue and watch with bated breath as she squeezes the bottle, sending a glob of glue flying through the air and onto her hair.

"Whoa, whoa!" I shout, rushing to her side and carefully wiping the glue from her hair. "Okay, maybe a little less force on the glue-squeezing next time."

Her giggles are infectious, and I can't help but smile despite my exasperation. This is becoming more of a comedy routine than an arts and crafts lesson.

With a deep breath, I guide her hand to the glue bottle, helping her apply a reasonable amount to the paper. She presses the pieces together, and miraculously, they stick.

"Great job!" I cheer, genuinely proud of her progress. "Now, let's add a stem."

I hand her a strip of green paper and watch as she attempts to fold and shape it. This time, her phasing ability seems to cooperate, and the paper remains solid in her hands. It's a minor victory, but I'd take it.

I watch from across the room as Lucy settles in for what should have been a simple reading session with a Tier 1 student named Jasper. The five-year-old boy with the uncanny ability to traverse reflective surfaces and manipulate reflections is proving to be quite the handful.

Lucy's expression is a mix of exasperation and determination as she holds up a colorful picture book. "Alright, Jasper, let's dive into the magical world of The Dancing Elephant."

Jasper's eyes sparkle with curiosity as he fidgets in his seat, his tiny fingers drumming against the table. But before Lucy can even start reading, a mischievous grin spreads across the boy's face.

In a blink, Jasper disappears from his seat, leaving a trail of giggles echoing through the room as he pops up in front of a mirror on the opposite wall.

"Jasper!" Lucy yells, her voice expressing irritation and amusement as she marches to the mirror. "We're supposed to be reading, remember?"

Jasper's reflection in the mirror mimics Lucy's stern expression, and he sticks his tongue out before vanishing again, only to reappear in a shiny ceramic vase by the window.

Lucy's sigh is audible as she hurries over to the vase. "Really? A vase? Come on, Jasper."

But Jasper seems to be on a mission, determined to explore every reflective surface in the room. He darts from mirror to window to a shiny metallic lamp, leaving Lucy to follow in his wake, the picture book forgotten in her hand.

"Okay, kid," Lucy mutters as she snatches Jasper from his latest escapade. "You're quick, I'll give you that."

Jasper's laughter fills the air, his infectious joy a stark contrast to Lucy's growing frustration. She settles him back at the reading table, her expression a mix of irritation and begrudging amusement.

"Let's try this again," Lucy says with a mixture of sternness and resignation. "We're going to read this book, and you're going to stay right here."

Jasper pouts, his bottom lip jutting out exaggeratedly, but Lucy is having none of it, as her patience is clearly wearing thin.

As Lucy finally starts reading the story, Jasper's attention wavers. He glances toward a nearby mirror with his eyes gleaming mischievously.

Lucy's eyes narrow, and without missing a beat, she shoots out her hand, summoning a gentle telekinetic pull that keeps Jasper in his seat, preventing his reflection-hopping antics.

"Hey!" Jasper protests, his attempts thwarted as he remains firmly in place.

Lucy's lips curve into a triumphant smirk. "Sorry, kid. You might be able to travel through reflections, but I've got a few tricks up my sleeve, too."

I watch as Dani, with an expression of a mix of patience

and agitation, sits in the play area with little Peter. Peter is a five-year-old boy with an extraordinary ability to control the structure of matter at the molecular level. In theory, it's incredible. In practice, it's often turned playtime into a chaotic experiment.

Dani's brows furrow as she watches Peter's little hands wave in the air, causing the toy blocks in front of him to shimmer and transform into colorful gummy bears. His delighted giggle fills the room, but Dani's audible sigh hints at her frustration.

"Peter, buddy, I know turning blocks into candy sounds fun, but maybe we can build something with the blocks instead?" Dani's tone is patient, though her eyes roll heavenward as the gummy bears bounce on the table.

Peter's innocent blue eyes meet Dani's, and he nods enthusiastically. "Okay, Ms. Dani!"

With a wry smile, Dani takes charge, showing him how to stack the blocks to build a tower. But, as fate would have it, Peter's excitement got the better of him, and a sudden flash saw the tower turning into a miniature Eiffel Tower.

Dani's muttered "Oh, for the love of…" is barely audible, but I hear it.

Not one to back down, Dani presses on, demonstrating again. This time, with meticulous care, they construct a tiny house. Peter claps his hands, thrilled with their creation. But, in a fit of contagious laughter, the house sprouts wings and flies across the room. Dani's face switches between amusement and disbelief.

"Peter, we're building a house, not inventing flying real estate," Dani mutters under her breath, but her lips curl into an affectionate grin.

Their third attempt is successful, and they managed to build a small castle made entirely of toy blocks. Dani's grin widens as Peter applauds their accomplishment and his face glowing with pride.

But then came the inevitable twist. Peter leans in close, whispering to the castle, and it emits a soft glow. Before we know it, the castle transforms into a life-sized, glowing replica of... Cinderella's Pumpkin Carriage.

Dani's jaw practically drops to the floor, and she mutters a string of curses that even I hadn't heard before. But she doesn't give up. Oh no, Dani has tricks up her sleeve. She waves her hands with a flourish, and the carriage shimmers, shrinking back into a regular toy castle. Peter's eyes widen in amazement, and his laughter echoes through the room.

"See, buddy? A castle can be just as cool as a pumpkin carriage," Dani says, with a blend of exhaustion and triumph.

I watch with a mixture of amusement and fondness as Vik sits down with Samantha, a five-year-old Tier 1 student with a unique animal telepathy ability. Samantha's wide eyes fixate on Vik, her small hands clutching a pencil while she attempts to form the letters of the alphabet on a piece of paper.

"Okay, Samantha," Vik says with a twinkle in her eyes and a voice that's patient and kind. "Let's start with the letter 'A.' Can you draw me a nice big 'A'?"

Samantha's brow scrunch in concentration, and she obediently draws the letter, but just as she finishes, a small bluebird lands on the windowsill, its feathers fluffed up in curiosity. Before anyone can react, Samantha's gaze locks onto the bird, and she reaches out her hand toward it. The bird hops closer, its tiny head tilting as if considering the invitation.

With a start, Vik leans forward, her voice a quiet

command. "Samantha, sweetie, let's finish drawing the 'A' first."

Samantha's hand freezes mid-air, and her eyes refocus on the paper. She blinks a few times, then looks down at the half-formed letter. With a sheepish grin, she quickly finishes the shape, the bird on the windowsill forgotten.

"That's perfect!" Vik praises in a warm tone. "Now, let's move on to the letter 'B,' okay?"

As Samantha dutifully starts on the next letter, a mischievous squirrel scampers along the windowsill, its little paws tapping against the glass. Samantha's attention wavers once again with her hand reaching out towards the window.

I stifle a laugh as Vik's eyes sparkle, and she clears her throat. "Samantha, sweetheart, let's focus on our writing, shall we?"

With a small huff of disappointment, Samantha turns her attention back to the paper. The squirrel chatters at the window for a moment before scampering away, apparently uninterested in competing for Samantha's attention any longer.

Vik leans in closer with a soft, firm voice. "You're doing such a great job, Samantha. Keep writing those letters."

Samantha nods and smiles widely at the praise. Her pencil moves across the paper, forming the letters with more confidence now. I watch as Vik's compulsion gently guides Samantha's focus, allowing her to concentrate on her task without being sidetracked by the animal visitors. By the time they finish with the letter 'Z,' Samantha is beaming with pride.

She looks up at Vik, her eyes shining. "I did it!"

"Yes, you did!" Vik's smile is genuine as she pats

Samantha's head affectionately. "You wrote all the letters beautifully."

Thankfully, the bell rings shortly after, and school is now over. We clean up the classroom before locking the door and heading home. I can tell we're all tired and frustrated from dealing with a bunch of five-year-olds today.

"I don't think I can take another week of that," Dani says as soon as we walk through the door.

"I wanted to compel them to nap the whole time," Vik adds as we sit on the couch. "Do you think the parents, or the Over Lords, would notice if I did that?"

I laugh a little. "I'm sure that would only prolong our suffering if they found out. You were already doing that with Samantha. Don't get caught, Vik," I stand from the couch. "I'm going to shower."

As I take a step, that familiar sensation happens, and a vision assaults my mind. The world around me blurs and twists as the vision washes over me, pulling me into a realm of shadows and whispers. I stand on the precipice of a dark abyss, my senses tingling with foreboding as I watch the scene unfold before me.

Axel stands in a dimly lit chamber, his silhouette shrouded by darkness. The air is thick with tension, and his presence seems almost diminished in the face of the ominous figures surrounding him. Something obscures their forms, their features concealed by the very shadows that writhe and twist around them.

Axel is in the same attire from the day they rescued me from his office, right before Dani blew him out the window. So, this happened already. I'm seeing something from the past.

"You have failed us," a voice hissed, dripping with malice. "The chaos you caused in your pursuit of those girls has drawn unwanted attention. The Dark Council is not to be toyed with."

Axel's shoulders tense, and his stance is defensive. "The Veil Society is formidable. I could have eliminated them if I wanted to."

The shadows move to constrict around him, their grip tightening as if to emphasize their displeasure. "Your arrogance blinds you, Axel. You underestimate their strength and the forces that protect them. Your Veil Society only exists because we allow it."

Suddenly, Axel lifts off the ground, his agonizing screams filling the chamber. My heart clenches as I watch, my breath catching in my throat. The figures channel some dark energy, their intentions malicious and unforgiving. Axel's cries echo as his form contorts in pain as whatever they're doing to him takes its toll.

"Consider this a warning," the voice hissed, the words laced with a chilling finality. "One more misstep, one more failure, and you will meet a fate far worse than you can imagine."

Axel's screams gradually fade, and a heavy silence coats the air. The shadows recede, retreating like a tide drawing away from the shore. As the darkness subsides, I find myself back in the living room with my breath in ragged gasps.

The weight of the vision lingers, the words of the shadowy figures echoing in my mind. Axel's involvement with the Veil Society is just the tip of the iceberg. There is a greater, more dangerous force at play, one that wields power beyond what we initially expected. Dread settles in the pit of my stomach. This is not good.

"We need to get to the Over Lords, right now," I tell the girls.

"What did you see, Liv?" Dani asks as she looks at me with concern.

"Axel is working with some people. I couldn't see their faces, but it's not good," I tell her.

She shrugs like it's no big deal. "We've got Axel. Aunt Ashley will interrogate him, and we'll end him and his little gang of misfits. Easy peasy."

"Axel is the least of our worries, Dani," I reply, eager to get to the Over Lords. "Whoever this group of people is, they are more powerful than we think. I have a terrible feeling about this."

"Are you telling me that this group of mysterious people can possibly take out my mom and aunts?" Dani asks, skeptical of what I just told them.

I nod, and quicker than I can blink, Dani teleports me to the main house to inform the Over Lords that they may not survive this coming fight with the Veil Society or whatever this Dark Council is supposed to be.

CHAPTER 24

JUST A LITTLE TORTURE

Dani and I teleport to the living room in the main house. The familiar scent of lilac and lemon surrounds us, and I roll my eyes at the sight that greets us. The Over Lords are lounging on the old couches, each holding a glass of wine, apparently relishing a moment of peace. Clearly, they were not expecting guests.

Over Lord Sydney arches an eyebrow at us. "Oh, joy. More interruptions. Just what we need. This had better be good because we're tired from cleaning up your shit in the city today."

I exchange a wry glance with Dani, fully aware that our timing isn't ideal. "Sorry to interrupt, but I wouldn't be here if it wasn't important, Over Lord Sydney. Trust me, I'd rather be in bed right now. Especially after the day I've had with the Tier 1's."

Over Lord Ashley smirks a little. "Oh, don't worry, Olivia. We were discussing world domination and how to redecorate the living room with more skulls. You know, the usual."

I stifle a chuckle before crossing my arms. "Well, I hate

to break up the party, but we've got a little situation on our hands."

"And what might that be, Olivia?" Over Lord Stephanie says as she puts her wineglass down and leans forward.

I took a deep breath, steeling myself. "I had a vision. Axel is not calling all the shots. There's a group called the Dark Council pulling the strings. They're the ones really in control."

Over Lord Annie raises an eyebrow. "The Dark Council?"

I nod. "Yeah. From the looks of it, they're powerful, and they're not to be trifled with. They've got Axel on a tight leash, and they're not happy with how he's managing things."

Over Lord Mary leans back, swirling her wine. "So, what? We're supposed to be shaking in our boots over these Dark Council assholes?"

I shrug, not knowing what to say. "Well, they do have an affinity for ominous names. It's kind of their thing."

Over Lord Miranda lets out a chuckle. "Right, because nothing strikes fear into the hearts of enemies like 'Dark Council.' But seriously, Olivia, how big of a threat are we talking about here?"

I sigh as my tone grows more serious. "I don't have all the details, but if they're reining in the Veil Society and Axel, they've got to have some serious power. Maybe they can cause some serious damage, even to you guys."

Over Lord Ashley laughs loud. "Us? Olivia, you forget who you're talking to. We've faced our fair share of challenges. A so-called 'Dark Council' doesn't intimidate us."

Over Lord Mary's lips lift into a smirk. "Yeah, last time I checked, we're the ones who kick demon ass before breakfast."

"I know you're all a force to be reckoned with, but we can't underestimate them. Especially after what happened when Axel attacked Orchard Landing. We need to gather more information and come up with a plan."

Over Lord Ashley hops up from the couch with a twinkle in her eyes. "Sounds like it's time for torture."

She snaps her fingers, and Torri and Jade pop into the room. They're in their pajamas and looking around in confusion.

"It's time to inflict some pain, guys," Over Lord Ashley tells them. "Jade, get the torture devices. Torri, bring your ugly face." She starts to walk away. "I'll meet you there. I have to change my clothes because I can't torture someone in pajamas. That's just crazy!"

Over Lord Ashley mumbles about whether to wear her battle gear or go with a grim weeper look for her torture session. I look toward the other Over Lords, wondering how they put up with Over Lord Ashley's craziness because I'm seriously concerned for her mental state. Everyone shakes their head at her retreating form, and suddenly, we're all standing in what I assume to be a dungeon.

I elbow Dani subtly. "You guys actually have a dungeon! This is cool, but in a scary medieval kind of way."

"Wait until you see the torture devices," she replies with a grin. "That's totally medieval."

I watch in amazement as Jade and Torri walk to a stone wall and push it open before entering the hidden room. My eyes widen when they walk out with so many torture devices, I feel like I'm in a horror movie. The atmosphere in the dungeon is thick with tension. The air practically vibrates with the anticipation of what is about to unfold.

As if on cue, the door slams open with a dramatic flair that can only belong to one person: Over Lord Ashley.

Dressed like the Grim Weeper, she exudes an aura that's both ominous and theatrical. White smoke billows around her, creating an ethereal curtain that shimmers with other-worldly energy.

The other Over Lords exchange weary glances as Over Lord Ashley saunters in, her form glowing with an eerie light that casts long shadows across the stone walls. She emits a low, haunting hum with every step, like an unearthly melody accompanying her approach.

With a look of bewilderment, I elbow Dani, "Um, why is she humming like that?"

"It's supposed to sound scary," Dani says as she tries not to laugh.

Over Lord Stephanie rolls her eyes, but a hint of amusement tugs at the corner of her lips. "Oh, great, it's the Queen of the Psychos. You'd better not have a bunch of corpses trailing behind you."

"Oh, for the love of all things dramatic," mutters Over Lord Mary, her voice laced with exasperation. "I swear, if she starts twirling around and belting out a song, I will kill her."

Over Lord Sydney chuckles softly, her gaze fixed on the spectacle before them. "Well, at least she's consistent. Can't fault her for that."

Over Lord Ashley's humming echoes eerily through the chamber, creating an odd backdrop to her entrance. As she strolls forward, her steps slow and deliberate, the other Over Lords exchange amused glances, barely containing their amusement at her over-the-top theatrics.

"We really should have gotten her help a long time ago," Over Lord Annie whispers to Over Lord Miranda, who simply smirks in response.

With a flourish, Over Lord Ashley extends her arm, the

sleeves of her cloak billowing dramatically. "Fear me, Axel, the asshole, for I am the harbinger of—"

Over Lord Stephanie crosses her arms with an expression of a mixture of exasperation and irritation. "Ashley, do you have to turn everything into a production?"

Over Lord Ashley shoots Over Lord Stephanie a mock-offended look before breaking into a playful pout. "You all lack appreciation for true artistry. Can't a girl embrace her theatrical side before a round of torture? Is that too much to ask?"

Dani rolls her eyes. "Artistry? Please, Aunt Ashley, you're one brain cell short of being put away in the looney bin. Seriously, have you always been this way, or is all the magic interfering with your mental stability?"

"Theatrical is an understatement. I half expect her to break into interpretive dance any second now." Over Lord Mary adds.

With an exaggerated sigh, Over Lord Ashley strikes a pose, her hand resting dramatically against her forehead. "Alas, my interpretive dance days are on hiatus. But fear not, for I bring you a performance of doom and gory torture! Where the hell is Axel?"

"Performance of doom and gory torture? Seriously?" Over Lord Stephanie says with a small laugh.

Over Lord Ashley pouts before, her glowing intensifies to emphasize her dramatics. "Yeah. Doom and gory torture for Axel. This torture will not be pleasant for him. You all lack appreciation for the finer points of theatrics."

"No, we lack the patience for your damn dramatic flair." Over Lord Miranda says as she shakes her head, her lips quirking into a grin.

"Seriously, can we not just get on with this?" Over Lord Annie chimes in with a roll of her eyes.

Over Lord Ashley's pout deepens, but she can't keep a straight face, and soon, her pout morphs into a mischievous grin. "Fine, fine. Ruin my moment."

As Over Lord Ashley's glowing aura fades and the white smoke dissipates, the room is in a slightly surreal silence, momentarily free from the tension that had been gripping the room.

"Now that we've had our nightly dose of Ashley's crazy, let's proceed." Over Lord Miranda finally says.

Over Lord Ashley sighs, but then quickly composes herself. "Alright, alright. Let's get down to business."

Axel appears in the room restrained and battered but stares at us defiantly. He must have put up a fight when he got here. The Over Lords encircle him, their expressions ranging from icy determination to smirking confidence.

Torri stands poised like a sentinel while Jade crackles with electric energy, her power a visible reminder of what awaits Axel should he refuse to cooperate. Dani and I watch from the side with our gazes locked on the interrogation unfolding before us.

Over Lord Ashley leans in close with an inquiring expression. "So, Axel, care to share your summer plans? Or are we just going to guess?"

Axel's lip curls in a half-hearted smirk, his gaze unwavering. "Not really. I've always been a fan of surprises."

Over Lord Mary's eyes flash with impatience. "We're not here to play games, Axel. We know you're not the mastermind behind all of this. Tell us about the Dark Council."

"I hear they're more powerful than you and your merry band of idiots. That they call the shots. Apparently, they are as powerful as us. Do you think we're scared of them?" Over

Lord Annie says. Her voice is crisp as her words cut through the air.

Axel's chuckle is strained, but there's a flicker of arrogance in his eyes. "They are, and fear is a powerful motivator. I'd give up, Olivia, if I were you."

Over Lord Sydney steps forward, her expression steelier than ever. "We're not afraid, Axel. We want information."

"Tell us about their plans. What is this pair of powers nonsense, and what do they want with it?" Over Lord Stephanie says.

Axel's defiance doesn't waver. "You think I'm going to break just because you threaten me?"

Over Lord Ashley's snarky grin widens. "Oh, honey, you've got us all wrong. We're not threatening you. We're just giving you... options."

A flicker of doubt crosses Axel's eyes, but his bravado quickly masks it. "I've faced worse than this."

"Worse than..." Over Lord Ashley says as a portal appears. She sticks her hand in and pulls out a clear case with mice. "This?"

"A glass box?" Axel says in confusion. "Is that an aquarium?"

"Not just a glass box, but the glass box," Over Lord Ashley answers.

When confusion still covers his face, she takes a seat on the floor in front of him, like she's talking to a child.

"Remember when you attacked the property as was like, 'I'm going to kick your ass,' as stuff?" She asks him. "I said you were going into the box?" She sighs in exasperation and points. "This is the box!"

When he still looks confused and doesn't answer, Over Lord Ashley gets up and stalks away. She mumbles about how he doesn't understand the significance of the box and can't wait to torture his soul for eternity because of it. However, she thinks she must first decorate the box to look scarier.

She proposes a few fingers and toes with an eyeball or two. Everyone in the room stares at her silently for a few minutes while she paces. We turn our attention back toward Axel when she finally calms down.

"Time's ticking, Axel." Over Lord Annie says as she cracks her knuckles, her patience wearing thin.

"Fuck you," he says as he spits at them. "Nothing you do will make me talk."

Suddenly, Axel screams in pain as Jade electrocutes him. Electricity covers his entire body as he convulses in the chair. When she finishes, sweat covers his body, and smoke seeps from his skin.

"Shall I continue, or are you ready to talk?" Jade asks him.

Axel's bravado wavers for a moment, but he quickly regains his composure. "Go ahead. I'm not afraid."

Over Lord Stephanie raises a hand, and Axel's eyes widen as she slowly sucks the air out of his lungs. He wiggles and strains in the chair as she slowly suffocates him. She stops before he can pass out from lack of oxygen, and air quickly fills his lungs. Over Lord Stephanie does this repeatedly until he's slumped over from fatigue.

"Still refuse to talk?" Over Lord Miranda asks again.

"Kiss...my...ass," Axel mumbles breathlessly.

Over Lord Mary leans in close with her voice dripping with venom. "You know, Axel, we can make this easy for you or very, very painful. The choice is yours."

Axel's lips curl into a dark smile. "You think a little pain will break me? You don't know who you're dealing with."

"Oh, we know exactly who you are, Axel. That's why

we're so curious about your friends." Over Lord Annie answers.

Over Lord Ashely claps with joy. "I love making new friends! Come on, Axel. I promise I'll be nice to them."

Axel's laughter is bitter and mocking. "You think I'm going to betray them? I'd sooner die."

"Well, Axel, lucky for you, we have a whole range of creative ways to make that happen." Over Lord Stephanie replies with a calm demeanor.

I can see his bravery wavering, but he remains stubborn. "Go ahead. I'm not afraid."

Over Lord Annie's hands glow with a brilliant light. "Or perhaps I can show you the true meaning of pain."

Axel's breathing hitches, the realization of the situation finally sinking in. Fear flickers in his eyes for a moment, but it's replaced with a stubborn resolve.

"Last chance, Axel. Give us the information we want, or things will get very unpleasant for you," she tells him as she moves closer.

He still keeps a defiant smile on his face. "Do your worst."

Just then, shadows, as if summoned by an unseen force, shadows emerge from the corners of the room. They flow like ink spilled in water, merging to create an all-encompassing darkness that seems to swallow everything in its path. The shadows engulf Axel's form, and a shiver creeps down my spine as the temperature in the room drops instantly.

The room becomes a void, an abyss of darkness that obliterates any sense of direction or distance. Panic flutters within me as I realize I can't see a thing. The shadows appear to have a tangible weight, pressing down on me, making it difficult to breathe. It was as if it had plunged me into a nightmare, a place where sight is meaningless and the only sensation is the cold, the darkness, and the eerie quiet.

A sudden movement catches my attention, like an extension of the shadows slithering toward me. My muscles tense, and I try to step back, to flee from the encroaching darkness, but it's as if an invisible force is holding me in place. My heart races as I struggle against the immobilizing grip.

Then, as if responding to my silent desperation, a bone-chilling wind sweeps through the abyss. It whips around me, tugging at my clothes and tousling my hair, carrying a haunting whisper that echoes from all directions. Fear tightens its grip as the coldness seeps into my very bones, and I feel like I'm being pulled in all directions by unseen forces.

Abruptly, the shadows recede, withdrawing like a tide retreating from the shore. As the darkness lifts, I find myself standing on unfamiliar ground. The ground is rough beneath my feet, and my surroundings are dimly lit by an eerie, otherworldly glow. Before me stand figures cloaked in shadows, much like the ones that had surrounded Axel in the dungeon.

My heart beats fast as I take in the scene before me. The figures are imposing, their features hidden within their dark shrouds. The air is thick with a noticeable tension, and an unspoken power emanates from them. My gaze flickers to Axel, who stands beside me, his expression a mix of confusion and apprehension.

I realize I'm not in the dungeon anymore. Somehow, someone or something transported me to a different place. The realization sends a surge of anxiety through me, but I steel myself against it. This is the room from my vision of Axel speaking to the Dark Council.

Before me, the figures cloaked in shadows move, their forms indistinct and foreboding. My heart pounds as I recognize the scene unfolding before me. Axel's stance before these shadowy beings is shaky, his demeanor far less defiant than it had been with the Over Lords.

"You disappoint us, Axel," a voice hissed, the words echoing in the void. "You were supposed to have them by now. We felt their presence when we rescued you the first time. We even told you who."

Axel's voice is strained, his expression a mixture of fatigue and fear. "I've been working on it. It's proving to be more difficult than expected."

Another figure steps forward, its presence exuding an eerie authority. "You nearly met your end at the hands of the Over Lords. Again! We had to spend considerable effort to ensure your survival."

Axel's shoulders tense, and a bead of sweat glistens on his forehead. "I assure you, it won't let that happen again."

The figures appear to bristle with impatience. "You're right. It will not happen again. The Veil is done! We'll grab the other half of the pairs of powers ourselves!"

Axel's voice wavers, a mixture of desperation and determination in his tone. "Please! We can do it! I swear it!"

There is silence, and Axel is shaking with anticipation as he waits for what they have to say.

"You will get one more chance. If you fail, we will end the Veil Society," a voice hisses. "We'd hoped to do this undetected, but we will finish this ourselves after we kill you should you fail again."

Axel disappears from the room, and now I'm surrounded by these imposing, shadowy figures.

"It's good to have you at last, Olivia," a voice hisses. "You are the Mai gani lokaci, time seer. And soon, we'll have the other pairs of powers to exact our revenge once and for all."

"I don't know what you want from me," I whisper as fear coats my tone.

"Soon," another voice hisses. "You will see soon."

I don't know what they mean, and I don't want to find out. Before I can get the courage to escape, everything goes dark.

CHAPTER 25

THE UNLIKELY BETRAYAL

As I slowly open my eyes, the darkness seems to press in on me from all sides. My head is heavy, as if I had been under some spell, and my heart races with confusion and trepidation. The surrounding room is thick with an impenetrable blackness, leaving me disoriented and unsure of my surroundings. I don't know how long I've been out, and that gives me anxiety.

I try to move, to stand up, but an invisible force holds me in place as if ethereal hands are pressing me down into the chair beneath me. Panic swells up within me, but I push it aside. I look around to find more chairs next to me.

A soft, almost inaudible murmur fills the air, and as my eyes adjust to the darkness, I realize that I'm not alone. Figures, shadowy and indistinct, surround me. Their presence is unsettling, reminding me they took me from Orchard Landing.

I squint, attempting to make out their features, but they remain cloaked in darkness. Fear knots in my stomach, and my heart races even faster, realizing I'm now face to face with them, or at least their shadowy forms.

"Who are you?" I whisper, my voice barely audible in the oppressive silence.

The figures remain silent, their aura of mystery and power permeating the air. I strain against the unseen restraints, feeling the weight of their gaze upon me. It's as if they're peering into the very depths of my soul and unraveling the secrets I held within.

Coldness seeps into my bones, making me shiver despite the lack of physical touch. The room pulses with an eerie energy, and the shadows dance around me like specters in the night. My hammering heart is a constant reminder of the danger that surrounds me.

With a suddenness that startles me, the figures move, their shadowy forms shifting and swirling like tendrils of smoke. As the shadows draw back, I gasp at what I see. Right in front of me are Lucy and Vik.

"Let us out of here, you piece of shit!" Lucy yells from a cage. "We are going to kill you when we get out of here, Felix!"

Standing in front of Lucy is a nerdy-looking guy staring at them with contempt. I look toward the second cage to see Vik unconscious with something covering her mouth.

"What the hell is going on?" I yell out. "Who the hell is Felix?"

Lucy looks at me and sighs with relief. "Olivia! Thank God you're alright."

"Who is that guy, and why are you here? How did you get here?" I ask, hoping that we can escape.

"You've been missing for a week," Lucy answers. "Vik and I were about to go out again to look for you. We got into a confrontation with Axel before Felix trapped us in one of his cages. I'm guessing by our sudden appearance here that

Felix is working with the shadow people, like the idiot that he is."

"I'm not an idiot!" Felix snaps in anger. "I managed to trap you, didn't I? Now, I can get the others so I can receive what they promised to me."

"Why would you do this?" Lucy asks him. "How the hell did you even get involved in this?"

"When the Veil attacked Orchard Landing, I came across someone named Barb," Felix starts. "She told me they could use someone with my ability to rid this world of evil. All I had to do was trap the pairs of powers and take them to the Dark Council."

"Wonder boy here can create impenetrable cages," Lucy says. "The only people capable of getting out of them are the Over Lords."

"Imagine my surprise when word got out that Axel escaped with Olivia," Felix continues, as if Lucy hadn't spoken. "With the Over Lords distracted in their attempts to find her, Axel could sneak back on the property to give me the information I needed."

"We were just about to kick Axel's ass when Felix trapped us," Lucy snarls in his direction. "When we get out of here, I'm going to make sure Over Lord Ashley puts you in the box."

Dani kicks her cage in anger. "Seriously. We will have to do something about the soldiers patrolling the property. There's no way so many people should have been able to get on and off Orchard Landing like they've been doing."

Felix leans his head back and laughs long and loud. "You all are so far out of your depth that it's funny. Neither of you has any idea what's going on or who you're dealing with. You're never getting out of here."

Dani laughs at Felix. "Suppose that is true. Whatever

you think you're getting out of this deal won't happen, either. Which means you're still a fucking idiot."

"Enough of this!" a shadowy voice hissed.

Shadows surround Felix, and when they disperse, he's gone. Lucy tries to break free of her cage. She's basically a goddess, and I'm hoping like hell she can break free despite what she said about the Over Lords being the only ones who can break out of Felix's cages. I fixed my gaze on Lucy, who's a whirlwind of determination within her cage.

I watch Lucy's hands press against the walls of her cage, with her fingers curling into tight fists. Her knuckles whiten with effort as she summons her abilities, and her eyes narrow in concentration. I can see the subtle shimmer of energy in the air around her, a telltale sign that her magic is at work.

With a surge of power, Lucy's palms push forward, and the air crackles with energy. The magical bars of her cage vibrate, a testament to the force she's exerting. Her face scrunches with strain as determination etches into every line of her features.

"Come on, Lucy," I whisper under my breath, my heart racing with hope and anxiety.

A low growl of frustration escapes her lips as the magical bars resist her efforts. I can see the beads of sweat forming on her forehead, her muscles taut as she pours her energy into the attempt to break free. It's a battle between her sheer force of will and the intricate magic that holds her captive.

A glimmer of movement catches my eye as the air around Lucy's cage warps and distorts. For a moment, it looks like the bars might bend, might give way to her relentless assault. But just as quickly, the magical energy within the cage seems to push back. Her expression shifts from determination to frustration, her telekinetic assault meeting an immovable barrier.

"Fuck!" Lucy yells with anger and disappointment, her hands falling back to her sides as she steps back, panting.

I can feel her frustration and powerlessness against the cage's magic. The shadows in the room move to close in around us, a reminder that we are at the mercy of those who trapped us. Lucy tries everything she can think of to escape. She throws energy balls and fireballs, trying to twist between the bars and more. She can't escape the cage.

"Your relentless attempts are starting to vex me," a voice snarls through the shadows.

"Well, excuse me for inconveniencing you. Heaven forbid I disturb your little shadowy gathering." Lucy snaps.

I watch her eyes blaze with anger, her chest heaving with each breath. And then, with a fierce determination, she spits out a response that drips with sarcasm and defiance. "Kiss my ass!"

The very atmosphere of the room shifts as the shadow figures' anger flares. The shadows writhe and pulse like living entities responding to their master's emotions. Our air grows stifling, heavy with an almost oppressive energy.

"Lucy, maybe now's not the best time for—" I begin, my voice low with caution, but I'm cut off as the room darkens further, the shadows merging into a more tangible form.

"You dare to speak to us this way?" another figure hissed, their anger emanating like a tangible force.

Lucy stands her ground with her jaw set defiantly. "Yes, I do. What are you going to do about it? Make it darker in here?"

Vik shifts beside me, her eyes wide as she assesses the escalating situation. The atmosphere has turned charged, a storm of power brewing around us. It's as if they caught us in the crosshairs of a battle far beyond our understanding.

Then, abruptly, the room grows still. The air hums with an evil energy, and I feel a sensation like icy tendrils snaking their way up my spine. Pain, sharp and sudden, lances through me, a response to the anger radiating from the shadow figures.

Lucy's defiant expression twists into a grimace of agony, and Vik lets out a muffled cry as she, too, is affected by the shadow figures' rage. The pain intensifies, a searing fire that consumes us from the inside out. I've never felt pain like this in my life, and Lucy's defiance is causing all of us this pain.

As the pain reaches an unbearable crescendo, darkness creeps at the edges of my vision. My body grows heavy, and the intensity of the pain muddled my thoughts from the pain the shadows cause. The room spins as the shadows dance in a macabre display before everything fades to black.

Consciousness slips away, the pain and the shadows merging into a haze of oblivion. As we succumb to the darkness, our strength waning, I can only hope we'll find a way to overcome this formidable evil and emerge from the shadow figures' grasp.

Slowly, consciousness returns, and I look around to find Lucy and Vik coming around, too. My head is killing me, and I just want to get some sleep the natural way.

"Next time, keep your damn mouth shut, Lucy," I growl at her as I wince from the pain in my head.

"Sorry, Liv," she replies. "I've got anger issues and whatnot."

I glare at her sorry excuse. "Learn to control that shit."

The oppressive darkness of the room seems to amplify

as a new presence enters. My heart skips a beat as I see Felix materialize in the room, with Dani in one of his cages.

"Felix, I'm going to skin you alive!" Dani snarls at him. She takes in her surroundings and gasps when she sees us. "Thank God you're okay."

I exchange uneasy glances with Lucy and Vik, wondering what the plan is now that we're all here. Vik's muffled grunts show her frustration at being unable to fully take part in the conversation as the gag is still over her mouth.

Dani's voice cuts through the tension, dripping with sarcasm. "Oh, Felix, you surprise me. Who would've thought your nerdy ass would have the courage to team up with these asshats?"

Felix's eyes turn to slits at Dani's comment, his serious demeanor faltering for a moment. "I've made my choices, Dani. I have great judgment and know when to align with the more powerful side."

"Judgment? Please, if you had any judgment, you wouldn't be cavorting with these shadow people, you bag of ass," Lucy throws out, quirking a brow.

Vik's eyes blaze with frustration, and she makes an exaggerated gesture towards her gag as if to say, 'Get this thing off me.' Her muffled grunts have turned into a low growl of impatience.

Felix's gaze shifts to Vik, and a hint of annoyance crosses his features. "Yes, yes, I know you're not thrilled about the mouthpiece. But I can't risk you using your ability."

As the imposing figures remain mysterious and silent, I take a deep breath as I attempt to assess the situation and devise a plan.

"Felix, what do they want with us?" I ask, trying to sound like a helpless victim.

Felix's expression turns serious as his tone becomes measured. "They want the pairs of powers, duh."

Dani rolls her eyes at the obvious intent. "Ah, the grand 'pair of powers' nonsense again. How original."

Felix's patience is wearing thin, and his words come out with a sharper edge. "Don't underestimate them, Dani. Their motives and power go far beyond your snarky attitude."

"So, what? We're their pawns now? Are we supposed to find the other half?" Lucy asks, since Felix insists on talking. Maybe she can get more information out of him.

Felix gives her an evil smirk. "You'll have to wait and see."

Vik's frustration grows, her grunts turning into more pronounced protests.

Felix's gaze flicks to her, and he finally removes the gag. Vik lets out a relieved sigh and rubs her jaw. Before she can utter a single word, her mouth snaps shut, and she uses her finger to pry it open, to no avail.

"These figures are not to be trifled with," Felix continues. "Your resistance is futile. Embrace your destiny or face their wrath."

The shadows take Felix once again. As the four of us stand together in the eerie presence of the shadowy figures, uncertainty swirls around us like a thick fog. We're left in silence for so long, time seems to blur, and we exchange bewildered glances.

Dani's voice cut through the tense silence. "So, any idea how long we've been gallivanting in this ominous nightmare?" she quips, her tone a mix of irritation and dark humor.

I shoot her a wry smile. "Oh, you know, with a casual stroll through the shadowy dimensions. Who needs a watch? I've never been out of the state before. Let me enjoy this."

Lucy smiles at my humor before adding her own. "Right. Time's a social construct, anyway. Who needs to know when the sun's coming up?"

Vik lets out an exasperated grunt and rolls her eyes with a mix of annoyance and agreement.

Dani's eyes sparkled mischievously. "Maybe this is the grand tour of otherworldly tourist destinations. Next stop, the Abyss of Unfinished To-Do Lists."

I can't help but chuckle. "Oh, and let's not forget the Tunnel of Eternal Potty Breaks."

Lucy raises an eyebrow, her grin sly. "And over there, the Hall of Perpetual Bad Hair Days."

Vik's grunt this time sounds both amused and exasperated, her eyes narrowing playfully at Lucy's comment.

As our laughter echoed through the shadowy space, Dani shrugs. "Well, if we're just here for some cosmic sight-seeing, sign me up for the 'Portals to Nowhere' package."

I gesture around dramatically. "And don't forget the 'Lost and Confused' guided tour."

Lucy throws her hands up with mock enthusiasm. "And the pièce de résistance: a chance to finally meet the elusive Dark Council, now taking reservations for eternity!"

Vik's eyes roll, her grunt punctuating the absurdity of our theories. If these dark figures are intent on keeping us here until they're ready to do whatever they're going to do with us, we'll annoy them to death. Dani and Lucy seem on board with the unspoken plan.

But during our joking, the shadowy figures remain silent, their mysterious presence untouched by our humor.

The air grows heavier, and the shadows around us shift in response to the figures' growing impatience. I can sense the figures' growing irritations as we continue to make terrible jokes and puns about our situation. When they finally speak, their voices carry a low, ominous edge that silences our light-hearted chatter.

"You seem to find this situation amusing," one figure hisses, their tone blending in frustration and warning.

Lucy's smirk falters slightly, and her eyebrows raise as she glances at us. "Well, you know, when you're stuck in the shadowy abyss, a little humor goes a long way."

I nod in agreement, and a sly smile appears on my face. "Laughter is the best defense mechanism against, you know, unknown cosmic forces."

Dani's lips twitch with a hint of defiance in her eyes. "And hey, if you guys ever decide to switch careers from ominous enigmas to stand-up comedians, let us know."

The shadowy figures' response is a chilling silence, and the atmosphere thickens with their growing displeasure. Usually, Vik grunts her displeasure because of the gag, but she only shifts uncomfortably as her eyes dart between us and the shadowy figures. Vik's grunt is softer this time, a subtle reminder that maybe now isn't the best time to push our luck.

As the tension in the room grows, the snarky remarks we use as a defense mechanism now feel like daring provocations. The shadowy figure's power presses down on us, their irritation manifesting in a palpable energy that sends shivers down our spines.

Dani clears her throat, her smirk replaced by a more cautious expression. "Alright, alright, we get it. Cosmic forces have no sense of humor."

Lucy's gaze shifts to Vik, and she gives her a sheepish

smile. "Sorry, Vik. Guess our charm doesn't work on everyone."

Vik responds with an exasperated but amused grunt, with her eyes rolling playfully as she acknowledges the change in tone.

We fill the dark room with apprehension, and anticipation weaves around us while we wait for the shadowy figure's next move. The snark and sass that had become our coping mechanism fade into unease, replaced by the gnawing sensation that we are indeed at the mercy of these enigmatic entities.

"Anyone else feels like we're the main course in a cosmic drama?" Dani says, with a mix of anxiety and dark humor.

Lucy's fingers tap against her thigh restlessly, her eyes narrowing on the shadowy figures. "If this is some cosmic entertainment, I'd give it a one-star review."

My expression grows tense, my gaze shifting between the figures and the dark expanse around us. "I've had enough of the ominous vibes. Can we get some answers, please?"

Vik's exasperated grunt mirrors our collective frustration, but her eyes flick nervously between us and the shadowy figures.

And then, just as the weight of the unknown starts to suffocate us, a familiar presence ripples through the shadows. The Over Lords appear, their forms cutting through the darkness like beacons of power. Relief washes over us, and the shadowy figures bristle in response.

"Oh, look who decided to crash the spooky party," Dani's voice drips with sarcasm as the Over Lords enter.

Over Lord Miranda's eyes flicker with amusement and

irritation. "You guys really do have a talent for attracting trouble, don't you?"

Dani holds her hands up. "Don't look at me. This is all Liv's fault."

"Yet, here you are. Trapped here just like me," I respond. "That's not my fault. You got here all on your own."

Over Lord Mary grins playfully. She's not the least bit worried about being in danger. "And here we were, thinking you could handle yourselves."

"Oh, don't worry," Lucy answers. "We're just here for the ambiance."

Over Lord Stephanie sighs with annoyance. "Can you try not to get captured every time we turn our backs?"

"As much as I enjoy this family reunion, we've got a score to settle." Over Lord Sydney's as she glares at the dark shadows, looking for the figures within.

Over Lord Ashley's laughter, slightly manic as always, echoes in the air. "Let's show these shadowy ass munchers what they're dealing with!"

The shadowy figures swirl in response to the Over Lords' presence. But then the atmosphere shifts, and the shadows themselves seem to coil with tension.

The Over Lords launch an attack, their power surging forward in a display of raw strength. But the shadowy figures are not to be underestimated. With a speed and power that is both astonishing and terrifying, they defend themselves and retaliate against the Over Lords.

Over Lord Mary moves her arms around, and her control over time manifests as a distortion in the air, freezing the very atmosphere around her target. The shadow's movements slow to a crawl as time seems to bend to her will.

Over Lord Stephanie conjures a powerful gust of wind

and fire that spiral towards the shadowy figures in a cyclone of destruction. Flames roar, and gusts of wind churn, forming a deadly whirlpool that seeks to consume the shadows.

Over Lord Mary weaves an illusion of false images, cloaking her movements and intentions. As she advances, multiple versions of herself appear, confounding the shadow figures and making it nearly impossible to predict her actual location.

Over Lord Sydney manifests tendrils of energy that extend from her fingertips. These tendrils weave around the shadows, binding them and restricting their movements with an almost tangible weight.

Over Lord Annie's electricity crackles with intensity, arcs of lightning leaping from her fingers to strike at the shadows. The air is alive as bolts of energy lance through the shadows, seeking their mark.

Over Lord Ashley's volatile power, always unpredictable, surges forth in a whirlwind of chaotic magic. Magic seems to wrap around her as she unleashes bursts of energy that explode like fireworks, bending to her will.

With an almost casual gesture, one figure extends a hand, and the surrounding shadows surge forward in a tidal wave of darkness. The Over Lords' magical assaults are met with an almost tangible resistance, the shadows swirling and twisting to counter their every move. In moments, the Over Lords' attacks have been nullified, their power and precision no match for the evil force that the shadowy figures wield.

A blinding wave of energy sweeps through the room, sending shockwaves rippling through the air. When the dust settles and the echoes of the clash fade, the Over Lords stand battered and injured, their expressions a mix of shock and disbelief. The shadowy figures remain unscathed, their presence untouched by the unfolding chaos.

The encounter has revealed the true extent of the shadowy figure's power. They're a force that transcends their understanding and leaves the Over Lords reeling. With grim determination, they realize that destroying the shadows is far more daunting than they could have ever expected.

Desperation encourages their movements as Over Lord Miranda's voice rings out. Her words are layered with urgency. "We need to get out of here."

"Open a portal, now!" Over Lord Mary says, and I'm surprised to hear a hint of fear in her voice.

Over Lord Annie's hands move with practiced precision as she conjures the portal, the swirling vortex of energy a lifeline amidst the chaos.

Dani's, Lucy's, and Vik's cages lift into the air as I'm teleported.

Over Lord Stephanie's voice is low and resolute as she tells them to hold on. "Get in, now!" She yells at me before pushing the cages through.

Over Lord Sydney's expression is grim as she glances between us and the shadows. "We'll regroup and come back stronger."

"There is no need to come back. We are coming for you," a voice hisses as the portal closes behind us.

CHAPTER 26
THE WRONG DECISION

As we materialize back on Orchard Landing, the air is heavy with the weight of our recent encounter. Though injured and visibly shaken, the Over Lords keep a sense of grim determination that resonates through their presence. Jade and Torri are waiting on the field when we appear, concern covering Jade's face, while Torri looks bored as usual.

Over Lord Miranda looks at them. "Secure the perimeter. We need to ensure they did not follow us."

"Are you all alright?" Jade asks with genuine worry as she looks at each of us.

"We're intact, if somewhat worse for wear." Over Lord Miranda nods as she replies.

A flicker of concern softens Torri's haughty expression. "What happened?"

"We had to rescue the girls, and those fucking shadow figures kicked our asses. That's what happened," Over Lord Mary says, her voice carrying a note of irritation.

"Yeah, but we're alive," Over Lord Stephanie adds.

Jade's relief is palpable, her shoulders relaxing as she

lets out a breath she didn't realize she was holding. "I'm glad to hear that. We've been busy on our end, too."

Torri's tone is dry as her arms cross. "We managed to capture Axel and a few others from the Veil. Those idiots were hanging around the perimeter of the property."

That didn't bother the Over Lords as their attention was clearly focused on more pressing matters at hand.

"Kill them. They've caused enough trouble for us already," Over Lord Miranda says in a voice devoid of hesitation.

Jade's eyebrows arch, her gaze locking onto her with surprise. "You want us to...?"

"We have bigger concerns than dealing with those assholes." Over Lord Mary snaps.

Jade and Torri exchange glances, as it's clear that the situation has taken a severe turn. The matter of Axel and his goons has taken a backseat to the looming threat posed by the shadowy figures and the Dark Council. They try hard to hide their worry, but I can see it clearly on their faces.

Over Lord Annie's gaze is firm, her words carrying a weight of finality. "Dispose of them swiftly. They're no longer a concern."

Jade's expression hardens with her resolve clear in her voice. "Understood."

Torri sighs with a hint of annoyance. "Fine. Let's get this over with."

Jade and Torri leave to fulfill their task as we go to the main house. We're inside now and just walked into the meeting room.

"That was one big cluster fuck," Over Lord Mary says as she sits in one of the chairs.

Over Lord Annie moves her hands with practiced precision to take down the cages that trap Vik, Lucy, and Dani.

With one last wave of her hand, the cages dissolve into nothingness, and Dani, Lucy, and Vik emerge, their expressions a mix of relief and trepidation.

"Well, that was a lovely cosmic vacation. Let's never do it again." Lucy says as her eyes shift between the Over Lords.

"If it weren't for Felix's dumbass, we wouldn't have been there in the first fucking place," Dani growls. "I need to find him because I'm going to snap every bone in his little weasel body."

"No need," Over Lord Annie says. "I've just sent word to Jade to take him to the dungeon. We'll deal with him when we finish this. You'll have your fun."

"Oh, how I've missed the sound of my voice," Vik says with gratitude and, accompanied by a playful eye roll.

"Well, we don't," Lucy replies playfully.

The room goes silent as everyone thinks over recent events. There is a mix of tension and anger as we all stare at nothing, lost in thought. The Over Lords' injuries are a sobering reminder of how strong those shadow figures are.

"We need to regroup and strategize. This isn't a fight we can win by charging in blindly." Over Lord Stephanie's voice interrupts the silence.

"We weren't completely recovered to begin with." Over Lord Sydney's expression is serious as she looks toward me. "If you would stop getting kidnapped, we wouldn't have to keep sending them to find you."

I lean back and frown. "It's not my fault. They took me on your watch this time." I point to Dani, Lucy, and Vik. "It's also not my fault they got captured in the process."

I know I shouldn't show such disrespect to the Over Lords, but I don't appreciate them blaming things on me. This entire situation with the Veil Society and the Dark

Council may have centered on me, but I did nothing to bring this on except for existing.

"Focus!" Over Lord Miranda yells as she slams her fist on the table. "We need to figure out a way to kill these shadow figures so we can get to the Dark Council. Not blame Olivia for things she cannot control,"

Over Lord Ashley's manic grins, wide with a hint of determination. "We are going to kick their asses so good they won't even know they're dead until I torture their souls."

As the room buzzes with a sense of purpose, Dani's eyes lock onto mine, her voice low but filled with resolve. "We'll find the other person for the pair of powers and take the fight to the Dark Council."

"Whatever it is you're thinking about doing, don't," Rebecca says as she materializes in the room. "You've all managed to cause quite the cosmic commotion."

"We don't have time for your shit right now, Rebecca," Over Lord Miranda snaps.

Rebecca's eyes flash in irritation. "And I'm not here to give you shit. I'm here because something has changed, and believe it or not, I don't want to see my best friends hurt."

"Too late for that. The only thing that's changed is us easily getting our asses kicked by a bunch of shadows. We need to retaliate quickly before they come for us like they said," Over Lord Mary replies.

Rebecca points at her with a shake of her head. "That right there. You know. You guys should really talk to me before changing tactics in situations like this."

"Are you going to be helpful for once?" Over Lord Annie asks as she puts her hands on her hips.

"Oh, I'm being helpful. Just not in the way you want, and you know why," Rebecca says as she looks around the room. Her eyes land on me, Dani, Lucy, and Vik. "The trio of troublemakers has now become a quartet, and you're stirring the bowl of shit. The result won't bode well for anyone."

"What the hell does that even mean?" I ask with a sigh of frustration.

Irritation covers Rebecca's face. "It means you didn't listen to a damn word I said before. Use your fucking ability, Olivia. Stop being a scared little bitch about everything."

"What you said was riddled bullshit that we didn't have time to decipher," Over Lord Sydney snaps.

"For fuck's sake!" my voice interrupts. "I am so tired of everyone telling me to use my ability. I don't know how. Not when people are constantly trying to kidnap me. I can't control it. Not when I'm scared of doing something wrong. I can't decipher her stupid riddles that are supposed to help me figure this out."

"We should just attack them before they attack us, kill them, and get this over with," Over Lord Stephanie says.

"Fine!" Rebecca yells. "Since you're so eager to change tactics and attack these things before they attack you, let me show you the outcome of that stupid ass decision."

I don't know what she means, but she starts to glow, and my body goes rigid. Her eyes close, her expression serene, as her ghostly form shimmers with an otherworldly light. All our heads snap toward the ceiling as her connection to the unseen deepens, and a vivid scene starts to unfold before us as we see what Rebecca saw.

Suddenly, we're transported to a dark, desolate landscape where shadows cling to every corner. In the distance, a group of figures emerges, their forms cloaked in darkness, an evil power radiating from them. Me, Dani, Lucy, Vik, and another figure I can't make out lay on the ground motionless as the battle rages around us.

The ground trembles as pieces of earth and stone emerge, charging into the fray with unyielding force as Over Lord Miranda's magic fills the air. Her brow furrows in concentration as she sends them charging towards the shadows. The ground trembles, and for a moment, it seems as if victory might be within reach. But the shadow figures are not so easily deterred.

The shadows shift and waver, coalescing into an imposing form that towers above Over Lord Miranda. Their presence radiates malevolence, a darkness threatening to snuff out the light she wields. As the stones and earth clashes against the shadow figures, Over Lord Miranda's eyes blaze with determination.

She summons walls of stone and barriers of earth, attempting to contain the shadow figure's attacks. Yet, they met each of her defenses with an unrelenting force. The shadows tear through the stones as if they are made of water.

Over Lord Miranda's breath comes in quick gasps as she fights to maintain her ground. Her hands move with practiced precision, her magic shaping the elements around her. However, the shadows seem to expect her every move, countering her attacks with a force stronger than her.

Gritting her teeth, Over Lord Miranda conjures sharp spikes of stone, launching them toward the shadows and attempting to teleport behind a shadow figure to catch it off guard. Yet, the shadowy being remains elusive, its form shifting and dispersing like smoke in the wind.

A surge of darkness lashes out, striking Over Lord Miranda with a force that sends her stumbling back. She staggers, her concentration faltering for a moment as she grunts in pain, and the shadows seize the opportunity. They coil around her, binding her in a vice-like grip that seems to drain the very strength from her. Over Lord Miranda's struggle is palpable, and she groans as she fights against the shadows' hold.

Her magic flares with renewed intensity, and the ground beneath her trembles as she attempts to break free. Despite her efforts, the shadows prove unyielding. Her defenses dissipate, her barriers shatter, and her attempts to escape their grasp are in vain. The shadow figure looms over her, its form twisting and writhing with a dark energy.

Over Lord Mary's illusions weave confusion, casting doubt and uncertainty upon the shadowy figures. Her illusions are so vivid and real that they seem to twist reality, affecting the shadowy beings' perception of the world. Illusions of blinding light cascade around her, creating a dazzling display that should have disoriented them. Yet, the shadow figures seem to flicker and contort, their form wavering as if untouched by Over Lord Mary's illusionary assault.

Her brows scrunch in frustration as she intensifies her efforts, conjuring images of blinding suns and piercing flames. Illusory beams of light shoot toward the shadow figures, each meant to penetrate their defenses and weaken their hold. But the shadow figures remain steadfast, their darkness resisting the brilliance of Over Lord Mary's illusions. The shadows advance with an unsettling grace, their forms shifting and flowing as they deflect her attacks.

Over Lord Mary's movements became more frenzied, her illusions more elaborate and vivid. Illusory chains coil around the shadow figures, meant to bind and constrain. Yet, the chains dissipate like smoke as the shadow figures slip through them like mere mirages.

The shadow figure's power seems to swell, its darkness engulfing Over Lord Mary's illusions and twisting them into grotesque forms. Illusory flames turned to inky smoke; blinding lights transformed into disorienting shadows.

Over Lord Mary's illusions shatter, leaving her vulnerable and exposed. The shadow figures advance as she grits her teeth, a fierce determination lighting up her gaze. She conjures one last illusion, a brilliant burst of light meant to blind the shadow figures.

The light erupts with blinding intensity, and for a fleeting moment, it seems that Over Lord Mary might have successfully fended them off. But then, with a surge of its power, the shadow figures push back, their darkness engulfing the illusion and snuffing out the light. Over Lord Mary stumbles back and falls to the ground, her strength waning from the blow.

Over Lord Annie tries to subdue the shadows by trying to enter their minds. The shadows falter as their own power is turned against them. Their emotions run rampant, and their minds cloud with doubt. Her abilities, usually a force to be reckoned with, are met with unexpected resistance as she attempts to manipulate their emotions and thoughts.

"Come on, you bastards. Let me in." Over Lord Annie says, her voice laced with frustration.

The shadow figure's response is a mocking laugh that echoes within her mind, an icy presence that sends shivers down her spine. The shadow's resistance to her intrusion shocks her. She pushes against their minds again, but a wave of searing pain surges through her mind, a counterattack that leaves her momentarily disoriented.

Over Lord Annie's head snaps up just in time to see the shadow figure's form morphing, tendrils of darkness lashing out in her direction. She tries to deflect the attack, but the shadow figures are relentless, lashing out repeatedly with an intensity that overwhelms her.

Over Lord Sydney's protective force fields shimmer into existence. They are forming barriers that deflect the shadows' attacks. However, even she's struggling to match the strength of the shadow figures she faces. The shadow figures move with an eerie grace, undulating and shifting as if they're composed of pure darkness.

Their attacks are swift and precise, each strike aimed at exploiting her defenses. The shadows warp and twist around, allowing it to slip through the cracks in her force fields.

With a sudden surge of power, the shadow figures launch a wave of darkness, shattering Over Lord Sydney's force fields and leaving her momentarily vulnerable. She staggers back, her breathing labored as she assesses the shadows. She conjures a brilliant sphere of light. The sphere expands, casting a radiant glow that pushes back the shadows and creates a light barrier between them.

With a swift motion, the shadows lash out with tendrils of darkness that wrap around her, and she grits her teeth, her palms glowing as she pours her energy into maintaining the barrier's integrity.

The struggle is clear on her face. Her features frown with strain as she fights to hold her ground. The shadow figure's power is overwhelming, and she finds herself at her limit as she strains against the dark forces that seek to overcome her. Sweat beads on her forehead, and with a last surge of strength, the shadows forge through the barrier, sending a shockwave of darkness that surrounds her. She staggers back and falls to the ground.

Water twists and churns, fire roars with intensity, and winds howl with fury as Over Lord Stephanie fights against the shadows. She raises her hands, and the earth beneath her responds as ripples of energy spread through the ground, causing the earth to tremble and quake.

Pillars of rock erupt from the ground, aiming to inflict harm. The shadow figures move with a sinister grace, shifting and weaving like smoke. They expect Over Lord Stephanie's every move, sidestepping the rocky pillars with uncanny ease.

Her eyes are narrow as her focus intensifies. She summons the power of the wind, willing it to her aid. Gusts of air howl around her, forming a protective barrier that deflects the shadow's advances. But the shadow figures are relentless, dark energy pressing against her defenses with an unsettling persistence. She reaches out to the surrounding plants, their life force intertwining with her magic.

Vines snake towards the shadows, their thorns seeking to bind and restrain. But the shadow figure's form seemed to blur, the vines slipping through its intangible shape like water through a sieve.

A cold, creeping sensation crawls up Over Lord Stephanie's spine as the shadow figures advance. Inky tendrils coil around her, a vice-like grip that tightens with each passing moment. She can feel the darkness seeping into her very being, sapping her strength and leaving her senses clouded. With a final surge of determination, she calls the energy of the earth, wind, and fire into a single, focused burst.

A brilliant light erupts from her form, a radiant burst of energy that disperses the encroaching shadows. For a brief, blinding moment, the battlefield is illuminated in a cascade of colors. The shadow figures let out a piercing howl, retreating from the searing brilliance. But they're not done yet.

Over Lord Ashley's control over the dead echoes with a chilling power, the undead rising to her command. With a wave of her hand, the shadows seem to recoil, a testament to the authority she holds over the forces of death. But the shadow figures are not so easily deterred. Their power surges forth, an enigmatic point that seems to drink in the very essence of the undead. The undead withers and dissolve, their ethereal forms crumbling to nothingness.

A flicker of uncertainty passes across Over Lord Ashley's features as they meet her efforts with unexpected resistance. She tries again but feels a chilling force pushing back against her, a tangible resistance that threatens to overwhelm her efforts. As the battle rages on, Over Lord Ashley's determination wavers.

However, she's not one to back down easily, and her resolve burns brighter with every passing moment. But the shadow figure's power is unyielding, its darkness intertwining with her, threatening to consume her very essence. Her breaths come in ragged gasps as she strains against the forces that seek to overwhelm her.

With a deafening crack, the shadow figure's power surges forth, overwhelming Over Lord Ashley's defenses. The burst of dark energy strikes her, sending her stumbling backward, her form shrouded in a cloud of fading necromantic magic. She hits the ground, her breathing heavy and her body bruised.

As the vision unfolds, I can't deny the gravity of our situation. The shadowy figures are a force to be reckoned with, their power beyond comprehension. Everything slowly comes back into focus as we all stand breathing heavily, trying to take in everything we just witnessed.

"Now you know the outcome of that decision," Rebecca says solemnly. "Don't say I never helped you, bitches. These people you're up against are not to be underestimated."

"Are we just going to skip past all of us getting our asses kicked except for Stephanie?" Over Lord Ashley says. "That vision would be more believable if it was me kicking ass and everyone else getting their asses kicked. We all know I'm the better fighter."

"Really, Ashley?" Over Lord Mary says with a shake of her head.

"Every ticking second carries the echoes of the past and whispers of the future. The threads of time could be woven in a way that the shadows are left with no refuge." Rebecca says. "Use that to your advantage. At one point during all this, you had everything you needed right in front of you. It's—"

Rebecca suddenly disappears, her statement left incomplete. We look around, wondering where she'd gone so abruptly.

"Rebecca?" Over Lord Mary questions.

Over Lord Ashley's eyes flash and she glows. "I can't feel her. I can't even call her here. What the fuck is going on?"

"Clearly, it's a bad idea to attack them, but what? We're supposed to wait for them to come to us?" Over Lord Mary says. "Because what the fuck was that Rebecca showed us?"

"Something is not right," Over Lord Miranda states. "Let's take a second to go over everything she said."

CHAPTER 27

REVEALING THE TRUTH

We sit around the table as we try to figure out our next course of action. But just as the conversation takes shape, the door to the meeting room swings open with surprising force. In strides, Linda and her presence command attention.

She's old, her form draped in flowing garments that carry an air of ancient wisdom. Her magical ability as a healer is well known, and she wields her power with a grace that belies her years.

"What in the hell are you lot doing?" Linda's voice is stern, her eyes narrowing as she directs her gaze at the Over Lords. "Do you have any idea how reckless and foolish you've been?"

Over Lord Miranda finds herself on the receiving end of Linda's wrath. "Linda, we—"

Linda raises a hand to silence her, her expression unyielding. "I don't want to hear excuses. Your impulsiveness has consequences, and it's not just your lives you're endangering."

As if on cue, Linda's magical aura shimmers to life, a

soft glow enveloping the Over Lords. The cuts and bruises that adorned their bodies mend, the healing energy knitting their wounds together.

"Every time you charge headfirst into danger, you leave a wake of chaos and destruction," Linda continues, her voice a stern echo in the room. "And don't think I haven't noticed your penchant for dismissing injuries as mere inconveniences."

Over Lord Mary's expression is a mixture of resignation and remorse. "We—"

Linda ignores her as her gaze turns, her attention shifting to Dani, Lucy, Vik, and me. "And don't think you four are exempt from this scolding."

I exchange a surprised glance with the others, unsure why we are being included in the reprimand. I don't wake up every morning wanting to be kidnapped or killed. Getting into hazardous situations may be Dani's, Lucy's, and Vik's typical day, but it's not mine. It's still not normal for me, even with being on Orchard Landing all this time.

Linda's tone softens, carrying an undercurrent of concern. "You may not be Over Lords, but you're just as integral to this fight and this world. Your well-being matters. Especially to me."

Dani's smirk is quick, her tone cheeky. "Don't worry, Linda. We're tougher than we look."

Linda sighs in exasperation, her magical aura humming as she directs her attention back to the Over Lords. "You all need to consider the consequences of your actions. The shadowy figures and the Dark Council are powerful, and your recklessness only gives them an advantage."

As Linda's healing magic completes its work, the Over Lords' injuries are nothing more than fading memories.

Linda's gaze holds a mixture of sternness and affection.

"You are leaders, yes, but that doesn't mean you're invincible."

"We know that, Linda. But our job is dangerous. We will get injured. We'll try not to be reckless next time." Over Lord Stephanie tells her.

Linda's presence seems to fill the room with unwavering authority. "Good. Because if you don't start heeding my words, I'll personally make sure you're confined to bedrest until you do."

A murmur of reluctant agreement ripples through the room as Linda's reprimand settles in. Her concern for our well-being is clear, and the reminder that our actions have far-reaching consequences is sobering. Satisfied that we won't drop dead, Linda leaves us alone to brainstorm.

As she's walking out, a group of men I've never seen before storm into the room. They look both worried and upset as they stride forward. I look on in amazement as each man envelops one of the Over Lords in a tight hug.

Dani leans over to whisper to me. "Those are my uncles. Uncle Noah is married to Aunt Miranda, Uncle Oliver is married to Aunt Stephanie, Uncle Lucas is married to Aunt Ashley, Uncle Ethan is married to Aunt Sydney, and Uncle Rafael is married to Aunt Annie."

"You guys have to stop getting yourselves injured," Noah says as he stands back and assesses his wife, Over Lord Miranda.

She smiles warmly at him. "It comes with the job. What are you guys doing here?" She thinks for a second. "Let me guess, Linda?"

I watch as they tell their husbands we'd been taken, and they had to rescue us, but it was more complicated than they thought. I love how the men dote on their wives. It's lovely to see people taking care of the Over Lords, since they're always taking care of everyone else.

They talk for about ten minutes before sending their husbands on their way, warning them that the impending battle is inevitable and that they may need their help. The men agree to prepare and leave us to continue discussing our plan of action.

"What did Rebecca say to you during her first visit?" Over Lord Miranda asks me.

"Uh, she said something about a thick veil and moving shadows, I think," I answer hesitantly. "Something about ancient powers on the eve of night."

As soon as I finish, I feel the familiar sensation that usually happens before a vision.

Before me stands Eve, her presence radiating a sense of calm familiarity. But it's the ethereal figure beside her that captures my attention. It's a being of otherworldly essence, shimmering with a faint light that seems to dance on the edge of perception.

Their conversation flows in hushed tones, each word carrying an undercurrent of purpose. Eve's demeanor is one of confidence as if she had been in the presence of this ethereal figure many times before. They center their discussion on me and my role in the events that had thrown my life into turmoil.

"You know what must be done," the ethereal being's voice is a soft echo, carrying a weight of wisdom beyond mortal under-standing.

Eve's gaze holds a mixture of determination and concern. "I do. But they need to be protected and guided. The Over Lords must understand the gravity of their mission."

The ethereal figure responds mysteriously, and their words carry a level of understanding that exceeds mine.

"They are capable, Eve. Their strength, love, and unity are their greatest assets," the ethereal being responds.

"And Olivia?" Eve questions. "They must take out the Dark Council without knowing the truth."

A solemn nod from the ethereal being is their response. "Her fate is intertwined with theirs. Trust that all will end well."

That's all I see as the vision fades away. The meeting room comes back into focus, and everyone stares at me. Fury surges within me as the remnants of the vision fade away, leaving behind a bitter taste of betrayal.

Eve, the one I'd trusted and considered a dear friend, has been keeping secrets. A sense of disappointment, a feeling that the very foundation of our friendship had been shaken, fuels the anger that rages within me.

"That lying bitch!" I yell out in anger.

"Wait, who's a bitch?" Dani questions in confusion. "What did you see, Liv?"

I'm pulsing with anger. "Give me a few minutes. I need to find somebody."

With a determined focus, I close my eyes, drawing upon the threads of my abilities and hoping this works. The visions come to life, swirling before me like tendrils of mist, each one a piece of the puzzle that holds the truth about Eve. The first vision unfolds, revealing a glimpse into the past, a moment shared with Eve when I was first kidnapped, now tainted by the knowledge of her hidden intentions. Anger within me intensifies as the vision shifts.

Suddenly, the ethereal voice yells out. "Do not look toward the future, for it will never be what it's supposed to be!"

I'm pushed back, and the meeting room comes back into focus. But amidst the anger, a surge of determination courses through me. With every ounce of concentration, I will the visions to guide me to Eve in the present moment.

The visions respond, converging on a single point, a fleeting glimpse of Eve's presence in the here and now.

Once I see her, I extend my hand and grab her by the arm. My grip on her is unyielding, fueled by the intensity of my emotions. With a determined tug, I pull her back through, drawing her from the vision into the tangible space of the meeting room. The meeting room materializes before me, and within it stands Eve, her expression a mixture of surprise and concern as I stare at her with fire blazing in my eyes.

Eve stumbles, her eyes wide with astonishment as she finds herself standing before me. "Olivia, what—?" She pauses, and her shoulders drop in resignation. "I knew you'd figure it out eventually. I was hoping for this to play out differently."

"Alright, what is Eve doing here, and why do I have to kick her ass?" Dani says.

Amid my anger, I ignore her and keep my focus on Eve. "You've been keeping secrets, Eve. Secrets that could help us. Why?" I ask, my voice carrying the weight of betrayal and hurt.

Eve's gaze holds a mixture of regret and earnestness. "I had my reasons, Olivia."

Over Lord Ashley let's lose her power, eyes, and body glowing. "I don't like the look on Olivia's face. It never ends well for those who hurt the people I care about."

She lifts Eve into the air. "How would you like to be maimed? Since you and Olivia used to be friends, I'm giving you options. So, what will it be? Decapitation? Dismemberment? Stabbing? Heart attack? Suffocation? It's your pick."

There isn't an ounce of fear on Eve's face. Suddenly, Eve waves a hand, and Over Lord Ashley yelps before falling to the ground as Eve floats back down. For a moment, we're all speechless. That only lasts a few seconds before the other Over Lords unleash their power as anger crosses their faces. Dani, Olivia, and Vik get into their fighting stances as well.

"I am not your enemy," Eve says, still without an ounce of fear.

"Well, you are something. So, you better tell us what that something is, or we're going to try our damndest to kick your ass," Over Lord Miranda says.

"I like you guys," Eve says with a smile. "I can see why she saved you. You'll keep Liv safe."

"What the hell, Eve?" I say, bringing her attention back to me.

"My name is Monteralia. I am part of the pairs of powers," she says.

"I don't understand. Axel tortured you to get to me. To force me to help them kidnap people. How did they not know you were the other half? Why did you lie?" I ask her, hurt still lacing my tone.

"I let them take me, Liv." She says calmly. "I never let on what I was, and I doubt that Barb lady could tell even if she could touch me. I had to know you were okay after they took you, and I had to see how much the Veil knew."

"You lied to me, Eve, or whatever your name is. You were my best friend. I trusted you!" I yell back at her with anger clear in my eyes. "Why couldn't you just tell me the truth from the start?"

She raises a brow. "Would you have believed me, or would you have thought me to be crazy? I've lived in this world long enough to know how humans react to certain things. I was slowly easing you into this world while fishing out the Veil and the Dark Council."

"So, I was just a pawn in your game?" I ask with sadness. "Just a means to an end."

"No, not really. It's all about the required perception, Liv," she tells me. "I must look and be something else. Pretend to be something while being someone else. It must look one way when, in reality, it's something different. It's all about how things are perceived. That's the only way this can work. But you've become a dear friend to me."

"If you were my friend, regardless of how crazy it sounded, you would have told me," I snap. "Is this the reason you were nice to me in college? You knew about this then, didn't you?"

"I do what I'm told, Liv," she says sadly. "It may have started out that I needed to keep you hidden and your ability a secret, but you really are my friend. A friend that I guided to the world of magic. To people in that world who could help you when I wasn't allowed to."

"What about me?" Vik asks, anger evident in her tone too. "How did I play a part in your twisted games?"

"I did use your circumstances to my advantage, Vik," Monteralia replies. "I made you believe we're related when I met you years ago. However, you do play a role in this inevitable encounter. One became a threat as soon as Liv's ability manifested. It is complicated to explain."

"You really played into the whole long-lost cousin story," Vik snarls.

"I don't care who you are, but you better start explaining," Over Lord Miranda snaps. "Cause I'm about to kick your ass all the way back to wherever the fuck you came from."

"I am Monteralia, Goddess of death. This is a tale that spans eons," Monteralia says, her voice distant as she remembers the story she's about to tell. "Long before your existence, the Earth was under siege by a great evil, a force of darkness that sought to consume all in its path. It was an entity born of chaos, an evil being that reveled in destruction."

A chill runs down my spine as I listen to Monteralia's words. The idea of such an ancient and frightening evil is difficult to hear about.

"In the middle of the chaos, it attacked our world Asteloria," Monteralia continues, her gaze distant, as if she were reliving the past. "A world woven from the very fabric of magic itself. Thodara ruled that world."

The mention of Asteloria brings a sense of mystique to the narrative, a world where magic was the essence of life.

Monteralia's expression grows somber. "Thodara and I were among the few who escaped the onslaught of that malevolent force. Unfortunately, our world was destroyed, but as we sought refuge, a division grew among us, those who believed in uniting our strengths to survive on a new world, and those seeking retribution."

"Thodara and I were the only ones who believed in unity. We formed a bond that transcended our individual identities and became more than just goddesses; we became of one mind, bound by a shared purpose," she continues.

Monteralia's gaze holds a mixture of sadness and determination. "The others decided to fight. The battle against the great evil was arduous, demanding great sacrifices. But they were no match and demanded Thodara and I help them, as they believed Thodara could have defeated this great evil if she chose to. Eventually, we managed to defeat the evil, but at a significant cost."

"And now," Monteralia's tone is resolute, "the darkness stirs once more, but in a different way. The Dark Council threatens our very existence. They seek the 'pairs of powers' to exact their revenge."

Another shiver runs through me as the puzzle pieces start to fit together. The ancient evil, the connection between Thodara and Monteralia, and the impending threat of the Dark Council.

Monteralia's gaze meets mine, her eyes carrying an unspoken understanding. "I once vowed to protect the balance of life and death. Thodara stands as my ally, just as she was in those long-forgotten days. Together, we ensure we defeat the darkness once and for all."

The tension in the room is high as the Over Lords, Dani, Lucy, Vik, and I, exchange glances, each grappling with the weight of the revelations Monteralia has unveiled. With a steadying breath, Over Lord Miranda's voice cuts through the silence.

"What exactly was this force of darkness you mentioned?" Miranda's gaze holds a mixture of curiosity and concern, mirroring the thoughts that surely swirl within us.

Monteralia's expression grows grave. "The Abyssal Devourer was an evil entity, a being born from the depths of chaos and darkness from magic. Its sole purpose was to consume and annihilate. It sought to extinguish all light and life in its path, leaving nothing but a void of eternal darkness."

Over Lord Mary's voice holds a touch of skepticism. "And what was the cost of defeating this... Abyssal Devourer?"

Monteralia's gaze is distant, her voice still tinged with a solemn note. "The cost was significant, a sacrifice that forever altered us. To destroy the Abyssal Devourer, we, the gods and goddesses who stood against it, agreed to surrender a significant portion of our powers. The very essence that defined us was given up to weaken the entity. In the end, all that remained was Thodara and I."

Over Lord Stephanie's voice rises in inquiry as the weight of the sacrifice settles over us. "But why would the other gods and goddesses agree with such a sacrifice? Weren't they already fighting it? What would giving up their power do if it already wasn't helping?"

A sudden realization surges within me. The pieces of the puzzle click into place with a jolt.

"They were tricked," I blurt out, my voice carrying the weight of revelation.

All eyes turn toward me, a mix of surprise and curiosity reflected in their gazes.

"They were tricked into thinking that giving up their powers was the only way to defeat the Abyssal Devourer," I continue.

My mind races to piece together the implications of what I'd just spoken.

Understanding dawn in Monteralia's eyes as she locks gazes with me. "Thodara," she murmurs.

"Why would Thodara trick them?" Dani asks in confusion.

"I think the better question is, if she could have defeated this Abyssal Devourer like the others believed, why didn't she?" Over Lord Mary asks instead.

Monteralia shakes her head sadly. "Because she could not."

"Why?" Vik asks.

"Because the Abyssal Devourer is magic, and magic cannot be destroyed. Asteloria lacked evil, anger, vengeance, and everything bad so that only the good remained. Which, as you know, does not create balance."

Monteralia replies, her tone giving way to her sadness. "That very essence has to go somewhere, and the Abyssal Devourer was born of everything bad that Asteloria lacked."

Over Lord Sydney's voice holds a hint of doubt. "So, Thodara tricked her fellow gods and goddesses into giving up their powers, believing it would empower her to destroy the Abyssal Devourer?"

Monteralia's gaze remains steady, her expression a mask of regret and acceptance. "Yes. She manipulated their need for retribution, convincing them their powers could be harnessed for the greater good. Instead, she performed an ancient ceremony that siphoned those powers and dispersed them into the humans of Earth."

A realization dawned upon me, connecting the dots between the past and the present. "The humans possess something that they did not," I state, my voice filled with awe and realization.

Monteralia nods again. "Yes, a quality that sets them apart, the capability to express empathy, compassion, and unity differently than we do. That is something that we lack, as we are very technical in our way of thinking. We become single-minded in our endeavors. Thodara saw that humanity had the potential to wield power not solely for destruction but for the protection and well-being of their world."

Over Lord Annie speaks with understanding in her voice. "I remember what Thodara told us now. She gave the magic to humans, entrusting them with the responsibility of safeguarding Earth, something she couldn't do for her own."

Monteralia's gaze meets mine, her eyes carrying the weight of her past decisions. "Yes, she saw in humans the ability to rise above their flaws, to be the guardians of magic and light. To rationalize where we could not. She believed that through their unity and care, they could serve as protectors against any darkness that threatened the balance of the worlds."

My heart races as the truth unfurls before me. "The shadow figures. The Dark Council. They are the same. They are the gods and goddesses who were deceived by Thodara."

"We suspect so," Monteralia answers.

"Why would all that lead them to target Earth, to seek the 'pair of powers'?" Lucy asks.

"What exactly is the pair of powers?" I ask. "We still haven't figured out and understood what it is."

Just as Monteralia opens her mouth to speak, a surge of energy suddenly disrupts the atmosphere. A brilliant flash of light illuminates the room. My attention snaps toward the Over Lords, whose bodies glow with an intense aura. Their eyes shimmer with otherworldly brilliance as their very essence pulses with power.

"There is a disturbance on the property," Over Lord Miranda states right before they teleport out of the room.

CHAPTER 28
THE DARK COUNCIL

My eyes are wide with shock as we take in the dire tableau before us. Darkness coils and envelopes buildings, trees, and residents, instilling terror. The air is dense with a sense of impending danger, and I can feel the unease radiating off the Over Lords.

There's a tangible reminder of evil's firm hold as the air vibrates with the shadow's ominous presence. The shadows are wreaking havoc upon Orchard Landing, trapping residents and structures alike in their chilling embrace.

Without hesitation, Over Lord Miranda moves to attack to push back the shadows as the other Over Lords move to secure our people. Her eyes blaze with anger, and she raises her hand. Bright beams of energy shoot from her pals, illuminating the darkness.

The energy cuts through the shadows like a blade, forcing them to move back. Her energy intensifies, creating a blinding sphere around her. The shadows hiss and move back as the energy causes them to jerk and twist.

"Let them go!" Over Lord Miranda shouts with anger in her tone. "Your fight is with us, not them."

The shadows surge forth, their darkness fusing into a concentrated mass that envelopes Over Lord Miranda's energy. She wavers and falters under the onslaught of the shadows before being pushed back, and she sails through the air. As soon as she lands on the ground, a powerful blast flows across the property, and suddenly, we're pinned to the ground.

"Who are you to command us!" a voice hisses as the shadows move and twist alluringly.

Over Lord Mary gains the shadow figure's attention by sighing loudly in irritation. "Listen, assholes. I know you're mad they tricked you into giving up most of your power, but look at the silver lining. You died fighting a great evil. Go down as heroes and not asshats with a grudge."

"Leave now before the Over Lords kill you," Monteralia tells them.

"Ah, Monteralia. We have been looking for you. You will pay for what you did to us," another voice hisses.

The air is tense as the shadows disperse, relinquishing their grasp on the unfortunate souls they had trapped. As the darkness lifts, the scene that unfolds before me is nothing short of surreal. The inky cloak dissipates, revealing figures that exude an aura of ancient power and ethereal presence.

My gaze locks onto the newcomers, my heart pounding as I process the sight before me. They stand tall and impos-ing, each radiating an aura of profound strength. Four powerful beings emerge from the fading shadows, their very presence commanding attention and respect.

"We are gods and goddesses of Asteloria," one woman

says. "I am Zara, goddess of life." She points toward her counterparts. "This is Darka, god of time, Valtor, god of earth, and Rika, goddess of nature."

Darka is a figure wrapped in mystery, his form obscured by flowing robes that seem to ripple like the very fabric of existence. His eyes hold a depth that speaks of the eons he has witnessed, a cosmic wisdom that transcends mortal understanding.

Valtor emanates an aura of steadfast determination. His form is solid and grounded, with an air of rugged strength that mirrors the essence of the earth he commands. His gaze holds an unwavering resolve, a testament to his connection with the very planet beneath our feet.

Rika stands with an elegance that mirrors the graceful flow of the world. Her presence is a symphony of flora and fauna, her eyes sparkling with the secrets of the wilderness she protects. She exudes an energy that is tranquil and fierce, a guardian of the natural world.

Zara radiates an essence of vitality and renewal. Her form seems to shimmer with a luminous glow, embodying the essence of life itself. Her eyes hold a depth of compassion, a profound understanding of the intricate web of life she weaves.

"Well, well, if it isn't the divine shit lumps that's been causing us problems," Over Lord Ashley says with a voice that drips with sarcasm.

Her eyes glint with an irreverent humor that clashes with the stoic presence of the Asteloria pantheon. "What's your band name? Snark Almighty? Mythic Mockingbirds? Idiotic Immortals?"

"What is this simple creature speaking about?" Zara asks as she completely misses the sarcasm.

"Who the fuck are you calling simple, bitch? Yeah, I don't know which one of us is with Olivia for this pair of powers business, but I'm willing to bet it's me," Over Lord Ashley replies. "But regardless of who it is, we'll kick your ass."

Everyone seems to hold their breath as Zara regards Ashley with an unwavering gaze. "You claim a partnership with Olivia? As part of the kungiyoyi biyu na iko?"

Before Ashley can respond, Monteralia's voice cuts through the tension, her tone measured and firm. "Enough! This is too dangerous. Destroy them and be done with it."

The gods and goddesses laugh long and hard. They don't seem the least bit worried about facing the Over Lords. I'm concerned because they're deities, and I'm sure they have much more power than the Over Lords.

"You are not a part of anything," Darka says as his eyes wrinkle with amusement.

Confused, I tilt my head to the side. "Isn't it biyu na iko? That's what Axel called it when he kidnapped me."

Valtor snarls at the mention of Axel's name. "He should have never been involved to begin with. He further proved how inferior you are. Biyu na iko means 'pair of powers'. Kungiyoyi biyu na iko means 'two pairs of powers'. They are different."

Realization hits me then. No wonder the shadow figures kept saying pairs of powers. At first, I was confused, but now I see Axel had it wrong from the beginning.

"There's more than one pair," I gasp. "I don't understand any of this. What do you want from me?"

"We want our power back!" Valtor snarls at me. "We want retribution for Thodara's and Monteralia's lies!" He points to us. "And you will die so that we may prevail."

"Can someone tell us what the hell is going on!" Over Lord Stephanie shouts.

Rika regards her with malice. "To correct early assumptions, yes, they tricked us into giving away a significant portion of our power, but we did not go down as heroes. Thodara and Monteralia left us to die."

I shake my head in denial. "No, it developed because it filtered all the evil out of Asteloria. It destroyed your world, and when it attacked ours, they tricked you into giving them to us so that we may fight it."

"That abomination of darkness was Thodara's creation. Isn't that right, sister?" Rika says to Monteralia.

I turn to look at Monteralia, and I can see the truth written on her face. This whole vendetta confuses me, and I'm not surprised by the lies we keep uncovering.

My angry gaze lands on Monteralia. "You lied to us. Again! What was the point of lying? You could have been truthful from the start."

Monteralia shakes her head. "You do not understand." She points to the gods and goddesses. "They were interfering with fate. Changing outcomes they had no business changing. Thodara created the Abyssal Devourer to take them down."

Over Lord Ashley snorts in disbelief. "So, she created a cosmic janitor to clean up your mess? How considerate."

"Unfortunately, it took a turn for the worse. Instead of targeting them, it targeted and siphoned evil. It destroyed our world in the process." Monteralia continues as if Over Lord Ashley hadn't spoken.

"Thodara led us to a secluded area, siphoned our power, and left us too weak to fight that abomination she created. It attacked us, and we were swallowed by the darkness," Valtor snarls. "Though she also weakened herself."

"Some mother she is. I'm sure creating a cosmic monster isn't listed in the parenting handbook," Over Lord Ashley replies. "Nothing says 'parental guidance', like unleashing an Abyssal Devourer."

Over Lord Mary whistles to get their attention. "You're here now, so that means you didn't die. How? And for all that is holy, tell us what the fuck this has to do with us?"

Zara bares her teeth like a rabid animal. "The Abyssal Devourer is darkness. Our anger and vengeance saved us, and we took control of the darkness. Became the darkness. We have searched long and hard for Thodara and a way to get our power back. We've finally found the right individuals to do that. Thodara and Monteralia knew who you were and tried to keep you hidden."

"Thodara weakened herself further when she saved you and gave you new life," Monteralia tells the Over Lords. "We knew this moment would come as fate dictated it. But she is still more powerful than them."

"Then let her fight them," Over Lord Annie replies. She looks at the gods and goddesses. "I'm guessing these pairs of powers are what you need to defeat Thodara? We're the most powerful of our kind. If it's not us, then who?"

The group of gods turns their gazes toward us. "Danielle, Lucille, Olivia, Monteralia, and Viktoria." Zara says.

"Hold on. Back it up," Over Lord Miranda says suddenly. "Make it make sense. Make. It. Make. Sense."

"Millennia back, during a time when realms and dimensions were interconnected in ways now obscured by time, we created multiple worlds. Our essence lives in every living being of the worlds we created. Though we did not create the earth. That was the goddess Alara. However, we are the inadvertent suppliers of your power, thanks to Thodara." Darka says.

"So, which one of you psychos created demons?" Over Lord Ashley interrupts. "Because that's seriously fucked up. Have you seen what they look like? Honestly, this speaks worse for Mary. She's the one who fell in love with one. I mean, how could she get jiggy with one of them and spawn their offspring?"

"Hey!" Dani shouts in outrage. "I'm the best thing that's ever happened to you."

"What about the turning, the prophecies, and all the bullshit we've been through?" Over Lord Sydney asks, skepticism clear in her tone.

"We have no control over the actions of living beings or what fate brings," Zara replies. "We are powerful, but even we cannot control all things, though we tried."

"Silence!" Darka shouts. "Danielle's dual heritage as a magic user and demon aligns her with the ancient forces that motivate creation. This resonance intertwines with Lucille's divine nature from another world, creating a harmonious balance between the primal and celestial energies."

He continues his explanation without missing a beat. "Olivia's unique ability to perceive time aligns her with me and grants her a glimpse into the past, present, and future. Monteralia's divine heritage links her with the cosmic powers wielded by the gods and goddesses. Their connection reflects the duality of time and eternity."

"Viktoria's power of manipulation and control over others serves as the catalyst in these pairings, though she's a conduit to magic itself. Her ability to compel, command, and influence aligns her with the manipulative aspects needed to complete magical transfers. Her presence acts—."

Over Lord Ashley cuts off his tangent by yawning loudly. "Story time is getting boring. We get it now. Are we going to fight or what?"

My eyes widen as the atmosphere around us shifts. The air grows heavy with an intensity that vibrates through every fiber of my being. The gods before us now show visible signs of agitation. It's as if the air crackles with their mounting anger, and an almost tangible tension hangs in the air.

Vik's form trembles involuntarily. A chill crawls down my spine as her trembling intensifies. Her body radiates with an aura of energy that connects with the very essence of the gods standing before us. Panic clenches at my chest as I realize what's happening. They're taking control of her.

A guttural cry erupts from Vik, and a scream of pain echoes in the space around us. Her features contort in agony, and her eyes squeeze shut as her body pulses with a force beyond her control. I feel her pain as if it were my own, a searing agony that leaves me gasping for breath.

Then her voice changes. A cadence, a rhythm, seems to resonate with a power that transcends our understanding. She speaks words I've never heard before. A series of syllables that feel ancient and potent. Each word is like a key turning a lock, and I feel an unfamiliar pressure building within me.

As Vik recites those words, her voice a desperate plea and an assertion of her will, something strange happens. A sensation unlike anything I've ever experienced overcomes me. It's as if a dam within me has burst open, and an overwhelming rush of energy surges forth from my core. Pain, power, and an intense connection to Monteralia coursed through me.

Beside me, Dani and Lucy also scream, their voices joining in a symphony of agony and release. Our powers flow, cascading through us and into the gods and goddesses. It's as if our essence is being pulled from us, drawn towards the towering figures before us. The pain is blinding, all-encompassing, yet there's a strange sense of calm beneath it.

And then, as suddenly as it began, it ends. A blinding light erupts across Orchard Landing, its brilliance searing through the air like a beacon of raw power. My heart races as my eyes burn, and I'm squinting against the intense radiance that envelopes everything around us.

During this dazzling display, a figure materializes, its form emerging from the very heart of the light itself. As the blinding light subsides, my vision gradually clears, revealing the figure that stands before us.

"Enough!" she thunders.

Her words resonate with a force that vibrates through the ground beneath us. Her presence alone thwarts the gods' attempts to seize our power as she pushes them back.

Over Lords Ashley's voice, ever bold and unapologetic, chimes in. "Oh, look who's graced us with her divine presence. Did you take a break from causing cosmic chaos to play with us mere mortals, Thodara?"

Thodara, the Goddess of magic, has appeared with an aura of authority that seems to command the very forces of the universe. Her presence is ethereal and awe-inspiring, a manifestation of cosmic power that holds dominion over all magic.

In her wake, Thodara held the gods at bay, who had been moments away from siphoning all the magic from us.

Thodara's gaze blazes with a fierce determination, her voice ringing out like a command that echoes across dimensions.

"Leave them be," she commands.

Our bodies are filled with tension, an unmistakable clash of cosmic energies as Thodara confronts the beings who sought to undo the balance of magic. Her form radiates a brilliance that seems to dwarf the other gods, and for a moment, time seems to bow before her authority.

"Dani, Lucy, Vik, Olivia, Monteralia," she says, her voice a melody that carries both reassurance and power. "You are not pawns in their games. Your destinies are your own, and no one may manipulate the threads of fate that weave your lives."

I finally snap, as I'm too overwhelmed by everything around me. "This is so stupid! Don't you get it? It's all fate. If what they said was true, this was always going to happen. It wouldn't have been a prophecy otherwise. They were always going to come for us. You were always going to intervene, and this moment was going to happen. You think that you're changing fate, but you're doing everything according to fate's plan. "

"Man, that's deep, Olivia," Over Lord Ashley says. "So, in reality, everything we do is according to fate's plan. We think we're going against it, but we're not."

Over Lord Mary growls. "You're wrong, Olivia. We're just supposed to accept whatever shit fate throws at us? Go along with whatever prophecy comes next? I don't accept that. We've beaten prophecies before, which means we can change fate. Nothing is set in stone. We can always change the outcome."

Thodara breaks up our conversation, telling us to stop talking nonsense. When she speaks, her presence ripples through the very fabric of reality, asserting her dominion over the forces that seek to manipulate our lives. The gods now appear fearful in her presence but still hold defiant gazes and stances.

With a last look at us, Thodara directs her attention back toward the celestial beings. "That evil should have killed you," she declares, her words carrying the weight of universal authority. "You are my greatest disappointment."

Thodara turns to us again as her gaze softens with understanding and compassion. "You are not mere vessels of power," she says, her voice a gentle reassurance. "Your strength lies in your choices, unity, and the unique qualities that make you who you are."

The gods are becoming restless. They don't like her interruption of the power transfer and are seething with anger. Thodara's intervention has not only thwarted their attempt to regain their powers, but has also provoked their ire, pushing them to the edge of fury.

"Even you, Thodara, cannot alter the tapestry of fate," Zara says, her voice unwavering as she addresses her. "Like the small creature said. This was destined to unfold because of the choices made long ago."

Voltar's eyes glitter with a magical sparkle as a bitter chuckle escapes his lips. "You interrupted us, Thodara, but you underestimate the power we've already stolen. Enough to best you, even in your weakened state, and to crush the so-called Over Lords."

The earth trembles beneath us, a tremor that mirrors the rising tension between the gods and Thodara. The ground seems to resonate with their anger, a reflection of the cosmic forces that now stand on the brink of collision.

Thodara's expression remains steadfast, with her gaze locked on the defiant figures before her. "Your actions have brought chaos and imbalance," she replies with a firm counterpoint to their threats. "You sought power at the expense of the harmony that should have prevailed."

Darka steps forward with eyes blazing with a smoldering fury. "You call us disappointments?" his voice drips with venom as he snarls. "Perhaps it was your inability to protect our world that led to this predicament. The great evil should have never succeeded."

"Even in the face of anger, Thodara, fate remains the same," Zara adds, her voice cutting through the air like a knife. "This conflict was woven into existence by your lies."

As the gods and goddesses prepare to unleash their fury upon Thodara, the clash of opposing energies intensifies, drawing the very elements themselves into the battle. The earthquakes with the weight of their power.

"You will die today," Valtor snarls. "And so will your precious Over Lords and their entire world."

Suddenly, I hear sighs, huffs, and puffs coming from the Over Lords. I turn to see them with looks of boredom and exasperation.

"Another day, another world-saving drama," Over Lord Ashley's voice drips with sarcasm as she rolls her eyes. "Because apparently, we're the universe's designated cleanup crew."

Over Lord Miranda let out a resigned sigh. "And do we ever get a thank-you card? No. Just more fucking trouble."

Over Lord Stephanie's voice joins the chorus as her words drip with irony. "You know, let's try not to die while saving the world this time. Okay?"

Over Lord Annie's laughter tinkles like a bitter melody. "And when we're done playing heroes, I suggest we crack open a few bottles of wine. Because, really, what's better after a cosmic battle than a little drunk celebration?"

"Absolutely. And how about an extended vacation? You

know, somewhere where the fate of the universe doesn't hang in the balance." Over Lord Mary adds with the same sarcastic tone.

"You won't be mocking us when you beg for death!" Valtor growls at them.

"Bring it on, motherfucker," Over Lord Mary answers.

CHAPTER 29

LET THEM FIGHT

The property seems to hold its breath in anticipation of what's coming. In an instant, the Over Lords shed their casual facades and don battle gear that glimmers with otherworldly brilliance. The transformation is swift, as if the gravity of the impending clash has ignited a dormant fire within them.

The earth trembles beneath the weight of anticipation as the grounds of Orchard Landing brace itself. In the distance, the rhythmic march of the Mutane Sihiri army echoes a steady cadence that signals the approach of thousands of magic users united under the Over Lords' command. The ground shakes beneath their determined steps, a tangible display of their collective power.

A portal blossoms to life as Over Lord Miranda raises her hand. Their demon brothers emerge from the portal, their forms exuding an otherworldly intensity. Each step resonates with power as they line up beside the Over Lords, their eyes fixed on the opposing force.

"Little sisters," Buranath says in greeting.

Astroloch looks around Orchard Landing with a frown

on his face. "There seems to always be a quarrel in which our assistance is required. I do not like this world very much."

"But you love us, so deal with it," Over Lord Annie says.

Another portal materializes, and from its depths emerges the husbands of the Over Lords'. They're dressed in armor that mirrors their wives, an unspoken unity that speaks of their shared commitment to this dire cause.

Shadows swirl ominously around the gods. Their forms contort in darkness as they conjure creatures from the very essence of the shadows themselves. The creatures emerge with a sinister grace, their forms twisting and menacing. Dark tendrils extend from their bodies, exuding an aura of malice that sends shivers down the spines of all who witness them.

A heavy silence settles over the battlefield, broken only by the heavy breaths of those gathered around. The tension rises until it's thick enough to cut with a blade. Both sides stand poised, assessing each other with wariness and resolve. The anticipation hangs in the air like a storm waiting to break. All hell breaks loose when the shadow creatures attack.

"Stay back while we handle this!" Thodara shouts as she blocks our side with a shield while they fight.

Over Lord Ashley screams out in frustration. "She can't just block us! What are we supposed to do, stand here and watch them have all the fucking fun?"

Over Lord Sydney pats her shoulder to keep her calm. "Relax and let them handle this. This should have been taken care of a long time ago."

"Then we shouldn't have been involved in the first damn place," Over Lord Ashley huffs.

I take in the fight happening between two groups of

powerful beings in awe. The clash of titans unfolds before my eyes, a battle of gods that shakes the very foundations of reality. Thodara's magic surges around her, a hurricane of vibrant energy that seems to bend reality itself. She uses her magic beautifully, creating barriers of shimmering light that deflect Darka's attempts to manipulate time.

Monteralia's presence is equally commanding, giving an air of deathly authority. She summons ethereal scythes from thin air, their gleaming edges slicing through the very fabric of the battlefield.

The clash of magic is breathtaking, like a symphony of elemental forces colliding. Thodara's magic crackles and bursts, manifesting as bolts of lightning that streak across the sky, seeking their targets with unerring accuracy. Monteralia's scythes swing with grace and power, leaving trails of energy in their wake. It's a dance of destruction and creation, each move calculated and precise.

Darka counters Thodara's lightning with flashes of temporal distortion. Time bends and warps, allowing him to evade her attacks with an uncanny grace. Valtor calls forth pillars of rock and stone from the very ground beneath his feet, forming barriers that shield him from Monteralia's onslaught. Rita manipulates the same elements, conjuring storms of wind and fire to disrupt Thodara's focus.

The earth trembles beneath our feet as the clash of godly powers reverberates through the air. We stand at the edge of the battlefield, a mixture of awe and anxiety filling our hearts as we witness the titanic struggle before us. The ground quakes with each impact, sending shockwaves rippling outward.

I can't believe what I'm seeing. The gods are clashing right in front of us, and it's like something out of a nightmare. Their powers are so immense it's hard to compre-hend. I exchange worried glances with Dani, Lucy, and Vik, and I can tell they feel the same sense of apprehension and fear as I do.

I turn to Dani, my eyes wide with amazement and fear. "Dani, this is insane! Have you ever seen anything like this before?"

Dani shakes her head, her expression mirroring my astonishment. "No, Olivia, this is beyond anything I could have imagined. These gods are on a whole different level."

"I don't even know where to begin processing all of this. How are we supposed to handle something like this?" Lucy adds.

Vik is just as wide-eyed as the rest of us. "I've read about battles between gods in ancient texts, but I never thought I'd witness one. We better hope that shield holds and that Thodara and Monteralia beat them. We're not equipped to get involved in this."

Monteralia's scythes whirl through the air, cutting through the very fabric of reality as they clash against Valtor's towering constructs of earth. She shoots a barrage of magical energy beams from her scythes, each bigger and more powerful than the last. The ground shakes as these two forces collide, creating more destruction that leaves us spellbound.

Rita's elemental storms swirl around her, colliding with Thodara's lightning in a dazzling display of power and chaos. Yet, Thodara and Monteralia are not easily deterred. Monteralia's scythes take on a life of their own, moving with an almost sentient determination, cutting through the elements that stand in their way.

Monteralia twirls her scythes in dizzying arcs, sending shockwaves of energy through the air. The scythes glow with a golden light as she twirls them around her. Rika takes a step forward, her eyes gleaming with an intensity that belies her calm demeanor.

Rika raises her hands, and suddenly, the very earth moves beneath our feet. Massive stone golems rise from the ground, their lumbering forms towering over us. It's a display of her mastery over the earth.

"So, I don't know about you guys, but I'm feeling wholly inadequate compared to them," Over Lord Stephanie says as she gestures toward the fighting gods. "My stomach is in knots just thinking about this fight."

Over Lord Ashley turns toward her with a look of concern. "Do you have to poop? Because now is not the time for that."

"What? No!" Over Lord Stephanie replies while rolling her eyes at the ridiculous question.

The golems spew molten lava that the Thodara and Monteralia dodge and deflect. Monteralia's scythes swing through the air and clash against the stone golems, but it has little effect. The golems hurl rocks the size of boulders, while Thodara conjures lightning bolts to strike them to pieces.

As the battle rages on, the clash of magic and power creates shockwaves that ripple through the air, leaving a trail of destruction in their wake. The sky crackles with energy, and flashes of light illuminate the battlefield. Thodara and Monteralia stand firm, their resolve unshaken, as they continue to channel their magic in a relentless assault against the godly forces before them.

As the earth continues to shake beneath us, we exchange glances filled with trepidation and admiration. The sheer magnitude of the battle before us is overwhelming, a clash of powers that spans the spectrum of existence.

We can only watch in awe, each moment filled with anticipation as the gods wage their fierce struggle.

As Voltar lifts his hand, the air ripples and shimmers like a mirage. A bolt of lightning crackles through the sky, followed by a deafening thunderclap that sends tremors through my bones. We watch in awe as power surges between his fingers like liquid fire.

The hairs on the back of my neck stand on end as though charged with electricity. Rika conjures a swirling vortex of water and, combined with the electricity, sends it soaring toward Monteralia. She successfully deflects it, twirling her scythes to create a barrier.

"Holy shit!" I shout. "Did you guys just see that?"

"It's both incredible and terrifying. The sheer power they wield..." Dani's voice trails off as she continues to stare at the gods.

I feel Vik's tight grip on my arm. "Liv, the consequences of this fight,... could be catastrophic. Thodara better end this soon, or everything will get destroyed.."

As their intense fight continues, an additional threat emerges on the battlefield. The shadow creatures surge forward with an evil intent. Their shapes contort and shift, each movement oozing with a sense of dread. I watch, my heart racing, as they converge upon the shield Thodara erected, separating the battle from us.

Dani's voice cuts through the tension, her eyes narrowing in focus. "Everyone, brace yourselves! They're trying to break through Thodara's shield."

Lucy stands beside her with her hands raised as if ready to channel her otherworldly power at any moment. Vik grits her teeth as she readies herself for the impending onslaught. We form a protective circle to ensure we have views from all sides. My body is tense as fear so strong shoots through my body. I knew this thing with the Veil Society and Dark Council would end, but I never imagined this scenario. I can only hope I don't die trying to aid in their defeat.

The shadow creatures slam into the shield with a force that causes the shield to waver and vibrate. A shiver runs down my spine as I watch their inky forms press against the magical barrier, their claws and appendages grasping for purchase. But the shield holds firm, shimmering with Thodara's magic and refusing to yield.

"They won't get through," Monteralia's voice carries a sense of assurance as her eyes lock on the shadowy assailants. "Thodara's barrier is impenetrable."

We continue to watch the relentless assault. The shadow creature snarls and hisses, their anger clear even from a distance. Their efforts to breach the shield become increasingly frantic, and their movements grow more erratic as they realize their attempts are in vain.

"Let them try," Over Lord Mary says with a mix of confidence and mockery. "We'll kick their ass to another dimension."

Over Lord Sydney smirks as she crosses her arms and leans against an invisible force field, her eyes fixed on the futile struggle unfolding before us. "They don't look so scary to me."

Even in the face of danger, the Over Lords remain calm. And through it all, Thodara's shield remains resolute, a symbol of her formidable magic. The battle against the shadow creatures rages on, and their attempts to breach the barrier continue to fail.

As the minutes stretch on, we can see that Thodara's shield will not break. The shadow creatures, once menacing, now appear like trapped insects, futilely banging against the walls of a glass jar. And we, protected by the goddess's magic, stand as a unified front, ready to face whatever challenges lie ahead.

Valtor pounds his massive fists on the ground, summoning colossal stone fists that raise from the earth to pummel Monteralia. With each impact, the ground trembles, and Monteralia's footsteps falter. The clash of powers, the crackling of energy, and the earth-shaking force of the gods' fight against Thodara and Monteralia create a surreal backdrop to the chaotic scene. My heart pounds in my chest as I watch, feeling a mix of anticipation, fear, and determination.

Theodora's laughter echoes through the battlefield. "You dare challenge us? Surrender now before we kill you."

Valtor laughs right back with a manic look in his eyes. "You will not win. We are simply reacquainting ourselves with our magic. It's time for your demise."

Darka stands at the forefront of the confrontation, shimmering with an otherworldly glow. With a mere gesture, he manipulates the fabric of time, creating ripples that distort the battlefield. I watch in fascination and horror as the space around Thodara and Monteralia warps and twists, causing their movements to slow and falter. Their expressions reflect their struggle against temporal manipulation.

Zara moves with a sweeping motion of her hands as she conjures tendrils of raw energy that dance and wiggle, manifesting into powerful, otherworldly beasts. These beasts attack Thodara and Monteralia from all angles, their forms shifting and morphing as they seek to overwhelm the goddesses. Thodara's magic clashes with Zara's creations, their power meeting in dazzling bursts of light and darkness.

Thick, gnarled claws slash through the air, seeking to break the shimmering barrier of magic Thodara has summoned. With each collision, sparks fly, and the air sizzles with energy.

The beasts snap their razor-sharp jaws, attempting to bite through the goddesses' defenses. Monteralia's dark energy flickers ominously in the face of these ravenous attacks, creating a stark contrast against the radiant hues of Thodara's barrier.

Valtor channels the very elements beneath his control. The ground quakes beneath Thodara's feet as Valtor commands the earth to rise against her. Geysers of molten rock erupt from the ground, creating a hazardous terrain that requires the goddesses to readjust their footing constantly. Monteralia counters with her power over death and decay, turning the earth against Valtor's efforts. The clash of their abilities forms a battleground that is as unstable as it is dangerous.

Rika weaves the forces of the natural to overwhelm Thodara and Monteralia. Vines and roots surge from the ground, ensnaring Thodara and Monteralia as if the very earth itself has risen to bind them. The air crackles with the energy of her influence as storms brew overhead, casting thunder and lightning across the tumultuous sky. I can see the strain in Thodara's expression as she battles against the powerful forces of nature, her magic flaring in response.

Despite their fierce resistance, Thodara and Monteralia hold their ground with unwavering determination. Their combined power is a testament to their strength and resilience, but it's clear that they're facing formidable opposition. As they continue to fight, I witness moments of brilliance and moments of despair, and now I'm not too sure of the outcome of this fight.

However, the tides of battle are ever-shifting, and as I watch, a realization dawns. Darka's manipulation of time erodes the fluidity of Thodara's and Monteralia's movements, sapping their speed and agility. Zara's creations gain the upper hand, as their relentless assault causes cracks to appear in the shields of magic that the goddesses wield.

Valtor's control over the earth strengthens, overpowering Monteralia's attempts to turn the very ground against him. Rika's forces of nature surge, entwining and ensnaring the goddesses with a ferocity that's hard to escape.

Bit by bit, the gods intensify their combined efforts, pushing back Thodara and Monteralia, weakening their defenses. The goddesses fight valiantly, but their magic is strained, their energy waning. Their expressions reveal the toll the battle is taking on them, the lines of exhaustion etched onto their faces.

And then, with one last surge of power, the gods' attacks converge, a merging of magic that overwhelms the goddesses. A blinding burst of light and energy envelops Thodara and Monteralia, momentarily obscuring their forms. As the brilliance fades, the two goddesses stand, weary and battered, as they stand with instability.

My heart aches as I witness their struggles. Thodara and Monteralia now appear vulnerable and diminished. The fight has taken its toll, and their power is diminished. Now, the gods' final assault comes.

A torrent of combined energy surges toward Thodara and Monteralia, a force that threatens to overwhelm them. The air vibrates with the intensity of the attack, and I watch with bated breath as the goddesses summon their remaining strength to counter the onslaught.

The clash is fierce, a storm of magic and power that shakes the very foundation of the battleground. In the aftermath, as the dust and energy settles, it's clear that the gods' attack has done its job. Thodara and Monteralia stand. Their forms weakened and are close to falling over. The gods' assault has left Thodara and Monteralia in a precarious state, their strength depleted and their defenses compromised.

The odds seem impossible that they will defeat them. And yet, as I stand witness to the aftermath of the battle, I also know that hope still burns within us, a fire that refuses to be extinguished even in the face of overwhelming odds.

Darka, his eyes blazing with triumph and fury, steps forward, his voice resonating with an air of superiority. "You thought you could defy us, Thodara, Monteralia. You thought you could interfere with our rightful reclamation of power."

Thodara squares her shoulders and meets his gaze with defiance. "We did what we believed was necessary to prevent the spread of your darkness."

"You meddled with forces you could not comprehend. And now, you shall pay the price," Valtor snarls a deep rumble.

Monteralia shoots a glare towards Valtor. "We will not yield to your evil desires. We fought to protect the worlds you threatened."

"You were always the disobedient ones, the ones who refused to see things our way," Rika says with anger and disdain.

"You thought you could change fate today, but you cannot alter fate," Zara states, her gaze cold and calculating as she fixes it upon the weakened goddesses.

Thodara's voice, though tired, holds a note of unwavering determination. "We may have made mistakes, but we did what we believed was right."

"Right? Your feeble attempts at righteousness are meaningless in the face of our power." Darka's laugh echoes through the air.

Valtor's hands clench into fists, his eyes narrowing with a vengeful fire. "You shall learn the extent of our power soon enough."

"And you will learn the resilience of those who stand against you," Monteralia says with a glint of defiance.

Rika's voice drips with contempt. "Resilience? You mistake it for foolishness."

Zara's gaze bore into the weakened goddesses. "It is time for you to realize the folly of your actions."

As the gods close in, their intent clear, and their power palpable, Thodara and Monteralia exchange a glance that holds a world of shared understanding. Despite the odds stacked against them, despite the overwhelming force that threatens to crush them, they stand unwavering in their purpose.

Thodara's voice rings out with a final note of defiance. "If it is our fate to fall, then we shall fall standing."

"We may be weakened, but we are not defeated," Monteralia adds with a note of finality.

Darka takes another step forward. His hands raise, fingers illuminating with magic as he channels his power. Valtor follows suit as the ground trembles once again. Rita, her hair entwined with foliage, joins them, her magic intertwining with theirs.

And Zara adds her strength to the mix. As they raise their hands, an eerie glow envelops their palms, a swirling vortex of energy forming between them. The air itself seems to tremble, bending to the will of their combined power.

The ground beneath them rumbles, echoing their

intent. Thodara and Monteralia stand defiant, their gazes unyielding even as their magic falters. I feel a knot of unease tighten in my chest as the vortex of power grows in intensity, a maelstrom of darkness and light threatening to consume everything in its path.

The shield that Thodara had woven to protect us from the shadow creatures fades. Its shimmering surface weakens, cracks spider webbing across its once-solid form. The air feels heavy, charged with the anticipation of what is about to happen.

"Stay close," Dani's voice breaks through my thoughts, and I realize she's positioned herself beside me, ready to act if needed. Lucy and Vik stand on the other side, united in their determination to face whatever comes next.

With a final surge of power, the gods and goddesses release their combined magic, a torrent of energy lashing out toward Thodara and Monteralia. The swirling vortex collides with them, and I watch in horror as their forms jolt and their magic is siphoned away.

Thodara's shield crumbles completely, dissolving into nothingness as her strength wanes. The gods' power envelops them. Their forms were wracked with the force of the magic being taken from them. I can see the strain on Thodara's face and the sheer effort it takes to hold her ground against this onslaught. They are losing the battle, which does not bode well for us.

CHAPTER 30
NOW ITS OUR FIGHT

As Thodara and Monteralia fall under the weight of the gods' assault, a tangible sense of dread settles over the battlefield. Thodara's shield wavers and eventually shatters in a cascade of energy, fading into nothingness. The moment the shield falls, the shadow creatures surge forward, their forms shifting and morphing as they advance.

The Mutane Sihiri soldiers, clad in their armor, move to intercept the shadow creatures with fierce determination. Their hands crackle with elemental forces, and as the first wave of shadow creatures crashes upon them, torrents of fire, ice, and lightning erupt, repelling the darkness that seeks to engulf them. Arcane shields shimmer into existence, providing a barrier against the relentless onslaught.

The Over Lords move with a grace that defies the chaos around them. Their unity is apparent, an unspoken understanding forged through years of battles and victories. As the shadow creatures surge forward, they meet the onslaught with a seamless display of power. The gods stand back and watch their creatures do all the work. Dani summons walls of earth, creating barriers that withstand the shadow creatures' attacks.

Lucy throws her arms in every direction, either yanking soldiers out of the way from a fatal blow or pushing the dark creature back. Vik's compulsion ability works to disrupt the creatures' coordination, causing confusion and discord amongst their ranks. With blinding speed, Lucy uses her agility to dart in and out of the fray, delivering precise and devastating blows.

Dani trades punches and kicks as her body is a blur of motion. One shadow creature punches Dani, sending a spray of blood into the air. However, she jumps right back into the fight. Growls and snarls fill the air as the creatures absorb the punishing blows, each strike delivering a symphony of pain. But the shadow creatures are relentless. With every fallen foe, they surge back to life, their forms reconstituting as if untouched.

Vik is holding her own against a creature attacking her. The brute lunges forward, fists clenched, aiming to over-power her with sheer force. His fists swing like wrecking balls, but Vik is quick and agile, ducking and weaving to avoid the crushing blows. With lightning speed, she retali-ates, landing a precise jab at the brute's ribcage, causing him to grunt in pain.

Suddenly, the atmosphere shifts with another presence. Striding right into the battle are Nash and Steel, followed by a larger group of people. I assume this is the Veil Society, and their arrival has added another layer of complexity to the frantic scene.

I watch their dark figures emerge from the shadows, their expressions a mix of malice and spite. My heart sinks at the sight, for we now face an even greater challenge: the convergence of enemies from every corner.

"Of course! Just what we fucking needed," Over Lord Miranda's voice drips with sarcasm as her eyes narrow at the incoming Veil Society members.

"First, gods with a grudge, then an army of shadow creatures, and now these self-entitled shit holes," Over Lord Ashley scoffs with annoyance.

"Can it get any worse?" Over Lord Mary's tone is a blend of frustration and exasperation.

"We've hit the jackpot in terms of terrible situations," Over Lord Stephanie chimes in as she grunts when one creature hits her.

I can't help but agree with their sentiments. The arrival of the Veil Society seems like a cruel twist of fate. The Veil Society members seem to relish in the chaos, and I can see their sinister grins visible even from a distance. They spread out, flanking the shadow creatures and the gods alike. I can hear their eerie whispers carried by the wind, an unsettling symphony of evil intentions.

Over Lord Sydney's voice is a mix of annoyance and resignation. "Who knew being a magic user would come with such drama?"

"If we make it through this alive, I vote for an extra extended vacation," Over Lord Annie mutters as she twists away for a kick.

"Agreed. After all, what's a little world-saving without a relaxing getaway?" Over Lord Mary says with even more sarcasm.

Despite the odds stacked against us, the Over Lords are leaders who have faced countless challenges before. They knew how to fight, strategize, and keep pushing forward, no matter the odds.

And as the Veil Society closes in, as the gods' powers rage, and as the shadow creatures threaten to engulf us all,

I know one thing for sure: we are in for a battle unlike any other. The Over Lord switches their focus toward the new group of magic users, intending to take them out swiftly.

"I really thought that once Axel was dead, you'd run away with your tails tucked between your legs," Over Lord Mary says to them.

"Axel was only a figurehead in this ordeal," Nash replies with a sinister smile. "He's no match for either myself or Steele with his ability to shed his skin just to heal himself. What good does that do for us? He's dead now, anyway."

Steele spreads his arms out wide, as if gesturing to everything around him. "This is bigger than all of you. Surrender now and let them take their power back. They have plans for all of us, and it will not go well for you if you keep fighting."

"You guys are even dumber than you look," Over Lord Miranda says. "They care nothing about you. They're using you. Once you finish being useful, they'll kill you."

Nash raises a brow. "Are you going to surrender or not? I'm really looking forward to a fight."

Over Lord Ashley looks at the battle raging around us. "It looks like our soldiers are putting up a good fight. We can spare a couple of minutes to humor them before killing them. After all, we've got a bigger threat to handle."

She looks toward Nash and Steele with a manic smile, with her hand on her watch. "Five minutes is all we can spare to entertain you. You better get some good hits in because, in the end, you'll all be dead."

I hear the beeping sound from the watch as she sets it, and the fighting starts. A large, muscly guy stomps toward me with an evil look that promises pain. I pull out the knives strapped to my sides and put them up, ready to defend myself.

He approaches me, and I swipe, trying to slash his chest, but he steps back, laughing as I miss him. He lunges forward, swinging his meaty fist in my direction. I move to the side, but I'm not fast enough as his fist swipes my cheek. Turning, I lodge my knife into his side. He doesn't flinch, as if he felt nothing at all.

"Three minutes left!" Over Lord Ashley taunts. "Majority of you are already dead. You guys really should have thought about this."

So far, no one, not Dani, Vik, Lucy, or the Over Lords has used any magic against them. There's no need, as they prove to be no match in any capacity against them. Over Lord Ashley's announcement distracts me, and the burly man grabs me. His hands wrap around my throat before he picks me up and slams me into the ground.

The impact knocks the wind from my lungs as pain radiates through my body. He climbs on top of me, pinning my arms beneath his knees as he chokes me. Panic rises, and I buck wildly, trying to knock him off me. I scratch and claw at his arms, but it has no effect.

"You may be fast, but you are no match for my super strength, little girl. I cannot kill you, but I will inflict a lot of pain," he says.

Something plows into him, knocking him off me. I sit up, gasping for air, and see Dani pummeling him in the face before holding him upside down by his legs.

"You may be strong, but I'm stronger," she says as he flails around. "Let me show you just how strong."

Her demon side takes over a little as she grabs his other leg. I watch with both horror and amazement as she rips him in half, from his groin to his head.

"Pathetic," she snaps and spits on his corpse before helping me up.

"One more minute until death do us part," Over Lord Ashley yells with a laugh. "You guys are pussies."

"Enough!" Nash snaps, anger clear in his eyes and tone. "We were just playing around."

Over Lord Ashley laughs. "What co-winky-dink. We were playing around, too."

"Let's kill them and be done with it. The gods don't need them alive." Steele says.

Over Lord Ashley raises a hand to stop the other Over Lords. "Stay back, guys. I'll handle these two idiots myself, and then they're going in the box with Axel."

"We don't have time for you to act extra, Ashley," Over Lord Miranda sighs.

Over Lord Ashley looks at her watch again. "Thirty seconds is remaining. That's plenty of time to kick their asses."

Nash's form shifts from solid to hazy as Steel conjures the elements, changing one element into another.

"Oh, intangibility and elemental transmutation," Over Lord Ashely says. "Guys, this just got juicier."

Over Lord Ashley teleports in front of Nash with a series of punches and kicks. He grins as he attempts to phase through Over Lord Ashley's attack. But he didn't expect her skill and control over death itself. With a flick of her fingers, she summons ethereal chains from the ground, dark energy coiling around Nash's form and anchoring him to the physical plane.

His intangibility is useless against her manipulation of death's power. Steele's hands crackle with raw energy, and he sends waves of molten rock hurtling toward Over Lord Ashley. The ground beneath her trembles as the molten earth approaches, but she remains unflinching. Raising her hand, she conjures a swirling vortex of souls around her, creating a protective barrier that absorbs the intense heat.

With a controlled exhale, Over Lord Ashley unleashes her own arsenal. The ground quivers as skeletal hands rise from the earth, reaching for Steele with grasping fingers. The undead minions she commands move with eerie precision, closing in on him from all sides. His elemental magic clashes against the necromantic forces.

Nash struggles against the ethereal chains that hold him captive, his intangible form flickering as he fights to break free. But Over Lord Ashley's mastery over death's realm was unyielding. She looks at them with her eyes burning with an unearthly fire. With a surge of power, she tightens the chains, binding Nash's form completely, rendering his intangibility useless.

Steele's attacks are growing weaker, his control over elemental forces faltering as the relentless undead horde closes in. Over Lord Ashley's power over death and reanimation is overwhelming, and her command of the undead army is absolute. As the final skeletal hand reaches Steele, he lets out a desperate cry, his elemental magic extinguishing in a burst of sparks.

With both subdued, Over Lord Ashley teleports in front of each of them, tearing their heads off quickly and efficiently. Her watch beeps just as she tosses Steel's head on the ground.

"Not a second after," she says as she looks at her watch.

"You are seriously deranged," I say before my eyes widen as I realize I'd spoken out loud.

Zara's voice rings out, her words dripping with condescension and amusement. "Well, well, what a delightful performance we have witnessed, Over Lords. Your struggle against the Veil Society was truly entertaining."

"We've allowed you to enjoy your little skirmishes for a while, but it's time for us to reclaim the stage," Darka adds with a sardonic smile.

Valtor joins in with an air of superiority. "You've played your part well, Over Lords, but now it's time for the true powers to take control."

As if responding to their commands, shadows converge around them, merging into a fresh wave of shadow creatures. Some creatures now have wings, and their forms twist and gnarl as they take to the air. My heart quickens as I realize the gods' intentions. They want to unleash these creatures upon the world, to spread chaos and destruction far and wide.

Rika gestures, and the shadow creatures obey as they fan out in all directions. The sky grows darker as the creatures take flight, blotting out the sun with their dark forms. Panic ripples through the Mutane Sihiri army, their shouts of alarm mingling with the anguished cries of the Over Lords outrage.

Over Lord Stephanie growls in anger. "Are you shitting me? As if we don't have enough to deal with already. Let's kill these fuckers before they cause irreparable damage to the world. "

Zara's gaze hardens to a dangerous glint. "Your insolence is tiresome, Over Lords. We've indulged your defiance for long enough."

With a wave of her hand, the shadow creatures disperse, vanishing into the distance as they carry out the gods' command. The world has suddenly become a battlefield on a much grander scale, with the gods themselves orchestrating the chaos. As the realization of the gods' true intentions settles in, a sense of dread fills the air.

Our defiance has drawn their attention, and now they

seek to assert their dominion over the very world we fight to protect. To carry out their original intentions from long ago. The Over Lords exchange glances, and their expressions are a mix of fear and concern as we prepare to face a new and even more difficult challenge.

"Hear me, Mutane Sihiri. Evil has come to our world. It is time to fight. Try to stay alive while we kill these pieces of shit," Over Lord Mary sends out through the calling.

"Really, Mary?" Over Lord Stephanie says. "That's your advice?"

She sends Over Lord Stephanie a look. "Shut up."

Suddenly, their husbands appear before them, battered and bruised from fighting.

"I will open a portal to the other factions. Tell them the world is being attacked. We need you to protect the people out there while we finish here," Over Lord Miranda says.

The men give objections but leave because they know the importance of doing what she asks. I watch the Over Lords' husbands and their demon brothers vanish into portals, carrying news of the impending threat to the world. They are off to rally reinforcements, to gather every ally in the desperate hope of stemming this tide of darkness.

Turning my attention back to the battlefield, I feel a shiver run down my spine. The Mutane Sihiri army that had once stood united is now dwindling because the number of shadow creatures is too many.

The Over Lords have grown serious as they prepare to take on the gods who so easily beat Thodara and Monteralia. However, worry still covers their faces, as the weight of the situation is undeniable. We had fought against the Veil and shadow creatures that seemed nearly unstoppable. The realization that victory is no longer assured hangs heavily in the air.

"Looks like this party just took an unexpected turn," Over Lord Stephanie mutters as she looks at the gods.

Over Lord Sydney's expression mirrors the concern in her sister's eyes. "This is the first time that I feel unsure about the battle we're about to fight."

Even Over Lord Ashley has a somber tone as she addresses the group. "Our army is dwindling, and those creatures... they just keep coming back. We need a plan."

As the Over Lords exchange glances, the gravity of what they have to do takes hold. They've faced countless challenges, but this is a new level of adversity. I feel the seriousness of the moment, the weight of responsibility pressing down on us all.

A tense silence settles over Orchard Landing, broken only by the distant cries of battle and the eerie rustle of the shadow creatures. The god's intent to plunge our world into chaos, to tear down everything we've fought so hard to build, will fail.

"Let's gather what remains of our forces," Over Lord Miranda finally says. "We need to hold our ground, protect our people, and figure out a way to kill these bastards."

Over Lord Mary nods in agreement. "We'll use every ounce of our magic, every strategy we've ever employed. We won't go down without a fight."

"And we'll give these gods and their shadow creatures an ass whooping they won't forget." Over Lord Stephanie adds.

The mocking laughter of the gods echoes through the air. Their voices carry a sense of arrogance, a belief that they hold all the power and that our resistance is futile.

"Look at them," Valtor's voice booms with derision. "These mortals truly think they can stand against us?"

Rika's laughter dances like an eerie melody. "It's almost adorable. Their feeble attempts to oppose us are laughable."

"Do they not realize the futility of their struggle?" Darka's mocking chuckle cuts through the air.

"Pathetic creatures who think they could ever challenge the gods," Darka replies.

Their laughter reverberates like a taunt, each note stoking the fires of determination within us. The gods have underestimated us, seeing only our human forms and not the power that surges through our veins. The Over Lords hold the magic of earth and the strength of countless battles. And as united as we are, we are far from feeble.

Over Lord Miranda's expression remains stoic as she looks into the gods. "You're idiots if you underestimate us. Kicking your asses will be so satisfying."

"Let them laugh. They'll soon learn the error of their arrogance." Over Lord Mary adds.

Annie's eyes glitter with defiance. "We've faced worse odds before. This is just another challenge to overcome."

Stephanie's smirk is razor sharp. "I can't wait to wipe the smirk off their dumb faces."

CHAPTER 31

THIS BATTLE ISN'T EASY

As they face the looming battle against the gods, tension hangs heavy in the air, a nearly tangible force that permeates their essence. Each Over Lord is glowing with power as they gather as much as possible to fight this brutal fight. They exchange furtive glances, and I can see the hesitation in their bodies. Once this begins, they must see this through, no matter what.

"We have a few tricks up our sleeves," Over Lord Miranda says. "We've developed a few weapons to aid us over the years, and you are perfect for testing them out."

Over Lord Miranda conjures an otherworldly bow flickering with energy and fire. A glowing sword, long and sharp, appears in Over Lord Mary's hands. I watch a thorn-covered whip, energy chains, and sharp, pointy daggers appear in the other's hands.

A chilling wind sweeps through the property, carrying the whispers of ancient prophecies and the echoes of battles long past. The Over Lords exchange a final, tense glance. With a collective nod, they step forward to engage the gods.

The shadow creatures are pushing back our army, and with their numbers declining quickly, their attention turns to us. Despite the fear that gnaws at the edges of my consciousness, I will fight because there's no avoiding it. My grip tightens around my weapon, and I exchange glances with Dani, Lucy, and Vik. We're united in purpose, bound by the shared resolve to protect this world from this sinister threat.

As the shadow creatures draw nearer, I feel a surge of adrenaline course through my veins. My heart pounds in my chest, each beat a testament to the impending clash. Time seems to slow as I focus on the approaching enemy, their forms flickering and distorting like shadows cast by an infernal fire.

An icy shiver traces down my spine as I raise my weapon, ready to face this relentless evil. My breath comes in short, controlled bursts as I steady myself. My senses heighten to catch even the slightest movement within the mass of darkness.

The battle cries of the shadow creatures fill the air, their chilling howls mingling with the fierce determination in our own voices. As they close in, I can feel the weight of their malice, a force that seeks to envelop and consume everything in its path. Yet we stand our ground, prepared to face anything.

Dani moves with a focused determination. As the shadow creature advances, she acts swiftly. With a sweep of her hand, the earth rises in sharp spikes, impaling the creatures and creating a barrier to impede their progress. She isn't holding back.

Her movements are precise and efficient, a dance of controlled destruction. But the shadow creatures are relentless, undeterred by the obstacles Dani has erected.

They push forward, their dark forms writhing as they attempt to bypass the barriers.

That's when Dani's powers shift. Her hands ignite with a flame that flickers with a demonic energy. She's resorted to using demon fire to give her the upper hand. She flings her hands forward, and the demon fire surges towards the shadow creatures.

The flames engulf them, their shrieks of agony filling the air as the inferno consumes them. The fire licks at their forms, leaving nothing but trails of dissipating shadows in its wake.

I watch Lucy spring into action. Lucy raises her hands with a focused expression, and a burst of blinding light erupts from her palms. The brilliance of it is almost blinding, and I have to shield my eyes for a moment. The shadow creatures recoil; their dark forms falter like light seared through their essence.

Taking advantage of their momentary disorientation, Lucy flicks a wrist, twisting and bending the shadow creatures in grotesque ways. She lifts the shadow creatures from the ground, their forms still contorting and twisting by her power. With a swift motion, she sends them hurtling through the air and crashing into each other with a sickening thud.

But Lucy hasn't finished yet. Her divine energy surges around her, imbuing her every movement with heightened grace and power. Her eyes glow with a radiant light, and her presence repels the darkness that once threatened to overwhelm us.

With a determined focus, Lucy unleashes a blast of power once more. The shadow creatures, weakened by the burst of light and their collision, are no match for the force of her divine energy. They shatter into shards of darkness, dissipating into nothingness.

"We are so badass," Dani says to Lucy.

Lucy smiles back and laughs a little. "You know we are. Let's finish this so we can assist the Over Lords."

Vik and I face off against three formidable shadow creatures. Vik grips her weapon tightly as she gets ready to spring into action. Her ability to compel and control others is useless against these newer shadow creatures, but she doesn't falter. Instead, she relies on her combat skills and agility, her body poised for swift movements.

A swift, spinning kick sends one of the shadow creatures hurtling backward, dissipating into nothingness upon impact with the ground. Without missing a beat, Vik pivots and delivers a swift elbow strike to another, shattering its form into a swirling mist.

One creature lunges at her with claws outstretched, but Vik sidesteps its attack gracefully, her nimble footwork allowing her to evade danger effortlessly. With a lightning-fast movement, she draws a small, gleaming knife from a concealed sheath on her thigh and plunges it into the creature's heart, causing it to dissipate into a dark mist that disperses into the air.

A shadow creature sets its eyes on me. I swallow the fear that threatens to rise, reminding myself that I have to stay focused. I don't possess the ability to conjure magic like the others, but I still had a role to play in this fight. My determination hardens, and I grip the hilt of my daggers, steeling myself for the confrontation.

The first shadow creature lunges at me, its form shifting and contorting as it reaches out with shadowy tendrils. Vik reacts with lightning speed, dodging its attack and countering with a quick, precise strike of her weapon.

"Fire!" Vik yells out.

Dani turns around, and demon fire flows from her hand onto Vik's blade before it impales in its chest. The creature lets out a distorted shriek as it dissipates into nothingness. But there are still two more to deal with. The shadows surge towards us at the same time as they seek to envelop us in darkness.

It's a relentless onslaught, and we're growing weary from the constant battle of fending them off. These two are not as easy to beat as the first creatures. But then Dani and Lucy step forward, an evil glint in their eyes.

I watch as Dani's magic surges around her, a blend of earth and demonic energy that seems to vibrate with power. Her eyes are ablaze with an intensity I had rarely seen before, and her hands crackle with energy. Beside her, Lucy's divine magic radiates a brilliant light, casting a warm glow that contrasts with the encroaching darkness.

With a synchronized movement, Dani and Lucy raise their hands, and their magic intertwines in a breathtaking display. As their magic blends, a shockwave of energy ripples outward, pushing back the approaching shadows.

The impact is astonishing. The shadows recoil as if struck by an invisible force, their forms flickering and dissipating in the face of the combined magic. It's definitely a sight to behold Dani's raw power and Lucy's divine essence working in harmony to repel the darkness.

As the shadows falter, Dani and Lucy press their advantage. Streams of earth and divine energy shot forth from their outstretched hands, lancing through the shadows with deadly precision.

While they're busy with that, creatures are still attacking me and Vik. I deftly sidestep an attack, my movements fluid and calculated. In response, I deliver a powerful punch to its dark, smoky form, my fist passing through it with an unsettling sensation of cold emptiness. My hand emerges unscathed, but the shadow creature recoils as its shape is momentarily disrupted.

The next shadow creature lunges at me from a different angle, and I twist my body to avoid its grasp. My foot shoots out in a sweeping kick, making contact with its amorphous body. It shudders and moves away again, its form shifting and undulating in disorientation.

A third shadow creature joins the fray, moving swiftly to encircle me. I know I can't rely solely on punches and kicks. However, Vik comes to my defense and stabs it through the chest.

Panting with adrenaline coursing through our veins, we exchange glances of relief. But the relief is short-lived, for in the distance, more malevolent forms are converging, a relentless tide of darkness that threatens to engulf us.

The shadow creatures are relentless in their pursuit to consume and destroy. The once-clear battlefield is now a furious battleground as we face a fresh wave of creatures emerging from the shadows.

"Fuck!" Vik yells as she looks at them. "These creatures are like roaches. Kill one, and five more appear. They just keep coming."

"We'll just keep killing them," Lucy replies.

The air is vibrating with unsettling energy as the encroaching darkness advances. Each step they take sending shivers down my spine. Despite our fatigue and wounds, we ready ourselves for another round, with our weapons poised at the ready. The shadow creatures reach us, attacking vigorously and quickly.

The anger and evil radiating from them almost make me want to throw up. We strike back with all the strength and skill we can muster. However, it's clear that the odds are stacked against us this time. The shadow creatures are chaotic in their attack, overwhelming us with sheer numbers and evil force.

We continue to fight, our movements fueled by desperation and fear to protect ourselves and each other. Every strike, every hit, is driven by the need to survive. But no matter how many we defeat, more continue to emerge, their dark forms twisting and writhing in a seemingly never-ending torrent. The battle is taking a toll on us, physically and mentally. Our breaths come in ragged gasps, and our muscles strain under the weight of continuous combat.

Yet, we refuse to back down. If the Over Lords are fighting for dear life against the gods, then we can't give up our fight. The sky seems to darken further as the shadow creatures amass a foreboding swarm that stretches as far as the eye can see. The realization strikes us like a blow. We're facing an enemy that seems boundless as they refuse to be defeated.

"This isn't looking good, guys!" I shout as I continue to fight the shadow creatures.

"Tell me something I don't know, Liv," Vik shouts, gritting her teeth from the pain of the hit she just took.

An idea crosses my mind. This whole time, I've feared my ability and this new world, never really embracing it. I have one last thing to try, to give us the upper hand before we succumb to these creatures.

My voice is loud as it rings out above the fighting. "I have an idea! I'll use my ability."

"What!" Dani shouts as she kicks a creature in the chest. "What the fuck have you been doing all this time, Liv?"

"Whatever it is, just do it already," Lucy snaps after a shadow creature punches her in the face.

"Alright! Alright!" I snap back at them.

With a deep breath, I close my eyes, letting the world around me fade away as I summon my ability. The familiar sensation of shifting through time and space envelopes me, and in an instant, I find myself standing in a future yet to unfold. I see the next few minutes of attacks and come back to reality. As we continue fighting, I tell them what to do when the shadow creatures attack, and we take them out quickly.

We continue to fight them with me, jumping back and forth through my visions and back to reality. My visions keep coming, showing the different outcomes of the fight. Whenever a vision shows an attack, I try to prevent it and kill the shadows. Unfortunately, I haven't learned to control my ability fully, and this method of fighting is getting out of control.

Soon, I can't control when the visions come, and they get longer every time, leaving me vulnerable during the fight. Dani and Vik had had to save my ass a few times.

"Stop, Olivia!" Thodara shouts weakly. "You cannot look into the future and stop fated outcomes. Control your ability."

She's been silent for so long, I thought she was dead. Unfortunately, the visions keep filtering through my mind, and I can't keep up. Maybe I can stop this altogether and skip to see when the battle ends. It's risky to try, especially with my ability going haywire, but I don't want anyone else to die. I try to concentrate more, willing my ability to take me to a future where this battle has ended.

It feels like someone opened a floodgate, and glimpses of what is coming overwhelm me. But the strain on my mind only increases. The visions are no longer within my control. They come unbidden, overlaying reality with glimpses of a future yet to happen.

I see the battle unfolding in different ways; the outcomes shifting with each vision. None of it is in our favor, and I can't tell which one is our actual future. It's as if time itself is unraveling around me. I hear Lucy's voice amid the chaos, calling out a warning.

"Stop, Liv!" she shouts. "We'll figure out another way."

My breathing is labored now. "I can't control it. I don't know how to stop it!"

And then something within me cracks. It's as if a dam had burst, and the flood of visions overwhelms me completely. Time itself seems to warp, merging the present and the future into a confusing, disorienting combination. I can feel reality shifting around me, the boundaries between moments dissolving.

I stumble, the ground beneath me feeling unstable, as if the very fabric of the world is breaking apart. The clash of battle, the shouts, and the roars of the shadow creatures all meld into a cacophony of chaos. I can hardly distinguish where I am or what is happening.

One moment, I'm lunging forward, my hands coming up to hit an incoming shadow creature. The next moment, I find myself several steps back, already expecting the attack and countering it before it even occurs. It's as if my actions are echoing through time, repeating in a strange loop.

Beside me, Dani's movements are just as disjointed. She'd strike a blow, her movements fluid and calculated, only to suddenly find herself back in her original position, poised to strike again. Her expressions shift rapidly from determination to anger as the dual realities clash.

"You broke reality, Liv!" Dani snaps, irritation apparent in her tone. "This is not what we fucking needed!"

Lucy adds to the chaos as objects levitate and propel themselves through the air. She'd throw a projectile at a shadow creature, only for it to loop back around and hit the creature from a different angle in a subsequent iteration. Her concentration is split between the present and the near future, and her efforts are mirrored and refracted.

Vik faces a test of her agility and combat skills as she evades the attacks of the shadow creatures. She moves with a grace that transcends time, anticipating their movements before they even make them. Her movements seem almost ethereal, as if she's dancing through the battle, each step a carefully orchestrated routine. Then, she repeats the fight as she gets trapped in the alternating realities.

And then there is me, trying to make sense of it all. My world sight ability has inadvertently torn open a rift in time, intertwining our actions in a never-ending loop. I would witness an attack, react to it, and then find myself right back where I started, reliving the sequence repeatedly.

The fight is a whirlwind of motion, a kaleidoscope of repeating actions and split-second decisions. The clash of magic and the swarming of shadow creatures create a chaotic backdrop for our disjointed movements. Each iteration feels both familiar and disorienting, like a never-ending déjà vu.

"You need to figure out how to fix this, Liv," Lucy yells. "We already had a hard enough time fighting them off without having to repeat our attacks."

"I can!" I cry.

No matter how hard I concentrate or try, nothing is fixing this rip in reality. As the fighting continues, the lines between the present and the future became increasingly blurred. We hop back and forth between the two, our movements becoming a dance of anticipation and reaction.

It's a dizzying experience that tests our instincts and abilities as we navigate this fractured reality.

Suddenly, everything freezes, and a haggard-looking Over Lord Mary appears in front of us. "Stop fucking with time, Olivia! You're screwing us up against the gods."

I look to the side to see the other Over Lords facing off against the gods, and it does not look good. Screwing up time really made it harder for the Over Lords.

"We can't afford to cover your asses while fighting them," she snaps at me before raising her hands.

Suddenly, Felix appears in front of us. "Put them in cages until we're finished," she commands him. "If you do this, and they don't die, we'll consider not killing you for your betrayal."

Felix shakes his head fervently and does what she says. Then we find ourselves locked in a cage with no way of getting out.

"Do not interfere, or I will snap your goddamn necks," Over Lord Mary growls before disappearing again. `

Dani looks at me with irritation in her eyes. "Well, this is just fabulous. I always dreamed of being on the sidelines during an epic battle."

Lucy's eyes flash with annoyance. "Thanks a lot, Liv."

Vik's usually composed demeanor cracks as she clenches her fists. "I can't believe we're stuck in cages. Again! This is beyond ridiculous."

My frustration gets the best of me, and I sigh. "I'm sorry, guys. I was only trying to help."

We exchange a few choice glances, our expressions conveying a mixture of annoyance and disbelief. That we're in this predicament is almost laughable if only the situation allowed it.

Lucy's fingers brush against the bars. "I mean, of all the

magical scenarios we've encountered, being locked in cages is probably the most underwhelming."

Dani shoots her a wry grin. "Well, you know what they say. Variety is the spice of life."

Vik shrugs in defeat. "And being a captive audience has its own charm, I suppose."

As they continue talking, my fingers dance along the bars, searching for any weakness or gap that might allow us to escape. It's a futile attempt, but it beats sitting idly by.

"They may have trapped us," I say, my tone more serious now, "but we're not exactly known for staying put."

Lucy's lips curve into a mischievous smile. "Agreed. We can still use magic even in these cages."

Vik's eyes gleam with delight. "When will the Over Lords stop underestimating our resourcefulness?"

"If we get hurt or interrupt them, my mom will kill us for sure this time," Dani sighs.

CHAPTER 32

ANGERING THE OVER LORDS

The Over Lords, who have always appeared calm and invincible, now stand before us in an utterly shocking disarray. Haggard, bruised and battered, they are living proof of the ferocious battle they are fighting. Their garments, typically pristine and adorned with intricate embroidery, are now marred by dirt, scorch marks, and the unmistakable stains of blood.

Despite their battered appearances, the Over Lords exude an air of resilience and stubbornness. Their unwavering commitment to protecting their people and the world is apparent, even in their disheveled state.

"Give up now and save yourself the embarrassment of dying in front of your people," Zara says.

"You give up and save yourself an ass whooping," Over Lord Miranda snaps back.

"Thodara and Monteralia, you two bitches are included in this ass whooping too," Over Lord Mary adds. "Because of you, our lives are changed forever. We didn't ask for this shit, but we're damn sure going to finish it. You can lay there and die, or you can fight back, but you will die today."

The gods loom before them, an ethereal presence that exudes power and danger. They emanated an aura that speaks of ages past and dominion over the elements. Their forms seem to shift with every breath, as if the very essence of the world obeys their will. Their snappy comment agitates them further, and they attack.

Over Lord Miranda faces off against Thodara with her magical bow in her hand. With a deft pull of the bowstring, she unleashes a torrent of blazing arrows; each imbued with the searing fury of fire. The arrows streak through the air like fiery comets, homing in on Theodora with uncanny precision. The goddess of magic reacts by conjuring a shimmering shield of arcane energy that deflects the arrows with a brilliant burst of light.

She retaliates by sending bolts of lightning and shards of ice hurtling toward Over Lord Miranda. She swiftly raises her Phoenix Bow, conjuring a barrier of flames to intercept the attack. The impact causes fiery explosions that illuminate the battlefield.

Over Lord Miranda conjures her special blade, something she created from the very essence of her magic. She lunges forward, her movements fluid and controlled as she aims for Thodara's side. Thodara counters by conjuring her shield to block the strike. If her renewed strength surprises Over Lord Miranda, she doesn't show it.

I'd have thought Thodara was too weak to fight and surrender, but I was wrong. Thodara sends a torrent of magical energy toward Over Lord Miranda. Undeterred, she notches another arrow in her bow with flames dancing along its length. She draws the string taut and releases the fiery projectile streaking toward Thodara. Yet, with a wave of her hand, Thodara deflects the arrow easily.

"You are no match for me," Thodara snaps. "I am magic!"

Thodara conjures a cascade of luminous spheres that swirl around her. With a sweep of her hand, she releases the spheres toward Over Lord Miranda in a brilliant flurry of magic. The orbs detonate on impact, casting blinding flashes of light and sending shockwaves rippling across the field. As the dust settles, Over Lord Miranda's form staggers, her breath labored as she teleports away for a reprieve.

Over Lord Mary faces off against the powerful Darka. Shadows dance around them, flickering like whispers of the unknown. Over Lord Mary's eyes narrow with intense focus as she readies herself for his next attack. She steps forward, her illusion abilities swirling around her like a cloak of deception. She conjures an illusory duplicate of herself, aiming to confuse Darka and gain the upper hand.

They dash towards Darka from multiple angles, obscuring his view and sowing confusion. Darka's stance wavers as he struggles to pinpoint the real version amid the phantasmal duplicates.

Darka's laughter cuts through the air like a blade. "You wield illusions, but can you truly tell what is real from what is not?"

He sidesteps her illusory attacks with fluid grace. His movements are seemingly unaffected by the distorted reality around him. Despite my screwing up reality, the Over Lords and the gods seem to fight reasonably well between realities. Just as that thought crosses my mind, the fracture in reality causes Over Lord Mary to stumble before falling forward into the future and falling back into the present.

Darka seizes this opportunity, exploiting the fractured reality to his advantage. With a calculated move, he channels the power of time through his form and sends a surge of temporal energy that envelopes Over Lord Mary. She stumbles as past and future blend into a disorienting whirlwind.

Time wraps around them. Shadows merge into tangible tendrils that wrap around her limbs, restricting her movements. She struggles against Darka as his smile widens at her frantic movements. He reaches out, but before he can touch her, a burst of energy flows from her body, sending him flying through the air.

She teleports over just as he lands and delivers a series of attacks, though he responds quickly. They trade punches and kicks, their bodies a blur of motion. A sudden flurry of blows erupts between them as fists collide with flesh.

Over Lord Mary punches Darka in the jaw, causing his head to snap back, with hair flying in disarray. Pain flares through his eyes, but he retaliates with a swift kick to her stomach. It connects with a thud, forcing the air out of her lungs.

Over Lord Annie finds herself locked in an intense battle against Rika. The air is alive with the energy of intertwined realities and their clash echoing through the dual existence that surrounds them. As Over Lord Annie raises her hand, channeling her power to manipulate emotions and thoughts, Rika's form shimmers in response.

Her brow furrows with concentration as she attempts to penetrate the intricate weave of Rika's thoughts. Yet, the fusion of present and future reality muddles her focus. Emotions and fragments of thoughts whirl in her mind, both her own and those of the goddess, creating a chaotic mental landscape.

With a sweeping gesture, she commands vines to erupt from the ground, trapping Over Lord Annie's feet. The earth seems to pulse with Rika's intent as she locks her in a botanical embrace. Struggling against her leafy restraints, Over Lord Annie summons her telepathic abilities once again.

But as her thoughts reach out, they encounter a distorted barrier, a rift between present and future that distorts the psychic connection. As she tries to infiltrate Rika's mind, an overwhelming surge of natural energies meets her attempts, sending shockwaves through her own consciousness.

The duel between emotions unfolds in parallel, as Rika's nature resonance clashes with Over Lord Annie's emotional manipulation. Her emotions intertwine with those of countless beings from different eras, creating a merging of feelings that threatens to overwhelm her focus. Rika maintains her serene control over nature's harmonious balance.

The relentless power of Rika's magic bears down upon her, a testament to the goddess's unwavering connection to her power. Over Lord Annie's strength wanes, her willpower unable to pierce the tumultuous weave of time. With a resigned breath, she stumbles, her form falling to the ground.

The battle rages on, a maelstrom of magic and weapons. Blades clash against staffs, daggers meet claws, and fists strike with bone-crushing force. The clash of energy and steel reverberates through the air, each strike accompanied by a burst of light or an eruption of shadow.

Amidst the chaos, the Over Lords' movements are a coordinated dance. They flow seamlessly from one attack to the next, their abilities intertwining in a dance of power.

But the Gods are not to be underestimated. Despite the break in realities, Darka manipulates time, causing the Over

Lords' attacks to falter and misfire, even within the dualist realities. Valtor's control over the earth allows him to reshape the terrain to his advantage, trapping the Over Lords in shifting prisons of stone. Rika's manipulation of nature summons vines and thorns that ensnare their movements, and Zara's power to shape creation alters the battle-field's landscape.

The battle continues, and the Over Lords' injuries accumulate. Gashes appear across their skin from Darka's blades, and bruises mar their bodies from Valtor's stone projectiles. Despite their valiant efforts, the gods are kicking their asses. Exhaustion and frustration take their toll. The Over Lords' breaths become ragged and labored, their movements slowing as pain gnaws at their limbs.

With each strike, they fight through the pain, their determination unwavering, but the gods' onslaught is unrelenting. Their attacks intensify, and the Over Lords find themselves overwhelmed by the sheer magnitude of their power. A fierce wind whips through the battlefield as Zara's creations clash against the Over Lords, the resulting shock-waves reverberating through the air.

The overwhelming power pushes the Over Lords back as they meet their every effort with an equal and opposite force. Their bodies scream in protest, wounds gushing blood, yet they fight on. But the gods' tireless assault is proving too much to bear.

One by one, the Over Lords stumble, their defenses faltering as their strength wanes. Finally, they lay sprawled on the ground, breaths coming in ragged gasps. Blood-soaked and battered, their forms radiate a fierce determination even in defeat.

The Gods stand triumphant, with their forms exuding an otherworldly power that seems to mock the Over Lords' resilience. But the Over Lords won't give up so easily. Slowly, they push their battered bodies off the ground and stand on shaky legs. They fought a good fight, even though this was a losing battle. Then, I realize the Over Lords will fight to their dying breath to protect their people and the world.

"Watch out, Mary!" Over Lord Miranda says before pushing her down, away from an unsuspecting sword.

She pushes Over Lord Mary out of the way, and now there's an enormous sword sticking out of her chest. Over Lord Mary snatches the blade out, and her sister falls to her knees.

"Miranda!" Over Lord Mary screams. "No, no, no!"

She grabs Over Lord Miranda, placing her hands over the wound on her chest to heal her.

"She's not healing!" she shouts.

Darka laughs at their pain. "My blade has stabbed her. No one survives the Voidreaver. My blade devours magic and energy, leaving those stabbed with it powerless and weak. She will die."

"It's okay, Mary," Over Lord Miranda says softly, blood leaking out the corner of her mouth. "Just finish kicking their asses. I'll be here when you're done."

By the look in her eyes, I know she doesn't believe that. She coughs a little, and more blood spills from her mouth. She gets a distant look in her eyes before her body becomes still.

"No!" Over Lord Mary cries. "Not my sister!"

She hugs Over Lord Miranda's body to her chest as she rocks back and forth, shaking from crying so hard. The other Over Lords cry silently for losing their sister. Their sadness and despair are thick in the air.

"We've let this little game of yours go on long enough," Zara says. "It is time for you to die."

Over Lord Mary's head snaps up, eyes flashing brighter than before. Time seems to freeze, leaving little sound on the battlefield. It shifts between freezing and not freezing as dual realities fight her control. She turns her head toward me, and I gasp in surprise as so much anger covers her face. She teleports in front of my cage.

"You!" Over Lord Mary snarls at me. She hits my cage with so much force it disintegrates from the impact. She grabs me by the throat. "All of this is because of you! My sister is dead because of you! You've been worthless during this entire ordeal. A complete waste of space."

"Mom, please stop," Dani yells from her cage.

Over Lord Mary ignores her as she squeezes my throat, and my eyes widen in fear. Her body vibrates as she tries to control her rage, but I can see it's a losing battle.

Time seems to start again, and the noise from the battlefield comes rushing back. "You may have the ability, but I'm the god of time. I control it," Darka says.

"You control nothing, bitch!" Over Lord Mary screams back, and a powerful blast shoots from her body.

The powerful blast hits the gods, and they fly back, landing on the ground with surprise written on their faces. The vibrations of realities are clashing violently now as Over Lord Mary's rage takes over. Her anger is a seething fire, fueled by her frustration and the belief that I'm responsible for their current predicament. As the battle resumes around us, her attention zeroes in on me, her gaze burning with accusation.

"Over Lord Mary, wait," I start, my voice trembling with fear.

But her anger seems to override any willingness to

listen. Her eyes glow with a fierce intensity, and I feel the familiar tingle of magical energy in the air. In that moment, a surge of power flows from me into Over Lord Mary.

It's a strange and disorienting sensation, as if a piece of my essence is being forcibly torn away. My magic responds to the touch, reluctantly obeying the call, drawn away from me like a puppet's strings being severed.

The siphoning process is not unlike what the gods had done to Dani, Vik, Lucy, and me earlier. Over Lord Mary's grip is like a vice, unyielding as she absorbs my magic. My vision blurs, and my head is spinning from the drain on my power. I feel weak and vulnerable as my magic slips through my fingers like sand.

As Over Lord Mary's grip tightens, my knees buckle, and I sink to the ground, breath coming in ragged gasps. I clench my fists to resist the assault on my magic, but it's as if Over Lord Mary's will is an unstoppable force. Around us, the Mutane Sihiri soldiers struggle to fight, chaos and magic clashing in a canopy of destruction as the rest of us fight against the shadow creatures.

But I'm too focused on my struggle to pay much attention to the broader fight. My mind races, desperately seeking a way to regain control, to fight back against Over Lord Mary's relentless onslaught. With a burst of energy that feels like a shockwave, the rest of my power drains from my body. She lets me go, and I fall to the ground, weak and breathless.

"You didn't kill me," I say breathlessly.

Over Lord Mary looks down at me. "Be lucky that I didn't. I may be powerful, but as you can see, we're no match for a God. I need your power to give me a boost for what I'm about to do."

The rest of the Over Lords teleport over to her with

questioning looks in their eyes.

Over Lord Mary looks at Over Lord Miranda's body with unshed tears. "I'm going to rewind time to save her. I'm going back to when all the gods showed up, and we're going to do the same thing they did to the girls, to them."

"Can you do that, Mary?" Over Lord Annie asks. "Olivia screwed up realities by messing with time. Do you think this could work?"

Over Lord Mary simply shrugs. "I think we can still go back. As for stealing the god's power, I don't know. At least Miranda will be alive, and we'll just have to fight this battle differently."

"We'll try to keep them busy while you try," Over Lord Sydney says.

Over Lord Mary soars to the sky, her body glowing brightly as she gathers her power. Below, the fight becomes even more chaotic as the Over Lords attack the gods again. As the gods attack back with fury, the Over Lords meet their onslaught with as best their battered bodies can.

The clash of powers is spectacular, the air crackling with energy as they battle against the gods. They calculate each move and infuse each strike with magic as they seek to hold their own against the formidable deities.

I can hear rumbles as the very earth itself shakes. Over Lord Mary has her arms raised, and power flows from her body as she attempts to separate realities and rewind time. As she continues, Darka spots her in the sky. Over Lord Mary's efforts to manipulate time become increasingly apparent the longer he stares.

The fabric of reality seems to shift and warp around her, the lines between past and present blurring. But Darks is not about to let her succeed without a fight.

Darka's powers of time manipulation clash with hers,

creating a dazzling display of temporal energy. The air wavers with distortion as their abilities collide, creating rifts in time that threaten to unravel the very foundation of the battle.

Over Lord Mary and Darka are engaged in a fierce confrontation, with Darka attempting to defeat her. Their powers collide in a dizzying dance, time-bending and warping around them as they struggle for control.

Over Lord Mary splits her focus between fighting Darka and wielding her power over time to rewind the events that had led to this point. Over Lord Mary's efforts allows her sisters to gain the upper hand as time continues to twist and collide. Their attacks become more precise, their defenses impenetrable.

Over Lord Mary's control over time grows stronger, and with a last surge of energy, she halts the gods' advances. Everyone and everything freezes as time comes to a stand-still. In a blinding burst of light, the timeline shifts, the events leading up to the battle, being rewritten instantly.

The god's expressions are a mixture of surprise and frustration. They exchange glances as the unexpected turn of events shatters their confident demeanor. Over Lord Mary's success in fixing time gives them another chance to defeat the gods as if the battle never happened.

Everyone is back to the start of the battle, us on one side of the field and the gods on the other. Over Lord Miranda stands with confusion on her face. She looks around as if piecing together the puzzle before her.

Over Lord Ashley, true to her manic and snarky nature, speaks first. "I can sense your confusion, Miranda. Let me offer a bit of clarity. You died. Mary stole Olivia's power. She fixed the realities Olivia fucked up and rewound the time to bring you back to life. All while fighting off Darka in the process. I'll admit, my big sister is pretty badass."

Over Lord Miranda's eyes widen in realization, forming an "o" of comprehension. A fire ignites in Over Lord Miranda's eyes as she absorbs the gravity of the situation. The Gods had claimed to be unbeatable, their arrogance and power unmatched. But now, the tables have turned.

With newfound resolve, Miranda's lips curl into a confident smile. "Well, well, it seems like my little sister just figured out a way to kick your asses," she muses.

"No time for shit talking," Over Lord Mary says as she grits her teeth. "I'm having a hard time keeping them at bay."

"You are more powerful than we gave you credit for," Rika says with a menacing smile. "We should have taken yours to begin with, then all of this wouldn't have happened."

"We'll rectify that right now," Valtor growls before

CHAPTER 33

TIME TO END THIS

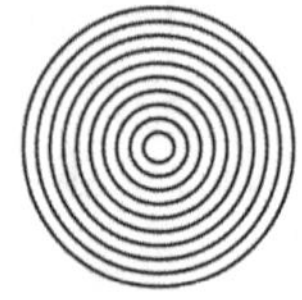

The Gods raise their hands, and the Over Lords scream in pain as they're encased in bright energy. Their power flows from them to the gods, and they turn pale, as if their very essence is leaving their bodies. They weren't expecting the gods to act so quickly, which caught them off guard. They stumble from the pain before righting themselves and preparing to attack.

A deafening crack splits the air as their magic siphons like a vortex into the gods. A blinding light erupts from the powerful entities. Their forms transcend the physical as their power ignites. The vortex of energy falters, and the gods jolt in surprise at the sudden reversal of power.

The Over Lords are now siphoning the gods' power, weakening them by the second. With an explosion that rocks the earth beneath us, the Over Lords release their magic in a burst of radiant light. The gods are thrown back, and the blast consumes their forms. The impact of the explosion sends shockwaves through the field, and for a moment, the world seems to hold its breath.

As the light fades, I glimpse the forms of the Over Lords

as they glow brightly. Their figures stand tall and resolute. Their eyes are blazing with an intensity that defies description. And with a sense of awe and wonder, I realize they've harnessed a good chunk of the god's power. Now that the Over Lords have more power, they can hopefully defeat the gods.

The Over Lords stand stronger than ever with the newfound power coursing through their veins and the sky crackles with energy as they face the gods who have wreaked havoc upon their world. The gods, once towering and formidable, are now faced with opponents who wield their very essence against them.

"What have you done?" Thodara screams at the Over Lords. "You were never meant to have this much power."

"Yeah, and clearly you were never meant to be a mother, yet here we are," Over Lord Mary snaps.

"I will not let this stand," Monteralia says. "Return the power, or we will be forced to take it."

Over Lord Ashley raises a hand. "I'll take option three, please. We pummel your asses into the ground and lock you away somewhere so deep and dark that you won't be able to tell your assholes from your faces."

Thodara simply nods. "So be it."

The gods attack, and once again, the battleground crackles with an electric tension as the Over Lords fight. The gods may be weakened, but it did not render them powerless, and they are still a formidable force.

As the Over Lords launch their initial assault, the gods expertly evade their attacks, displaying a synergy born from countless battles fought across the ages. Over Lord Miranda, embodying the strengths of Thodara, engages in an intricate dance of agility and precision against her divine counterpart. Each strike is a testament to her dedication to the craft of combat, a testament that even without magic, she remained a force to be reckoned with.

Over Lord Miranda spins and kicks Thodara in the face. Her head snaps back, but she turns quickly, punching Over Lord Miranda in the stomach. They go back and forth, going blow for blow against each other, both giving as good as they're getting.

Over Lord Miranda flips out of the way of Thodara's kick before summoning her energy bow. She fires arrows rapidly, with three of them hitting Thodara in the torso. She grunts from the pain before disappearing.

The ground shakes and I look around the carnage to see Over Lord Mary shoot a blast of energy from her eyes. She yells out before squeezing her eyes shut, and time shifts. There's a rip, and suddenly, they're right back at the beginning of their fight with the Gods.

"Control that shit, Mary!" Over Lord Miranda snaps. "Now is not the time for you to spaz out!"

"Sorry!" Over Lord Mary shouts before they attack the Gods again.

Over Lord Annie engages in a fierce confrontation with Valtor, and she's struggling. With the Over Lord Mary's control over time slipping, causing realities to cross, and his ability to control time, she can barely keep up with how to attack.

She takes hit after hit, trying her best to protect herself against his manic attack before falling to the ground. Luckily, before he can deliver a fatal blow, lightning strikes him. Over Lord Annie quickly teleports away.

Over Lord Sydney clashes against Zara. Despite the enhancement of her magical prowess, she relies on her quick thinking and adaptability to keep pace with the goddess. She conjures energy whips and slashes them toward Zara, leaving lashes across her skin.

Suddenly, Over Lord Sydney twitches, and then she's underneath Zara, getting hammered by her. Zara freezes for a few seconds before she's standing across the field.

Over Lord Sydney stands up, wiping the blood off her face. "This fragmented reality is really starting to piss me off. If I'm going to jump between realities, at least put me in the one where I'm not getting my ass kicked!"

She teleports over to Zara to resume fighting. My focus switches to Over Lord Stephanie. She's fighting against Rika, and a crackling surge of energy ripples through the field. Over Lord Stephanie raises her hands, and the ground beneath them trembles as the trees bend to her will, their branches twisting into intricate patterns.

The branches soar toward Rika, but she blocks them. She unleashes a barrage of mystical bolts, each imbued with a different elemental force. Fire, ice, lightning, and earth rain down upon Rika, creating a dazzling display of colors and sparks. She responds by blocking the assault with fighting skills I didn't know she possessed.

Throughout the fierce fight, they met the Over Lords with a resistance that defies their newly acquired powers. The gods show unparalleled combat skills, their every move a calculated dance of evasion and retaliation. However, the Over Lords are driven by a relentless sense of purpose, their unity a formidable weapon in itself.

As they continue to fight, their synergy grows stronger, each complementing the other. Slowly, they overpower the gods, exploiting gaps in their defense and countering their moves with precision.

Still, the gods prove they are still powerful as the sky blazes with swirling torrents of magic. The Over Lords stand at the epicenter of the chaos, joining their powers in a last-ditch effort to end the reign of the Gods. Over Lord Mary, her eyes blazing with commitment channels the essence of her stolen world sight ability, its energy coursing through her veins.

Beside her, the sisters lend their strength to help subdue the gods. Their very being trembles under immense pressure, but they have no choice; the gods' tyranny must end. The gods unleash their remaining power in devastating blasts of divine energy. Thunderous roars shake the earth as beams of light and fire descend upon the Over Lords. The ground beneath them cracks and trembles, threatening to swallow them whole.

"Focus!" Over Lord Mary shouts, her voice cutting through the chaos.

Over Lord Stephanie conjures a protective barrier of swirling air and stone. It quivers under the gods' assault but holds, thanks to their combined power. Over Lord Annie projects waves of calming energy, attempting to soothe the anger of the gods and prevent their attacks. She strains under the weight of the collective emotions assaulting her mind, beads of sweat forming on her forehead.

Over Lord Mary weaves a web of intricate illusions to confuse the Gods and divert their attention away from the converging of powers. Her concentration wavers as she struggles to juggle multiple realities simultaneously and strains from exertion.

The Over Lords feel their strength waning as the gods' attack intensifies. Desperation crosses their faces, but they can't afford to falter. With every ounce of their being, they channel their magic into a swirling vortex of energy that spirals into the heavens. Above, the sky darkens as if the very cosmos acknowledges the cataclysmic clash below. The Over Lords' collective power grows more potent, drawing upon the gods' essence.

"They're too strong!" Over Lord Stephanie grunts, beads of sweat trickling down her face as he struggles to maintain the power.

"We can't give up!" Over Lord Mary's voice rings out, her eyes locked onto the celestial prison forming high above. "We didn't go through all this shit just to lose!"

The gods' rage intensified as they realize the Over Lords' intentions. Their assault grows more frenzied, and the heavens seem to weep at the impending doom. Over Lord Annie's knees buckle as she fights to maintain her empathic shield.

She clenches her fists, determination in her eyes, and presses on, her heart aching with the weight of the gods' anger. Over Lord Mary's illusions fray at the edges, revealing glimpses of the chaos beneath. She grits her teeth and weaves the illusions tighter, sweat streaming down her face like a river.

The moment of truth arrives as the god's prison nears completion. The Over Lords are almost out of strength, and exhaustion is causing their bodies to shake. Each god unleashes one final, desperate assault on their divine power.

Over Lord Mary cries out as her vision blurs. "Now, together!"

With a final, incredible effort, the Over Lords pour more of their magic into the prison they're constructing. The celestial prison above them shows brilliantly a beacon of hope amid chaos. It pulses with power, drawing the Gods into its ethereal embrace. The god's power falters. They struggle in vain as something inexorably draws them into the prison.

Their screams echo through the field, a haunting lamentation of their fall from grace. The celestial prison seals shut, the sky clears, and the explosive magic dissipates. The Over Lords stand there, breathless, and drained, their gazes locked upon the now-quiet heavens.

"We did it," Over Lord Stephanie whispers.

The Over Lords turn their attention to the cages that still trap Dani, Lucy, and Vik. The impenetrable barriers that hold them captive dissolve with a mere thought from the Over Lords.

Dani, Lucy, Viktoria, and I cling to each other, relieved that we all survived this ordeal. I'm sad to say I can't say the same for quite a few soldiers. Our quiet embraces don't last long because Over Lord Miranda turns her gaze toward me.

"Olivia," she says, her voice tinged with anger, "you almost unraveled the fabric of reality with the reckless use of your world sight ability. Do you have any idea how close we came to losing?"

"I... I'm sorry, Over Lord Miranda. I didn't mean to..." I say before lowering my gaze, ashamed that I almost ruined things for everyone in my attempt to help.

Over Lord Miranda cuts me off with a raised hand. "Sorry isn't enough. We were fortunate this time, but we cannot afford such risks in the future. You must learn to control your powers more responsibly."

I nod, hoping my remorse is apparent. I've always struggled to harness the full extent of my abilities, and my recent actions have nearly cost them everything. The aftermath of their battle with the gods leaves the Over Lords drained and vulnerable. Over Lord Mary, in particular, feels the weight of my stolen magic like a storm raging within her.

She clutches her chest, gasping for breath as waves of magic surge through her being. Over Lord Sydney turns her attention to Over Lord Mary, who has remained far from the group. Over Lord Sydney's keen eyes widen in alarm as she notices something wrong.

"Mary," she calls out with concern. "Mary, are you alright?"

Over Lord Mary turns toward her sisters as her form shimmers and vibrates with unrestrained magic. It's as if the stolen world sight ability within her is pushing her to her limits.

Over Lord Sydney approaches cautiously. "Mary, you're glowing. Something's not right."

The other Over Lords, sensing the disturbance, turn their attention to their sister. They watch in alarm as her magical aura intensifies, bathing the surroundings in a brilliant, pulsating light.

Over Lord Mary clenches her fists as she struggles to contain the overwhelming power within her. "I can't... it's too much. Olivia's magic is tearing me apart!"

Over Lord Mary's form continues to vibrate as the magic threatens to consume her entirely. The air crackles with energy as the other Over Lords try to figure out how to help. Over Lord Mary tries to speak, but her voice catches in her throat. Her world sight ability, once mine, now swirls chaotically within her. She can see glimpses of countless realities, each one a dizzying kaleidoscope of possibilities.

Over Lord Annie reaches out to steady her, and her empathic powers sense the turmoil within her sister. "This is bad, guys. We need to help her."

The Over Lords exchange worried glances. The stolen

magic is destabilizing Over Lord Mary's very existence. She's wavering between realities, her form shifting and flickering like a mirage in the desert.

"I can't... control it," Over Lord Mary gasps, her voice echoing from different planes of existence.

Over Lord Miranda extends her hand, attempting to lend her support, but it passes through Over Lord Mary's flickering form like smoke. The concerned look turns into frantic worry.

Over Lord Stephanie gasps. "We need to do something. Mary's being torn apart!"

As Over Lord Mary's instability intensifies, the stolen magic within her builds to a crescendo. The world seems to warp and twist as if reality itself is in flux. My eyes widen as I see what's happening to the Over Lord.

"Mary, hold on!" Over Lord Sydney cries out as she steps closer with fear in her eyes.

And then, in a blinding flash of light, it happens. A massive blast of energy erupts from Over Lords Mary's body, arcing toward me. The force of it sends me stumbling backward with my eyes wide with shock. The magic courses through me, wrapping around me like a warm embrace. For a moment, the world stands still as the power surges within me.

I gasp, feeling the familiar rush of the world sight ability returning to me. The chaos within my mind settles, and I can once again see the threads of fate and possibility. As the brilliant light fades, Over Lord Mary's form stabilizes, as does reality, and her breathing slows to a steady rhythm.

She blinks, disoriented, but no longer lost in the tumultuous sea of realities. For a few brief seconds, visions filter through my mind too fast for me to see before ending.

My body hums with newfound power, and I look at Over Lord Mary in surprise. "You gave it back to me."

Mary nods weakly before rolling her eyes. "I couldn't hold it any longer. It was tearing me apart. I'd rather not die, thank you very much."

I can't help but feel a surge of gratitude toward her. I thought I'd lost it forever. A part of me forever stolen, but Over Lord Mary's magic spit it back at me before it tore her apart.

I approach her with my voice filled with sincerity. "Thank you, Over Lord Mary. You've given me back a part of myself I thought was gone forever. I'll be forever grateful."

She quirks a brow, and I'm sure she's still thinking about the problems I've caused. "Yeah, well, you're welcome."

As I turn away from her, I overhear the conversations of the other Over Lords, their voices low and contemplative. They speak of the arduous battle we've just endured, a battle they never believed they would win.

Over Lord Miranda, her usually stoic demeanor softened by exhaustion, "I never thought we'd see the day when we'd face the gods themselves. It definitely was a battle for the ages."

"The power they wielded was unimaginable. It's a miracle we survived."Over Lord Annie adds with relief and weariness.

"But we couldn't have done it without everyone here. We lost a lot of soldiers today." Over Lord Stephanie chimes in.

Over Lord Sydney interjects with a mischievous grin, "And let's not forget Mary found a way for us to steal the gods' magic and whoop their asses with it."

We all share a chuckle at Over Lord Mary's expense, her

unconventional methods having played a vital role in our victory.

Over Lord Mary herself takes a bow. "What can I say? I'm the queen of kick ass, and those gods didn't see me coming!"

The camaraderie and lighthearted banter provide a much-needed respite from the gravity of our recent battle. Despite the odds stacked against us, we emerged victorious, united in purpose and determination.

Over Lord Mary's voice breaks through the chatter. "Hopefully, that's all the action we see for a very long time."

"Yeah, I don't think I can take any more fighting until I soak my body in Epsom salt for a few months," Over Lord Miranda jokes.

As I stand among the Over Lords, I can't help but feel a sense of belonging. We may come from different backgrounds and wield different magic, but today, we shared a common goal—to protect the world from the dark forces that sought to consume it.

We walk among the carnage on the field. Bodies of the soldiers litter the ground, and a sense of loss overwhelms me. I may not have known them personally, but they still mattered. They had a family, friends, and maybe even children, and their loss resonated with everyone.

Just then, Jade steps forward, looking worn from battle. Her voice carries the weight of authority as she addresses the Over Lords. "My Lords, we have defeated the shadow creatures that dared to encroach upon our lands. "

Torri adds her voice to the report. "The cursed remnants of the shadow creatures are gone, and we have banished the malevolent energies that animated them from our property."

"Thank you," Over Lord Miranda tells them. "Prepare

the burial grounds with the utmost care. We shall lay the fallen to rest with the honor they deserve. Please clean and restore Orchard Landing to its previous state."

Jade and Torri exchange a tired glance before accepting the task at hand. "It shall be done, my Lords," Jade affirms.

"You girls head home to get cleaned up, and some much needed rest," Over Lord Mary tells us. "Despite your fuck ups, you did well."

The words of Over Lord Mary still echo in our minds as we make our way back to the cozy house Dani, Lucy, Vik, and I call home. She had told us we did well in the battle against the ancient gods, but there's an unspoken heaviness in the air—a weight of uncertainty that hangs over us.

We walk in silence, with our thoughts clearly elsewhere. Despite winning against the gods, I wonder how the shadow creatures affected the outside world. The battle may have been on Orchard Landing, but I wonder if anyone saw or felt what was happening.

I break the silence of our walk. "We did alright, didn't we?"

Dani glances at me briefly, offering a small smile. "Yeah, Liv, we did. The Over Lords said we held our own, and that's no small feat considering who we were up against."

Lucy nods in agreement, with her voice carrying a hint of relief. "It's true. I mean, those gods were ancient and powerful. We survived, which is more than we could've hoped for."

Vik finally speaks up. "I just wish I could've done more. My magic felt so... insignificant compared to theirs. We've never been in something like that, and I'm thankful for the Over Lords insisting on the type of training we go through."

I reach over and give Vik's hand a reassuring squeeze. "Your magic is unique, Vik. It may not be as flashy, but it's important. You helped to protect us, and that counts for a lot. And yeah, I thought you guys were paranoid, and now I see there's some merit to all the shit you do here."

As I walk back to the house with Vik, Lucy, and Dani, the weight of everything that's happened settles heavily on my shoulders. The sky above is a canvas of stars, each a reminder of the magical world I've found myself in. Yet, despite the friends I've made and the family I've grown to love, doubt gnaws at the edges of my mind.

Vik strides beside me with her arm linked with mine. Lucy and Dani talk to each other ahead of us. They've accepted me as one of their own, a part of their magical family. I cherish them, yet a sense of inadequacy nags at me. Can I truly belong in this world when I can't control my powers?

As we continue walking toward the house, my mind races, thinking of leaving this magical world behind and returning to my normal life. They are so at home here, so certain of their place in this enchanting world. But I'm different. I've always been different.

The power within me is like a wildfire, unpredictable and uncontrollable. I've tried so hard to fit in, to learn the ways of this world, but it's like trying to grasp the wind. I've caused more harm than good, and I can't bear the thought of putting my newfound family in danger again.

As we approach the house, the lights flicker in the windows. I can't help but wonder if this world is too much for me to handle. My heart aches with the fear of disappointing those who have shown me kindness and acceptance. I want to be a part of their world, but my powers remain a wild, untamed force. How can I ever fit in when I can't control the very essence of what makes this world so enchanting?

As we step through the front door and into the warmth of our home, I take a deep breath, trying to banish the doubt that threatens to consume me. Perhaps with time, with the support of my friends and family, I can learn to harness my power. Perhaps I can find my place in this world after all. Or maybe returning to my everyday life is the right thing to do.

CHAPTER 34
BACK TO NORMAL

The scent of victory still clings to us with a heady mix of sweat, magic, and adrenaline from the battle with the Gods. Dani, Lucy, Vik, and I stand outside our modest home as we yearn for a hot shower, fresh clothes, and a hearty meal. With that in mind, we turn the handle and walk inside.

I sigh with exhaustion and run a hand through my tousled hair. "I don't know about you all, but I can really use a shower right now."

Lucy nods in agreement as she takes in our battered state. "And I think we could all use some clean clothes."

Viktoria chuckles at how awful we look. "I wholeheartedly agree. A change of clothes will do wonders."

With a collective understanding, we go through the house to our respective areas. After luxuriating in hot showers and donning fresh clothes, we reconvene in the kitchen. The aroma of freshly cooked food wafts through the air as Viktoria prepares a simple yet comforting meal.

As we savor our meal, Dani clears her throat. "I hate to

interrupt our much-needed relaxation, but we're being summoned to the main house."

We exchange curious glances, momentarily forgetting our exhaustion. Summoning from the main house right now is not good and usually signals important matters.

I put down my fork and frown. "Summoned? What could it be about?"

Dani shrugs, her expression serious. "I don't know, but we better find out."

With the taste of food still on our tongues, she teleport us from our cozy home to the main house. The transition is seamless, and we find ourselves standing in the living room of the Over Lords'. The Over Lords sit on the couch, looking refreshed and dignified. It's a stark contrast to the battle-weary group that had left just moments ago.

Over Lord Annie approaches me with an expression of a mixture of understanding and concern. "Olivia, we need to talk."

I already know what they want to talk about. "I know, and I've been thinking about it."

Over Lord Annie gestures for me to follow her to a secluded spot away from the others.

"Olivia," she begins gently, "your world sight ability is a gift and a curse. We have witnessed how it can be used for good, but we have also witnessed the chaos it can unleash. It's time for you to make a choice."

I take a deep, steadying breath. "Well, I've already made my decision. I can't keep this power because it's too dangerous."

Her hair catches in the light as she nods. "I understand. Surrendering such a gift is not a simple choice, but it's the responsible one."

Over Lord Annie's cerulean magic illuminates the living

room as she extends her hand. With a touch of her fingers to her own forehead, she channels her magic to bind my magic. The ethereal energy flows from her hand, forming an intricate pattern that encircles me.

My extraordinary world sight ability dims. Its brilliance slowly fades as Over Lord Annie's binding magic takes effect. The room holds its breath as Over Lord Annie's binding magic seals away my potent gift, concealing it deep within me. Her hand withdraws from her forehead, leaving my magic dormant and hidden. The cerulean glow recedes and the regular light to illuminate the room.

"It's done," Over Lord Annie says gently. "Your power is no longer a danger to you or others."

With my emotions in turmoil, I nod. "Thank you, Over Lord Annie."

She places a reassuring hand on my shoulder. "You're welcome. Now, you have another choice to make."

I raise an eyebrow, curious as to what she means. "What choice is that?"

"You can choose to erase your memories of this magical world so you can live a normal life without the burden of this knowledge. Or you can remain aware of it and stay in contact with us. The choice is yours," she says.

I consider this carefully. The idea of a normal life is tempting, free from the complexities of magic and other-worldly battles. But I have formed deep bonds with the Over Lords, Danielle, Lucy, and Viktoria. They've become like a second family, and I can't bear the thought of losing them.

After a moment of contemplation, I finally made my decision. "I want to keep my memories. I want to stay in touch with all of you. You've become important to me, and I don't want to lose that."

Over Lord Annie smiles as her eyes fill with warmth. "Very well. We'll ensure that you can maintain contact with us, even in the outside world."

With that last statement, I'm teleported back home as if none of this ever happened. I sit on the edge of my bed, the morning sun casting a warm glow through the curtains of my small, modest house.

My reflection in the mirror seems different today, as if the weight of the world has finally lifted from my shoulders. I sigh, thinking of the extraordinary adventures, the battles, and the magic I'd been a part of. But it's time to return to my normal human life.

I leave the house and get behind the wheel, thinking this trip is long overdue. The drive is short, and I'm unsure how this visit will go. Before I know it, I'm parking in the driveway and getting out. Steeling my nerves, I knock on the door.

"Olivia, dear, is that really you?" Mom's voice quivers with a mix of disbelief and joy.

"Yes, Mom, it's me. How are you?" I ask.

She pulls me into a tight embrace, tears filling her eyes. "I thought you were never coming home. You never answer your phone. I thought your seizures had taken you away from me."

I hesitate for a moment, debating whether to reveal the truth about my abilities and the world I'd been a part of. But I can't. It would be too much for Mom to handle.

Instead, I offer a reassuring smile. "It's a miracle, Mom. I'm better now. The new treatment I was on worked."

I made up a story about starting a new treatment while I was away. I hate lying to her, but luckily, she believes me. Our relationship is still strained, haunted by unspoken truths and the distance that had grown between us. I can only hope that time will heal our relationship.

In the days that follow, I settled back into my old life. I return to work at Sutton Engineering, which is now under a new boss who seems entirely unaware of the mysterious disappearances of Axel, Nash, Steele, and Barb.

No one asks questions, and I'm finally able to relax. After about a week of living a normal life, I'm startled when Dani, Lucy, and Vik pop into my living room while I'm watching TV.

"Liv, you are coming on a mission with us tonight. So, get your lonely ass dressed right now," Dani says.

"Dani, you know I don't have my world sight anymore. I can't even do magic. What good am I on a mission?" I ask, wondering what the hell is going through their heads.

Lucy smiles and lets out a little laugh. "Liv, you underestimate yourself. You've got other skills that are just as valuable. Remember, we taught you how to kick ass."

"Lucy's right. Besides, we miss having you with us. It's not the same without you around," Vik whines.

I offer a small smile. "While I appreciate that, you guys are the ones with the magic. I'll be a liability."

Dani puts a hand on my shoulder. "Liv, you're not a liability. You're family. And family sticks together, magic or not."

"Plus, you know you can always rely on your uncanny ability to talk your way out of trouble. I remember how well that went," Lucy laughs.

"Ha, ha, you're hilarious," I tell her. "Alright, I'm in. But if things go south, it's on you!"

"Deal!" Dani shouts quickly. "Now, let's get ready to show this new magic user that we mean business."

With a wink and a nod, Dani leads us through a

concealed portal into a hidden part of the city. We're on a mission to apprehend a rogue magic user who's been causing havoc, and I've become an honorary member of their secret team. The mission takes us to the heart of the city, where they pursue their target, a recently discovered magic user named Adrian.

His magical ability is the manipulation of shadows, a power that allows him to blend seamlessly into darkness and strike from the unseen. As if we need to deal with any more shadows after the battle with the Gods. As the night descends, they track Adrian through the labyrinthine alleys and dimly lit streets of the city. His power gives him a distinct advantage, making it challenging to expect his next movement.

My heart races with each shadowy flicker, my anxiety mounting as I realize my limited contribution to the mission. I can't help but feel like dead weight. The tension peaks when Adrian springs from the shadows in a sudden, calculated ambush, launching a barrage of shadowy tendrils at us. I barely have time to react before the tendril grazes my shoulder, leaving a searing burn in its wake. I wince in pain and clutch my injured arm.

Lucy responds by conjuring a blinding burst of light that momentarily stuns Adrian. Dani and Vik rush forward, forming a protective barrier around me. Despite my injury, I can't help but admire my friends' teamwork and skill. They're a force to be reckoned with, magic or no magic. Lucy subdues Adrian with a combination of her light-based magic and Vik's compulsion.

They bind him in magical restraints, ensuring he can't escape. With him secured, we quickly transport him back to Orchard Landing. They place Adrian in a containment chamber before turning their attention to my injury. They rush me to the infirmary, where Linda greets us with a stern expression. She scolds them for taking unnecessary risks and endangering my life. I don't know why Dani or Lucy didn't heal me. We could have avoided Linda's scolding.

"Did you think your abilities alone would be enough to protect you?" Linda chides as she examines my wound. "You're lucky it's not more serious."

I wince as Linda's healing magic mends my injured shoulder, the pain slowly receding. Dani, Vik, and Lucy exchange guilty glances, knowing that Linda is right.

Linda sighs, adding, "I must alert the Over Lords about this incident. They need to know what happened."

Dani, Vik, and Lucy groan in unison, well aware that they are about to face the consequences of their reckless actions. The Over Lords are not known for their leniency, especially for the safety of their team. As Linda leaves the infirmary to contact the Over Lords, I give them a weak smile. Despite the danger and the impending trouble, I can't help but feel grateful to have such a devoted and daring group of friends by my side.

Over Lord Ashley walks in, rolling her eyes and mutters sarcastically. "Didn't you learn anything while on Orchard Landing? Because if you did, how could you let that magic user get a cheap shot in?"

I roll my eyes at her rhetorical question. "Nice to see you too, Over Lord Ashely. Have you taken your meds today? You look a little crazier than usual."

Dani, Vik, and Lucy laugh as she fakes outrage at my dig. I know she knows I'm joking. She relishes in people believing she's crazy and plays into it to the fullest extent.

Her eyes flash as she unleashes her power. "I'll show you crazy, Olivia. Come on, let's go a couple of rounds."

"Aunt Ashley, that's enough. Leave Live alone," Dani

says.

"Oh, lighten up. I'm just fucking with her," Over Lord Ashley replies. "If you can't take the heat, Liv, then you have to grow some balls if you want to hang out with us."

Over Lord Miranda steps forward. "Dani, Vik, Lucy, care to explain why you thought it was a good idea to involve Olivia in this mission?

Dani actually looks embarrassed. "We thought... well, she's still a valuable member of the team, even without her magic."

"And she has other skills that could be helpful. We just didn't expect how dangerous it would be," Vik says.

Over Lord Ashley scoffs. "What other skills? Surely, you can come up with a better excuse than this?"

"We underestimated our target," Lucy says, ignoring Over Lord Ashley's comment. "Adrian's power is unlike anything we've encountered before."

"Oh, I see. So, you brought Olivia along for her charm and strategic mind, did you?" Over Lord Ashley says.

I can't continue to sit here and let them take all the blame. "Look, I insisted on going with them," I add. "I missed you all and wanted to come, even without my abilities."

"Olivia, you should have known better. Your safety is our top priority, and you put yourself at unnecessary risk." Over Lord Miranda snaps.

Over Lord Mary shakes her head, disapproving. "And you three, Dani, Vik, Lucy, you should have prioritized the mission's success over sentimentality."

"We know, mom. It was a mistake, and we take full responsibility." Dani says.

Vik nods her head in agreement. "We won't make that mistake again."

"Damn skippy," Over Lord Ashley adds. "Now, what about those consequences?"

Over Lord Miranda nudges her shoulder. "Not now, Ashley." She looks at us. "While we appreciate your dedication to the team, we cannot afford such lapses in judgment. We have rules and protocols for a reason."

Over Lord Mary nods. "From now on, no one participates in a mission unless they are fully prepared and trained. And that includes Olivia. We won't allow anyone to put themselves or the team at risk."

"I understand, Over Lords. This won't happen again." I say sadly.

They teleport me back home after my wounds are healed. It's late, so I head to bed to prepare for work the next day. Weeks slip by like grains of sand through my fingers, marking my return to the mundane life of a chemical engineer. I had traded the wonderful and magical world for the sterile walls of my laboratory, and the transition had been as abrupt as it was disorienting.

The memories of my time with Dani, Lucy, Vik, and the Overlords weigh heavily on my mind. The battles against shadow creatures, the binding of my world sight by Overlord Annie—they are all too vivid, too surreal to be merely a dream. But here I am, back in the ordinary world, with my extraordinary abilities locked away. I think I regret my decision to come back.

Equations and experiments, test tubes and beakers now consume my days. The world of chemical reactions and scientific hypotheses was once my passion, my calling. But now, I yearn for the rush of magic and the thrill of being with my friends. The silence from Dani, Lucy, Vik, and the Overlords is deafening. No messages, no calls, no cryptic summons.

It's as if they had wholly erased me from their magical world. Perhaps they are moving on to new battles, new challenges, and I am merely a footnote in their story.

As I continue to work, the days become weeks, and my ache grows. I can't help but wonder if I would ever be called back to Orchard Landing. If I would once again be a part of their world. Until then, I can only yearn for the return of magic and the whispers of fate that had once defined my life.

There's nothing unusual about work today. As much as I expect some excitement, nothing ever happens, and I disappoint myself all over again. Life has a peculiar way of returning to normalcy, even after the most extraordinary experiences.

I'm hunched over the lab bench, engrossed in running a group of tests on the new fuel compound. My focus is so intense that I barely notice the soft chime of the lab door as it opens. It's not until someone clears their throat that I look up, startled.

A young intern, Sarah, stands there with a sheepish smile. "Sorry to interrupt, Olivia, but I have a few questions about the chemical tests we're running."

I return her smile and motion for her to come closer. "No problem, Sarah. That's what I'm here for. What do you need help with?"

She pulls out a notebook and opens it to a page filled with handwritten notes and diagrams. "Well," she begins, "I'm a bit confused about the procedures for checking particulate contamination, viscosity, and water levels in the new fuel. Can you walk me through it?"

I nod, glad to see her enthusiasm for learning. "Of course, Sarah. Let's start with particulate contamination." I pick up a beaker filled with a fuel sample and a syringe.

"First, we take a sample of the fuel and pass it through a filter to separate any solid particles. Then, we weigh the filter before and after to determine the mass of particulates trapped."

Sarah follows my demonstration closely, jotting down notes as I explain each step. "Got it," she says, her confidence growing.

"Next, viscosity." I grab a viscometer and show her how to immerse it in the fuel sample. "We measure how quickly the fuel flows through the viscometer. The thicker the fuel, the slower it flows."

Sarah nods, her eyes focused on the instrument. "Okay, that makes sense."

"Now, for water level." I hand her a specialized test tube with a clear bottom and a stopper. "We add a small sample of the fuel to this tube and let it settle. Any water present will separate and settle at the bottom."

As I explain, Sarah performs the test, inspecting the tube. She smiles as she notices the water droplets collecting at the bottom. "I see it now. Thanks, Olivia."

With a sense of accomplishment, I move on to the next test, explaining its principles and procedures. Sarah is an eager learner, absorbing each piece of information like a sponge. Her questions become more insightful as we progress, and I'm impressed by her grasp of the concepts.

As we wrap up our session, I can't help but feel a sense of pride in having helped another aspiring scientist. Sarah's passion for the work reminds me of my journey into this field.

"Great job, Sarah," I tell her as we finish. "You're picking this up quickly. Don't hesitate to ask if you have more questions or need help with anything else."

She thanks me and leaves the lab, eager to apply what

she's learned. I return to my tests to finish before writing up the reports. As I sit at my desk surrounded by the hum of machinery and the chatter of my coworkers, I can't help but feel disconnected from it all.

The memories of my time on Orchard Landing still linger in my mind, a stark contrast to the sterile, fluorescent-lit reality before me. I try to immerse myself in the world of chemical equations and laboratory experiments, but it's a struggle to find the same sense of purpose and fulfillment I once had.

The days blur into one another, a monotonous cycle of work and sleep. I find solace in the simplicity of my mundane life, in the absence of magic and prophecies. One evening, as I'm preparing to leave the office, I catch a glimpse of myself in the mirror.

The reflection staring back at me is the same Olivia who once had visions and wielded magic, but now I'm just an ordinary woman in a city that knows nothing of the hidden world beneath its surface.

I make my way home to my small house, the quiet solitude a stark contrast to the chaos of my recent past. There are no battles to fight, no gods to defeat, and no visions to guide me. As I settle into the stillness of the evening, I can't help but wonder if this is where my journey ends, if I'll forever be caught between the mundane and the magical, between the ordinary and the extraordinary.

For now, I'll embrace the simplicity of my life, grateful for the moments of peace it offers. But deep down, I know that the echoes of my extraordinary past will always linger, a reminder that the world is full of mysteries waiting to be uncovered and that I am forever changed by the adventures I've undertaken.

CHAPTER 35

BEING NORMAL SUCKS

I rush through the gleaming corridors of our state-of-the-art research facility, my heels echoing in the pristine hallways. Today is a big day—a meeting with the new CEO to update him on our company's progress in developing the revolutionary new fuel that could change the world. The weight of responsibility presses down on my shoulders, but I'm determined to deliver positive news.

As I enter the CEO's office, I'm met with an aura of authority. He's a sharp-minded individual known for his innovative approach to business. We exchange pleasantries, and he gestures for me to take a seat. The room is awash with the soft glow of natural sunlight filtering through tall windows, offering a view of the bustling city beyond.

"Olivia," he begins, leaning forward with an expectant look. "Tell me where we stand on the development of the new fuel."

I open my notebook and take a deep breath. This is my moment to shine. "Sir, we've made significant strides in the past few months. Our latest tests show a 20% increase in energy efficiency, and we're on track to reduce carbon emissions by 30% with the new formula."

His eyes brighten with approval, and I feel a rush of relief. My team's hard work is paying off, and it's an honor to deliver these favorable results to the CEO. We discuss the next steps and timelines, and I leave his office with a sense of accomplishment.

Later, I meet with the management team to listen as they discuss the company's achievements and express their appreciation for the dedicated employees. It's heartening to hear their recognition, but a part of me can't help but wonder if they truly understand the long hours and hard work that goes into our research.

Once the meeting concludes, I head to the training room, where a group of new employees awaits. Their eager faces fill the room with anticipation. I begin the class by taking them through the various levels of our facility and explaining the intricacies of our research.

We start in the labs, where I show them the cutting-edge equipment and share insights into the tests we conduct. Their fascination with the science behind our work is unmistakable, and their questions flow freely. I'm grateful for the opportunity to inspire and educate the next generation of researchers.

As we move from one area to another, I can't help but feel a sense of pride in what we've accomplished as a team. The challenges are immense, but the promise of our research keeps us motivated. I watch as the new employees absorb the knowledge I impart, their enthusiasm a reminder of why I chose this path in the first place.

The tour with the new employees wraps up, and I hand them off to a colleague, ensuring they're in capable hands. Duty calls, and I need to get back to the lab. My team has been diligently refining our new fuel formula, and I want to oversee the last tests before we present the final results to the CEO.

As I enter the lab, my heart sinks at the sight before me. My team is in disarray, frantic whispers echoing through the usually focused space. Something has gone terribly wrong, and the tension in the air is palpable.

"Olivia, we're glad you're here," one of my colleagues says, her face etched with worry.

I don't waste a moment. "What happened?"

They explain that during the last phase of testing, the results were wildly unexpected. The fuel exhibited unstable properties, a far cry from the efficiency we had achieved earlier. Panic had taken hold, and no one knew what to do.

I can't hide my frustration. "Why didn't anyone alert me sooner? We could have caught this earlier!"

My team members exchange uneasy glances, their expressions reflecting a mix of regret and apprehension. They should have reached out to me immediately when the issue arose. We dive into a frantic effort to identify the problem. Test after test, analysis after analysis. Hours pass, and the lab is enveloped in the late-night stillness. The clock on the wall ticks past midnight, and fatigue takes its toll.

But then, a breakthrough. I notice discrepancies in the additives used in the last batch of fuel. My heart sinks as I realize the magnitude of the error. Someone on my team had mistakenly added the wrong additives in significant amounts.

I confront the team member responsible, a mixture of anger and disappointment surging within me. They admit their mistake, their face drawn with remorse. It's a costly error that has set us back significantly in our research and could impact our company's progress.

With a heavy heart, I made a mental note to address this issue with the team. We'll need to learn from this mistake and put measures in place to prevent such errors in the future. It's a painful lesson, but setbacks are part of the journey in the world of research and development.

Mistakes happen, but it's how we learn from them and adapt that defines our progress. We'll press on, more determined than ever, knowing that our work has the potential to change the world, one fuel formula at a time.

The following days are a whirlwind of analysis and recalibration. We work tirelessly to rectify the error and bring our research back on track. My conversations with the CEO are less optimistic, but I am determined to regain his trust. We revise our timeline and set more rigorous quality control measures to ensure such a mistake won't happen again.

As I sit at my desk, the hum of the lab equipment providing a steady background noise, I can't help but reflect on how things have changed at work. The chaos that followed the mishap with the fuel formula has finally calmed down, and we're back on track with our research. But as I glance around at my colleagues, chatting and laughing with each other, I can't shake the feeling of loneliness that has settled over me like a heavy fog.

My life has become a solitary routine, and it's hard not to feel like an outsider among my colleagues. There was a time when I had a friend to eat lunch with, someone to share a joke or a quiet conversation with during our breaks. But now, those moments have become a distant memory. I sigh softly, my gaze fixed on my computer screen. It's not that my coworkers are unfriendly; they're quite the opposite.

They're a tight-knit group, and they've taken to my introverted personality with understanding and respect. They appreciate my dedication to our work, and I can't fault them for that. But it's made it difficult to break through the shell of my solitude.

Lunch breaks are the loneliest part of my day. I watch my coworkers head out together, forming bonds and friendships that I can't seem to penetrate. They invite each other to gatherings to celebrate achievements and milestones, but the invitations rarely extend to me. I'm the quiet, reserved scientist who's more comfortable with test tubes and data analysis than with social interactions.

As I wrap up my workday, the sense of isolation haunting me lingers like a shadow. With a sigh, I gather my belongings and head out of the lab, joining the stream of colleagues as they bid each other farewell and make plans for the evening. The drive home was quiet and quick despite the tiny bit of traffic I encountered.

Once inside my cozy home, I kick off my shoes and collapse onto the couch. My thoughts drift to the upcoming evening, another quiet night by myself, with nothing but the soft glow of my reading lamp for company. Just as I'm comforting myself to the solitude, my phone rings, shattering the stillness.

I glance at the caller ID, and my heart sinks as I see my mother's name flashing on the screen. We haven't spoken in a while, and her calls usually mean she's calling to ensure I'm not messing up her image. I reluctantly answer the phone, bracing myself for what's coming.

"Hello, Mom," I say, my voice carrying a hint of weariness.

"Olivia, darling! How are you?" she says in her usual professional voice instead of sounding motherly.

"I'm fine, Mom," I reply, trying to keep my tone even.

She doesn't seem to notice my lack of enthusiasm. "That's wonderful to hear, sweetheart. I was thinking, it's been ages since we had lunch together. How about we meet up tomorrow at The Garden Bistro? You remember that place, don't you?"

I hesitate for a moment as I consider how to respond. I've been avoiding social gatherings with her, not that she wants me to attend, anyway. The thought of making small talk and navigating through the complexities of her constituents is exhausting. But my mother can be quite persistent when she wants to be.

"Mom, I appreciate the offer, but I'm really swamped with work right now," I begin, attempting to decline her invitation gently.

She doesn't seem to be deterred in the least. "Nonsense, dear. It's been too long since we caught up. I've already made a reservation for us at 1 p.m. The Garden Bistro, tomorrow. I'll see you there."

Before I can protest further, she cheerfully adds, "I can't wait to hear all about what you've been up to, Olivia. It's a date, then. Goodbye for now, dear!"

With a defeated sigh, I hang up the phone and set it aside, feeling a mix of frustration and resignation wash over me. My mother's unwavering determination has won again, and I'm left with no choice but to meet her for lunch tomorrow at The Garden Bistro. It's not that I don't love my mother, but the thought of being out with her leaves me feeling drained already.

As the weight of the impending lunch settles on my shoulders, I can't help but scream my frustration into the nearest couch pillow. It's a minor release of the pent-up emotions that have been building within me. The isolation, the solitude, and the constant struggle to find my place in a world that often feels overwhelming.

After a moment of catharsis, I take a deep breath and try to shake off the negative feelings that have taken hold. Perhaps this lunch with my mother will be a welcome change of pace, a chance to reconnect and share some semblance of normalcy. It's been a while since we've had a semi-normal conversation, and maybe, just maybe, it's exactly what I need.

I get up from the couch and head to my bedroom to prepare for a night's rest that hopefully clears my mind of the lingering frustrations. As I settle under the covers and close my eyes, I remind myself that even during solitude and the challenges of social interactions, there are moments of connection and understanding waiting to be rediscovered. With that thought in mind, I drift off to sleep, hoping lunch with my mother will bring a glimmer of light into my otherwise solitary existence.

I sit across from my mother, the clinking of cutlery against fine china the only sound breaking the uneasy silence. "Why do I keep doing this?" I wonder as I've done countless times before.

Why do I keep trying to reestablish a relationship with a woman who will never change? My mother, always over-bearing and only ever concerned with her image, is in full swing, her voice carrying through the restaurant as she talks animatedly about her latest accomplishment.

"I told my publicist that you're finally cured of that... condition," she says the word like it's dirty, something to be ashamed of. "And everyone is just so thrilled, Olivia. I've never been happier!"

I nod absently, barely registering her words as I pick at my salad. She's always been more interested in appearances and her social standing than in any genuine connection with me. It's infuriating.

"And you know what, dear?" She leans in closer, her tone conspiratorial. "I think it's high time you accompany me to more events. You've been so reclusive lately, and I need my daughter by my side."

Her words hit a nerve that's been raw and exposed for years. She hadn't wanted to be seen with me when she thought I was sick, when she felt my life was over. Now, she wants me to be a part of her perfect world. Anger manifests within me, and I can't contain it any longer.

"Mom," I snap, my voice sharp and cutting. She blinks, taken aback by my tone. "You never cared about me when you thought I was sick. You couldn't distance yourself from me fast enough."

Her brows furrow, and she attempts to play innocent. "Olivia, I don't know what you're talking about."

I can't take it anymore. The frustration and years of feeling like an afterthought all boil over. I slam my palm on the table, causing the dishes to rattle and the other diners to glance our way.

"You never cared because I was never sick!" I practically shout, my voice filled with anger and despair. "It was magic, Mom, not some disease! There's an entire world out there that no one knows about, a world of magic, and I'm a part of it!"

Her eyes widen in shock, her perfectly painted lips parting in astonishment. "Magic?" she sputters. "Olivia, you've lost your mind. You need serious help. I'll find you the best mental institution to fix whatever this is."

My mouth drops open in disbelief. I just revealed my

deepest secret to her, and her response is to have me committed. The anger courses through me like a wildfire, consuming any remaining thread of patience I had.

"You're impossible," I hiss, pushing my chair back with a screech of metal against the floor. "I can't do this anymore, Mom. If you ever want to have a relationship with me, then try caring about someone other than yourself."

I storm away from the table, leaving her sitting there, her expression a mix of shock and disapproval. It's the first time I've ever stood up to her, and though it's liberating, it's also heartbreaking. I don't dwell on it as I make my way home to prepare for work in the morning.

I will no longer dwell on my fractured relationship with my mother. I will no longer let regrets of giving up my magic and choosing to leave the magical world get to me. This is my life and I will start living it to the fullest extent. Things are going to get better for me. One way or another.

EPILOGUE

I sit at my desk, my fingers dancing across the keyboard as I type a report. It's a normal workday filled with spreadsheets, meetings, and the hum of fluorescent lights. Mom has tried to call me many times, but I've declined each call, and I'm not ready to speak to her yet.

My anger is still simmering below the surface, and I need to cool down some more before hearing whatever nonsense comes out of her mouth.

As I click the "Save" button on my computer, my phone vibrates with an incoming call. I pick it up, expecting it to be my mom again. Maybe if I answer and let her say what she has to say, I can go back to ignoring her again. Instead, the voice that greets me is one I haven't heard in months, and the tone sends shivers down my spine.

"Liv, it's Dani. We need you at Orchard Landing now."

Before I can respond, the phone slips from my hand, clattering onto the desk. My surroundings blur, and a disorienting rush of vertigo sweeps over me. I blink, and suddenly, I'm no longer in my office. I'm standing in the living room of the main house on Orchard Landing. Dani and Lucy stand before me, their expressions a mix of urgency and relief.

"Liv, I'm sorry for the abrupt teleportation, but we're in a dire situation," Dani says quickly.

Now, I'm worried because this isn't like them at all. "What's happening? Why did you bring me here?"

"Vik is missing," Lucy cries frantically.

At my stunned expression, they explain what happened. They were on another mission, tracking a group of rogue magic users who had been causing havoc in the city. Dani, Lucy, and Viktoria moved stealthily through the shadows. As they approached a narrow alley, the tension in the air was palpable.

Dani and Lucy took the lead, their magical abilities at the ready. With precision and coordination from years of working together, they confronted the rogue magic users, sparks, and magical energy crackling in the night air.

Viktoria moved to flank the rogue magic users from behind, hoping to catch them off guard. But then, amidst the chaos, Lucy noticed something was amiss. Viktoria, who had been a blur of movement and power just moments ago, was suddenly nowhere to be found.

Panic surged through Lucy as she realized Viktoria had run off to chase after one of the rogue magic users, separating herself from the group in the heat of the battle. Dani and Lucy fought with magic users, but couldn't spare a moment to search for Vik.

When the rogue magic users were finally subdued, they turned their attention to finding Vik. Frantic, they scoured the alley, called out her name, and even used magic to locate her, but there was no response, no sign of Viktoria. Days turned into a week. Vik remained missing.

The Over Lords joined the search, using their magic to summon her back, but their efforts proved fruitless. The only certainty they had was that Vik was not dead otherwise, Over Lord Ashley's intuition would have alerted her to the tragedy. Yet, despite their exhaustive search and growing desperation, Vik remains an enigma, vanished into the night without a trace.

Lucy paces the living room as she pulls at her hair. "We've tried everything we can think of, but nothing's working. You're the only one who might have an idea."

My heart races as I realize the gravity of the situation. They need me to use my ability. Standing in the center of the room, a faint shimmer of uncertainty in my eyes as I weigh the gravity of my options. On the one hand, I've waited to join them again. On the other, I never expected to have to use my ability again.

Especially since the chaos I created the last time I tried to help. I wait patiently for the Over Lords, hoping I have an answer when they come. As the doors to the house swing open, the Over Lords enter one by one, their presence commanding and powerful. Over Lord Miranda approaches me with a solemn expression.

"Olivia, we are deeply sorry for what has happened to Viktoria. We have exhausted all our magical means of locating her, but she's still missing." She tells me.

"I know, Over Lord Miranda. That's why I'm here. I want to help find Viktoria, no matter what it takes." I reply.

Over Lord Annie grabs my shoulder to get my attention. "We have a proposition for you, Olivia. We can unbind your world sight ability temporarily. You can use it to find Viktoria's location, and once we do, we will bind your powers once more. Will you consent to this?"

My decision was swift, my determination unwavering. "Yes, I will do whatever it takes to find Viktoria."

Over Lord Annie nods and unbinds my ability. A soft, iridescent glow envelopes me, and I close my eyes, focusing all my energy on my world sight ability. Visions swirl in my mind, a kaleidoscope of past, present, and future. I see glimpses of Viktoria, my friend's face, and the path she has taken. I zero in on the images, piecing together the puzzle of Viktoria's whereabouts.

Time seemed to stand still as my concentration deepens. The room falls into a hushed silence, the Over Lords watching with bated breath. Finally, my eyes snap open, my gaze fixed on a distant point in the magical map of the world sight. The vision has taken me to the location of Viktoria, but what I see leaves me both shocked and puzzled.

I'm standing before the old, abandoned cathedral on the outskirts of the city, a place shrouded in eerie silence and draped in the fading light of the setting sun. As I enter the cathedral, I'm met with a scene that defies explanation. Viktoria is here, but she's not alone.

She stands at the center of a circular chamber, her eyes closed in concentration, surrounded by a shimmering, otherworldly portal that seems to connect to lead to another world. The chamber pulses with magical energy, and I can feel powerful magic, both benevolent and malevolent, on the other side of the portal. It's as if Viktoria has become a conduit, a bridge between worlds. I approach Viktoria cautiously, my heart pounding with relief and bewilderment.

"Vik, it's me, Olivia. Are you alright?" I ask softly so as not to startle her.

Viktoria's eyes snap open, and she turns to face me, her expression a strange mix of determination and exhaustion.

"Olivia, you shouldn't have come here. It's dangerous, and I can't control it." She says breathlessly.

"Control what?" I ask hesitantly.

"I must answer the call, Olivia. Something is summoning me, and I can't resist its pull." She murmurs.

I walk closer. "Vik, please, you don't know what this force is or what it wants. We need to find a way back home."

Viktoria's eyes glow with an otherworldly light, and she appears to be in communion with the very fabric of the cosmos. Suddenly, a swirling vortex appears. Amidst the chaos and uncertainty, Viktoria whispers in a voice that resonates with power, her words both mesmerizing and cryptic.

As the mysterious force pulls Viktoria into the vortex, I feel an irresistible pressure pushing me away. Helpless, I'm forcefully expelled from the vision and sent hurtling back through the cosmic vision.

With a jolt, I find myself sprawled on the floor of the main house. The world around me seems stable and real once more, and the comforting presence of the Over Lords replaces the chaos of the inter-dimensional abyss. I sit there momentarily, stunned and disoriented, my breath coming in ragged gasps. The memory of Viktoria's resolute expression and the enigmatic force that had summoned her lingers in my mind.

"Olivia, did you find Viktoria? Where is she?" Over Lord Miranda asks, interrupting my thoughts.

I struggle to find my voice, my mind still reeling from the surreal experience I'd just endured.

"I found her, but... she's... she's gone," I stammer. "She's been pulled into some kind of vortex. I couldn't stop her, and something pushed me out."

"What?" Over Lord Stephanie says.

I nod. "But she whispered something just before it sucked her away. "

"Well! Don't leave us in suspense. Spit is out already," Over Lord Ashley shouts.

"She said, the threads of magic weave beyond our realms. An ancient force calls me to where light and shadow converge. Remember, the bridge must hold, for the fate of worlds hangs in the balance."

"What the hell does that even mean?" Over Lord Annie asks.

"It means a powerful, ancient, and mysterious force exists outside the boundaries of conventional reality. Viktoria is being summoned by this enigmatic force, which seeks to use her unique ability as a bridge between worlds. To find the answers to this cosmic mystery, one must seek the convergence point of opposing forces, where forgotten realms and their histories intersect," comes Rebecca's reply.

"Just fucking great," Over Lord Miranda shouts.

Rebecca simply shrugs. "I don't know what the hell those gods did to Viktoria in the process of reclaiming their power, but they just opened a new can of worms. My vision has shown me that those gods, yes, all of them, were keeping something at bay. And locking them away the way you released whatever hold they had."

Over Lord Mary sighs. "Why can't we catch a fucking break?"

Over Lord Annie looks over at me. "I know this is a big ask, but are you in or out?"

For a moment, I hesitate, with my heart racing. I've yearned for a normal life away from the complexities of the magical world, but regretted it immensely. I had second thoughts, and now it's clear that destiny had other plans.

There's no way I'm turning my back on my friends, my responsibilities, or the potential danger that looms.

I look toward my friends and the Over Lords. "Looks like I'll hold on to the world sight ability a little longer."

I don't know what's waiting out there for us, but I know that if we work together, we'll have Vik back home safe and sound and defeat whatever this new evil is. It can't possibly be that bad. I mean, the Over Lords went against the gods and defeated them. So, I'm sure whatever is out there will be a piece of cake.

I hope.

Afterword

Thank you for reading Disguised Perception. I hope you enjoyed this magical, kick ass journey to save the world. If you truly enjoyed the book, please leave a review!

Tiffany

Acknowledgments

I have to start by thanking my awesome husband for his ever lasting patience and support. I want to thank my children for their encouragement and love. Lastly, I want to thank my sister Monica. From reading early drafts to providing advice on what the book needs, you were there. I want to thank my husband Jason for keeping the children busy so I could write and edit. I also want to thank my mother for her love, encouragement, and support. You all were as dedicated as I was to getting this book completed. You all are very important to me and I wouldn't be where I am without you. Thank you.

Tiffany

About the Author

Tiffany Kahapea lives in Texas. She's retired Army veteran with a thriving aerospace engineering career and a pilot who loves to fly in her free time. She seamlessly balances her adventurous pursuits with her cherished role as a devoted mother of two. Beyond her professional accomplishments, she's an enthusiastic reader, a crochet virtuoso, and a budding writer. Her bookshelves are a testament to her love for literature, while her crochet creations reveal her artistic flair. In her quiet moments, she crafts captivating stories, inviting readers to embark on literary journeys with her. Her life is a testament to resilience, creativity, and a relentless pursuit of passion. She truly hopes to ensnare readers with her new book series

Also by Tiffany Kahapea

Hidden Magic: The Call of The Prophecy

Secret Prophecy: Institute of Magical Arts

Unknown Legacy: Secrets of The Divine